THE UNDERSTANDING OF JENNER RANSFIELD

Imogen de la Bere divides her time between England and New Zealand, where she writes on a diverse range of subjects, from theatre, through opera and rock music, to matters of religion. Her first novel, *The Last Deception of Palliser Wentwood*, was published in 1999.

GN00724768

ALSO BY IMOGEN DE LA BERE

The Last Deception of Palliser Wentwood

Imogen de la Bere

THE UNDERSTANDING
OF JENNER RANSFIELD

V

VINTAGE

Published by Vintage 2000

2 4 6 8 10 9 7 5 3 1

First published in Great Britain by
Jonathan Cape 1999

Vintage
Random House, 20 Vauxhall Bridge Road,
London SW1V 2SA

Random House Australia (Pty) Limited
20 Alfred Street, Milsons Point, Sydney
New South Wales 2061, Australia

Random House New Zealand Limited
18 Poland Road, Glenfield,
Auckland 10, New Zealand

Random House (Pty) Limited
Endulini, 5A Jubilee Road, Parktown 2193,
South Africa

The Random House Group Limited Reg. No. 954009
www.randomhouse.co.uk

A CIP catalogue record for this book
is available from the British Library

ISBN 0 09 928944 X

Papers used by Random House are natural, recyclable products
made from wood grown in sustainable forests. The manufactur-
ing processes conform to the environmental regulations of the
country of origin

Printed and bound in Great Britain by
Cox & Wyman Limited, Reading, Berkshire

To my one true love
Sorry about the steak & kidney

I

NOTHING IN ENGLAND looked as it should. There were far too many fields for a start, but also far too many roads, with unthinkable numbers of cars busying where, for heaven's sake? And the villages, so long admired in *The Glories of Olde England,* were even more stuffed full of quirky public houses and outgrowths of thatch and casually ancient monuments than you could imagine, but were overridden by stockbroker suburbs, petrol stations bright with plastic, and the litter-strewn forecourts of closed-down shops. A cluster of loveliness would bob up for a moment amid the sea of semi-detached brick and then be lost to sight.

All this Theodora noticed as she was driven from Bridgwater station to the Ransfield farm, which rejoiced in the name Nightingales. From a distance of ten thousand miles the name had suggested a place impossibly lovely. It was not lovely. It was not even picturesquely shabby. Presuppositions toppled one by one, from the moment she was hailed on the platform by the lanky woman in a raincoat to the moment they entered the avenue of descent to the farmhouse. She had gotten it all wrong; she was to continue to do so, each misunderstanding more subtle and serious than the last, until the dreadful, exhilarating hour came when she knew that she knew nothing. This is our story.

It was bull semen that had brought Theodora Potts –

twenty-six, blonde curls, blue eyes, white smile, doctorate in veterinary science, little and neat as a sea-horse – from Melbourne to Bridgwater station. She was to study with the great Dr Jenner Ransfield, and she was quite sure that she had got that bit right. She had been told all about Dr Ransfield's terrific work, when he was at Melbourne, in applying the nascent technology of image processing to the study of bull semen. The Cattle Breeding Association of Victoria had given him a lavish grant and taken out a patent, but no one could tell her what happened after that. Scarred by the experience with Dr Ransfield, the cattle breeders decided to invest in someone more accessible, and had lighted gleefully upon the very bright and personable Dr Potts. She might not be a scholar of the Ransfield marque, but she was a good deal nicer to take out to lunch. So Theo found herself a post-doctoral fellow, on generous terms, analysing the effectiveness of different methods of harvesting (for want of a better term) semen from bulls. But Jenner Ransfield was still the man with all the ideas, she was told. Her friend and mentor, Prof. Betsy in Zoo., was always dropping his name. *Ransfield once told me. Jenner Ransfield gave a lecture on this when he was here. Jenner Ransfield broke the ground on this one.* No one disagreed with the assertion that Jenner Ransfield was a distinguished scholar; somewhat *applied*, they said in the more esoteric faculties; in the applied schools they contended that his work was so theoretically demanding as to be unreadable. Theo read everything of his she could lay her hands on – his ground-breaking paper on prions and his detailed epidemiology of scrapie in Southland. She had had described to her his brilliant design engine for storing and displaying DNA diagrams, which allowed you to produce difference charts, so you could see the relationship between one structure and another in a variety of representations. But when Theodora did a search for papers he might have written in her specialist area, the results were a tad disappointing. Prof. Betsy said maybe Theo's search was not quite rigorous enough, for the great Dr R. was bound to have published in the area: he'd done so much amazing work. Unsettlingly, Prof. Betsy was ambivalent about Theo's proposal that she visit the grand old man in his cave. The President of the Cattle Breeding Association, however, was firmly in favour.

Dr Ransfield spoke in the most wonderfully fruity Olde Englishe manner on the telephone. He made a joke about her accent, pretending not to understand the word *heven't*. But being at the wrong end of the day and the wrong end of the world, Theo didn't feel it appropriate to take offence. He did sound so frightfully like the real thing.

Plus he lived on a farm in an English village. Theo imagined one of those farms you saw on English TV, with steamy fields and dry stone walls, and an eighteenth-century stable yard, a shiny stud horse being led out at dawn. A man with a voice like that just had to have a groom or two.

Where might she stay for the duration of her post-doc? she asked him, fanning enthusiasm for the project she felt was lacking from his e-mails. Was there a university flat perhaps, or a room in a student hostel nearby? A sort of snort greeted this, which Theo decided to interpret as static. There was not. There was no student accommodation nearby. She was told that people in this dark corner of the world regarded students as aberrants, a slightly lower form of life than those sad sweet creatures who hung out of trees and burrowed underground to protest against the march of progress. Theo had no idea what he was talking about. However, Dr Ransfield continued, as if he had to dredge the offer out of mud, there was a caravan at the bottom of his farm which she might use, if not alarmed by the proximity of badgers, foxes, rubbish dumps, New

Age travellers, protesters, tramps and other English wildlife. She laughed, and buoyed up by the vision of the average Australian farmer's caravan, an oceangoing barge fitted with refrigerator, microwave, television and double water bed, said it would suit her very well and thanks heaps, Dr Ransfield, I'm really excited about coming over.

'Indeed,' he said, but what he meant was hard to determine. Theo reckoned you can't be too accurate about intonation over ten thousand miles.

So naturally, when the woman, wearing a long brown mac like an army surplus body bag, and green rubber boots, her odd-coloured hair scraped back into a large green rubber band, came up and addressed her, Theo thought she might be one of the grooms with which she had peopled Nightingales Farm. Of course, she thought afterwards in justification, the accent confused her – she didn't know that people spoke like that in real life. All the Scots she'd heard speak before were policemen on TV of one species or other. As words rolled out of the woman's mouth, Theo found herself entranced by the mere sound of it, and had to smile extra hard to make up for not paying attention.

'Elspeth, I'm Elspeth,' she said and grabbed firm hold of Theo's pack without question. 'Welcome to the West Country. We're so pleased to see you.'

And she did seemed pleased, extraordinarily, inappropriately so.

'I managed to get the car,' she said, weaving through the station car park towards a reverend vehicle, also green, the body reinforced with strips of wood, from which the varnish had long since pined away. Theo had a vague memory of having seen such cars depicted in magazines at the dentist's.

'I didna think the egg truck was quite the thing.'

A splendid plaid blanket was thrown over the passenger seat. On opening the door, Elspeth whipped this

4

blanket out. The seat underneath had been re-covered in leatherette, painstakingly stitched by hand.

'Dog hairs, we can't have that now,' said Elspeth as she put the blanket in the back with Theo's pack, shuffling cardboard boxes of paper, empty wine bottles, and a tarpaulin, to make room.

The passenger seat had a dangerous list, but Theo sat upright amid a decade's litter, and looked out the window, her head going to and fro like a mechanical doll, determined to miss nothing of the rural beauties.

There wasn't much to see between Bridgwater and the farm: dull grey roads, slews of ordinary houses, fantastically punctuated by medieval church towers, so sharp and bright that they could not be real. Theo, who had been in England barely a week, looked and looked, finding even the supermarkets of a different country a source of fascination.

Elspeth talked all the way with the brittle enthusiasm of the form captain to the new girl, hoping that *this* one is not going to join the piss-takers. Theo picked up about half of her speech, but smiled her sweetest at the whole. She was trying for clues as to where Elspeth fitted into the scheme of things. Jenner was mentioned regularly, rather than Dr Ransfield; there was considerable detail about Robin and May Margaret of whom Theo knew nothing. But she smiled anyway.

They passed into countryside – rather flatter and more grey than she'd hoped for – wide empty fields, dead sky pierced by the four turrets of an improbably tall church tower. Among the trees in the distance was a mess of colour – flags, tents, banners; in the tree tops structures and swathes of cloth. Evidence of encampment was scattered about: an old van painted orange; a Bedford lorry converted into folksy caravan with stained wooden flanks and a Grimms' fairytale chimney; two big brown horses; smoke from a bonfire sauntering straight up into the sky.

Was this a travellers' encampment, New Age or ancient Romany? Such things were known about in Australia, but viewed with the same ethnic curiosity that a Yorkshireman reserves for an Aboriginal dance. Theo craned her neck to get a better view, so as to be able to write home and tell her mother what she'd seen. They turned down a side road, lost sight of the camp and then suddenly came almost upon it. A huge banner, made of sheets sewn together, was draped across several trees, making a kind of entrance arch. THE BATTLE OF SEDGEMOOR was painted in good green letters.

'Oh,' said Theo, 'one of those historical battle reconstruction things. Where people run at each other shouting with wooden pikes and roll over groaning. I saw one on the British Living History video on the plane. Lots of wigs.'

'Oh no!' cried Elspeth. 'That's an environmental protest camp, against the new superstore and leisure park complex that is being built. You should hear Jenner on the subject!'

Hearing Jenner on the subject was about to become Theo's least favourite pastime, but of this she was, as yet, unaware.

She was aware, however, of being more sorely bumped and chilled than you might have expected, having been picked up from the station in a prosperous country on behalf of a famous person.

By the time they arrived at the farm gate, Theo had enough material for a letter to Mum (*shops in Hong Kong, size of Heathrow, dirtiness of trains, tallest church tower in Somerset*), for an e-mail to her best friend Juliet (*a drunken sleaze on the plane, blast of London, cutest pubs, protest camp wow!*) and some left over for her fella, Tom (*missing you already, football crazy, ten varieties of beer on tap, none of them cold*). But all at once the inclination to write to anyone drained out of her. For disappointment only becomes humiliation when it is made public. She could just hear them, sympathetic, but chortling inside – *Well, I did have my doubts, Theodora! – Thought it was a bit strange all around. – Honestly, babe, you are the last of the innocents abroad.* They'd be all condolence, but they'd love it – Theo had finally made a mistake.

Theodora Potts didn't make mistakes. She always knew what she was doing, from the time at school when it was discovered she was clever as well as cute, and she made best friends with Juliet Marsden (as she was then called, before the shedding of the patronymic). Mum wasn't at all sure about Juliet, eight inches taller than Theo and an evangelical feminist. But it worked out brilliantly, their friendship a mutual defence against the hordes of the average. From Juliet she caught rabid feminism, less as an intellectual conviction than as a weapon against boys, men, fellas, blokes, fathers and brothers, the great joking ribald rowdy crew, hastening to change your tyre when you got a flattie, and then ribbing you afterwards about women being useless. Dad said it was a mistake, a feminist would never get ahead, but she'd proved him wrong. Then Vet School – Juliet was appalled – *an Australian vet school has got to be the chauvinist stronghold of the world! They'll treat you like a bimbo, they'll destroy you, it's so boring! For Christ's sake, go to a real university, and do a real subject; we've got a world to change!* But Theo had shaken her curls defiantly – *I always wanted to be a vet; I've been going to be a vet since I can remember. And Dad thinks it's brilliant. And they make heaps of money. It's just a meal ticket, I'll do something afterwards. Besides, it'll really piss them off when I get top of the class; which I will.*

Which she did, and went on to a doctorate in veterinary science, thus being able proudly to mention that she was really entitled to be called Doctor, unlike all the other vets who just pretended.

Contrary to prediction, her attendance at the wimmen's events that Juliet organised grew more passionate every

7

year that passed. She practically lived in the Wimmen's Room, perching on the side of the big purple couch, as if she were at a tea-party. Her brothers thought this was a big mistake – *you'll never get a man, hanging out with those hairy-legged dykes in overalls*. But they were wrong. Alone of the wimmen's group she had a boyfriend for her entire stint at university, and the same boyfriend at that. He was big and rangy and represented the province in the various Aussie Rules age groups; he had even been trialled for the nationals. He could be taken to events requiring a partner, and would stand loomingly at Theodora's side. The sisters thought Tom a disaster area, until they found that he could be safely ignored, loved to cook, and enjoyed mowing lawns. *You can keep that one, Theo, as long as I can borrow him.*

Getting it right so often had not made Theo insufferable, but neither had success equipped her to deal with Nightingales Farm, Jenner Ransfield, Elspeth, Fergal, and all the events which fell jingle-jangling off her decision to come to England.

From the moment the terrible old car turned down the drive of Nightingales Farm, Theo saw that she was not in any place she ever expected to land up in, nor did she have the vocabulary to communicate what she found – the texture of the air, the atmosphere, the graininess, grimness, peculiarity. She had no method to convey to those cheery folk back there, living their wide open lives in the sun, the existence of this parallel universe. By crossing the world she had dropped through into another version, where people spoke and acted in recognisable ways, where trees were trees and cars were cars, but interpreted by another advertising agency using the same specifications.

She got out to open the gate. It was five-barred, green

and slimy to the touch and had an intricate metal clasp. Words were carved into the wood, starting at the top with NIGHTINGALES FARM and continuing down the side post and along the bottom rail, by this time upside down. Theo tried to read them, but gave up after ABANDON because of the difficulty in reading slimy green words upside down. There are some things you just don't want to know about.

'One of May Margaret's jokes,' said Elspeth as Theo got back into the car. 'Jenner threatens to take a chisel to it, but so far the threat is all.

'May Margaret is so gifted,' Elspeth continued. 'Though it's a pity what she does with her talent, either dishonest or obscene. Jenner gets very upset about the attic, knowing that she'll never let him look at her work. As if, he says, she were ashamed. But one can't deny the ability. I think it might be from her grandfather who was wonderful with his hands. He made much of the furniture that's in the house.'

May Margaret's jokes continued all the way down the track to the farmhouse door. The track, overwhelmed on either side by murky trees, was mud, with occasional pools of downtrodden gravel, and many large brown puddles, so deep that it was necessary to drive around them, one at a time. Elspeth wound her way down with the concentration of one attempting a road skills test. The incline of the track was considerable; the exercise of descent might have been mildly exciting in itself, had not Theo's attention been entirely taken up with the sentinels of the track. All May Margaret's work, she was told.

Clearly May Margaret was an experimenter: the statuary, for want of a better word, was nothing if not varied. Theo wondered if she would have been more or less affected if they had all been in the style of the first pair – two life-size warriors, newly painted glossy black, very crudely hacked out of wood, except for their huge grimacing masks, and protruding spears, which were highly detailed and made of coloured plastic and bits of painted metal.

Jenner, she was informed, *had* taken a saw to those, but in what respect Theo couldn't tell. Besides, she was bumped away too fast for a critical appraisal, and the next creatures reared up, cows and deer and a horse made of corrugated iron and scrap metal, painted yellow and primer pink. Life-size, but brighter than life, they receded into the forest.

She had the impression of others scattered through the trees, but equally well she might have caught sight of miscellaneous farm implements and caches of rubbish and taken them for art works.

At the bottom of the track, just before they came to rest in front of the farmhouse, stood a weathered set of plaster statues – four knights and ladies, wearing their never-never medieval garments with a grace that belied the streaked and flaked paint of their surface.

'Gosh,' said Theo. She negotiated herself out of the car amid a sea of hens. Copper, glossy black, shaggy white, speckled silver, hound-dog yellow, they ran scattering and petitioning by turns. Two Great Danes, chained up by the house, clambered to the extent of the chains and roared discouragement.

The farmhouse of Nightingales, dingy white with a mould-red roof, was so hemmed in by trees that it seemed to sag under the burden of dark green. It had the air of a dispirited old person who has settled back into his armchair. Before the house, where a nice cottagey front garden should have been, was a cleared area of gravel, pitted with puddles. On either hand were sheds of black wooden board and red tiled roofs; their dark interiors gave nothing away.

Below the farmhouse the track descended downwards into shadow. In the distance Theo could see the flat of

Sedgemoor, criss-crossed with channels of water, glinting purposefully in the afternoon light, and a church tower poking upwards. The sky was low and the horizon unnaturally close. Her jacket, green and purple, which had seen her cheerfully through two ski seasons, seemed inadequate against the infiltration of the damp. Somewhere over there was the camp of the protesters, defiantly bright, forlornly hopeful, a scrap of colour in a grey world.

The plaster statues had started life bright and cheery too. Theo went over to look at them. On their plinths were carved names, originally picked out in black, now just discernible. Sir Jenner, Lady Elspeth, Lady May Margaret, Sir Robin. *Oh Jesus!* thought Theo, *the family portraits.* Sir Jenner, magnificent of profile, swarthy of skin, wearing a black surcoat and the latest in chain mail, stared out across the woods into a mystic future, his fine aristocratic profile heightened by the nosepiece of his helmet. His mailed hand toyed with a red rose. Lady Elspeth, recognisably the woman in the mac, was represented here in blue clingy stuff; she inclined her head yieldingly, her hands clasped together, holding a little white-sailed boat as delicately as one might hold a dove. Lady May Margaret, young, beautiful and bold, in a smashing red dress, black hair in real Ivanhoe-type plaits, rested her hand nonchalantly on the hilt of a sword. Sir Robin, a long-haired youth in blue tights and a gold tunic, stared with great intensity at his pointy particoloured shoes.

'Aren't they lovely?' said Elspeth. 'I thought them a little strange at first – May Margaret having the sword and Jenner the flower. But Jenner likes them. I think he likes them because they are old-fashioned. She did them as an art project for school, but they were too big to take. But they gave her an A for them, nonetheless. Of course, she doesn't do that sort of thing now.'

The Ransfield family. Standing here, under the plumb

sky, Theo's faraway family seemed a bit of the best thing in the world – her big, smiling, self-satisfied brothers, her mother with hair permed and brow creased, her infuriatingly smug dad. She thought of them all at her farewell barbecue: her father in his embarrassing apron in the form of a woman's body, presiding over the barbecue of his own construction, her brothers building pyramids of empty beer cans and bowling at them with oranges, her mother propped up over the kitchen island, deep in gin and a huddle of gossip with her daughters-in-law, coleslaw destined for the table outside forgotten in their midst. Barefoot amid the grown-ups, a taggle of nieces and nephews, bronzed and lean, in their kidz designer jeans and parrot-coloured T-shirts, shot in and out, the head of the chase catching up with the tail. Up the trees, into the house, out again, round on to the street, in twos and threes, screeched at by mothers – *Darren, come and get some food now! Brad, for Christ's sake catch that boy will you? And make him eat something.* When she went to these gatherings, Theo never knew whether she liked family or not. Tom, standing to one side, grinning, can in hand, universally respected because of his sporting prowess – her family wouldn't mind if he were a moron and a complete chauvinist, just so long as he could catch a ball. If she married him, which she supposed she would, they'd love him to bits. You could just see Theo and Tom's kids, couldn't you? Blond and brown-skinned, good-looking like their parents, sporty like their dad, but bright like their mum, smiling their shy white smiles at Grandma when she complimented them on winning a race or getting the Computer Prize at school. Enough to make any mother's heart turn over with love. Football kit, ballet gear, guitar cases in the back of the Holden, endless activities, swimming swimming swimming, *Gosh you must be proud of them, Theo! How's Tom's job?* Yeah, family life.

Theo was quite sure she would find Elspeth's family delightful, when she got to know them. Sir Jenner, Lady May Margaret, Sir Robin. *God speed thee, dear brother. Your humble servant, sir. Sweet sister, I prithee, mine own esteemed Father. Mother, Oh Mother. Your hawk's blood was never so red, My dear son, I tell thee oh!*

She looked sideways at Elspeth, hoping she hadn't made some sort of irredeemable conversational gaffe in the short time she had imagined her the groom or handywoman. She scanned for signs that this was indeed the Lady Elspeth, wife to the great Sir or Dr Jenner, then remembered a comedy sketch on television about two old upper-class biddies and their dogs, who conformed to the same model of scruffiness as Elspeth.

'Come in, come in, you must be starved with the cold.'

It wasn't so much the cold as the whining damp that got to her; inside the farmhouse was no different. The whine, if anything, was more shrill. They went in through the back door, passing a ramshackle of outhouses and sheds, and into one more add-on to the house, which turned out to be the kitchen, and the living centre of the house, insofar as it could be said to have such a thing. The floor of the kitchen was on the same level and of the same concrete as the yard beyond, as if someone had simply dumped walls down on to an existing space. Consequently the old and mangy rugs, much in need of a shake, which lapped over one another all over the floor were simply hosts to the dampness creeping up from below. Elspeth rushed in and proceeded to do something arcane to a stove in the corner.

Jenner, she heard, did not approve of central heating; he said there was a clear correlation between the spread of central heating throughout England and the decline in academic standards.

'Let's go mad,' Elspeth said, with a giggle, and turned the gas heater up to full.

Theo sat down, but felt no call to take off her coat.

'We'll have a coffee before I take you down to settle in,' Elspeth said in the voice of one promising a great treat. 'Unless you'd like something stronger? We could raid Jenner's whisky cupboard.'

Whisky at three o'clock in the afternoon was a new idea to Theo, as was raiding anyone's cupboard, except as a student prank. Some mates of Tom's pulled that one off. Snuck into the office of the Vice-Chancellor (*neat name, eh?*) when the cleaners had just left and replaced all the spirits with different shades of tea. Good little stir afterwards, drinking the proceeds, and imagining the expression on the faces of the VC's guests. Now that seemed like a scene from someone else's life.

This is your life, Theodora Potts! Sitting in the dingy kitchen of a man who might have won Australia's first Nobel Prize, had he stayed put. So they say, but talk in the Staff Club is cheap.

The kitchen was long and narrow, with a cluster of stove and whiteware down the dark end, an old pine table filling up the middle, and a strip of windows, which would have let in a certain amount of light if they had not been blocked by the detritus of years. There was no evidence that they had ever been cleaned; perhaps they had been occasionally sluiced down with a hose from the outside. Most of the fourth wall of the kitchen was non-existent, the kitchen giving straight on to a dark carpeted hallway, a good step up, from which were visible the dark staircase to the next floor and two dark closed doors. The hall was panelled in oak and cluttered with several large pieces of furniture of the sideboard variety, one with candle holders and speckled mirrors. On one of the sideboards, all by itself, sat a bible of mammoth proportions. In the small spaces left by the furniture hung two coats of arms and a rusty stag's head. Theo thought that making your way through the hall without banging into an awkward corner would require sobriety.

'How old is this house?'

'Oh, not very old, about 1550. There's a picture some-where.'

On the small stretch of wall left over from kitchenware and window, Elspeth had a pinboard layered inches thick with cuttings and pictures. She unskewered two of these piles and put them on the table before Theo. Leafing through them she found that practically everything related to the sea or sailing on the sea; articles torn from magazines and papers about round-the-world races, the diagram of a yacht race, photos of yachtswomen standing proud, advertisements for nautical supplies, a brochure from a marina near the Isle of Wight, a diagram for tying *a better bowline* . . . snapshots of people in small boats, people in jerseys standing by small boats, people in wet-suits half in the water, people grinning and holding up a trophy and a champagne bottle. In among this marine memorabilia were other family bits – school reports, a PTA notice dated 1986, postcards from America and Scotland (*Predictably disgusting weather here. Recalcitrant air conditioning. Obtuse conference organisers. All the usual delights*), articles torn out of the newspaper about Jenner Ransfield, one with photo, his dark visage grainy and indecipherable: LOCAL BOFFIN UNVEILS THE CHICKEN OF THE FUTURE.

'There it is!' said Elspeth, pointing over her shoulder at the pile.

Theo looked at the postcard, sharp crinkly edges, well yellowed away from its original black and white. In spidery white writing down the bottom was written *Nightingales Farm, Somerset*. It was such a pretty place, whitewashed, hollyhocks, delphiniums, with a thick thatched roof.

'Thatch!' cried Theo, like one catching sight of the Holy Grail.

'Yes, wasn't it lovely? I fell in love with it at once. But Jenner says it was environmentally unsound and far too expensive. He says the preservation of thatch is as pretentious and wasteful as driving a Rolls-Royce. Chance would be a fine thing, say I. Though not to his face of course.'

'Of course,' murmured Theo, wondering why it went without saying. She was quite unable to comprehend why anyone would actually remove a thatch roof.

'Tiles are so much more practical, and quite pretty.'

'Amazing. In Australia we think anything a hundred years old is just fascinating, and we slap a preservation order on anything pre-war.'

'Well, Jenner's views are complicated – too complicated for me to follow. You had much better ask him directly.'

So Dr Ransfield wasn't quite so Olde Worlde as all that.

'Have you finished your coffee? We can go down to the caravan now.'

Fortified by a single cup of milky coffee, Theo was led down the track towards the caravan. It grew dark as they descended. Theo reckoned this was not twilight but the crowding in of oaks and beeches. The caravan wasn't easy to discern, being dark green like the rest of the grove. It sat on bricks in a little clearing, next to an extensive vegetable patch.

Theo looked at the green tin exterior, and her notion of the caravan as the luxurious bauble of the rich shimmered for a moment in the Somerset twilight and popped.

'I built this myself!' said Elspeth, and somehow you could tell.

She opened the door with pride, apologising for the musty smell which she hadn't been able to drive out.

There was a welcoming vase of wild flowers on the fold-down table. She turned on the light, a low-wattage bulb powered by a black cord draped through a whole procession of trees. She showed Theo how to ignite the gas ring in the tiny kitchen area, and explained how to tell when the gas in the bottle was running out. There was a narrow divan which doubled as a bed, upholstered in that ribbed nylon that you do not want to lay your cheek upon and underneath it a pair of wooden drawers. The floor was linoleum, orange and brown zigzags. There were net curtains against peerers-in, but nothing against the cold. Behind a plastic curtain there was a handbasin, a square inch of mirror, and a shower which drew rainwater from a tank in the roof. On the wall were four coloured prints of sailing ships, long Sellotaped to the tin.

'I used to be a shipwright,' said Elspeth.

'Gee, thanks,' said Theo and plopped down her pack, thinking it was just as well she had a mountain-proof sleeping bag.

'I'll leave you to settle in. Come up to the house when you're ready. We can have some high tea in a little while. Robin will come downstairs, I expect. May Margaret comes and goes, one can never tell. She's away at the present time. Supper is about eight, or nine, all depending on when Jenner comes in, which isn't very predictable, I am afraid. But you can pop up for an egg any time really, though Jenner doesn't like the children having what he calls *ad hoc* meals.'

The vision of virgin white sheets and central heating, and a genial Dr Ransfield, smelling of tobacco and chuckling into his tea, shrivelled up and slid out of the door as Elspeth slammed it behind her — it not fitting terribly well, you see.

Theo stood where she had been left, in the gloom, and could not prevent a tear sliding down alongside her nose, right down into her mouth. Theodora Potts, who at twenty-six had never done a creature a moment's voluntary harm, except to dent the pride of a boy or two, and cause a few experimental bulls some pleasurable surprise – what had she done to deserve this, except exhibit a little naïvety? She knew that she had no right to misery, having seen a beggar at the station, his beer can clutched like a comforter, a barrier of cardboard against the world; she knew she had no right to misery, having a credit card in her pocket and kind friends at home. But she experienced one of those moments of pure unhappiness which overcome us in the midst of plenty, which, like a nightmare, we cannot reason away. Who is so large that they can confidently declare that the death of a small hope is not, after all, a death?

The house, Theo is to discover, consists of six rooms, excluding passages and services, in which the reader and writer are not generally interested until it comes to matters of sex or concealment – or murder. But murder mystery this story is not. On the ground floor, across the dark hallway from the kitchen, are two rooms, their doors tight shut: the dogs' room and Jenner's room. Upstairs, their doors equally shut, but with less violent overtones, are the bedrooms of Elspeth and Robin. May Margaret inhabits the upper quarters, sleeping on her truckle bed, if she sleeps at all. There are no living rooms as such. When the house was previously inhabited, by a jovial farmer, his wife and family, before a dementia, contracted by affection for his doomed cattle, drove him to impale himself on a pitchfork in the byre and die in a darkened room two days later, there were two dark but comfy family rooms adjoining the hall, all blowsy hot from the fires which burned windfall timber, morning, noon and night. There was a dining room and a living room: a dining room for eating around the dining table in, and living room for sitting in, and for fire, television, armchairs. This room still has fire, television and armchairs, but they are enjoyed by the dogs, who reportedly have quite clear views on which television programmes they prefer. Jenner's dogs, two female Great Danes, one tawny, the other piebald, are ill-tempered, lazy dogs, rather noisy for their breed. They lollop from the car wreaking daily havoc among the chickens, straight into the house and into their chairs, as if the journey from the Agricultural College had been oh so wearing, my dear. They raise their wondrous voices when they feel that dinner time approacheth, and lo, the woman lays forth meat and mash, while the man dispenses powders. Short-haired, they crave heat, and lean, they love warmth. And the lord their master provides for them, in the room that is set for them he provides comfort. In the other room, once the dining room, Jenner Ransfield conducts his life. No one goes inside, not even the dogs, but through the momentarily opened door there is evidence of many books, a table loaded high with paper, a narrow bed, dark pictures in massive frames, and a permanent cloud of tobacco smoke. Clothes issue forth to be washed; glasses to be rinsed. Here the chequebook lives, and here whisky is enshrined. The door has an excellent slam.

Theo observes the narrow bed in Jenner's room and the chaste white bed in Elspeth's, and is disconcerted. Her parents' bedroom has a pink bedspread made of candle-wick, furrowed in neat lines across its vastness. They have bookshelves on either side, and matching bedside lamps, with separate controls, as well as a shared control for the dimmer on the main lights, the radio and the television. They do not argue over these. In bed Theo's mother reads palatable works of history – the life of Mary Queen of Scots, the tragedy at Mayerling, Ludwig of Bavaria and Hildegard of Bingen. Her books are large format with glossy colour plates, but have a proper critical apparatus and bibliography, to make it clear they are not for dullards. Theo's father dozes over his bedtime reading, and watches television with headphones or with no sound at all, but when he reads, he reads White Papers on medical reform, the *Lancet*, the *General Practitioner*, and the last book on fly fishing or racing he got for Christmas/birthday/Father's Day from one of his children. Every night he contemplates scaling the citadel of satin, but most nights sleep overtakes him before his thoughts translate to action. He awakes happy in his clean smooth bed, the sun through the curtains, the birds bright, the lawn smiling under the automatic watering system.

With so divergent a background, it takes Theo some time to get to grips with the Ransfields, though they are but four in number. Afterwards, when she described them to her friends, she wondered if she ever got the hang of them at all. She said it was like living in that TV comedy about aliens in human bodies who have been inadequately briefed about life on earth.

The morning after her arrival, she wakes in confusion, uncomfortably early, having fallen asleep after tea, overcome by jet lag. The discomfort and disappointment of her surroundings immediately assert themselves, but she realises as she lies in her warm nest of sleeping bag that it is the dread of meeting Dr Ransfield that chiefly troubles her. And to think that only a day ago she was looking forward to the privilege more than anything since walking up to the podium at Vet School graduation to collect her *summa cum laude* statuette in the form of a brass bull.

It is far too dank and grey to consider going for a run; she curls up again and dozes and thinks of Tom, warm and ordinary. Some time later she hears singing outside.

I wish I wish but it's all in vain

I wish I was a maid again
But a maid again I ne'er shall be
Till apples grow on an orange tree

She peers out through the haze, still cuddled in her sleeping bag, and considers that the wet stuff slicing downwards is probably called spring rain. It must be spring because the vegetables are poking up through the red soil and white stones, little feathery carrot tops and other things Theodora doesn't recognise but that must be vegetables because they are appearing in such tidy rows. Elspeth is coming down the garden path, wearing a yellow oilskin and sou'wester and green wellingtons. She skirts around the caravan, politely not looking in to see if Theodora is stirring, and ventures on to a new strip of the garden, already roughly dug over, bends down and starts to pick up stones. She carries an armful to the side of the patch, arranges them, and goes back for more, bending over, picking up an armful, then back to deposit them.

Theodora watches this gawky ballet for a few minutes, then impelled by shame, grits her teeth and gets up, skittering in bare feet on the linoleum. She puts a saucepan of water on to heat, and though crying out for a shower, throws on her clothes, anything, anything to keep in the precious warmth. She sends up a prayer to the household gods that there will be a shower at the college. She has already learnt that the house has a problem with its hot-water supply, due to Jenner's passion for switching off the power.

When she emerges, Elspeth smiles at her radiantly, as if she had half expected her guest to flee in the night.

'Jenner said not to disturb you. I am to take you to the college after you have had a spot of breakfast.'

Elspeth insists on porridge, which Theo eats for the cultural experience and the comfort. While Theo is ploughing through her helping, Elspeth goes outside to get the egg truck started. Theo realises that she is going to encounter the great and now apparently terrible Dr Ransfield with unwashed hair. She feels this will put her at such a psychological disadvantage that she will never recover, and wonders how this could be happening to her.

After breakfast, clutching her bag, with towel, soap and shampoo, nice clean pad and pen, and a respectable novel to cover all eventualities, Theodora is driven to the college in the egg truck, which is marginally less comfortable than the green car, but free from dog hair.

The North-West Somerset Agricultural College is housed in a fine Georgian mansion, once home to some obscure branch of the squirearchy. From the front the illusion of stately grandeur has been preserved, so that Theo, arriving at the imposing portico from the sweep of driveway through magnificently landscaped gardens, says *Wow!* a number of times. Only afterwards does she find out how extensive and mean-spirited are the modern buildings behind the gracious walls of eighteenth-century brick.

Elspeth explains, shouting over the noise of the engine, that she dare not stop the truck, in case it will not start again. Theo climbs out and goes into the entrance hall, where all pretence at elegance ends. Utilitarian vinyl, chrome chairs with ripped seats spewing out pieces of foam, big plain noticeboards, as found in every institution in the world, with the same notices: posters for college events, disco, fun run, fund-raiser for Animal Rights, College Chaplaincy For Your Every Need, Pastor Rick, On Campus Every Monday Afternoon.

It turned out to be a long day.

She found her way to Animal Husbandry easily by following the college map, although she could not quite believe that the great man himself was located in so lowly a place. The department was housed in a large prefabricated hut, most of which was an open-plan computer laboratory. Six offices were partitioned off along the south-facing wall for the staff members; beside the main door was a glass cubby-hole inhabited by a harridan of the class Academic Secretary, with which Theo was well acquainted.

She went into the common room, where half a dozen students were slouching over the computer terminals, and machine-gunned them all with her superiority. She found them narrow and spotty specimens, shrill with spurious wit and throbbing with ill-controlled hormones. Theo never had any unease about the speed with which she arrived at conclusions.

She found a door labelled DR J. RANSFIELD and knocked. Knocked again. Started to feel uncomfortable. Knocked again.

One of the girls detached herself from the group. She had streaked ginger and blonde hair and full pouty make-up.

'He won't answer, you know, even when he's there.' Theo decided the look on her face could best be described as a smirk.

'How the fuck do I get in touch with him, then?'

'Caroline knows. Caroline, do you know where Jenner is, then?' She giggled as if this was a huge joke.

A second girl peeled herself off the computer terminal and came across to look Theo over.

'Hi. You must be Dr Potts. He's been talking about you.' She rolled her eyes. She was as skinny as everyone else in England, pretty and neat like a doll made when materials are short, with hair washed dark red, and magenta lipstick. She had four studs in her ears and a tiny one in her nose. She wore a skimpy little top, which showed her midriff, a little black skirt, and monster black shoes.

'He's in there,' she said, 'but he won't come out. I'll tell him you're here, shall I?'

'Oh great,' said Theo, 'and meanwhile?'

The girls shrugged as if synchronised.

'There's a coffee machine at the caff.'

Theo marched into the harridan's cubicle.

'Hello, I'm Dr Potts. Could you tell Dr Ransfield that I shall be in the library when he is ready to see me. I guess it doesn't take all morning for him to put on his make-up.'

The departmental secretary, a woman of solid worth, with a bosom suited to opera-going, and no sense of humour, said merely, 'Bear with me, please, and tried Jenner's extension.

'I'll let him know,' she said.

Theo went to the Students' Union and tried to get a shower. She was told that yes, she certainly could. Her heart sang. First she would have to fill in this form to join the Students' Union and when it was processed and her ID card issued, she could have one any time she wanted.

'But I want one *now*!' she cried. It made no difference.

No one could bend the rules, and no amount of cajoling or swearing or reasoned argument had any effect. Theo's hair stayed greasy, and she felt like cinders.

She found the library, a rectangular block of grey-brown brick, without proportion or adorning feature. She applied for a library card, and filled in another form, was told to return in a week. *I'm getting the message*. She then asked, without any expectation of a cheering answer, if she could use the Internet, and was given two more forms, one for a user code, and one for Internet access, to be authorised by the Head of Department and one's Personal Mentor, and full of disclaimers regarding prosecution for illegal purposes and any claims for emotional damage. *And would this also take a week? It can take up to three.* But she was told the mission goal of the IT department was to turn all applications around in a week. Theo explained succinctly and colourfully to the librarian exactly how easy it was to set up a new account, but did not think thereby that she had improved the reputation of Australians in the Mother Country.

She bought herself a nasty cup of coffee and took it back to the library, which was strictly forbidden, and sat down in the reading area by the new periodicals with her feet on the occasional table. This too was bound to be forbidden, but, deep into the latest *Journal of the American Institute of Agricultural Technology*, she ceased to give one.

She'd given up on Dr Ransfield; she'd already decided to cut her losses, collect what data was on hand and hightail it back home, by way of Amsterdam and Barcelona. She would then produce a sexy-looking report for the Cattle Breeders, based on what material she already had, and offer to refund the travel grant. They would smile at her benignly and say *No, no, Dr Potts, we couldn't do that. This is an excellent report. Have some more money and do some more work for us.* She'd got it all worked out by the end of the Table of Contents of the *Journal of the American Institute of Agricultural Technology*. She had dismissed him so completely that when her concentration was interrupted by his voice, she did not at once know who it might be. The mere sound of his voice was also a new experience.

Jenner Ransfield's voice, rich and rolling as the Welsh countryside of one's fantasy, rigid with the authority of Oxford, jagged with a slight overlay of Australia, deep and musical and unnerving, was to become a major influence in her life. *It's his voice that gets you*, she'd say, trying to explain the Ransfield effect. *Once he starts to talk you can't stop listening to it, no matter what sort of specious or crazy stuff comes out. And to make it worse, about half of what he says is absolutely brilliant.*

But on the dreary day of their first meeting, she knew nothing about this, only that she heard an extraordinary voice saying things she didn't quite understand.

'Dr Theodora Potts. You are Dr Potts, my gracious

visitor, and I have treated you despitefully. I am a worm and no man.'

Her image of cuddly Dr Ransfield, with a round owl face and round owl glasses, a twinkly smile and cardigan of thick brown wool, had been with her so long that she didn't immediately realise that the real Dr Ransfield was addressing her, and he didn't look like that at all.

He looked, in fact, rather like the statue of himself as a knight which stood at the entrance to his farmhouse. He was remarkably tall, belying any expectation about Welsh stature, and towered over Theo as she sat slumped in the easy chair. He was very dark and hirsute, but clean-shaven and trimmed, quite unlike the disordered image projected by his home. His nose was pronounced and beaked; with his wild dark eyes it gave him the appearance of a buzzard tied to its perch in a run-down wildlife park. Though Theo was not much given to metaphor she felt herself a furry animal under the intelligent scrutiny of a vivisectionist.

She didn't have time to decide on a suitable approach. Perhaps there wasn't one, for Jenner Ransfield was completely outside her experience, and slightly outside the real world as she understood it. His feet, in his brown brogues, were firmly planted on the nylon carpet, but his personage seemed to inhabit a different plane of existence. Who the hell talked like that? *A worm and no man*, for God's sake.

But Jenner Ransfield did talk like that, and at length. He was a man possessed but Theo couldn't figure out exactly what it was that possessed him. He took her on an extended walk around the college grounds, and talked and talked and talked; almost, she reported to Juliet later, without hesitation, deviation or repetition.

During the walk, Theo often felt as if she wasn't really there, that his rant – the first of many she was to endure – was directed all around her, and she was a place-holder who allowed him to vent the wrath inside him. But then, suddenly in full flood, he would direct a saying at her which made it quite clear that he knew precisely whom he was talking to. This rhetorical device meant that it was impossible to switch off and be carried along by the flow of his lovely voice.

'Look around you,' he said, waving his arm around from a great height. 'This so-called college typifies all that is appalling and disjointed about Britain today. I would use the word dysfunctional, if I did not so abhor its currency. Look at these gracious grounds, these lawns, these trees, the elegance of this lakeside, the breadth of vision, the enlightenment of the designer and, though it chokes me to say it, the generosity of spirit of the Croesus who endowed it. That is England, admirable and mighty. And now, look over there – those mingy, narrow-minded, jerry-built prisons of the spirit called lecture rooms and offices, that hideous library stocked with sociological verbiage of caring and sharing, scarcely fit to wipe an arse withal, and barely a philosophy text or a mathematical treatise worthy of the name. And yet they place the one within the other – the mean within the mighty. Somewhere, a faceless bureaucrat, in a soulless office facing over the railways, with a stroke of his pen thrust this college into this setting, motivated no doubt by a race memory of beauty married to usefulness, but ever since that one moment of inspiration, the philistines have acted as if they occupy a different aesthetic universe from their forebears. Those zombies you see there – they are Yahoos in the country of the Houyhnhnms. That is one of the handful of good things about Australia: there you do not pretend not to be philistines. Do you regard yourself as anything other than a philistine?'

'Me? You'd need to define the term before I'd answer that!'

'Well answered, Dr Potts! I see we shall be entirely

compatible. Matthew Arnold, though he is not a man for whom I have any personal affection, combining as he did the worst aspects of the English middle classes in the nineteenth century, Arnold divided society into Barbarians, Philistines and the Populace . . .'

And so on around the lake, through the shrubbery and back again.

His anger was all-encompassing. He could find cause to rail against everything and everyone. Theo naïvely thought she might be exempt, as his guest and his collaborator, as a much younger person, well-intentioned, who had done him no wrong. In this she was mistaken, as she found out later.

The day's work that followed the walk around the lake was the most intense and extending Theodora had ever undertaken. Later she wrote to Prof. Betsy that Jenner Ransfield's mind ranged over so many disciplines that it seemed almost unfair to ordinary scholars, and in each area his reading and conceptual grasp was positively scary. He also knew about technical matters like the working of the image analyser and the best methods of capturing data from microscopes and video cameras, which really ought to be left to lowlier forms of life like technicians. However, he was not, Theo reported, one of those tiresome know-alls that clutter up university staff rooms trying to bore the pants off you. He assumed that the same attitude of rigour and thoroughness was natural to everyone, and while she was running to keep up with him, Theo found she really wanted to do so.

After the walk around the lake he allowed only one break in the day, to eat white sandwiches in the caff. He described this food as having been extruded out of plastic tubes and reconstituted into sandwich shapes in the kitchen. Theo laughed, but wasn't sure whether it was a joke. The rest of the day he poured them both endless cups of decent coffee from the pot which stood attentive on the lab bench. Theo noticed that the students did not help themselves to this coffee. All the work was done at the bench; she did not see the inside of his office.

In the evening he loaded his dogs into the back of the green car and drove her home. This was to be a defining experience in the life of Theodora Potts.

'You must tell no one what we did today!' he said, once they were out of the college environs. 'No one!'

They flurried through side roads, ducking and diving through mean streets to avoid any suggestion of delay. But in spite of this precaution, they washed up in a sludge of traffic, a vast population of red tail lights bobbing on its surface, waiting to be released. Jenner leant on the horn, which gave only an apologetic squawk. He pressed harder to elicit a volume commensurate with his frustration, but the mechanical device refused to pay heed to its master. He began to call down imprecations on the motorist ahead who was straddling what Jenner perceived as two lanes; then he pushed up beside him, nearside wheels on the pavement, achieved two car lengths of advantage and was again impeded. He saw a side street ahead, aimed for it, cutting in front of a cyclist. Theo had a brief flash of the cyclist throwing up her hands in alarm, and another brief flash of a No Exit symbol by the opening to Jenner's escape route.

'Why?' she said. 'Why must I tell no one?'

'Because,' he said, roaring down the empty cul-de-sac with all the force of his released anger, 'the world is full of jealous mediocrities who build their careers, their fortunes and their reputations by stealing the work of others. It is not a theft that they, self-righteous ones, recognise as such, which makes it more insidious, more evil. It is a self-deceptive theft, like a blind parasitic worm, which hears a discussion here, a lecture there, a result the other place, leeches on and sucks away the blood of originality into itself, drunken with the taste of it, until it does not know what is its own and what it has stolen.'

'Gosh,' said Theo.

Her hair brushed the front window as the car reached an unexpected crisis.

'Go and look for a way out.'

Wondering at herself the while, Theo got out of the car, and walked along the hedges looking wistfully into the lighted front rooms, where people with central heating were watching television. She knew they had driven into a dead end, but she didn't know how to get back in the car and tell him. She stood hesitating at the end of the cul-de-sac where a bicycle path led off into the dark. He flung open the car door and came towards her.

'There's a sort of bicycle path,' she proffered.

He subjected the opening of the path to examination, while the tawny dog, Abishag, took the opportunity to shit on a nice new stretch of verge. He discovered that the bollards were removable. Theo found herself helping to uproot concrete barricades without any sense of a jape or a protest. The bicycle path was just wide enough for the car to pass down, and they passed down it at a good speed. But when they reached the end, the bollards blocking their exit refused to be removed, and eventually the car reversed up the path, back down the cul-de-sac and forced its way into the pool of traffic again.

This was not really a good moment to have a debate with Jenner.

'But I still don't see why the secrecy,' Theo pursued. 'I'm doing exactly what I set out to do in my research plan. The images and the statistics were known to be available; you stated as much in a letter to the Cattle Breeding Association. All we're doing is correlating them.'

'You are a simpleton. They shouldn't have let you out. They shouldn't let an innocent abroad with a post-doctoral fellowship. They should have withheld your doctorate until you were old and ugly and suspicious like me.'

'Fucking paranoid, I call it,' said Theo in a mutter.

He leant over, while the car was still moving forward, and threw open her door.

'Out!'

'I'm sorry. That was a bit rude.'

'You may call me paranoid, you may call me maniacal, you may call me any such epithet of mania you please. It has all been done before. You may call me a mountebank, or a hothead, you may call me a dinosaur or an aberration of nature. All those terms I have heard and shrugged off my well-developed carapace. But you are not to use that other word in my presence, not under any provocation, or in any context, neither in quotation nor description. Not even if we are engaged in an act of fornication together shall you use it.'

'That,' said Theo, slamming the car door shut, with herself still on the inside, 'would not be fucking fornication; that would be fucking adultery. And, incidentally, rape.'

No further word was uttered for the rest of the journey back to the farm. Three months spread in front of Theodora like an eternity, half nightmare, half farce.

II

MAY MARGARET, ELSPETH and Jenner's daughter, had possession of the top of the house. At the head of the upper stairs was a door, and on the door a precisely carved notice which read 'MEN, BEWARE!' Beneath the wooden words was a smoothly finished bas-relief, of a woman's face, grinning like a Bacchante, her cheeks stuffed with things which might or might not have been testicles.

May Margaret had returned from a jaunt away, but neither of her parents would say where she had gone. She was in great good spirits, and on the first Saturday morning she invited Theodora to step up, issuing the invitation by hollering down the stairs. Elspeth pressed a two-litre bottle of Coca-Cola into Theo's hand and sent her up.

Theo ascended into the gloom of the first staircase, seeing only closed doors on her way, and then up into the light at the top, where she was warmly welcomed by May Margaret under the watchful eye of the woman on the door.

'Gosh, it *is* nice to have someone sane in the house. I imagine you are sane? Though coming to stay here one might wonder. But being Australian how were you to know? The father probably seems quite all right from all those miles away. O goody, did she send up some Coke? She does like to feed one, but I think she's finally getting the message. Drugs, in whatever form – sugar, caffeine, alcohol, chocolate – anything but food.'

May Margaret, twenty-one, towered over Theo. She grabbed the bottle and shook her hand. The grip was impressive and would not have disgraced a cattleman back home. She had black hair streakily hennaed, cut in a pudding-basin bob, as exact as the lettering on her door. She wore a black jersey riddled with holes, and black corduroy pants which hung about her hips like a curtain before a children's makeshift stage. She poured them both a Coke, reusing disposable plastic cups.

'Sit down somewhere, and just let me hear a normal person talk.'

Theo checked around for somewhere to sit. The upper storey of the house had been transformed into the set for some kind of avant-garde sitcom. The walls that had divided servants' rooms from boxroom and dingy corridor had been stripped back to the timbers, so that the whole floor consisted of a series of spaces divided by struts. The windows were draped in black, and the whole was lit by a pair of Anglepoise lamps trained on a work in progress at the far end; the rest of the space was cast into shadow, and it was hard to make out what there was to sit on. Theo felt that parking her bum on one of May Margaret's mistressworks would not help the germination of their friendship. Trouble was, everything in the area was carved. The timbers of the house were a riot of figures and colours, each upright a different piece of design, two or three flourishes of an idea worked out and then abandoned, as if the house itself were her sketchbook. The apple boxes which served for chairs, the one table, which was stacked with tools and paint pots, the windowsills, everything had been practised upon. The effect was unsettling, as one design was superseded by another, the ideas jostling for attention, squabbling among themselves. Monkey men with tumescent genitalia fresh from the pages of *Heavy Metal* rubbed up agaisnt smooth buttocks of Venus in the style of Eric Gill.

May Margaret sat down on a box by the table, and cleared a space for her elbow and her cup. Theo followed suit.

It was exceptionally draughty in the studio; cold air streamed under the blackout curtains, and up through the cracks in the floor. May Margaret's jersey was next her skin, and she wore no socks under her black boots. But neither did she keep still. She sat on the apple box and tapped her fingers and her feet as if she were a wind-up toy stuck in the corner.

'What on earth brought you to England? Really, what a dead-end hole – why not America? Have you seen what passes for art in this country? Pickled animals and bits of embroidery. Oh, and videos of people standing still. And concrete casts of books. You have to admire the effrontery, but one questions the skill. Skill is what it's all about, application of skill to an idea. And fun. Where's the fun in chopping up a carcass?'

'Do you have fun?'

'Absolutely. I have the blessedness of the dotty. Maybe I'll show you the attic, then you'll see how much fun I have.'

She pointed upwards. Theo, shivering over her Coke, looked up for enlightenment, and noticed a wooden ladder, carved beyond the point of safety, leading up to a trapdoor. It was padlocked shut.

'I tried to make my area man-proof, but you can never be too careful, not after what he did to my Warriors at the Gate.'

'What did he do to the Warriors at the Gate?'

'Aren't they jolly? They were much more jolly before, in a rather excited state, ready to take on the post lady any time. He emasculated them with a saw — I mean an axe would be forgivable, don't you think? Crime of passion, unstoppable penis envy, righteous indignation, *something*. But a saw is premeditated. Like burning books, I told him. You can imagine how well he liked that comparison!

'Anyway I took the opportunity to give them a nice new lick of paint, and tidy up their private parts, poor old chaps. And gave them a few more coloured plastic bits on the face masks to compensate for the bits they'd lost. I often wonder if chaps generally wouldn't mind that sort of trade.'

'You don't like men?'

'*Au contraire!* I love them. Some time you must meet my friend Elgin and his merry crew, all chaps. My friends tend to be male. I did have a girlfriend or two at school, but when you can't bring people home, it does blight such friendships. Made a lovely friend at art school, but then she decided she was in love with me, which made things a bit awkward. You don't mind me telling you all this? How about you?'

'I have a fella at home. Tom. He's awfully sweet. But I don't know . . .'

'They're either insignificant or they try to run your life. Robin or Jenner, that's the choice.'

'There might be a third kind,' said Theo wistfully.

May Margaret made a sound between a snort and a shout that was already becoming familiar to Theo. Happily in May Margaret's case it was not followed by a hell-raising sermon. She pulled out a flattened packet of smokes from the back pocket of her jeans. They were the long thin donkey-brown kind.

'Does your brother ever come out into the light of day?' Theo asked. 'Ever since I arrived he's been in his room, except for monosyllabic appearances at meals.'

'I am sure you can understand why one is monosyllabic

in this household,' said May Margaret, lighting her cigarillo with an antique mother-of-pearl lighter. 'Actually, you will observe the Lesser Spotted Robin in the daylight if you are a keen ornithologist and rise at dawn. The Robin is the newspaper king of Bridgwater. He flies out at dawn on his bike and does every newspaper round in the district. He has it all plotted and planned how to deliver the most papers in the shortest time. Any shop with the sign Wanted: Newspaper Delivery Boy or Girl – in he dives and takes on the job, then he flutters home and enters the detail of the round into his computer program which interfaces with road maps and calculates the routes. A masterpiece of operations research, of which his father might justly be proud, if he stopped talking for long enough to notice. And all the money Robin earns goes to pay his Internet telephone account, because one month the bill happened to be very large, and paterfamilias happened to see it, and there was a jolly old stink. I'm sure you understand – you have siblings?'

'Oh yes, heaps.'

Theo had a rush of affection for her brothers. There were only three of them, though often it seemed like more; hardly an hour passed at home without an extra boy turning up on his bike, or later his motorbike or car; that was before the girls started in earnest, and the brothers were less likely to be home. Sometimes she would wish they were a little less predictable, electing for something other than cricket in the summer and rugby in the winter, swimming on every conceivable occasion, tall blonde girlfriends and professional careers. But right now their implacable ordinariness seemed like a shaft of heaven.

'Does Robin ever get off the Net?'

'Almost never. He's designed, according to himself, the most beautiful web page in the world. It rejoices in the name love dot inn dot org. Can you guess what it is?'

37

'I dunno. One of those soft-core porno sites?'

'Exactly what you are supposed to think, and like thousands before you, surfing in search of boobs, you are confronted by a picture of Jesus. It's terrifying. And the clever little sods, once you visit the site, you can never get off the heavenly mailing list.'

'Born-again type? *Jesus!*'

May Margaret found this very amusing.

'Poor Robin, he takes the pater's global disapproval personally. He has retreated into the great maw of religion in order to find absolution for the sins of his father, which are heaped upon his head. It's a great shame as well as a great cruelty, because he's an exceptionally clever little fellow, my brother.'

'Who pays for Robin's gear – and his website and all that clobber?'

'American money. Very suspect. You can imagine what the tyrant has to say on the matter.'

'You'd think they might finance another phone line, so you can live like civilised people.'

In truth Theo was longing to talk to Tom, a feeling that took her by surprise. She felt that she would combust if she didn't talk to somebody normal, and catch the tenor of an ordinary day.

'We are not civilised. We do not need a telephone. Who would risk ringing the Ransfields? *He* might answer the telephone.'

'What about your friends?'

'Oh, I do all my communicating with the world through Elgin. He arranges all my commissions and all my social life. It's extremely satisfactory. Do you like my current *chef d'oeuvre*?'

May Margaret's work in progress was a gnome. He was almost finished.

'Life-size, though I'm not sure what life-size is with

gnomes. I decided that gnomes are eunuchs and generate by means of gnome-spores, sneezed out of the nostrils in the general direction of lady gnomes.'

Otherwise, she said, she'd have had to suggest tiny gnome apparatus which her client wouldn't like.

'When I explained all this, I think my client thought I was serious. Specially when I told her to be careful around him if he started to sneeze . . . I'm a bit sorry he's going, actually. I've got to paint him, which seems a shame. He'll lose a lot of detail, but she insists on his having bright red pants.'

The gnome leered at Theo from underneath his heavy eyelids, while his fingers played meaningfully with his fishing rod.

'He does look as if he's about to sneeze, or something male and nasty.'

'Yes, it's fun making things that take on a life of their own.'

The two women walked around the gnome.

'What do you do, Theodora?' May Margaret asked, in the voice of a polite relation.

'I'm researching. Artificial insemination in beef cattle. I did my doctoral thesis on it – the correlation between the way bull semen is harvested and the results. Now I've got this grant to follow up an idea, using imaging technology to analyse the quality of the semen –'

May Margaret threw back her head and laughed and laughed, so that her fringe quivered all round her head like a bobbly lampshade.

'*He* must just adore you!'

'I don't think I want to find out, either way.'

May Margaret laughed mightily at this also. Then she said she'd better get to work on the gnome because Elgin insisted the little chap be delivered to his new home at the day and hour agreed. How bourgeois they are, these men who love gain. It was especially galling, May Margaret explained, because it was Elgin who had delayed her with his scheme for visiting an empty cottage in the wilds of Cornwall stuffed full of neglected furniture.

'And of course he could not let the erotic opportunity slip through his manly fingers,' May Margaret said, 'however late we were running. Tiresome creatures.'

Theo could stay if she wasn't too cold. May Margaret said that she was never cold these days, not since her father complained about her burning electricity through the night. She made a decision then that she wasn't going to be cold, and, she said, it's amazing how easy it's been since. The trick is to remember that at any moment you can stop work, go downstairs, burst into the dogs' room and be instantly warm. Then you never have to do it.

'It's all for the escape fund,' May Margaret explained, as she yanked off the lid of the red paint pot, 'this commercial stuff. My real work is in the attic.'

She'd get a hundred pounds for this little man, she said, stirring the paint as delicately as a master chef, which worked out to about a pound an hour, but it was a hundred pounds she wouldn't otherwise have: a hundred pounds into the escape fund.

'Silly thing, though, I have this fatal weakness for Mother. Silly woman looks so downtrodden when a big gas bill comes in. One can't not help her out. One should be strong, and leave her to face the consequence of showing him the bills. After all, it's his bloody dogs that keep warm in this house, no one else.'

May Margaret chatted as she worked. She'd never travelled, she said. She'd like to go to Oxford and see all the stone carving on the buildings. Like to go to Hatfield House too, and see the carved staircase, with the bird catcher and the windmill. And Germany, Meister Bernard's altarpiece. Bourg-en-Bress. And Kilpeck, all those Greene Men and the Sheila-na-gog. But there is no money forthcoming from the parental coffer for such unnecessary expeditions.

'His theory is that, having spent all Grandmama's legacy to send me to that god-awful school, he shouldn't have to spend a penny more. Especially as he is denied access to his own attic, a cause of great distress to him. On this matter alone, I agree with him – why should he support me? I am an adult, capable of earning a living. Three pounds an hour wiping tables, why not? If I choose to freeze up here and carve things, rather than wipe tables, that's my choice, don't you think? That's the sort of reasoning my father prides himself on.'

'His reasoning often seems to be intellectual justification for what he feels.'

May Margaret turned around from the gnome, paint-brush in mid-air. 'Gosh, he *will* adore you. I'd take great care, if I were you.'

'He seems to thoroughly dislike me.'

'Split infinitive. Now those he *does* dislike. No, he'll adore you, but the manifestations will be contra-indicative, if you follow me. Treat him like a tube of phosphorus – steaming away quietly to itself – add something quite harmless like a bit of sunlight, and boom. Destruction.'

Cold drives Theo downstairs after a while, in search of a coffee. May Margaret has declined the offer, say-ing that coffee must be heated with electricity, must it not? Theo curls herself around a mug of coffee and reads a selection of Saturday papers that Robin has left on the kitchen table. She is impressed by the literacy and seriousness of the big papers, but understands the context of about a quarter of the articles; this makes her feel disconcerted and depressed. It astounds her that Britain, which nobody at home takes very seriously, should generate so many column inches, and so much of it concerning itself.

Nobody's about. When Theo's father had guests, he would get up on a Saturday morning bristling with ideas for the day. *Golf? Tennis? Sightseeing, a nice long drive? Into town and ride on the trams?* And here, where there is so much to see, no one wants to show it to her. She decides she will have to blow her careful accumulation of a Canberra-sized mortgage, and hire a car.

Things can't go on like this. She'd kill for a long hot bath. She has managed a shower almost every day – the shower in the caravan can be persuaded to run warm by turning on the gas and waiting for the blast of hot water which suddenly turns to cold again, before changing its mind and again searing whatever small portion of the body it can reach. She has also braved the musty showers at the Students' Union which are uniformly lukewarm; after such a shower, one is clean but chilled. She feels she must examine herself for mildew in unexpected places. She dare not ask for a bath at the farmhouse, because she knows the desperate state of the hot water. Jenner insists that the kitchen range be the only form of water heating, but equally insists on a regular supply of clean clothes, clean sheets and even clean tablecloths. Though she washes everything in cold, it is Elspeth's lament – her only lament – that there is never enough hot water. Theo observes that Jenner has his bath each morning and Robin his shower. Elspeth cannot endure anything stained or sticky about her person, but claims to believe cold water good for one. So Theo puts up with the shower in the caravan. At least, she argues, the water is lovely soft rainwater, which makes her hair as soft and downy as a day-old chick. She thinks she will call this sort of reasoning the Elspeth Syndrome.

This Saturday morning Jenner is embattled in his room, the only sign of life a seeping of pipe tobacco under the door, and the faint buzz from the gramophone of Tito Schipa stealing *Una furtiva lagrima*. Theo drinks her coffee on tenterhooks for the sound of his door opening. There's a cough from his room, and Theo finds she cannot bear the thought of being found alone in the kitchen when he emerges. She takes off into the farmyard to hide.

The dogs greet her with their usual show of animosity. Theo likes animals, in spite of what she does to bulls, and has tried to make friends with the dogs. This is not a good idea; they regard her as a rival for Jenner's favour. Theo asserts her dominance over them as a self-respecting vet must, and so stand-off has been achieved. The dogs and the chickens comprise all the stock on Nightingales Farm; there is not even a pig for her to scratch the back of. She roves around the farmyard looking for cats or squirrels or even perhaps a mouse.

It's very peculiar behaviour, she thinks, as she strolls across the farmyard towards the surrounding wood. Every day this week she has worked in the lab with Jenner, has talked agricultural science and statistics and genetics and behaviouralism and bio-ethics and the theory of image analysis over lunch. She has lived through three journeys to college and three journeys home again, though opting for the student pub and the bus home on Friday. And yet, after all this proximity and hours of talk, she flees at the very thought of his coming out of his room and saying good morning. She decides it must be jet lag, because nothing else makes sense.

The trees close in on every side. It's as if she were miles from habitation, rather than yards. She finds herself working out the statistical likelihood of a wandering rapist in the vicinity. Being of an analytical bent, she takes the comparative crime statistics of England and Australia, the relative population density, and does calculations well into the thicket. She recalls a paper she read recently which

43

examined the sexual violation statistics from all OECD countries and found that one is eight and a half times more likely to be raped by someone whose name one knows than by a stranger.

Her attention is diverted by a group of plaster gnomes, like tropical fungi freakishly transported. She squats down by the little family. There are four gnome children and their parents, and although they are brightly painted and rotund, they are not whimsical. The gnome mother sadly proffers an apple which a gnome child rejects. The gnome father is swishing at a bare-bottomed child with an evil horse whip. The other two children are engaged in fisti-cuffs, their faces suffused with rage. Theo wonders if she might buy them off May Margaret, not to grace her parents' fishpond, which they would scarcely do, but to act as a visual aid when she tries to describe Nightingales back home. Already her limited vocabulary of similes is all used up. She has run out of ways to explain what it's like without alarming them. Because she would not like them to think it was *seriously* weird.

There's nothing seriously weird, she tells herself, about hunkering down in a dark wood looking at dysfunctional gnomes, wondering about rapists, but it's not behaviour that she finds easy to explain to herself. She's not seriously afraid of Jenner Ransfield; she's not seriously disturbed by his household. But she feels uneasy. She tries to frame a description for Juliet: *dislocated*, she thinks, *diffracted*, *polarised* . . . some sort of effect. If she were as sensible as she knows she is, by now she would have treated the whole thing as an enlarging life experience, like living for a week in a hippie commune, have politely thanked the Ransfields for their hospitality and moved into a bed and breakfast. But instead, she feels trapped here, powerless and somehow involved. None of these states is familiar or desirable. She doesn't feel like Theodora

Potts at all, and it isn't just her body crying out for a bath.

Beyond the trees, in the farmyard, there is a familiar voice raised, with barking and slamming of doors. Theo hears the car storm up the track behind her to the gate; she contracts herself so as not to be seen. She hears the car putter and kick into the distance. Jenner is off somewhere. It's now safe to go back into the house.

When she enters the farmhouse kitchen, she finds Elspeth struggling with the washing machine, which has refused to spin and is full of water and greyish sheets. She has a collection of buckets, into which she is disgorging the water and the wet sheets, but still, water pours out on to the floor all round her. She is trying not to cry. 'It was just this moment fixed. It was such a bill. I shall have to have him back.'

Theo goes to her aid; a grown woman crying over her washing is a hideous sight.

'It's going to rain,' Theo says. 'These will never dry outside. Do you have a dryer?'

Such a question does not need an answer. Elspeth's shaking of the head is more mourning than response.

Theo's mother has a laundry of most sparkling whiteness. It is connected to the house by a glassed-in corridor full of shelves and cupboards and incidental sunlight. Here are kept the not-quite kitchen, not-quite laundry, not-quite garage items, like the preserving pan and the portable barbecue and the picnic hamper, with six plastic settings in yellow and green. The corridor is paved in white vinyl, as is the adjoining laundry, in which everything lines up in perfect right angles, and not a murmur of dust is to be seen. The lint from the dryer is deposited into a white swing-top bin which is emptied every day into a larger bin. The stray dust which accumulates around the mouth of the dryer is wiped away with a white paper from the holder on the wall above the dryer, and the paper towel goes into the bin. The pegs, which alone are not white, sit in neat compartments in the peg holder inside the laundry basket. Sometimes the pegs are colour matched, red in one compartment, pink in another; mercifully this is not a common practice. A broom hangs from a hook by the door, alongside a squeegee mop and a long-handled dustpan. The muck just doesn't stand a chance.

Theo squashes the sopping washing into the receptacles and hauls them out into the yard, where she tips out the gross water and squeezes out some more. She goes back inside and hauls the wet rugs into the stable yard, then finds a broom and dashes a mixture of soapy water and dust rolls and good old-fashioned dirt across the kitchen floor and into the yard. She seizes on a pile of newspapers, ignoring Elspeth's yelps, throws them on the floor and jumps on them to make them absorb the rest of the water. Then she drags up all the wet papers and crumples some into the kitchen fire, where they smoulder with a great satisfactory steaminess. She puts the rest of the wet papers outside the door to deal with later. Then she disposes the drier rugs over the wet area, and dragoons Elspeth into the yard to help her wring out the sheets. They laugh as they stand either end of a dripping sheet and twist it round and round, a domestic parody of a tug-of-war. They empty the buckets and put the washing in them.

'After lunch, I'll go to the launderette,' says Theo. 'There must be one in Bridgwater somewhere.'

But Elspeth insists that she must come, as she has some errands in the town. Also, she adds, the egg truck might refuse to start in the High Street, and how embarrassing that would be! Theo agrees wholeheartedly and asks why they can't take the car, which, though deeply uncool, is at least reliable. Jenner might need it, she is told. Saturday afternoon – who knows where he might want to go?

Theo does not want to spend her second Saturday in England at the launderette. She has visions of Stonehenge and the Lost Gardens of Heligan and briefly fantasises that Jenner might suggest they all go on an outing. She quickly dismisses this as fanciful; at that moment, it would have been quite impossible for her to imagine the circumstances in which she and Jenner will eventually visit the beautiful and magical parts of western England.

Elspeth and Theo stow the buckets of laundry in the back of the truck for afters. Then they get on with preparing the lunch, buttering bread and washing radishes. This is a tricky procedure as Elspeth doesn't know how many of the household to expect. Robin may or may not come downstairs; May Margaret may or may not take a break from her work; Jenner may or may not reappear from wherever he has disappeared to. Elspeth says she doesn't know where he's gone, though he muttered something about college business. Often he goes on long walks, she says, across the moor, and far beyond, with or without the dogs; he drives to little villages and looks at the churches; he goes fishing; country shows, he often goes to country shows.

There is a clatter on the stair, and Robin descends. He wears laced-up riding boots and a white Hamlet shirt; his flesh, insofar as it is visible, is the same colour. Long black hair cascades into his eyes and down his shoulders.

'We received our one hundred thousandth hit!' he cries. His eyes are shining. He spreads out his arms to embrace the errant world.

He's younger than May Margaret, about nineteen or twenty, and parts of him still gangle with adolescence. His accent differs from that of everyone else in the family – where May Margaret is cut-glass, Jenner theatrically and musically educated, and Elspeth defiantly Scots, Robin has a light flat voice, flatter than Theo's, with a marked local accent, the accent to be heard in the supermarkets and bus queues.

His mother is loud in congratulation and wishes she could share the glad tidings with Jenner.

'I *would* like it if Father came and looked at my page,' says Robin. 'I'm particularly proud of the Scapegoat. I got the image from the museum direct, so it's very fine. Then I tidied it up – simplified it a little. People often download it.'

'Can I come and look at your page?' asks Theo.

'Oh yes, oh certainly, yes,' says Robin ducking under his hair, 'when it's finished, but it's not quite – there are a few things . . .'

'OK, fair enough.'

She recognises that he's petrified of her entering his room. And she knows just what his room will look like; it will resemble the rooms of a dozen studious, mouse-trained men of her reluctant acquaintance, toppling piles of bright software packages, some still shrink-wrap intact, scatters of discs, music and otherwise, pizza wrappings indiscriminate among the printed dumps of images of blood-streaked warriors and battle-maidens overburdened with cleavage, the screeds of unconsulted read-me files, crumpled up Coke cans, complete sets of favourite science fiction writers in alphabetical order, the lubricious babe posters adorned with puckish speech bubbles. The universal culture spread by telepathy rather than contact, for the inhabitants of these rooms rarely venture forth from their dens into each others'. Theo knows that she is unlikely to be invited inside, blonde curls notwithstanding.

Robin joins them at the table. He refuses a coffee, asking instead for hot Bovril. Theo reckons this concoction smells like the sort of thing she'd give to a sick cow.

'Praise the Lord,' he says. 'A hundred thousand hits. A hundred thousand chances for the Lord Jesus to enter into people's hearts. Drawn in by the clever links and the great story. Into the heart of the Good News!'

'What sort of visitors are they?' asks Theo, determined to get on well with this household. 'I mean, are they just drifting by, or intentional?'

'Dwight is analysing the visitors' book. I'm just debugging my auto-mail program. It detects the e-mail address of anyone who visits and sends them a Gospel Update.'

'How do people get off the mailing list?' asks Theo, all innocence.

'I haven't quite perfected that part. But we shouldn't let them go too easily. The Lord never lets go of us.'

'I hope you get paid for all this hard work,' Theo says.

'Oh no! There's no profit in it for anyone. After all, what shall it profit a man, if he shall gain the whole world, and lose his own soul?'

'Do you go to a local church?' Theo asks, burrowing into the range for warmth.

'No no, oh no. The traditional churches have sold their soul to Mammon long ago. Sexual misconduct and corruption and worldliness are everywhere.'

'Not at my kirk there isn't,' says Elspeth, 'whatever Jenner has to say on the subject. His father was Chapel, you know, and they are very uncompromising.'

'Grandpa was too bound up in the tradition,' says Robin. 'For them the tradition has become more important than the gospel.'

'Whereas you have the dinkum gospel?' says Theo, and then wishes she hadn't. It doesn't sound quite like the question posed by the perfect guest. Fortunately, the irony slides harmlessly off Robin's glazed exterior.

After lunch, the egg truck got Elspeth and Theo to Bridgwater. Elspeth didn't like driving in town on Saturdays. It was a little foretaste of hell, she said. It was easier to keep the egg business to the week. On all fronts, Theo guessed, for she had heard Jenner on the subject of the egg business. The whole enterprise, he asserted, was typical of the peasant approach to life which persists in the race memory of women: the jam–jar school of investment. Scrape together the minimum from the minimum for the minimum return, treating labour as having no value: thus spake Jenner Ransfield.

They visited the launderette and they shopped. Theo wrote to Mum afterwards about the shopping – after all, what do you put in a letter to Mum? For example, you do *not* write:

Dear Mum, Dr Ransfield propositioned me in a very complicated way but I don't think he is violent but is certainly a little mad, but I came out of it OK, and am not at all scared of sleeping in a caravan at the bottom of his farm, oh no, not at all. It has a bolt on the door. Sort of.

Rather you write:

Dear Mum, Went shopping in Bridgwater with Elspeth in the egg truck. She calls her eggs Nightingales' Farm Fresh Completely Free Range Organic Eggs and she sells them to a market stall which sells out of them every week. We know this because we went to the stall and had a chat to the market trader. You'd love the market – it's wall to wall bargains. Elspeth only gets half the takings from the sale of her eggs, which I think is a big rip-off. She's really proud of the fact that she bought this terrible old truck with the proceeds. It was very broken down, but she knows how to fix things, having been so often called upon to tinker with ships' engines! She doesn't seem to make much profit from the eggs, judging by the general state of the household.

We went to this wonderfully olde worlde grocery shop.

The man behind the counter had a full-length white cotton apron and served us individually, item by item, and chatted the whole time about the weather and local affairs. He and Elspeth spent ages on sorting out the suet for the Steak and Kidney Pudding which is my Big Treat for Sunday dinner (which is lunch, by the way). I told her she should sell her eggs through this shop exclusively, and put them in poncy baskets with clean straw, but she reckons she can't let the chap on the market stall down. She is too nice for her own good. After that we went to the butcher's and repeated the whole thing with the steak and the kidney. The main subject of conversation (apart from the rain) is the occupation of the site of the battle of Sedgemoor (don't ask me when that was) by a bunch of protesters – a bit like land-rights protesters, except they want to stop roads and new developments eating up the countryside. I'm not sure I see the point because the towns are absurdly congested, and the houses ridiculously small with teensy gardens, and there is absolutely heaps of lovely countryside, far more than we are led to believe. Not like home, of course, but still more than enough . . .

That's how you write to mothers.

Theo has elected to buy the drink to go with the special lunch. She has been given a shopping list: 1 bottle sweet cider for Elspeth; 1 bottle good burgundy, French, none of your Australian gutter dregs, for Jenner; whisky for May Margaret, the cheapest available and as much as you can afford; Welsh spring water for Robin. She decides to add a good Australian to the haul, on the grounds that Jenner might drink some by accident and be forced to approve it. She suspects that he will contrive simultaneously to drink and despise it.

She stands in the drinks section of the supermarket reading Australian wine labels with unstinting affection and thinks about buying booze at home. Always got to be careful about the brands of beer, cos the guys are as partisan about their beer as the English are about their football.

She lugs her choices to the express checkout, foolishly expecting express service, and stands for twenty minutes shifting her load from arm to arm while the checkout girl tries to rip open a little plastic bag of fifty-pence pieces with her fingers, a plastic pen, and finally her teeth. When none of these is successful she summons the supervisor, who sails towards them across the vast marina of the checkouts, and then sails away again in search of a pair of scissors. All the while, the customers at the express checkout, with their hen's-nest-warm bread and their tiny tins of gourmet catfood, redispose their handfuls and wait. Theo wonders why it is not possible to give change in smaller denominations, of which there are plenty in the till.

As she dumps her purchases in the back of the egg truck, Theo remembers loading up a rolled-gold Holden for a beach party. She remembers the back of the wagon sagging under the weight of supplies, and the debate as to whether the extra space the glasses would take up was really worth it, when you could stow some extra piss. She remembers later unstacking armfuls of cardboard casks, balancing one atop the next, building ziggurats of beer cans next to the coolers. Take one out, put one in, that was the rule, until it was just too hard to co-ordinate the hand and the lid. She remembers well into the party telling Tom to get stuffed because he was boring, and a lovely South African guy, lecturer in constitutional law, weeping into his wine because his wife wouldn't join him in Australia. Then she remembers putting her arms around him because he was sad, and him transferring his weeping to her left breast, and her wondering why one breast and not the other, then the memory is obliged to sort of fade out . . .

*　　*　　*

Not as far away as it seems, Fergal floats naked in the top of a tree watching the branches weave in and out, like a dancing basket. He lifts his hand up to look at it against the fledgling green of the leaves, and wonders about it. Why does his hand seem to be made of something quite different from the tree, like a bad piece of superimposition in a TV advert? Does it just look different to him because he thinks of it as human and therefore soiled? Or is his hand formed by a different set of processes – starting from when it popped out, balled into a fist, waving uselessly at the green-masked men who shouldn't stare like that, and warped from then on, by grabbing at hard objects, someone else's toy train, the edge of the TV cabinet, twisted into vicious conformity to spoons, pens, handle-bars, joysticks, knives. His hand will never melt into the tree, even though a clever film editor could do it easy as reviving a dinosaur.

Why the fuck has he started thinking he wants to be a tree? And lose the very things that make him Fergal – slippery, faster than the fuzz can see, round the corner and into the window, down the chute and through the back door, melt into shadows and emerge kicking a can, like nothing harder could ever be contemplated, looking like a dozo and never missing a trick – his dodge, his slide, his feint, his wile, his getaway. What has got into him? Must be all the nothing, all the smoke, turning him into a turnip-muncher, a tree-hugger, like they call them, when he is a warrior, an urban rebel who has absolutely his cause.

Just that, right now, his cause is to lie in the hammock, naked in the rain.

'Moonbeam,' shout several voices from below, 'Moonie! Moonbeam! Snappers! Paparats!'

Fergal sighs and slips his wrists and ankles into a contraption of manacles which give a convincing appearance of being inescapable. He checks for the keys concealed on a twig nearby and snaps the locks shut. Moonbeam gives good press. He smiles obligingly at the cameras which zoom up towards him, and rattles his chains to show that they are not plastic. He refuses coyly to cover his balls when requested. 'Cut em out,' he shouts. 'That's what a computer's for, innit? Doctoring the evidence!'

'Don't blame us,' the cameraman shouts back. 'We'd put you on the news, balls an' all.'

And accompanied by such happy banter, Fergal carries on with his task of saving one lovely but sadly insignificant corner of the world.

III

SATURDAY EVENING – WHAT do you do? You go to
the pub, especially when you are newly in England, the
home of the picturesque pub comfortably full of friendly
yokels and horse brasses. Theo asked her hosts whether
they would come down to the local, which, she had
ascertained, was called the Bleeding Heart. Jenner replied
that under no circumstances would he darken the doors
of a public house, and that she would find it stuffed with
bumpkins, closet drunkards, New Age masturbators, petty
Hitlers and male Thatchers.

Now that she had some acquaintance with Jenner,
Theodora took this as a recommendation. She smiled
sweetly at his miscellaneous wrath and said in that case
she might just go for a walk towards the moor, since
it was only raining a *little* bit. Apparently unaware of
any irony, he retreated to his room in the height of his
dudgeon, slamming the door. Shortly afterwards the strains
of a Welsh male voice choir singing 'Speed your Journey'
burst forth, and Theo took this as cue to persuade Elspeth
to accompany her down to the pub. She didn't know the
way, and she'd so much like to try the famous English
pub, and was it safe to walk around here alone? Elspeth
said a walk would be nice, as it was not too wet, and it
wouldn't do to drive after a drink, even a little one. Theo
considered the various states of drunkenness in which she

had driven home, times when she could not even recall having done so. How many other things, she sometimes wondered, had she conveniently forgotten?

Once safely inside the Bleeding Heart, Theo bought the drinks. Cider was Elspeth's choice, on some dim remembrance that cider was safe. Compared perhaps to whisky, which she had been conditioned never to consume, despite deep personal and cultural devotion. To come home cheerful on cider might provoke scorn; to be even the slightest nip the worse for whisky would bring down the heavens. This she tried to explain to Theo after the first cider, but the accent and the ellipsis furred the meaning. Theo pretended not to know who the referent was, who was the authority that decreed what might or might not be drunk. Theo drank exactly and as much as she pleased, having been coached in this virtue by her friend Juliet. First gender liberation, then social and sexual liberation – that is: do what you want, wear what you want, get drunk when you want, ask anyone to bed if you want. *Does that mean I can wear lippie to wimmen's meetings? – Yeah, I guess, if you must.* Theo hadn't got all the lessons perfect yet – she still needed a drink or two before she'd ask a yummy man to bed with her, and she still thought carefully about what to wear to a meeting with the Cattle Breeders – but she had no compunction in ordering a double vodka even though she was already distinctly blurred.

That night she stuck to beer, since the fellas in the pub insisted on buying her pints of Real Ale in all its earthy forms so that she might taste the true liquid. Keen to imbibe as much cultural experience as possible, she smiled and smiled her pretty white smile and obliged by downing more pints than it was generally felt her small person could hold.

Yes, but we know about Aussies. Especially Aussie girls. –

What do we know about Aussie girls, then? Cue for general laughter.

After an hour in the pub, Theodora felt obscurely deflated, like a puppy that has been patted too much. The attention was all wrong; being Australian wasn't a special talent, and being a cute Australian female wasn't a licence to tell endless weasly jokes. Theodora thought she preferred the heavy-handed jests of her homeland. At least you knew when the bastards were getting at you.

She tried to explain this to Elspeth, but the vocabulary of feminism was new to this sister.

Nonetheless the evening was rich with womanly confidence. After one genteel glass of cider Elspeth embarked on her life story.

'Do you know the Demon Lover, in the ballad? That's how he looked to me, you know? Like the Demon Lover. I remember that it flashed through my mind when I saw him waiting on the pontoon. It was such a surprise, that, to see him so. I had been thinking of him so hard, you know, you know what I mean, all day, while I was working. I was fitting out a ketch. She was about a hundred years old, but all new fittings. She had to shine, the master said, shine. I loved to make the old ships new, better than building new ones. I liked to take a yacht out when she first arrived all battered and I'd sing to her, you know, and tell her how beautiful she was. Ships have a personality, though I wouldna say that to Jenner.

'I never thought I'd see him again, not after the first time. I was such a girlie, though I was all but thirty. I never understood it then, and to this day I don't.'

He stands on the end of the pontoon, the wind is whipping up his black hair, he's wearing a full length black-brown stockman's coat from Australia, so becoming on his tall figure. He looks like an advertisement for aftershave. But it's the Demon Lover she thinks of, coming to take her away, irresistible and deadly, and the thought strikes terror into her heart, that she should associate the most adored form in the created universe with the bogeyman. She thinks she has conjured him up, thinking about him so hard and so long, never expecting to hear again those rolling tones, like a film actor who has taken to the pulpit.

> *I am now married to a ship's carpenter,*
> *To a ship's carpenter I am bound*
> *And I would not leave my husband dear*
> *For twice the sum of twenty thousand pound.*

What has brought him to stand in the wind and wait for her to come ashore, after the excruciating first evening? Even Elspeth, with her ignorance of dates and evenings out, knows it was a one-off, a no-hoper, a blind date that should have stayed unseen. Two people thrown together only by the ineptitude of a new computer dating system, a system which, had she known it (and Jenner did), had so woefully few people aboard that everyone was paired off with everyone else on the off-chance. All they had in common was their height, and their completely differently motivated desire to be married. On their date, he had talked and talked and she had goggled and giggled. Then he had taken her back to his flat and continued to talk while he attempted, without preamble, to undress her, and she had ceased to giggle and fled into the night, unable even to scream. But she had left behind her bag, newly purchased for the evening, and found herself in the bleak streets of Southampton with no means of getting back to Hythe, many miles away. She was forced to knock on his door; he answered it in his dressing gown, apparently naked else, and while she was phoning for a taxi she thought she would pass out from terror at the sight of him, black and hairy beneath the dark blue wool.

She does not understand, and will never grow to understand, what brought him here, to the waterside, to seek her out, and nor, if the truth is to be told, could he have given an accurate explanation of his actions. *I cannot account for it, m'lud; I started my car and drove in the direction of Bucklers Hard. Perhaps I was inflamed by the breasts of a female student. Perhaps I had caught sight of an article stolen from my work. I was dreaming of a different, more innocent world, a world that her simplicity embodied. And embodies to this day.*

All that Elspeth sees is Jenner Ransfield standing on the pontoon, against all hope or reason, and her heart does not know whether to leap or to dive. She shakes like a day-old puppy, and knows that she is lost.

How did it go from there? Theo wanted to know, she wants to know everything about the love lives of the previous generation; they are so deliciously different. She loves it when her dad and mum get sentimental over a bubbly or two on their wedding anniversary and talk about how they met. Stories like Mum and Dad's are great because you know about the happy ending and all that; Jenner and Elspeth – well, maybe not . . .

It was not quite Mills & Boon. Elspeth, in her jeans and guernsey, a bit salty and reddened from the wind, gauche, androgynous, unprepared with shiny new bag or matching smart shoes.

'You left your scarf,' he says, holding it out, horrid chiffon thing she had tucked on at the last moment, and regretted. He has had it for three days, three days to reflect on her cheap taste in scarves. 'Can I buy you a drink?'

They go to the nearest pub, the Heart of Oak. It's full of smoke, full of sailors and tarred memorabilia. He buys her whisky and she talks about Scotland and her family.

'That's all I ever wanted,' she told Theo, as she tells Jenner twenty-two and a half years before, 'to be part of a family. When Mother left us, and then later after she died, once we'd got over the loss, it was Father and Jenny and I, and, you know, it was happiness itself. For years, I never wanted anything else, except to mess about in boats with Father and sit down to family meals, everyone round the table, Jenny and her David and her children, and me and Father, and a steaming dish of potatoes and a big roast with gravy. And the jokes and the silly kidding and the games. All children together, Swallows and Amazons, you know?'

But idylls are not built to last. David grew prosperous and went to London, dragging the crew behind him; Jenny grew sad and could not be talked to, and Father, it transpired, had been eaten up with cancer for years without letting on. *A couple of months to go, old girl, didn't want to ruin our last years. Chuck me over the side, will you?*

Since then it's been hard, she tells Jenner, the tears unceremoniously mixing with her whisky. I have been living in a sort of underworld.

'But you know, Theodora, I shouldna say this, but then I had my job, and I had my sailing and I had my friends. But I thought nothing of them because I hadna family. I thought to be a virgin at thirty was the worst thing in the world; and now I know there are worse things.'

Who knows what motivates Jenner? Who ever knows that – but on several whiskies, much emotion and no food, he follows in her wake, up two flights of stairs to her rooms in Market Street, creeping absurdly so as not to alert the landlady. He shuts the door on her bed–sitting room, looks about him and pays her one of his two compliments, the two crumbs of praise which she will feed on for more than twenty years.

He leans against the inside of the door, having shut it

most masterfully behind him, and looks around. There is nothing in the room; this is Elspeth's secret. Everything that can be painted white is painted white, and everything else is varnished. The curtains are sailcloth. Every stowable item is packed away. The bed is as tight made as a demonstration bandage.

'How lovely,' he says.

'"How lovely," he said when he saw my room, and he stood quite still.'

He stands quite still with his hands splayed out as if demonstrating her room to an unseen class. She busies herself unstowing the gas ring to make coffee, but he moves too fast. He is violent and he hurts her, but she accepts this as the price one must pay for being a virgin at thirty, and not taking enough interest in these things. He goes on and on hurting her, but by then he has paid her the second compliment, and so she cares less.

This part Elspeth did not tell Theo.

He looks at her naked and says, 'Jesus Christ, a Michelangelo, pure white, and so lean, like a man with breasts. Jesus, what a gift.'

It is not clear to whom he says this.

Elspeth sits up in bed after Jenner has left, hugging herself together, unable to move, longing for a bath, and yet unwilling to wash away the physical traces of his presence. It is necessary to hold some piece of evidence to reassure herself of what has happened. There is the evidence of her own body, never to be restored to its former state, nor ever to be seen with the same indifference, but that is not quite enough to hold the image of his person, burnt black by the Australian sun, hairy and dangerous against hers. She gathers up what hairs she can find, pubic and otherwise, and holds them in her hand, wondering if women normally keep mementoes of this nature. She cradles them in her fist, knowing that she is lost for ever, and will make no bones about it. No matter what happens to her hereafter she is an incurable case. The terror of Jenner has burnt him into her, but in the process, the perversity of the emotions has transmuted the terror into passion. She has become his devotee as she became his victim. It is exquisite sweet pain, comparable only to the whip of the wind off the sea as you turn into the strait, quite out of breath, chilled to the bone, and winning. At four o'clock in the morning she begins to write him a letter.

She wrote three drafts of the letter, not being a great one for letters generally, and at school having been among the dim ones at English. The letters they wrote at school didn't come in very handy either. *Dear Sir, With regard to yours of the 13th inst.* They had not done love letters as a class subject, though maybe, she said to Theo, it would have made English a lot more fun.

'He has the letter still, you know. I saw it last time I went into his room. Where it always was, behind the spotted dog on the mantelpiece. I almost took it out of the envelope and read it. But then I remember every word, so long did I spend writing it.'

'And it did the trick!' cried Theo, still caught up in the story.

'I canna tell. You never know why Jenner does what he does, you know?'

'But you know what he thinks,' said Theo. 'Though I suspect his opinions are more emotional than rational.'

She was alarmed to hear the words glide out as glib as a two-bit counsellor's.

'And one knows what he feels,' said Elspeth, 'but it's not always good to know that.'

The two women laughed over the pub table.

'I didn't have a clue what to write, not reading the right sort of books, but I knew I had to tell him how I felt. It makes me blush now. After one date, as they call it now, well, two dates, to swear undying love! And I wasn't even a chit of a girl, I was a grown woman! Promising that if he married me, I'd be the most loyal wife in the world. So you see that's why . . .'

It's too far to the place where he lives, so she gets on her bicycle, sore and sleepless at six o'clock in the morning, and sets out for the university. It is a jewel of a morning, sharp and sparkling, and her heart is high, but after three miles even the glory of the sun on Southampton Water cannot distract her from her crumpled state. It is too far; but she must get the letter to him today.

'Isn't it funny to think,' she said, 'that one day seemed to count so much, when now we've been married for twenty-two years. And how many days is that?'

'Eight thousand and something. Eight thousand and thirty.'

'Eight thousand days!'

Theo tried to imagine waking up beside Tom on eight thousand consecutive mornings and her heart sank.

'Another round?'

Elspeth gave a little laugh. 'I will turn into a real tippler,' she said.

No harm in that, Theo thought, if there's no other way.

Her mother had a depressed phase. It was entirely predictable, her father explained, with the departure of the boys and the loss of her womanhood – a double defeminisation, he said. He prescribed suitable drugs, to save her the trouble of going to his colleague who treated her little ailments of flu and backstrain. And lo, she was cured, throwing herself into the gardening and taking up golf (an expensive therapy, grumbled Dad, but he didn't really mean it) and helping Theo get her flat nice. And planning weddings, which eventually obliged. And grandchildren. So now she was fine, and didn't take anything, except heaps of gin.

The trouble with the feminist manifesto was this: it was perfectly consistent in the Wimmen's Room, but the minute you took it outside and tried to apply it, the plans didn't line up with the kitchen. Theo remembers sitting at the island, forced to take a break from study, with her hands cupped around a milky coffee, picking at a fresh scone, and trying to impress upon her mother the necessity for making her own life.

'But I don't want to be a social worker. Or a teacher. No, Theo, I don't want to be a lawyer. I want to be a grandma. I'm good at it.'

'No, Theo, I'm not dependent on your father. Yes, he gives me housekeeping and an allowance, but that's perfectly reasonable for what I do. And I've got the money that Nana left me, you know, dear, so I can actually pay for the golf myself, if he does refuse, which he won't. And I bought the Mitsubishi myself, as you know. I am perfectly all right as I am, dear, you know. I don't think a career makes a person happy at all, look at that poor dentist who killed his wife and children, and as for Dr Harrison – I did tell you, didn't I? –

'–Well, maybe I do live my life through other people. But what's so terrible about that, dear? I think that's quite normal. Your father does the same really, you know. He is enormously proud of Colin, and of you, dear. It makes him feel that everything he's done has been worthwhile. And I'm no different. I am looking forward to the day you get married.'

How could you explain to mothers? Even about something as straightforward (in Mum's book) as getting married? Theo would rail at Juliet. How could you tell her, in terms that she'd understand, that you couldn't marry a guy who wasn't completely liberated, and you couldn't marry a guy who wasn't a total turn-on, and the two things just didn't go together?

And how could you explain to Elspeth, seated across the sticky wooden tabletop, that the only happiness she could expect in life would derive from rejecting the thing that filled her life? Until she left Jenner Ransfield she'd be miserable; but how was little Theo to put that into blunt words?

Elspeth was talking again, still about Jenner. Theo wanted to explain why this had become the wrong subject. But even Theo's directness stopped short of telling a relative stranger that she was married to an irredeemable bastard. Besides, the story was addictive, like those terrible cartoon love stories in cheap women's mags, illustrated with black and white photos and stilted conversations in sans serif type and cutout boxes.

'He's such a brilliant man. I sometimes wonder why he puts up with us, none of us clever at all. Not in the way he is, and you are. I think Robin is brilliant, in his own way. And May Margaret, of course . . .'

It had been a hard ten years, she said, from the time they married till they landed at Nightingales Farm, and the solid job at the Agricultural College; years which passed in a fog of acrimony and sleeplessness, of uncertainty and passion, moving from pillar to post, without room for the furniture. Nothing that happened to Jenner made any sense, his papers, his conference successes, the international phonecalls – that was before the Internet of course – foreign scholars who sought him out because – *well, you understand, Theodora, do you not?* – and at the same time, the difficulty with tenure, the short-term contracts, two terms teaching here, a six-month research fellowship there, and then a good placement, suddenly clouded. By what? Jealousy, incompetence, lack of imagination, how could one tell?

Theo had spent enough time in universities and places of research to understand how easily an able man is swept aside and rendered ridiculous by jealousies and vested interests. But she also understood enough of the wide world to know that persistent self-indulgence of Jenner's brand was bound to bring its reward. It was not enough to be brilliant; you had to be just a tiny bit diplomatic as well.

Elspeth was so happy when he bought the farm. She remembers standing in the kitchen with the two children, perished with the cold that comes up through the floor, for the house has been empty a sad time. She weeps with joy. It's a plain kitchen, workmanlike, begging for a roaring fire and bustle to save it from gloom, but it is undeniably a kitchen, and it is hers. She wipes away the memories of hand-washing nappies in a shared bathroom, of lines of wet socks across the foot of the bed, refusing to dry, of the winter-time cry of children – *I haven't anything to wear. It's all wet and muddy* – of Jenner coming home late and thrashing into the clothes horse and cursing it ripely before throwing the clean clothes on to the floor, of sleeping in sheets rigid with semen because the launderette was just too far away, two buses and a walk – she discards all those memories, because they are small things, and all behind her, because now she is going to be happy. She has her own washing machine, her own house, and nobody is going to drive her from it.

The children run into the hall and up the stairs, wildly excited at so much space; they squabble over who shall have which room, but there are so many rooms, with all those little ones on the top floor. And the attic! *Can we actually climb inside the thatch?* She hears their voices pealing from a distance, and her heart leaps like a fawn. Room for the children to run in – a house full of rooms, a maze of sheds, moor and fields, a forest full of trees.

She's never cared for the countryside, being so devoted to the sea, but Jenner's heart is in the soil, so that's good. Being here will make him happy, he can keep pigs and scratch their backs, a few cows, a pony; Elspeth will get a cat. She bends down and starts work on the fire. Having no experience of the country, she is also ignorant of the workings of such devices, but her happiness buoys her up in spite of damp twigs and smoke which billows back into her face. The concrete is hard and cold on her knees, but she presages a thick carpet with lots of underlay against the cold. On the walls two thick coats of white paint, and bright yellow curtains, not dissimilar to those which danced at the kitchen windows at home.

No, no, she tells herself sternly, this is home! That was my parents' home.

She's surprised at how stiff she's become. Forty, her life scarcely started, and already she's starting to creak. But soon she'll be back in sailing trim! She'll need a new wet-suit; she was induced to throw her old one away two moves ago, though a wet-suit should last twenty years at least. But anyway it surely wouldn't have fitted her? Two children, married life, she'll have grown stouter. It's inevitable, married women grow comfortably plump, though she isn't aware of any of her clothes not fitting. She wishes they would fail to fit her, so she could pop into Marks and Sparks or Oxfam and get something new. Maybe she hasn't grown stout, but something has slipped in her appearance, because of the way Jenner looks, or doesn't look, at her. She is conscious of not appearing in his eye as she did. But then sometimes she thinks it is easier not to appear in Jenner's eye.

She straightens up, the fire quickened. She imagines herself in a new dress, a summer cotton, white with a small collar and a broad red leather belt. She has new red sandals and a red velvet ribbon tying up her hair. Jenner comes into the house through the front door, puts his arm around her waist and swirls her round . . . Well, she can dream; after all, she has the house, the farm, it is all signed and sealed, and Jenner's contract at the Agricultural College is permanent, only drunkenness or crime can unseat him now. Now they can commence to be happy.

'It's funny, isn't it,' she said to Theo: 'it's funny how your notion of happiness changes.'

She thought that to be married was the only thing. To have a family. Then to have a home.

Theo, whose philosophy of happiness was to do extremely well at things and enjoy every single moment, nodded sagely. She knew it was her duty to explain to Elspeth the monstrous regiment of men, the way that they dominate everything women do and think, the way they determine what you value, what is art and what is science, how you read books, how you conduct business, whether you are allowed to get drunk. But words failed her to tell of these things.

Words failed, as they failed Theo to explain why being housewife to a grown family, when you are a qualified and ardent shipwright, is a sin against the Holy Ghost.

Theo knew that in this argument she was up against Jenner, and he had cheated by causing this excellent sister to fall in love with him.

'There are people,' said Elspeth, 'who are blessed with talent. And the rest of us whose job it is in life to support them. I have no difficulty with that.'

What can you say? What *can* you say?

Theo was standing at the bar, while the publican, Harry Simmons, prop., engaged her in banter, his eyes flicking from face to breasts. She was about to order another round when Jenner Ransfield chose to arrive. He stood in the pub doorway, holding the swing doors at arm's length before him, because he was barred from entry. Somehow it had poured with rain while Theo and Elspeth sat snug and drinking, so that Jenner's dark brown horseman's coat was glossy with the wet. The noses of his dogs prodded at his heels, their heads bowed with the tiresomeness of it all.

'Look at the bitches!' he cried.

It was always a mistake to understimate the physical effect of Jenner Ransfield, six foot two and dark as the devil. He stared at Theo with such palpable anger that she felt herself tremble.

'Here I am scouring the countryside for you, even so far as to venture into the camp of the holy joes, in the rain, and all the time you are here as snug as ticks, getting yourselves drunk.'

'Can I buy you a drink?' said Theo, trying to get a grip on herself.

'You can't, I'm afraid, my dear,' said the publican, 'because he is not welcome in this house.'

'I shall wait for you outside,' said Jenner and let the doors slam.

Elspeth was on her feet already and on her way out. Theo hesitated, torn between sisterly feeling and distaste for the scene that awaited her.

'Now, you have another, my dear,' said the publican. 'Don't you let that man intimidate you.'

'No, no,' said Theo, bravely, 'he doesn't intimidate me. It's just that he's my host.'

'I'm surprised he knows the meaning of the word. Whereas I do. I am mine host. Why don't you bring your things up here instead? Nice dry back bedroom.'

Theo looked at him. He was about thirty, dull blond, starting to show signs of wear, behind-the-bar pallor and gut, but had a nice smile. You wouldn't know what his hands were up to, but a nice dry bedroom sounded so delicious that Theo would have hugged him had the bar not been between them.

The car horn sounded loud and long. Theo thought of Elspeth, for whom she felt some responsibility, bearing the onslaught of Jenner's wrath alone. She dragged herself away from the Bleeding Heart and the little back bedroom. And predictably, all the way from the pub car park to the farmyard Elspeth and Theo sat silent through a tirade against their thoughtlessness. Neither of them proffered a defence; there were no gaps in the fabric of his speech. They were heartless indeed and stupid to go and sit in the pub without leaving so much as a note, so that he must go haring off into the night, into the lap of those lost souls up on the moor, making a fool of himself. Theo, crouching in the back with the dogs, wonders what prevents her from launching straight back at him. Is it fear, or politeness, or just the pointlessness of countering irrational behaviour with argument?

'I'm sorry, Jenner,' said Elspeth. 'We should have told you we were going out.'

'Sorry!' he cried. 'Sorry! What a pusillanimous, mealy-mouthed sort of response is that? An appropriate penance would be to wade your way to the moor and back, as I have just done.

'And a fine return on my hospitality to make my wife a drunkard!' he added to no one in particular.

You could feel the anger in the car, vibrating against the glass. Theo was overcome by the urge to giggle, but she recognised that there was nothing amusing in Elspeth's plight. One of the dogs, Lilith, the piebald one, growled in an indiscriminate way. They arrived at the farmhouse to find light pouring out of every window.

'Who in damnation has turned on all these lights? The mindless extravagance of the girl, why doesn't she flounce off and pay her own electricity bills?'

When they went into the house, May Margaret was standing on the staircase, holding a large chisel by the blade and tapping the wooden handle into her palm.

'Back from your whoring, are you?' asked her father.

May Margaret smiled and ignored him.

'Any coffee, Mother?'

'I'll make it, I'll make it,' cried Elspeth.

'None of your women's piss.'

'And what exact objection do you have to women's piss?' asked May Margaret. 'Is it in some way inferior to male piss? Certainly the latter has a headier aroma.'

Theo started to make the coffee while Elspeth went around the house turning off lights and Jenner and May Margaret traded insults of increasing scatology. Better than a play, thought Theo grimly, kicking one of the dogs out of her way to the fridge. Not her sort of play.

Jenner took his coffee from Theo's hand and went immediately to his room.

'Why have you turned off my light, woman?' he shouted as he opened the door.

As he shut the door firm behind him, he heard a new sound from the kitchen – a sound he had never heard before in his house. He could not immediately decide whether he hated or loved it. It was the sound of women's laughter.

IV

FOR AN HOUR on Sunday morning there was the threat that Jenner would go out, and imperil Elspeth's plan for a proper Sunday lunch, with the whole family and their guest gathered around the table.

Jenner knew perfectly well how much effort Elspeth was putting into the lunch, for he was in the kitchen while she bustled about the preparations, attempting to pack his fishing basket with the makings of a picnic. He was only persuaded to stay by his daughter repeatedly encouraging him to go.

Thank God, thought Theo, *we can get this over with. And tomorrow I can break the news and get the hell out.*

There was much steaming and flapping in the kitchen; the room seemed crowded even though only Theo and Elspeth were busy in it. Jenner retreated into his lair. Robin was sitting at the kitchen table, although it was already laid for dinner, with white linen napkins, carefully ironed, and the best cutlery, not matched, but still good and some of it quite old, from Elspeth's family home, and five glasses, each one different from the next, but each one a decent piece of crystal. He had pushed the mats and cutlery and flowers out of the way, and was studying an unnaturally large bible, complete with footnotes, cross-references in the margin and commentary in a separate column. He was reading from the Letter of James.

May Margaret went out to stride about in the rain.

'Call me when lunch is ready, Theodora, would you, dear chuck?'

'Dinner,' said Robin.

May Margaret snorted and left the kitchen door ajar. From Jenner's room came forth the sounds of crackled opera, *The Pearl Fishers*, which no one recognised, and why should they?

'His father's records,' said Elspeth. 'I remember the old man bowed over them as his hearing went. Apparently his mother would flee the room; she couldna bear to hear them.'

'Did she really hate opera that much?'

'No, no. She was as musical as an angel. She taught music, beginner pupils only; she'd never play herself, though Mr Ransfield bought her the best piano in Europe, if he was to be believed. She had been a pianist in Europe, wherever it was she came from, Poland, was it, or Austria? But she wouldna play a note except baby tunes; and screamed at him if he turned up the gramophone, though you could get barely a word out of her above a whisper.'

'Poor woman!'

'I think there was too much theatre in it!' said Elspeth. 'Other people suffered too, without making such a show.'

'You didn't like her much,' said Theo, scraping away at the carrots.

'I never knew her. She was dead long before.'

O souvenir charmant! O souvenir charmant!

'So all this is what Jenner says?'

'And his dad. They talked about her without cease. They must have loved her to death!'

'Didn't he grow up on a farm in Wales or something? Somewhere terrifically remote?'

'Well, coming from Scotland, I don't regard Monmouth

as remote. But it was a dark little valley. I suppose remoteness is how isolated you feel.'

'Glasgow, Mother, is not remote by any definition.'

'Read your bible!' said Theo, 'or I'll give you a turnip.'

O souvenir charmant! O souvenir charmant!

And what a spread it was, when all five of them sat down to it at last. Steak and kidney pie and Yorkshire pudding, and gravy and boiled carrots and roast potatoes and steamed cabbage and braised leeks and field mushrooms. The pudding was a magnificent decorated trifle, slurping with proper custard, which Elspeth and Theo had stirred with infinite care, topped off with hundreds and thousands and chocolate buttons and Smarties, like a children's party cake. But the trifle was not destined to be touched until that evening, when Fergal fixed it with a hungry eye, and had his way with it.

Jenner opened the French wine, but declined to do the honours with the Australian, so Theo got up from the table, took the corkscrew and opened it herself.

'It would be a wasted exercise, I imagine,' he said, 'to ask you to sample a genuine wine? Possibly quite a good one,' he added, holding the label up to his eyes.

'If price is commensurate with quality, I guess so,' said Theo. 'And I was planning to try some French, as long as you drink the comparable amount of the Australian.'

'Perhaps later, when my palette's dulled by English food.'

'Shall I be mother?' cried Elspeth, poised over the steak and kidney pie. She took the knife in one fair hand, and in the other seized the bowl

> *. . . and she's cut out her true love's heart,*
> *and to perdition sent his soul.*

75

And it's alack, my own true love,
And it's alas, my dearie,
For I'm condemned this day to hang
For loving one who hates me.

The portion of pie was cut and passed down the table to Jenner. Elspeth continued to serve pie, while Jenner was handed vegetables. Halfway through the proceedings, 'What's this?' he said.

'Steak and kidney pie, of course. Especially for Theodora.'

'But you know that I detest kidney! That it makes me vomit! How dare you serve it up to me at my table? You stupid, thoughtless woman! How long have we been cloistered together, and still you don't know that of all the things that I most loathe, the most loathsome is kidney!'

He roared for his dogs, pushed his chair back across the floor, and rose to his feet. He grasped the plate and scraped the contents on to the floor. The dogs gobbled it up, so that it was gone in a moment. He leant forward from his great height across the table to seize the pie dish from Elspeth's hands, but she hesitated to let go. In the moment of her hesitating, Theo stood up, placed both her hands firmly on the dish, and pressed down with all her weight to keep it grounded on the table.

'Well, I helped to make this pie, and I want to taste some of it, so you can fuck off.'

He let go, as if the dish was suddenly live, towered over her, glaring, but she would only look at him sideways. He stepped back, turned on his heel and sent his chair clattering across the kitchen. He made for the door, dogs at his elbow, then turned and fixed her with his eye.

'It's a mystifying code of behaviour you have down there, in the shrivelled-up arsehole of the world. Take what you can get and spit in the face of the giver – that is the Australian creed. I remember it well; I shall not forget it, the arrogant ingratitude coupled with viciously unprincipled behaviour. The grasp and swear mentality, it is etched on my mind by pain. It might have been hoped that one to whom nature has been so kind might have escaped the syphilis of Australian manners, but not so. I weep for this generation, I weep for my country and for yours.'

And with that he departed. Robin fled from the table, taking the stairs two at a time until his door was slammed tight behind him.

'Why, he's left his bible behind,' said May Margaret, grinning and eating like a misericord of gluttony.

Elspeth crossed her arms on the table, put down her head and wept.

'Eat up, Theo, it'll only get cold,' said May Margaret, 'and there's absolutely nothing you can do about it. They've made their bed, but they're not going to stop me lying in mine.'

The two girls proceeded to demolish the dinner. Theo, unable to think of anything to say to comfort Elspeth, drank a satisfying proportion of her bottle of wine. Nobody really felt like the trifle.

Elspeth went into the hallway and brought back to the table the enormous bible. She opened it, not at any comforting passage, but at the front, where a family tree spread its thin black branches down the page. Theo, glancing at it, saw that it represented Elspeth's side of the family, and that the latest generation, Elspeth's children and her sister's, were all carefully entered.

'I should apologise to him, I really should,' said Theo, a little blurry. 'But then I should do the dishes.'

'I shouldn't do either,' said May Margaret, but Theo had rolled up her sleeves and begun to clear the table.

At Christmas, at her parents', they were jostling to get

the dishes inside and into the dishwasher, so they could get the cricket started. Her brothers and their wives tripped over each other in their enthusiasm to restore everything to its natural cleanliness. *No, Mum, don't you move, you just sit there and relax*. And Mum, glowing with a meal well cooked, did just that, sat there in the sun with her tea and her sunglasses, and her sandals off, and gossiped to Auntie Jeanette about prostate and hysterectomy, while the grandchildren, great-nephews and great-nieces used them as the base for tag. Or Power Ranger Gladiators, as the game was called officially.

As Theo toiled her way through the dishes, constantly refilling the kettle and replacing it on the stove, to replenish the lukewarm water, she listened to Elspeth meekly sniffing behind her, and wished she could cut out a piece of that superabundant Christmas cheerfulness, and bring it here. Or one single piece of whiteware from her parents' home; or some small helping of the bountiful supply of hot water which sprang from the taps in her flat. She knew that material things do not bring happiness; but she was learning that physical discomfort adds considerably to the sum of misery.

Theo disposed of all the food, to the chickens and the refrigerator, but refused on principle to put any of the leavings out for the dogs. No one offered to help her. May Margaret sat at the table by her mother and drank whisky. Theo scraped and rinsed, washed, dried and put away. It felt like a suitable penance, but it did not take away from Theo the pitiful desire to apologise, as if she had caused the ruination of the meal. So she rolled down her sleeves, shrugged on her coat and went out.

The rain had eased to a polite drizzle, which it was warm enough to ignore. The Morris Countryman was in the shed, which implied that Jenner had walked away in his fury. There was no saying which way he had gone.

Up the hill, and along the road? Down the hill and on to the moor? Or had he struck out into the forest, or across the fields? Fruitless to look for him. *Well, thank God for that reprieve*. She leant her back up against Sir Jenner's mailed feet and wondered how to get through the afternoon.

A brown hen came out of the undergrowth trailed by a scuttling fluffy white chick, with baggy trousers and a bright eye. They darted forward to Theo's feet and then back, then forward, then back. She watched them feinting and pecking, growing inches bolder, and saw how the chick followed the hen's approaches with variations of his own, as if he were already practising for cockhood. But he imitated and took cover under her, the moment Theo's foot stirred, then pranced out again, doing what Mother did, only fiercer now, now more timid. Theo pondered their behaviour. How much was learnt, how much part of the generalised henniness of hens? Did the mother hen have a concept of him as her charge, or was he an adjunct, a fluffy attendant to her feet? Did she have a concept of anything, or was she just a stringbag of reactions and genetic predispositions? If you took a chicken from its dam, did it know about foraging and dust baths, and the fear of the human foot? She wondered, if it came to know these things, whether it was programming in the creature or a lucky combination of fowly guesses. In what sense did it matter whether animals were conscious, whether hens learnt or were programmed, assuming there were a true distinction? Jenner's thought processes had got to her already.

What about masochistically washing dishes, then? How did you end up as a person who did that?

From down beyond the valley, a long way away, came the baying of dogs. It wasn't the familiar didgeridoo of the Great Danes, heralds of anger, but was high-toned and snappish. To Theo, the agitation of dogs generally

79

suggested the presence of other dogs. Lifting the burden of necessary apology – *got to get this over with, so I can get out gracefully tomorrow* – she started to walk towards the sound.

Ordinarily she would not care to take the path through the trees, finding the overgrown solitude full of vague threat, but she comforted herself with the thought that Jenner Ransfield, if lurking Heathcliff-like in these woods or on the moor beyond, was more frightening than any shabby tramp nurturing a hammer inside his charity great-coat. And as she walked, one white leather trainer boldly in front of the other, she worked on analysing the constituents of his frighteningness. Was she afraid he would attack her with his walking stick? No. She was faster, fitter and trained in martial arts; besides there had never been any indication that he hit his wife or family. Theo had been on a course; she knew what to look for in a wife-beater. Was she afraid he would rape her? He wouldn't *dare*! Let him so much as breathe warmly in her general direction, and she'd have him hung so high that his eyeballs and his testicles would bounce when they hit the ground. She was sure that he knew this, if not instinctively, at least as a learned response that had become instinctual. His sexual threat was more generalised; Theo recognised it, but could not classify it in any way that was useful to her. It could therefore be discarded as evidence. Of what, then, was she afraid? Of being shouted at? Of being cursed? Well, really, Theodora, grow up, sticks and stones. He's good at shouting and has a large vocabulary in which to curse. *So?* as they used to say in the playground, reducing all claimed superiorities to arbitrary nothingness.

The forest around her was no longer lugubrious old trees, but a bright modern picket of young firs, planted in pursuit of some obscure subsidy. Through the young growth reared up here and there an ancient tree, which had stood in this hollow and watched peasant farmers come and go and scratch a living and fall to dust. Through this light growth there was no sign of its owner, nor of his dogs; Theo decided to walk on, towards the darker forest beyond.

She was running over in her head the arguments on rural subsidy, pro and con. A good Australian, she knew that nothing was gained economically by dinky little holdings with three sheep and a cow; but as a first-time traveller and new world nostalgic, she lamented the reduction of an ancient forest to prickly hectares of cloned pine. This interesting debate, which might have kept her mind busy against all sorts of gloomy threat, was interrupted. She heard a new sound, not the hallooing of Jenner's hounds, nor the rural chorus of tractor and pump; she heard a little pattering like a swift secret dog or one of those funny mouse deer that now run wild in England. A little splashing in the puddles. She looked about her at once, and then saw a young man flying through the trees towards her. He was stark naked.

She was not afraid. He was a little man, skinny and pale, and his cock, which jiggled about as he ran, was too pathetic a thing to threaten. She stood her ground, square in the path, facing him as he ran briskly down towards her. Her attention was taken by the discomfort that must be caused men by running naked with their bits flopping about. She remembered discussions about male ballet dancers and jockstraps, and the titters at the sixth-form outing to *The Firebird*. She remembered when she first saw a boy naked, Barry Grayson, in the sand dunes behind the caravans on Robson's beach, and the awful temptation to giggle at the unlikeliness of his construction. It was far too big and then went far too small, as if he had over-inflated it to impress her, and caused it to burst into sad little Eeyore fragments.

Boys in general were too easy to laugh at, men too, by

and large. Except Jenner Ransfield, whom it would be a relief to find funny. However, the little guy approaching, although white and stunted as if he had grown up under a stone, did not appear absurd. He ran with communicable intensity, and yet without any of the usual indications of desperation.

He slowed as he approached the thinning of the trees; clearly they offered him inadequate camouflage. He hesitated, caught sight of Theo, veered to one side and shimmied up a spreading oak, and disappeared. The tree, dressed in her finest spring gauds, modestly drew her garments together to cover him.

It was a highly impressive performance, and for physical dexterity alone Theo was prepared to give him the benefit of the doubt. She observed as he bounced up the tree, for all the world like a squirrel, that he was not entirely naked; he carried on his back a little black bag with two straps securely in place over his shoulders. Then he was invisible in the tree. She was about to address him in her most strident Australian, when around the corner, from the lane on to the path, came two policemen in full gear, with bright yellow jackets, black helmets with visors, and wondrously priapic batons held before them.

It was a happy accident for all concerned that Theo had taken trouble to prepare for the special Sunday meal. She had vigorously gelled and brushed her curls into approximate magazine shape; she had applied make-up. She had donned her best jersey (baby-blue lamb's-wool), her smartest jeans and whitened her trainers. Then afterwards, to brave Jenner and the elements, she'd put on her jacket – emerald green and imperial purple, rustling with expensive extras and gargantuan black zips, proclaiming her irrefutably a foreigner with more money than knowledge of the conditions. In this garb she could not be mistaken for a protester of any shade of belief. So that, as she stood dickering in the middle of the path which led to the moor, the two policemen who pounded towards her lowered their batons and made a conciliatory approach.

'Have you seen him, then, seen a man coming this way?' said one.

'Naked,' said the other. 'Couldn't mistake him, stark naked.'

'No, I don't think so,' said Theo in a long slow voice, reminiscent of Cousin Jim from Yackandanda. 'What's going on around here?'

'Where are you from, miss?' said one.

'I'm from Australia. I'm staying at the farm over there, Nightingales. I just came out for a walk after lunch and I heard all this barking. What's going on? Got a holdup?'

'Just a protest camp, nothing important, my dear,' said the other.

'Now, did you hear or see anyone come down this way?' said the first.

It was hard to take them seriously with their cuddly accents and their double act, but Theo was a veteran of protests – anti-nuclear, pro-abortion, anti-grant cuts – and she knew there was nothing endearing about any policeman at any time. Unless a sister had been unequivocally raped, and you wanted the rapist bastard taken apart, of course.

'No, I guess I would have seen him? Wouldn't I? I just walked down from over there, by this path, and you can see right through the wood in both directions. I'm looking for a tall man in a big brown stockman's coat with two Great Danes; have you seen him?'

This diversionary action had the required effect on the policemen. They frowned at each other through the plastic of their visors.

'Is this person associated with the protesters, my dear?'

'I don't think so. I don't know. I don't know about the protest, you see. He just went off.'

'A missing person? You'll need to go down to the station. We're on Wilful Obstruction at present.'

'Oh, no, mate, not a missing person. I think he's in possession of himself. He's very angry, though, but not armed. I think the dogs are fairly harmless.'

'Well, my advice is, miss, go down to the station at once. Stay away from him, if you're concerned. Our victim-protection people will take out an order to protect you, but we're on a different mission. You quite sure you haven't seen our charlie?'

'Are you concerned, my dear? Is this man dangerous? With the protesters running about here as well, you're best to go home.'

'Yes, I think I will, thanks a million, I will.' And she made as if to turn around and walk off back towards the farm.

'Miss! You haven't seen anyone else? Little chap, running away? Might look harmless to you, like a kid out of school, but he's not, believe me.'

'No, I don't think so.' Real slow. 'I'd have noticed, wouldn't I? Naked and all that?'

The policemen were ill at ease. They felt they should believe her but they didn't want to; they felt they should protect her, but they knew they had a higher duty. 'We'll lose the bugger,' said one and they tore themselves away and trotted back towards the moor.

She waited until they were completely out of sight before wandering into the forest. When she got to the neighbourhood of the tree that the young man had climbed, she stopped and called out. Her voice sounded out of place, stripped of context like a voice recorded in a padded studio, later to be bodied out with electronic reverberation.

If anyone heard her calling out she would be embarrassed. To keep quiet seemed the proper behaviour in a wood, and to call out peculiar, and slightly disgusting, like burping on the radio.

'You can come down now. They've buggered off.'

There was no response. OK so he was there and hiding. Or he wasn't there and she was sounding like a prat. But unless Jenner Ransfield was lurking behind a tree, who gave one?

'Look mate, I know you're up there. You can stay up there for ever if you want, and freeze your balls off, for all I care, but anyway the pigs have pissed off, so if you come down now you'll miss them. Not that I give a shit what you do, OK?'

She waited – maybe for ten seconds, maybe a minute, it was impossible to tell. There was no response, not even an answering rustle or an echo, so she started to stump off home.

He slid down the tree, practically without sound, and trotted up behind her. He was clothed now, in khaki combat pants and a black T-shirt and trainers. He had mousy black-brown hair, very straight and fine, falling over his eyes, pale skin, dirty fingernails, what was left of them. He was the same height as Theo, maybe fractionally shorter, and about the same age, twenty-five, twenty-six.

'Thanks,' he said, although he pronounced it 'fanks'. Theo, though ignorant of English accents, guessed this was working-class London. He looked half starved, like an engraving out of a sociology textbook.

'It's OK. I mean, two pigs, helmets and visors; it must be serious.'

'Yeah.'

'Are you coming my way?'

'Seems so.'

'You might live to regret it,' she said, though regret, it turned out, was not precisely the right word for it.

He grinned. He had lovely greeny-grey eyes and awful stained teeth.

'Why naked, for Christ's sake?'

'Gets them going,' he said. 'Gotta fag?'

'Do I look like the sort of person who'd smoke?'

'I'd kill for a fag.'

'We could go into the village. There's nothing in the village except the pub and a gas station, but I guess they sell cigarettes. And crisps.'

'Rural England, yeah?'

They walked in a silence broken only by disembodied shouts and the barking of dogs. The young man showed no nervousness, but his attention was concentrated on the path behind him; he was sensitive to the first tremor of law-enforcing foot. The farm buildings reared up before them, from the chimney a tentative flurry of smoke signalling distress within.

'Let's steer clear of the house.'

'Australian, innit? *Neighbours, Home and Away*.'

'Right on. *EastEnders*? *Minder*?'

'Don't know it, *Minder*. Me grandad was a miner in Sunderland.'

They cut through the trees and took the footpath towards the Bleeding Heart, ten minutes' walk away. He said nothing, and she couldn't think of an opening. She stole glances though, to ascertain whether he was as harmless as he seemed. She concluded that he posed her no threat of any kind.

'I'm skint,' he said as they stood outside the doors of the pub, looking at the painted bill of fare, maroon and gold. *Traditional Fair Ploughman's £2.95 Steak Sanwich £3.50 Old Englishe Beef. Chicken Tikka £4 all with chips from 12 oclock. Families Welcome Harry Simmons prop.*

'*Now* you tell me.'

'Yeah, well, there's no money in protests. There's a living.'

'Well, it so happens that I have a few pounds. But when it's gone, that's it.'

''S OK.'

And apparently, for him, it was OK. Theo, keen to understand the customs of the country, thought that perhaps it was fair enough that a martyr for the cause should be bought cigarettes and junk food.

There was a certain gloating pleasure in dropping by the Bleeding Heart with a bloke, even if he was a half-starved and inarticulate specimen. He was indisputably a bloke, one who spoke a dialect of their language, and probably knew all about football.

His name was Fergal, but he wasn't Irish, at least not recently. He didn't see the point in surnames. Theo didn't either, but for different reasons. She bought him cigarettes from a machine. She'd never bought cigarettes before; marijuana very occasionally, but never nicotine. She also bought two halves of beer, contrary to her better judgement.

'Why am I doing this?' she said. But Fergal was watching television.

They had crisps and beer.

'I had to leave me sleeping bag.'

'I could fetch it.'

'They'd get you. Five hundred pound fine and throw you out the country. Let's go in the sun.'

By some charming coincidence the rain clouds had lifted, and straggly sunlight lit up the little courtyard out the back. The rustic bench was wet with rain, but Fergal spread his purple anorak out for them to sit upon.

They had another half sitting in the pale sunlight. The concrete paving was concrete criss-crossed to look like flagstones. Half-hearted roses scrambled out of wooden tubs. There was no one else in the pub. Fergal had a second cigarette. He smoked like a woman, languorous, using his lips. Nice lips, almost pouty.

He'd been at the protest two months. The winter was no good for protests, the well-wishers didn't come out to visit, and only the real tough could take it. Too much mud, and no good for his trademark nakedness.

He had spent the winter at his mother's, sleeping on the floor. Painted the flat, and her neighbour's. Painted the stairwell too, but that was a waste of time. 'Looked good for a minute.'

Inside his little leather bag a telephone rang. He made no hurry to attend to it, unzipped the bag, pulled out some rolled-up clothes, then the phone. By the time he answered it had rung perhaps twenty times.

His conversation was laconic. The person on the other end was voluble.

'Yeah, well, they gutted us. We was ready at dawn, yeah? Didn't come at dawn though, eh, did they?'

The other end was full of advice and consolation; Fergal yipped monosyllables and cemented plans with a brevity that would have thrilled management consultants the world over.

'How do you afford a mobile phone?' Theo demanded.

'I don't. We all got given them by a well-wisher. He pays the bill too. Or she.'

'A well-wisher? I didn't know such people existed any more.'

'Well, there you go.'

He drained his glass and initiated a conversation.

'There's loads of them actually. I've never ate so well in me life since I started on the protests. Pies, pizzas, buns, apples, stuff straight out of people's gardens. Course, it helps that I do the gardening for them.'

'You do gardening?'

'Why not? Me grandad loved his allotment more than night and day. In fact he had three in the end. I can grow anything anywhere, me.'

'I can't even keep a geranium alive in a pot.'

'Well, geraniums get lonely, see.'

Theo laughed, but saw he was perfectly serious.

'I do a lot of gardening,' he went on. 'Get to a place, go round the Vicarage, offer to weed the border for a cuppa tea, and there you go. Beer and ciggies for life.'

'They trust you around their houses?'

He cocked his head on one side and grinned at her under his fringe.

'One look in me bonny green eyes and they know they can trust me. Vicars' wives, stockbrokers' wives, doctors' wives.'

'Screw them, do you?'

'Na, I'm not into sex.'

'Aah,' said Theo. 'Want another?'

'Yeah. And some nuts, peanuts, yeah?'

Standing at the deserted bar, she waited for Harry Simmons prop. to complete his slopping of a sticky cloth over the sticky surface and serve her. His interest in her had cooled since last night – such predictable creatures, men, come in trailing a fella, and they decide you're his property. *As if.* She studied the row of horse brasses rippling down beside the upended bottles of spirits, seeing and not seeing crude cutout representations of a dog, star, hunting horn, horse's head, plough team, wheatsheaf. The sun had already started its descent and filtered in on to the surface of the brass. Theo had seen things like that in Australia and assumed they were cheap attempts to recreate another world. Now she was in another world, and they were here. Here too was a funny little waif, so full of self-possession that he had her buying him a third drink in the middle of the day, when all she wanted was an honest sandwich.

He was on the phone again. She plonked the beers down in front of him.

'I'm going home after this,' she said. 'I've got problems to sort.'

'Me too. How to get me bag.'

'Do you live anywhere?'

'Here,' he said.

'Oh, very funny.'

Defusing her neatly, he grinned. 'Yeah, pseud, innit?

'No, really,' he went on. 'I used to live at me girlfriend's, but she threw me out. Lived on me grandad's allotment for a while, get a shower down the centre. Sometimes I go home to me mum's.'

'Doesn't sound much of a life.'

'It's better than sitting at a desk saving up for the deposit on a house that you have to work for the rest of your life to pay for.'

'There's got to be a flaw in that argument, but right now I'm too pissed to think of it.'

Fergal came with her, more or less as expected. His company was a totem against disaster. There was nothing Jenner Ransfield could say now that would shake the confidence of being young and *with* someone. It was a bit like picking up a dog walking home, when you were little, really comforting and kind of fun, but at the same time you couldn't help being anxious about your home-coming, and then the awful dread of *what if I am allowed to keep him, and then he belongs to someone else?*

They arrived at the farm gate.

'I'd better warn you,' she said, 'this is a weird place.'

He stopped and read the words carved on the gate, something Theo had not yet wanted to do.

'Abandon hope all ye who enter here. Lovely,' he said.

'Except it doesn't,' said Theo and laughed. 'Look, it says *Abandon hop*.'

'Never did learn them big words,' said Fergal.

They walked down past May Margaret's warriors and reconstructed animals. Fergal said he thought they were great and if she lived in Camden she'd be employed by the council as part of the recycling scheme. They arrived at the feet of the plaster statues. Theo introduced Fergal to the family.

'And this is Sir Jenner, who is the strangest man you ever met or hope to meet.'

'Hop to meet,' said Fergal.

'He's a right royal bastard. He won't like you.'

'He won't see me. Once it's dark I'll go and get me stuff, then tomorrer I'll do some gardens for the well-wishers and fuck off out of here. We're regrouping with a new plan.'

Theodora wondered why it was that she felt so obscurely disappointed, as if the puppy had eaten the whole gleaming tin of dogfood, wagged its good cheer, and ambled off down the street, tongue out, tail sweeping, friend to all.

V

FOR FERGAL THE loss of his sleeping bag was catastrophic. He tried to explain this to Theo, quite gently, in terms that she would understand. As soon as he saw her setup, he saw that Theodora was a middle-class girl from a want-nothing background. These people, he knew, have a different concept of *not afford*. *Not affording something*, in the vocabulary of affluence, meant not feeling it was quite right to buy it – this month.

But Fergal had no means of support, nor any way to gain a means of support. Once an object was gone, it was irreplaceable, except by gift or theft. For an indigent such as Fergal, whom even the government declines to acknowledge, there is no credit card company proffering a material paradise; there is no rich sister with a house in Billericay and smart company Jag; no nest egg tucked away in Mum's building society for a really wet day. The sleeping bag, bought with Fergal's honestly earned but now completely exhausted money, could not be replaced. Without it Fergal was practically impotent.

'If you're on the streets and you don't have a bag, you die,' he said. 'In the end, you die. Yeah, newspapers, blankets from charity handouts, yeah. But you're going to die. And even if you don't die straight away, you get so cold you want to, so you do things to make it happen quicker.'

He thought this sounded raw, too far outside her experience, so he tried again.

'A bag's not like a car, see? Without a car you can still catch the bus or walk places. Without a bag, you're just about a stiff.'

Theodora was walking about the caravan in a towel, daubed dry from the shower, but wet and prickly from the cold, brushing her hair vigorously to remove all traces of the stuff she had applied. Outside the afternoon had drawn in, but they were snug inside.

'But you aren't on the streets,' she said. 'You're very snug in this caravan with me.'

He saw her brow furrow with the effort of understanding him. He wanted her to understand, because he couldn't spend time on her if she was insensitive to the cause, if she was ignorant of the other half and refused to try and learn. He wanted to spend time on her, because he couldn't take his eyes off her. He thought she was the most beautiful creature he had ever seen. Not in the traditional sense, of exquisite prettiness or perfect feature, for Theodora was merely a conventionally agreeable girl; but in Fergal's eyes she had stepped straight out of the Garden of Eden. This was how people were supposed to look – glowing with health, pure skin, springy hair, teeth white and shiny, limbs which folded and unfolded when bidden. He looked and looked for a blemish, a spot, a roughness artfully concealed, for any indication that corrective action had been taken to achieve this perfection. Of course he had seen such creatures on American high school dramas on TV, but had always assumed that the daunting perfection was an artifice. He could detect no artifice in Theodora; she did not seem aware of how she charged the room with her aliveness. He thought if she took her clothes off she'd look just the same, a body as it ought to be, spilling energy and beauty but all the while unconscious of its glory.

It was his business to notice things, and he noticed everything about Theo. He saw that her sleeping bag was expensive and very warm, that her mountaineering jacket was about as good as you could get, that her personal stereo was the best on the market, that her camera and notebook computer cashed in would keep him for months. He felt no resentment; there was no reason in his belief system why those with money shouldn't have proper possessions. Why would you buy a cheap sleeping bag when you could afford a good one? Only a raving loony socialist would do that. Fergal looked at Theo's possessions as an enthusiast looks at a museum, with consuming interest but without envy.

He looked at her person in the same way: he had no desire to have sex with her; that was not in his canon, but he filed away the shape of her forearms and the true blondeness of her hair, the precise helices of her curls, the insolent perfection of the ear.

He also observed the caravan, its quirky welding and palpable leaks, and was confused by the contrast between Theo's belongings and the housing in which he found her. Very few things confused him. If someone had that sort of financial backing, why stay in this scummy little dive? Was she in love, was she stupid? He didn't think she was in love with anybody, else why'd she be walking around in a towel waiting for him to make a move? And she wasn't stupid, not from the way she talked. Did she think she was camping, then, laboriously boiling up water for coffee on a bed-sitter gas ring? Perhaps she thought of England as a great big camp site – damp, inconvenient, but kinda fun, a lark, something to talk about back home.

'What's with this caravan, then?'

'This farm belongs to a guy called Jenner Ransfield, who's a mega-distinguished agricultural scientist, if you know what that means. I came over here to study under him, because I'm a vet. Not your James Herriot kind of vet, I'm a nasty scientific one. So here I am, studying under Jenner Ransfield, which is a sick sort of joke. And he offered me accommodation, which is another joke, this one. I'm here, but I won't be here long. Somewhere a nice dry bedroom is just hanging out for me.'

'Why is studying with this guy a joke, then?'

'Oh God, I can't start to explain.'

'Yes, you can. I went to college.'

'You did? I still can't explain. There isn't anything you can put your finger on. It's just that he's mad – no, not mad exactly, he's sane, but he chooses not to be. He just doesn't live in the same world that I do.'

'I don't neither.'

'I could say, I rest my case, but I'm not that much of a bitch.'

He grinned at her good humour, her magic teeth; he lay warm under her sleeping bag, cigarette in hand, because she'd let him smoke inside. He was about as comfortable as he could imagine. He knew he had to move though, reclaim his one and only possession, though it seemed like the last thing he wanted to do. His body screeched at him that getting out of the warm and the comfort of this little hidey-hole, with this perfect girl, was a small madness – which was why he had to make himself move before he lost the will entirely.

'It's dark enough. Better get up there.'

'You're fucking mad.'

'Look, it's me livelihood. You really got no idea, right?'

'I'll buy you a new sleeping bag.'

'Well, I wouldn't say no, but the thing is, if I can get it back, then you could just give me the money instead.'

'But it's wet out there.'

'Yeah, that's the real problem, innit?'

'Too right, mate. I'm sick to death of this rain. But you'll never call me a wimp, so I'm coming too.'

She was pulling on her jeans, expensive thermal socks, zipping and buckling her coat.

'They'll get you,' he said in protest. 'Throw you out the country. Don't do it.'

'I've got a much better plan. We'll get May Margaret to help us. She talks like one of their bosses – you know, Lord-Lieutenants and Lords of the Manor, and that lordly stuff.'

It was raining in that niggling, inconsequential way he had got used to since he'd been down here, as if it thought raining was the normal thing to do, like scratching your head all the time whether you had lice or not.

Theo didn't want to go inside the house. She threw stones at a window until a head appeared.

Nothing bothered Fergal much, but he wondered about this place. He was a townie, even though he'd spent three summers on the protests, up trees mostly. The country gave him the creeps, all that silence that wasn't. In a city you knew what lurked in the shadows, what was waiting round the corners to get you and hurt you bad, and where you might run to hide from it.

They waited beside the big grey truck. Fergal took out his last cigarette and smoked it with all the lovely tragedy of a person condemned.

. . . it's mostly nettles, now, the little garden. The outlines are visible, a double line of rocks, one terraced an inch or two above the other, the sweet pool, fringed with black dragon and buttercups, a concrete birdbath, covered in small-leafed ivy. Someone made an effort here, some starry-eyed schoolteacher, taking her class outside on balmy days, transforming the patch of gravel and weeds by the old staff room prefab into a snippet of paradise. *See what can be done, a person can transform anywhere, even forgotten corners like this, into a haven of peace and beauty. Remember this, when you are surrounded by concrete, stuck in a tower block with the lift broken, remember this place, when you look out of your window and can't see a tree – you too can make the wasteland bloom.* And then home to her neat semi with three square feet of lawn mowed to perfection, and flowers in wooden tubs symmetrically arranged on the gravel by the front door. The dream was good, but dreams are dreams, and no one comes to enjoy the little garden, the staff room is condemned as being riddled with asbestos, inside ashtrays overflow by the armchairs too nasty to keep in the school and too solid to throw away. No one comes here to contemplate the sweetness of nature; these walls are steeped in sourness, cheating, sneaking, pain and misery. An ivy-covered birdbath is no defence against the meanness of the human spirit, O schoolteacher.

Fergal is leaning against the wall in the sunlight, smoking a cigarette, up to his knees in nettles. He knows the nettles afford him no defence, any more than the birdbath and the niceness occasionally observable in teachers. He is going to get done over, so he smokes his cigarette the way he imagines a condemned man would, millisecond by millisecond, amazed at how long and delicious a smoke can be. He can't remember what particular set of miscalculations has led him to this end: grinning at the wrong moment, giving someone lip, having an Irish name? Who cares anyway? He knows his place in the universal pecking order that is school, and his place is to be bashed.

He sees that his hand is shaking; he didn't know he was scared. Yes, he did, he knew he was shit scared, but he didn't know his body was scared without him. His mind has been full of excuses – *I ran into a tree, sir. Me stepdad came in drunk. I fell down the stairs in the dark, the lift's broke.* And then an excuse for Mum – but why make one up? Tell her, and tell her to stow it?

How bad did it hurt when they really did you? More

than when Dad did? Did you cry, like you couldn't help it? Fergal never cries, but then he mightn't be able not to, if it really hurts. Did it hurt more after or at the time? How many of them were coming to do him over, and if he just crumpled up would they leave him alone? If he cried and called out, would they tell everyone he was a girl, do what Dad used to, repeat the treatment till he learnt not to? He leans over and is sick. The weeds cover it up.

There are only two of them, as it happens, and they come round the corner all casual like they are going to join him for a smoke. Fergal grunts as if he's vaguely surprised to see them and starts to light another cigarette. This is pretty stupid, because of his hands shaking. They start to say things, things that would alarm no teacher overhearing, things quite simple, harmless but for the tone. He doesn't know what he says back; nothing he says is going to make any difference.

He gets the new fag alight, puts away the lighter. Starts to smoke. Looks them in the eye, thinks, what the fuck – they're going to hurt me, so, who the fuck are they anyway? If they kill me, they'll suffer. They'll get raped in jail, not me. I ain't here, me, I ain't here.

The big boys advance across the garden, approaching Fergal one on each side. He goes on smoking. One of them steps in his vomit, bends down to look, comes up disgusted and swearing. The other one laughs. Mockery makes the first one angry, he raises his voice, shouts that he'll get Fergal.

Never did though, not then, not never. For out of the old building, lazy, like a lioness woken up after a feed, comes Keeshmal, otherwise known, deceptively, as Quiche. Wot real men eat. Six feet tall, with shoulders and breasts to match, she rules the school, because of her knife, because of her girl gang, and because of the backup afforded by her great brothers.

'Fuck off, you cunts,' she commands, and they don't exactly run but they would've, if they could've.

'Not you,' she says to Fergal.

He stays where he is, still working on the same cigarette.

'I reckon you owe me.'

'Reckon so,' he says, Clint Eastwood to the last.

That was where he learnt, among the abandoned armchairs and carved-up desks, that things are not how they seem, that a runt like him had the magic to make a goddess quiver and moan. Under the posters decrying smoking, posters urging Teacher Solidarity against the forces of capitalism, posters exhorting sexual continence, he learnt that beauty is everywhere, that the greatest is no more and no less than a human being, that the unconsidered, slipping around the corners in darkness, keeping his nose and his cock clean, may yet be the influencer of policy, the holder of a whip hand. He learnt to take nothing for granted.

'Dr Potts!' came a voice of the type that caused every hair on Fergal's body to stand up. 'You summoned me.'

'Hi, yes, May Margaret, emergency time – this is Fergal, a friend of mine,' said Theodora as if she were talking to any old girl friend not some great towering duchess. 'Can you borrow the egg truck?'

Briefly she explained why, leaving the tall girl in the ragged black clothes and the cut-glass voice no room to argue. To her credit, May Margaret took to the challenge with great enthusiasm. After listening to the rise and fall of her voice a bit longer, Fergal decided she was probably all right.

'I say, what a truly Enid Blyton adventure!' she cried. 'I'll get the key!'

'Torch!' Fergal's tone carried half across the yard, but was still classifiable as a whisper.

'And your smokes,' he added, cos he could tell a mile off.

Theodora started to laugh. The sound was lovely. Fergal forgot everything for a second. The need for a cigarette nudged him, but he nudged it back. Piss off, he said, this is Eden.

Lots of ideas sloshed around in Fergal's head – nicked from commercials, picture books, lessons he once listened to, catechism class, soaps, arcade games – a word, a picture, a notion, all by itself, loosely connected by the clear jelly inside his head to all the others, but having nothing specifically to join up with. Connecting them was what professors did, sticking pins right through lovely ideas and setting them in a pattern that was right for all time. But Fergal didn't like that; he liked them to slosh around, keeping their space, colliding, slopping away again, coming up against another one. Here was Eden, up against a cigarette. Cigarettes were pleasure neatly packaged with no befores and afters, cigarettes were smoke of hell, cigarettes were freedom and Marlboro Man, and in your face, social worker. Eden was naked Eve, mysteriously pink and short of body hair, cupping fig leaves over her bits, to the sharp poking in the ribs of Joseph Patrick Donovan. Eden was some farm out West in a black and white movie. Eden was a big black woman singing reggae.

Theodora was restless, eager to be going, body fired up; he liked Action Woman, her plastic limbs oiled, Cat Woman, coiled for the spring, Lara Croft, all pixels, but great boobs and look at them thighs. But she had a mind, bright spark in the eyes, evaluating him, checking him out. That was OK; he stood up to being checked out, got used to it in the protest business – meeting all sorts. Girls who were current, they wanted to know where they stood, whether you were going to jump them, whether you were clean, whether you were gay. This one, Theodora, she was trying to figure it out, thought she had the data. She'd have to ask him in the end, they all did: that was part of his marketing strategy.

'Got it!' hallooed May Margaret through the darkness.

Theo shushed her frantically. What was the big deal about secrecy?

'Don't fret, Theo! My father hasn't returned from his afternoon ramble. Poor Mother is in a state, but rather relieved that you are not only safely returned, but have a young man in tow.'

'Jesus! You don't think Elspeth thinks –'

'Yes, I'm afraid so. The mindset of the enslaved woman. A silly woman, my mother, but she holds no animus towards you because you are young and lovely and my father lusteth after you in his heart.'

'Oh for God's sake, May Margaret!'

'Fear not, sweet chuck; my mother is an irrational, romantic soul. She will die a thousand deaths from misery but never say a word. However, I assured her you had not run off with the male parent, and we were going to search for him in the truck. Sedgemoor's as good a place to look for him as any other.'

'But where the fuck is he?'

'Well put, Theodora, well put, if grammatically idiosyncratic. I might have asked, Where is his asterisk? Or, Where is he asterisking? Since that terrible word never pollutes my maidenly lips.'

'*Jesus*,' said Fergal under his breath.

Theo seemed defeated by this conversation. She climbed into the cab, and made Fergal sit in the middle. She stared out of the window. Processing, thought Fergal. The idea of Theodora spread out before him like a warm lagoon nestling a beach in Paradise, captured in vivid blues and yellows by the travel agent's local photographer.

May Margaret started the truck by free-wheeling down

the farm track and suddenly engaging the gear. This proved as exciting as a fairground ride – one of those that trundles the country evading the safety inspectors. They drove out of the farm gates, on to the road and off towards the battleground.

'So you're an eco-warrior,' said May Margaret, '*soi-disant.*'

'Is that French for somefin?' asked Fergal.

'He's been in the protest. The police were after him.'

'How terrific. Are you one I'd have heard of? Do you have one of those nicknames? Laa-Laa, Tinky-Winky?'

'I'm Moonbeam.'

May Margaret almost stalled the truck, a very unwise reaction in practical terms.

'You are Moonbeam? The naked one? Can you prove it?'

'Who's Moonbeam?'

'Me. It's me stage name. See me in the *News of the World* on Sunday? It was a real stunna. I could autograph me bum for you, if you like.'

'I don't understand a word you're saying,' said Theo. 'I've been in this country for three weeks, and it seems like ten years since I saw a clean surface or had dry feet, and then it seems like I've just got off the plane into the Appalachian Mountains, it's so weird.'

May Margaret found this funny, but Fergal felt obscurely disturbed, like when someone stuck a chewing-gum bogey up the nose of Queen Victoria on a poster in the Tube. It was essential to explain.

'It's like this, see. The newspapers and the TV used to love us protesters, like we were the seven-day wonder that lasted a year, down tunnels, up trees. And we were all young and sweet and had long hair and kooky nicknames. Didn't last though, cos we were too serious and didn't screw each other often enough, and don't make any money. But for a while there, yeah, we were headline country. An' one day I'd taken off all me clothes to dry because some stockbroking prick had turned a hose on me. It was a sunny day, lovely. There I was up a tree, starkers, me clothes spread all round the branches, soaking up the sun, and some snapper's been taking pictures. And some of the others spun him this line about nudity being my form of individual protest. And they give me a nickname and all, Moonbeam, and it got in all the papers. Not the TV so much, family viewing and that. And what I noticed was, when I had me clothes on, no one recognised me at all.'

'Oh yes, Moonbeam is quite a celebrity,' said May Margaret.

'I don't think if I wrote home and said I'd met Moonbeam that anyone in Australia would be mega-impressed. They'd think I'd gone soft. Caught the English disease – cutesy.'

'Cutesy? Is that how you think of us?'

'Don't even know what it means,' said Fergal.

'I used to think England was cute,' said Theo. 'I did. Bobbing to the Queen, soldiers in furry helmets, judges in woolly headgear. But not any more. Not since I met you guys.'

As they bumped along Fergal rolled around in his head the notion of cute. Cute he'd have called Theodora, first off, round-eyed girl off *Friends*, collectable china thatched cottages, like those in the locked glass cabinet in the house of his sister's mother-in-law if you could call her that, kittens. He had a kitten once, but he didn't know what he called it. It musta had a name, because he named everything then, even the shoe box on a chain that was a dog. Black-heart Fido; one of them shoe-box dogs was called. He got burnt, did Black-heart Fido, one day when the wood was too damp to catch. Kitten musta had a fate too, other than taking fits and dashing into dark corners.

'Nothing cute about judges,' said Fergal. 'Nastiest group of people on God's earth.'

'No judges on your gardening round, then, mate?' said Theo.

'You garden?' said May Margaret in simple amazement.

'Yeah. I'm champion. Gimme a greenhouse I can grow Chilean bell flower, even. Salsify, red peppers, sugar snap peas, the best tomatoes. You name it, I can grow it.'

'I don't see gardening as a way of making one's mark. Write poems, paint great murals on derelict buildings, walk around Essex with a pole on your head, but not gardening!'

'I don't wanna make a mark.'

They rolled off the dark and narrow lane leading up to the protest site and on to the battlefield by way of a muddy track, over which Royalist trees bowed their faithful heads.

'What *do* you want, Fergal?' asked Theo.

A long silence was observed as May Margaret negotiated the dips and furrows of the neglected roadway. Ideas tumbled around in Fergal's head looking for words to attach themselves to. He longed for a cigarette. He wondered about the question, but did not immediately find an answer.

They came to a barrier of metal stakes and plastic netting, and notices from the police. There was no sign of life. May Margaret stopped the truck, and the three clambered out. They stood in a row staring in the torch beam at the crumpled remnants of human activity beyond the barrier.

'First up, I want a smoke.'

May Margaret said nothing. She gave the torch to Theo, extracted two flattened cigarettes from a packet in her back pocket, lit one from the other and handed it on to Fergal.

'Thanks.'

They drew on the cigarettes in silence. Fergal thought about the question.

Theo stood by the netting and scanned the site with torchlight. BUTLIN BIG ONE read a sign, painted in splotchy red, smashed in half, the jagged edges of the break forced downwards into mud. A purple tent stood upright, its plastic flanks flapping. A pair of green Wellingtons had been neatly placed by its wide opening; they were still waiting. A washing line ran from the apex of the tent to the neighbouring oak tree, a dark T-shirt and two pairs of white underpants still pegged up. Next door was a big khaki canvas tent, veteran of a hundred Scout camps, half standing, half broken, as if it had been run over in the mud while beating a dignified retreat, wooden poles struggling doggedly to stay upright and still offer shelter from the unspecified perils of outdoors.

Up to this point Theo had regarded the protest, the rescue of Fergal, and the expedition to salvage his possessions, as a few more episodes in a series of running japes against Establishment Man. She had been playing this game for years – organising protests, writing memos, calling meetings, issuing press releases – and she took it very seriously, the way you take a computer game seriously – lots of strategy, lots of discussion, lots of time. But when it starts to go against you, you have a laugh and a drink, wipe the scores and start again.

But now, looking at the remnants of Butlin Big One, she felt a new creeping dampness in her heart. She felt it was possible, looking around her at the hard and homely evidence, that everything did not turn out OK in the end, that not all stories had a happy ending.

She felt shocked at the sight of people's possessions ground into the mud, the realisation that Fergal's worldly goods were somewhere in that mess, and that he was not going to abandon them, because they were all he had. No possession had ever raised much passion in her heart, except perhaps her first tennis racquet, first lipstick, and her Secret Diary for the year 1985. Anything that got lost, she replaced with a better one. But to own almost nothing and to risk the complete destruction of that pittance suggested a dedication that was almost mania. She had known many dedicated campaigners in her time, but they all went home to a comfortable flat at the end of the day.

Fergal and May Margaret stood perfectly still, two dots of concentrated combustion, close together, one a head taller than the other, a primitive signalling system, the key to which has been lost.

Fergal broke the silence. His answer hung in the air, like the words from a Zen master, meaning very little and far too much.

'What I want,' said Fergal, grinding the butt of his cigarette carefully into the mud, 'is – I want to want nothing.'

I want to want nothing. Theodora Potts's house of cards held its structure for a moment, then slid silently into a neat pile on the floor of her life. For ever afterwards, whenever she tried to build it back into its proper shape, Fergal's subversion came out of nowhere and caused the structure to quiver and fall once more.

He told them to stay put and pretend to be sightseers having a gawk. If anyone came, they were to drive off and leave him. Then he ducked into the wood, up a convenient tree, over the largely symbolic barrier and into the debris of Butlin Big One.

May Margaret and Theo had a go at being sightseers. They read the brass plaque marking the battlefield by the light of the torch. English history meant nothing to Theo, and why should it? They'd studied the United Nations and Japan and Australia 1740 to the Present Day in Social Studies. And that was enough history for anyone. Chaps in wigs with mistresses were just for television dramas. They had no relevance to a modern Australian. Theo tried to figure out why anyone, particularly someone like Fergal, would care about a flat expanse of mud and grass, presumably under which lay a few shards of shattered limbs and rusted helmets, but which, as far as the torch could make out, had in itself no feature or beauty to distinguish it from a thousand other stretches of English countryside.

'Who the hell was James Duke of Monmouth?'

'The pretty result of Charles the II's asterisking.'

'May Margaret, why can't you say fucking like everyone else?'

'Because he has forbidden the word to sully my mouth, and I make sure to obey him. Your reaction to that ban is more satisfying but less amusing.'

After they had read and reread the account of the battle they stared into the blankness, listening for the scurry of Fergal or the tread of the law. A vehicle with double headlights came slowly up the lane behind them.

'God, let's hope it's not the same cops I met before!'

It was, however, the vehicle of a security firm, men of a much more menacing stamp. They wound down the windows and looked at the girls. Their car was sleek and black, with grilles inside the back windows and mean-looking aerials. Theo walked right up to it.

'Hiya!' she said in the slow tones of Cousin Jim from Yackandandah. 'I'd never heard of the Battle of Sedgemoor before, though I suppose you guys know all about these things. Your history is just so amazing, it's so old.'

'Mostly we're interested in the here and now,' said a coal-black voice from the car, with no identifiable accent.

'Well, that's lucky, because I'm really trying to find a real English pub, but my friend here is only interested in old battlefields and churches. Preferably a pub with some real English fellas in it.'

'We're not here to give advice to tourists, we're here to keep everybody, repeat everybody, off this site. But I will give you one piece of advice: stay out of trouble if you want to stay in this country.'

'I never get into trouble,' said Theo with her best shot at a giggle. 'Not that kind, anyway! Come on, Maggie, let's look for some action.'

The security guards watched them, in silence broken only by the crackle of their RT. The young women piled into the truck, which, as they should have foreseen, failed to start. May Margaret produced every swearword in common parlance except the one forbidden, but Theo climbed out again and waved down the security men as they were sliding away down the track.

'You flirted with them!' cried May Margaret afterwards, as if Theo had been caught *in flagrante delicto* with a donkey.

'Got the flaming truck started, though. And we gave Fergal more time to find his stuff and get away. But remind me never to go anywhere in this crate again. I'm going to hire a car tomorrow if it bankrupts me. What with Jenner's car and this truck I've really had the Ransfield vehicle experience. Let's hope those goons don't cross-reference their information with the pigs kosher.'

'The *what?*'

'Pigs kosher, the genuine police. It's a sort of Aussie joke. A paradox.'

'Tasty, very tasty. I say, I wonder where little Fergal is?'

'He'll be right as rain; those pig substitute men didn't have any dogs with them. They're more interested in strutting up and down and terrifying the locals than catching people.'

But when they arrived at the embouchure of the farm, dogs were very much in evidence. A great barking was in progress, the farmyard was brightly lit, by magnificent police-issue torches. Jenner's Great Danes were standing in the midst, barking for everything they were worth, while two policemen strained on the leashes of two equally aggressive, if rather more high-pitched, Alsatians. Jenner stood by his front door, still in his stockman's coat, horse whip in hand, loving every minute of it. The policemen, much at a disadvantage, whipless and in yellow, were trying to explain themselves over the hysterical baying.

Jenner, the women could well hear, was not accepting any explanations. He was a God-fearing, tax-paying citizen of the United Kingdom, who slaved and laboured to pay his dues, who abode by the laws of the land, earning his keep by the very sweat of his brow, so that parasites might wax and grow fat! A man who gave his life-blood, his bodily essence, the substance of his soul, to stay on the land, and preserve it, who had not stinted a day from toil, yea, not in his lifetime – and who could say as much? As a boy he rose before dawn to drive in the cows, loading the milk cart before school, poring over his studies, and never slackening in his duty to his father and to the land – as he never had, in all the years that followed, always passionate for the country, for farming, for the proud life of the independent farmer, and yet holding, yea more than holding his place in the great world of learning! How dare they! How dare they infringe the liberty of a Briton? How dare they, sneaking, snivelling, paid-by-the-hour civil servants in yellow jackets, come wheedling on to his land, with their overbred neurotic dogs, and demand anything? Let alone to search his farm, his very person – tantamount to rape, yes, tantamount!

Did they have a search warrant? No, he thought not! Britain was made great on the rule of law! On habeas corpus and the right to be silent, the right to be innocent, the necessity of a search warrant! Strip those rights away, and what do we have? We have Fascism, brothers, Fascism; we have Hitler, and Mussolini, and Mosley; we have anarchy and every man and dog for himself. Those rights make us just; those rights make us human; those rights make us proud to be British, and neither you nor your jumped-up superiors, nor your hysterical hounds, shall diminish that proud heritage! Now, they are to be removed, until warrant is served, or by God I shall set my hounds upon you, gentlemen, and heaven take the hindmost!

'Gosh, he's good when he gets going,' said Theo, leaning out of the truck window.

'Heard it all before. He's only got so many rhetorical techniques,' said May Margaret. 'Don't be taken in by the poor little farm boy eristic. He only stayed with his father at weekends, and on Sundays, being the Sabbath Day, they did not labour nor disport themselves. A boyhood of Saturdays now translates into a lifetime of drudgery.'

The police could not exit from the farm, with or without dignity, until the truck had desisted from blocking the exit. After they had performed the slow *pas de deux* of truck and police van, and May Margaret had neatly stowed her vehicle under cover, she felt the need for another cigarette. She slowly brought out a fag, tapped it ceremoniously on the dash, and slowly commenced to light it. She sat in the cab, drawing deep breaths as if she had been engaged in an exhilarating act of sexual connection. Fergal crawled out of the back of the truck, squeezed in beside her, and helped himself from the packet.

'You little shit!' said Theo. 'I've been worried about you all the way from that bleeding battlefield.'

'Bloody good fun, innit? Fuck, he's good. Who is 'e?'

'He is an entrenched old conservative who makes Thatcher look liberal and Enoch Powell benign. He is, for good measure, an intellectual anarchist and a born-again blood-red socialist. If there is a position to embattle yourself in, Jenner Ransfield will hole up there, all guns blazing. He is highly intelligent, sexually demented and not quite clinically mad. He is also biologically, but in no other sense, my father.'

'Jesus. Makes my father seem quite a darling, really.'

'Why?' Theo asked. 'What's he like?'

Jenner's dogs, having seen off the upstarts, surrounded the truck and curtailed this conversation. Jenner was walking around below, smiting the sides of the truck with his whip and demanding an explanation of recent events.

'You or me, doll?' asked Theo.

'You. His anger with you is not anger at all.'

'Possibly. As we say in the clinical world, it exhibits as anger. Which is quite unpleasant enough.'

Meanwhile Jenner was demanding an answer. *Thwack, thwack, thwack.* Theo leant out of her window, looked down upon him, and smiled. He stopped still, dogs beside him.

'Hi,' she said. 'Bloody amazing evening. Those cops giving you gyp?'

'Theodora, I prefer it if you speak English. Get out of that vehicle and explain yourself. You also, May Margaret. Out, now!'

Thwack, thwack-thwack.

'Jenner, this is Fergal. Fergal, Dr Ransfield, my host.'

Jenner paused for a moment.

'And what is Fergal – some plausible piece of flotsam, some rent boy, some guttersnipe extortionist with an eye for the irredeemably naïve?'

Theo looked him in the eye and wondered how you decided another person was mad. The face of the man who looked back at her did not seem mad in the lock-em-up sense. She thought of him as solemnly excited, as if he had set fire to a great bonfire of fripperies and was circling it with grim delight. He was recognisably the same man with whom she had ordinary serious conversations. At the same time, he was allowing these words to come out of his mouth, as if he were deliberately using words as a species of game, designed to damage, or perhaps had engaged a speech engine to produce these utterances, emissions from his mouth in which his person was not involved.

Jenner started once more to beat the side of the truck, a rhythmic crazy flailing. Theo saw that this was intended to intimidate, and noted how effective it was. She hesitated over the most appropriate manner in which to answer him; sassy, meek and mild, or fantastical? Every approach had the potential to make him madder. She cowered with indecision.

'Well?' he demanded, as the blows assailed the paintwork. 'Well?'

Fergal leant over Theo's lap, popped his head out of the window, and extended his non-cigarette hand towards Jenner.

'Moonbeam. Environmental activist. Thanks for seeing them cops off. Not that I've broke the law, not since I started on the protests. That don't matter to them, of course. Thanks, anyway, mate.'

Jenner stopped hitting the truck at once, took one look at Fergal, reached up and shook the proffered hand.

'Honoured to meet you,' he said without any irony that Theo could detect. 'A man of principle. Handsome arse on you as well. Come inside and partake.'

Out of the depths of the truck Fergal brought his belongings: a magenta sleeping bag, mountain conditions, on which was painted a plump white M; a canvas duffel bag; an armful of distraught green nylon, jumbled with cords and pegs, which was once a tent. All of these were disfigured with mud, and unpleasant to the touch. Theo helped carry them inside, and laid them out in the hallway, as reverently as a pall over a coffin. It was clear that vehicles with deep-tracked tyres had driven all over these items, with the intention of embedding them in mud.

Fergal took several books out of the duffel bag, and examined each one. *Culture and Anarchy, The Dispossessed, Pocket Wildflowers of Britain, The State We're In, The Anarchist Reader, Down and Out in Paris and London.* Then he turned out on to the kitchen table a collection of cassette tapes, home-copied, careful handwritten covers, cracked to pieces, slivers of plastic everywhere. Elspeth hovering around in great confusion cried out with the sorrow of it, but Fergal grinned and shrugged.

'Get new ones on the insurance, won't I?'

Jenner poured him a very large whisky and prowled around the damaged chattels speculating out loud on how the perpetrators could be made to pay.

''Snot worth it,' said Fergal, settling comfortably at the kitchen table. 'Me sleeping bag is OK, me books are OK, and I haven't got anything to play me tapes on anyhow. Got nicked. Making a fuss lets them know where I am. I don't want the cops to know I'm here.'

'Are you here?' said Theo.

'Have you had any supper, Fergal?' asked Elspeth.

'Tell the truth, I could kill a slice of toast, missus.'

'Toast! We can do better than that!' Elspeth opened the fridge in ecstasy. 'We have some boiled potatoes, left over, and some steak and kidney pie.'

'Champion!'

Elspeth, May Margaret and Theo paid little attention when Jenner bade them goodnight. They sat down with Fergal at the table and watched while he ate his way through all the leftovers of their Sunday lunch, fried up and liberally coated in tomato ketchup. Theo picked bits off his plate. She thought they might as well finish off the booze she had bought for lunch. They had wine, the remains of the cider, rather flat, and the whisky Theo had bought for May Margaret. Fergal told them funny stories about the protest and the police.

Then Elspeth remembered the trifle. Robin was summoned from above, and all five of them tucked into it, until the bowl was wiped clean.

Fergal caught Theo's eye and grinned.

'Looks like I'm here all right, don't it?'

VI

FERGAL KNEW THE police would come back looking for him. It was in the nature of the policeman to ferret out the Fergals of this world, as it was the nature of Fergal to avoid the law at all costs.

The question was: when? How long could he risk staying here, in the best hideout he could imagine? Here he was, curled up warm in the daybreak, snug as a kitten in a slipper, happy as a rat in rubbish. Everything he could want. And if he had sex with her, he would be doubly sure of being looked after: warmth, food, cigarettes, clothes, transport. If he still did that stuff like he used to do it. When he was at school he learnt how to be fucking good. He knew that, because otherwise Quiche would've dumped him after the novelty wore off, like she dumped all his rivals.

But sex, like money, belonged to that other life. Still, he couldn't prevent the pictures forming in his head, Quiche's wide pink pussy and the whole catalogue of her lascivious sisters, the Lady Whiplash, New Busty Brunette, Submissive Swedish doll. Bleeding stupid to let these images squirm to the surface when lying warm under Theodora's sleeping bag, comfortably conformed to Theodora's body. She might wake up, take one look at him and condemn him for ever as a liar and a cheat. He didn't lie and he didn't cheat; it was important that she understand that, even if he never saw her after tomorrow. He wanted her goodwill because of her loveliness, the way you want the giraffes in the zoo not to avert their great heads as you approach.

Asleep she was unchanged, slept with such soundness and containment. Her skin was as pure on close examination as you could dream; he wanted to stretch out and touch her naked thigh. He did not want to do this from any sexual motive, for sex was dirty, hole-in-corner, unhealthy, and Theodora was all cleanliness; he wanted to assure himself that the skin felt as lovely as he knew it would.

'You can stay here,' she had said last night, curled up with cocoa, both of them too cosy to move anyway. 'As long as we sort some things out.'

'It's OK, I told ya, I don't do sex.'

'Not gay, are you? Got something transmittable?'

'Nope. Neither.'

'Permanent relationship?'

'Nope.'

You could see she was puzzled. Should he struggle to explain? Explanations were boring, but worse than that, they crammed into dreary little compartments called words, things that were big and messy and wild. No words would serve to convey to Theodora why Fergal did not do sex.

'If I was a girl, and you were a bloke, and I said No, you'd have to take it.'

'I have to say,' said Theo carefully, 'that that is a perfectly fair answer.'

There was one sleeping place in the caravan, a surface described as a fold-down double bed in the plans Elspeth had used to build the caravan. Whatever minute persons the caravan designers had in mind to share this double bed, Fergal and Theodora, diminutive people, were larger than they. Theo had spread a bedsheet over the surface, and arranged her one pillow and a cushion from the drawing room, and opened flat her sleeping bag.

Like a little housewife, she patted down the bed she'd made, a bit too precisely, because of all the drinking. Then she went into the tiny curtained corner that contained the shower and basin and came out wearing a white T-shirt that came down to her knees. On the front was printed MY BODY IS MINE. On the back he read the words BUT I SHARE.

'I'm pissed and I'm going to bed. You keep some clothes on, and if you try anything on, without asking, I'll get May Margaret to carve you up and feed you to Jenner's dogs.'

She curled into a shell under the sleeping bag.

That man, Fergal thought in the dark, that man. He was a ravening wolf. He was an emotional bandit. He looked at Theodora as if he were hungry and she was food. It was not healthy; he was dangerous, dangerous in the complicated way of the needy, those eternally damned to desire and never be satisfied. Fergal had seen with his own eyes the self-justification of the rapist – *the pain of my need is greater than the pain of your violation. You cannot know what I suffer – yes, you suffer when I punish you thus and thus, but you are whole, you are strong, you cannot know a fraction of my anger and the eating away of my being that is my hate.* Fergal knew all this from one long stare interchanged with the man, called her boyfriend, who was raping his sister, the longest moment of his life, the moment at fourteen when his understanding was complete, where he saw pain and degradation and drew them into his own heart, when he saw raw evil in a face he recognised, where he saw the face of the devil and knew it to be a man they had called mate. He was his sister, he was every living thing that was battered and humiliated and ground down because *there is no pain like the pain of my need.*

In the face of Jenner Ransfield he had seen that evil. Theodora needed to be protected from him.

It was too easy for that man to get at her. Walk out of

the house for a stroll in the woods, warm night, stop by for a chat. No one would hear. Nothing would be said. But not while Fergal was here, because under the pillow, reliable as ever, the knife, which Quiche acquired for him, the best knife she could source for him, slice off a man's balls in seconds. It had never been used, but was always ready to defend his sisters, Quiche, in the unlikely event that she should need defence, any girl who needed defence. And now Theodora.

But he couldn't stick around, that was the bad bit. One day, two days, get her out of here, get away himself. When he was gone – well, they had to look out for themselves, didn't they? Fergal couldn't get tangled up in things, he had a world to save. He slept, one hand flat against his knife, the other as close to Theodora's body as he dared.

Morning. She was awake, and giving him that speculative look.

'Never screwed a little man before. Should I give it a try, do you think?'

'I told you –'

'And you meant it. Amazing. I guess I'd better go back to sleep.'

'I'll make us a coffee.'

'Yeah, thanks, I guess that's not a bad substitute.' She yawned deliciously. 'I don't really want to show my face before Jenner's left for the college. Otherwise I'll have to take a ride in that god-awful car of his. It was ghastly enough last week, but after what we went through this weekend – *Jesus*! We had a monumental scene on Saturday night because I took Elspeth to the pub. And then we had another, even worse, on Sunday because she cooked steak and kidney pudding. And I have to face him after all that.'

'Scared of him, are ya?'

'No, no, I don't think so. Not scared exactly, just deeply uncomfortable. He rants. And then suddenly he's perfectly rational and interesting, like the rants were a performance for my benefit, and I'm supposed to applaud.'

'I'd watch him, if I was you.'

'Just cos I took a risk with you doesn't mean that I'm generally stupid around men. Remember, I went to Vet School in Australia. I've done self-defence till I'm practically a walking Jackie Chan movie.'

'Not much use if he's got a knife.'

'That's the whole point of self-defence.'

Fergal declined to argue, suspecting that he had been in many more perilous situations than she had, but it would do him no good to get all superior.

He climbed over her as carefully as if she were a cathedral made of matchsticks. He filled the pan with water and lit the gas. He thought about cigarettes.

'You gotta bloke out there?'

'Yes I have, not that it's any of your business. Six feet tall, built like a brick shit-house, hung like a horse, good in bed and sweet-natured.'

'And you still wanna screw around.'

'Jesus God, what possessed me to pick you up? You might have been a sex maniac and carved me up in the night.'

'Look, it's OK, I'll piss off today. You knew I was OK. And you haven't caught nothing off of me, not even a lice.'

'Louse. I'm sorry,' she said, taking the coffee from him. 'That was fairly foul. No, really, I knew you were OK. I trust my intuition absolutely on these things. Of course you're welcome to stay. It's nice to have company.'

'It's nice to be warm,' he said, and got in beside her. He thought he'd take the risk of the cops arriving this early.

*　　*　　*

121

In spite of her stated reluctance, Theo did go up to the house before Jenner had left for work. Was he late leaving or had she miscalculated? Either way she reckoned she needed a solid hit of sugar and carbohydrate to conteract her hangover, and because it was raining, she accepted a ride from Jenner. Might as well get the awful bit over with. As soon as she got into the car, crouched up in discomfort, she found herself submissive.

'I guess I should say sorry,' she started. 'In fact, I guess I should pack my bags and bugger off, really, I've been so consistently rude.'

'No, no,' he said, turning a lugubrious face towards her. 'No, no, no. That would intensify my mortification. It is I who owe you an apology. I have behaved abominably. I have roared by reason of the disquietness of my heart.'

Theo guessed this was from somewhere in the Bible, but it didn't help.

She sat on the edge of the passenger seat, her knees tucked away towards the door, partly to avoid the muzzle of Abishag in her neck, partly to minimise the chance of accidental contact while the gear lever was manipulated or the handbrake yanked – this latter a constant hazard, since the regular brakes seemed to have given up the unequal struggle with Jenner's driving.

'Well, I'm still sorry. I think it would be better if I found a bed and breakfast place. Having me around is obviously putting you all under stress.'

The rain, as was often the case, was localised over Nightingales valley. They had left the farm early. There was little traffic about, and none on the winding country lane through which they passed. On either side the hedgerows bristled up to the sky, and the trees behind them bent over to touch, but every now and again there was a window in the greenery, and through these shafts of heavenly sunlight appeared. The effect was magical, and for a moment Theo was prepared to forgive England.

'You must not do that,' he said. 'You will destroy me.'

For Christ's sake! she thought. *How do I deal with this at quarter to eight in the morning?*

Practically. She had found this was always the best way when men got emotional. Be the nice vet with the rubber gloves, even at quarter to eight with a hang-over.

'Jenner, I don't think we are going to be able to work together if you take that line.'

'Don't talk of leaving and I shall promise to contain myself.'

It became clear to Theo that extricating herself from Nightingales was not going to be as simple as she'd expected.

They passed under a skylight in the green and into pure, brilliant light, all the more wonderful for being in contrast to the waves of the hedges. Through the portholes, Theo saw a field steaming in the light. A rabbit sat stock still in the middle of the field, crystallised in the beauty of the morning.

'Moonbeam, Fergal,' said Jenner, 'this boy who has washed up in your bed – he matters?'

Theo caught his eye, and was disconcerted to find that Jenner Ransfield was no longer a stranger.

'It's not what you think.'

'Never assume that you know what I think. I may conclude that you and the boy are fornicating. I may conclude otherwise. But what I imagine about you remains in the privacy of my head. That was not my ques-tion.'

'I don't know,' said Theo. 'I don't know if he matters. Logically speaking, how could I answer that question when I only met him yesterday?'

'You spent a night in bed with him on as little acquaintance. There was a more innocent time when that mattered a great deal.'

'I don't see that it's any of your business,' she said. 'You're not my father. Not that I'd put up with him interfering in my sex life.'

They came out of the tunnel of trees into brightness. A field of lucerne, brilliantly yellow against the lapis lazuli sky, assaulted the eye. Theo looked away from the light, looked at Jenner stooped over the wheel, and felt unaccountably sad.

'But yes, I guess, I shall be a bit sorry when Fergal goes. Well, not sorry exactly – I don't really know the word for it. Pissed off.'

Jenner emitted the classic Ransfield snort, turned his head towards her sharply, and back towards the lane ahead. They came to a leafy crossroads with four white fingers pointing apparently at random, where he completely failed to slow down.

'You must not expect what passes for a rational reaction from me, Theodora. People of my generation, especially men, suffer dreadfully from ambivalence. We can recall the sexual torments of youth, but we cannot abide the images of young people, especially those in our care, enjoying the sexual freedom we were denied. We remember enough not to wish to forbid them, but we are consumed with envy, both of your freedom and your youth.'

'It's not as much fun as it's cracked up to be.'

'Yes, and that makes it altogether more painful – I can never forget the moment my boy's hand touched a woman's breast for the first time, the ecstasy of it, not simply the softness of the skin of her breast, its perfect warmth and life-giving fullness, even a young girl's breast has that – complete in itself, and yet the promise that it held of pleasure not to be dreamt of – it was not simply the sensual delight, but the achievement it represented – the long pilgrimage of devotion that had led me to that shrine, the cajoling, the wooing with words, the breaking down of barrier beyond barrier – and then the reward, the great leaping certainty that the glory was greater than I had promised her it would be, and she knew it also.'

It's too early in the morning for this, Jenner.

Theo folded her arms tight across her chest, and moved a centimetre further towards the door, but she kept watching his osprey profile as he talked.

'And then I see young people casually taking what we struggled for, doing it all before they can drive a car, and enjoying nothing. You discover no ecstasy, find no divinity in sex. Can you deny that?'

'God!' said Theo. 'Don't you think that rather a personal question?'

'Your generation, not yourself.'

'Well, maybe,' said Theo. 'Maybe it's better our way. Who needs that ghastly struggle to get laid?'

'Yes,' he said, calm, reasonable. 'And who needs ecstasy?'

They drove up to the college in a complicated silence, for all the world like lovers who had had a tiff. He parked the car in its special place, where it was visible through his office window, and opened the back doors to allow the tethered dogs to come and go. Theo filled up their water bowls from the garden tap and set them down, though she knew they'd slop all the water out on the first slurp, and someone would have to trek back and refill them. She and Jenner walked in the same silence towards the horticultural plots where Jenner selected, for the vase on his desk, two or three flowers and a sprig or two of green, as he did every morning. The chief gardener, a man tolerant of eccentricity, nodded good morning.

Two students were already in the lab when they arrived,

a beautiful Chinese boy, crouched over a computer with absolute concentration, and the girl called Caroline. She was wearing a tiny little dress made out of the Union Jack and sandals with cork heels four inches high. She was chewing her fingers and fiddling with the computer mouse, and waiting for them to arrive. She crossed her legs on the lab stool as soon as Jenner walked in through the door.

'Jenner,' she said, 'can you help me with this?'

'Dr Potts will help you,' he said and disappeared into his office, flowers in hand.

Theo had established herself in a corner of the lab with a computer more primitive than any she had ever used. It was the best the sorry collection afforded. She switched it on and while it was cranking itself into life she poured a coffee.

'What's the prob?' she asked Caroline.

Caroline had decided that she could do no work until her nails were in better shape. 'Don't worry about it,' she said. 'I'll wait till Jenner has time.'

'I've got a minute now,' said Theo, determined to do as she was bid. 'I really don't mind; we're all a bit rugged this morning. God, what a weekend!'

But Caroline was not to be deterred nor chatted with.

'Really,' she said, and got out of her bag a maroon mobile phone, the colour of her nails.

Another of the girls sauntered in and threw her bag across the lab bench. She flung off her jacket and revealed a lime-green top covering the upper part of her ribcage and black flared polyester pants. She had a silver stud in her navel.

Theo started to describe her weekend in an e-mail to Juliet, but the events became more surreal as she wrote. She still felt the need to talk. She was tempted to recount her adventures to the students, because at least they would understand what she was talking about. Then she remembered that the police were still interested in Fergal's whereabouts.

'Who's this Moonbeam character?' she asked.

The two girls broke off their undertone conversation.

'Oh, *Moonbeam*!' said the girl called Mel. 'He is *so* cute. My friend Fran went over to Sedgemoor to get his autograph, but he couldn't get out of those chain things. She got a picture, but he covered himself up.'

'Those people just lie around smoking dope all day,' said Caroline. 'They think they're ever so cool, but they're just layabouts really. Dirty and lazy. They all want to get themselves arrested so they can have a shower and a meal on the government.'

'Gee, is that so?' said Theo, and gave up on the conversation.

She finished her e-mail, spread out her papers and set to work. She was currently engaged on cleaning and organising the data that Jenner's students had collected for him over the years. Soon she would start on the analysis. Though tired and much the worse for wear, she worked with speed and concentration, shutting out the banter and garbled information that passed between the students. But every time a door opened, she registered the activity, for it might indicate that Jenner was about to swoop. The staff members came and went, to tutorials, lectures, faculty meetings, Jenner more than anyone else, because his room was sacrosanct, and those matters normally conducted in the lecturer's office had to be conducted elsewhere. He also was much more likely to go to the library than his colleagues, and was the only one who was given to walking around the grounds by himself.

On some of these forays, he would come and stand over Theo and start to talk to her on matters relating to their work. He would bring her a journal article or a reference or the address of a website. Sometimes he would sit down and work with her, examining data and discussing methodology for an hour or longer. Or he would take her on walks around the lake while he shared the secrets of his latest work. In the midst of this professionalism he would jerk back into his other persona, delivering a florid compliment or a barbed personal remark. Worse still were the rants against random selected targets. Theo would grow tense all over, and try to keep silent until the fit had passed and he was back to his working self. When these moods took him in the lab, any students present would exchange glances and coded gestures.

But today he seemed inclined to avoid the lab. He came out of his holt and made for the outer door without pausing. Theo called him back because she wanted to complain. So in a sense what happened was her own fault.

'Look here, Jenner,' she said. 'This program's poked. I don't think it's written to an algorithm at all, I think it's a random pattern generator, thrown together by some lazy sod to justify a research grant. I mean, look at this!'

On the screen she had displayed in a window a grainy image which, although in fact a hugely magnified portion of the semen of a venerable Aberdeen Angus bull, might have been anything at all.

'Look what it makes of that,' she said, jabbing with her finger at a subsidiary panel, where a logical analysis of the image was displayed. 'Look at the numbers, look at the pattern it produces.' Jenner bent forward obediently, looked and absorbed.

'Now, look at this one! I mean, this is ridiculous!' She double-clicked on an icon on the screen; the computer grumbled and clanked to itself, and eventually spat open a second window, displaying another blur of enlarged semen, and another set of analyses.

'Look at the analysis – look at the picture.'

Jenner complied, bending close to the screen.

'The analysis is practically the same,' she said. 'It hardly differentiates materially from the other one, and yet look at the images – look at them! They are clearly different, discernibly different! This programmer of yours didn't know pussy.'

For a while, Jenner bent in silence then straightened up and turned on her. The students present in the lab, especially Caroline and Mel, waited with breath indrawn to see how he would react.

'What sort of scholar do you call yourself? You are nothing but an arrogant child. Why do you assume that what you think you see must be the correct interpretation? You stare at images, you believe that you see certain things – but you have failed to understand the fundamentals of our work – we do not make assumptions based on what we think we know. How can you presume to trust your eyes? Discernibly different, you say. Discernible by what? By your mind, by your assumptions. Therefore the computer must be wrong, because your assumption about what you see cannot be wrong! That supposed difference you see in that image and this – how do you know it is not an illusion based on preconceptions inside your head? As in everything else – you believe that you *know*, and that your knowledge is by some divine mandate, the absolute itself – The Knowledge of Theodora Potts. But in truly objective terms you know nothing at all!'

As suddenly as it began, the rant was ended. Theo was blushing – had not done so since school, since the day the French master made her translate into French, in front of the whole class, the note that Kevin Barraclough had just passed her, while he, the master, smiled and supplied the slang terms for the words she didn't know.

Jenner walked away from the computer as if nothing had happened, and poured himself a coffee. He began to drink, slow, speculative, as if he had just delivered a seminal lecture, impromptu.

Then he became conscious of the expression of delight on Caroline Hayes's face and turned on her.

'And by what right do you smirk, young woman? Are you conscious of any respect in which you are superior to Dr Potts? She should be your exemplar in open-mindedness and application. If you were to spend as much attention on imitating Dr Potts's example as you do on the nurturing of your inconsiderable attractions, it is remotely possible that you might meet with some measure of academic success.'

Jenner took his coffee to the far side of the room and sat down at a vacant workstation. Caroline Hayes had turned the colour of her nails. Theo grimaced at her in sisterly conspiracy against the tyranny of men in general and Jenner Ransfield in particular. Her commiseration was met with a look of dislike powerful enough to strip varnish.

The police didn't come that day. Bureaucratic hassles with the warrant, Fergal reckoned, never once dropping his guard.

After Theodora got up and left for work, he was inclined to sleep in and make the most of this little holiday of comfort. He had one secret cigarette left, and he thought about smoking it. He thought about Theodora and what she reminded him of: Saint Barbara, all sleek plaster and don't touch me, and strawberries that were just so poppingly red you couldn't not pinch them. He thought too of squirrels and those little birds that came and eyed him up, so mean and so edible. He thought about Perfect Miss Just 19, Just 38–24–36 Just Waiting for You.

Then he heard Elspeth come down the path to the vegetable patch. She was singing. He couldn't make out a single word, but she had a nice voice. Fergal would bet anything that that man never told her so. He thought she was a really nice person, and wondered how he could tell her so.

> Dinna ye see yon bonnie white house,
> Shining on yon brae sae bonnie?
> And I am the Earl of the Isle of Skye
> And ye –

He got out of bed, dressed, and went outside. Gotta pay your way.

While he helped in the garden, Fergal told Elspeth all about his grandad's allotment, and how he liked to garden, and scratched his living that way. She told him about growing up in Glasgow in a big stone house with three floors, always cold, and nothing in the garden except shrubs and bitter grass, but no one caring because they were always somewhere else, in a boat, and being cold was being alive. And how when she was forced to stay at home, she would sit up in the yew tree and sail across the lawn. Vegetable gardens, are they strictly necessary? You buy your vegetables from the man in the van. But Jenner has a passion about chemicals and sprays, and won't eat vegetables from the supermarket, even the expensive ones labelled Organic. It fills in the day, she says, better than washing the kitchen floor.

'But you've had no breakfast,' she cried suddenly. 'I'm so sorry. Come now, we can look to these vegetables later.'

'What I'd really like is a shave,' he said. 'I feel like Fred Flintstone. I lost me razor somewhere in the mess. Don't fancy digging around in the mud for a razor, not really.'

Up in the house she packed him off to the bathroom, where he found disposable razors – May Margaret's perhaps, for Jenner used a cut-throat. There was no way he was going to touch that. There was soap, towels, even some warmish water. He felt pretty good going down to breakfast.

She cooked them both a bumper breakfast: fried bread, onions, several eggs, a rasher each of bacon. She cooked it all up like she really wanted to, really enjoyed having him there to talk to. It was fun. You could see her unfold, like one of them fast-track films of flowers opening. As he ate, between mouthfuls, Fergal talked about his mum, about what a laugh she is, about the dad who is never mentioned, but you always used to feel his hand in the air, poised to hit, but how you don't any more, about how the girls saved up one Christmas and bought her a night class – any night class, Mum, cos you always wanted to learn something. And how she went and did calligraphy, can you believe it, calligraphy, and turned out to be real good at it – all those years cleaning and she still got her hands perfectly under control. And you should see her, sitting there at night, working on something, a certificate or a birthday poem. Happy, that's what she is. Tired out, living in three rooms, but you see her like that, working, and, well, it's lovely. Never charges enough. When you slave wiping toilet bowls for three pounds an hour, a hundred pounds for a bit of writing seems wrong. Specially when every second of doing it is heaven.

Elspeth's eyes shone as he told this tale, as if he were describing someone swept away to a fairy castle, not a working-class woman stuck in a tower block penning birthday doggerel.

After breakfast, they cleared up the dishes and then went to work on the muddy things that were still spreadeagled over the hall. They put Fergal's sleeping bag in the bath and bent over it together to wash off the mud, and talked about how they hated launderettes and shared bathrooms and outside toilets. They hoovered the drying mud and bits of twig up from the hallway. Then Fergal said he'd have a go at the dogs' room, which you could see was one of those jobs that only an outsider can face.

Elspeth let him get on with it, singing away all the while, in her porridge voice; snatches were decipherable.

> First they ate the white puddin
> And syne they ate the black
> And aye the auld wife said to hersel
> May the devil slip down with that!

During the day, first May Margaret and then Robin appeared downstairs. Elspeth stopped whatever she was doing to make them coffee, Bovril, sandwiches, lunch. In the afternoon Fergal and Elspeth collected eggs, and cleaned up the nesting area a bit, and weeded the vegetable garden, and dug some new potatoes for supper. The sun shone on them benignly.

About two o'clock a large van came down the drive. Fergal was by the garden tap washing mud off the spuds. He froze and then ducked inside the dark implement shed nearby. He stood motionless among rakes and buckets, until he heard voices outside which assured him that it was a delivery for May Margaret. He stayed concealed until the object was taken indoors. The process seemed to take a long time, because the object, from all the swearing, was heavy and cumbersome.

After the van had gone, he took the potatoes inside and started to scrape them. Elspeth was making a bread-and-butter pudding. This, she thought, would be a treat for Theodora. Fergal wondered if it fell into the same category as steak and kidney pudding, but didn't say so.

'How long will you be staying, Fergal?'

'Just get me things dry, charge me phone, and I'll be gone. Tomorrow, day after. We're washed up here; there's a new thing going down in Norfolk.'

He didn't want to take the shine out of her eyes and put the moil back in her voice, but long experience of leaving had taught him to prick these balloons before they got airborne.

'Nice in Norfolk,' he said invitingly. 'They do lots of sailing. In fact that's why we're going. Some bugger reckons he's got the right to enclose some of them Broads.'

'I used to know a man who ran a sailing school in Norfolk,' said Elspeth. 'Zachary Bryce. A lovely man, an American. Like a bear in sunglasses.'

'Old flame, was he?'

'Oh no!' said Elspeth. 'He had a very nice wife. He was just a friend. I wonder if he's still there.'

'You should come with us. It don't rain much in Norfolk.'

Elspeth looked up sharply, her fingers poised over the layering of stale bread.

'Me?'

'Yeah, why not?'

There was such a long silence that Fergal had to look round from the potatoes to see if she was still there.

'It's such a nice day, I should have washed the sheets,' she said.

Do I give one? Fergal asked. *No, I do not.*

In the late afternoon, Fergal is sitting in the frame of Robin's window propelling his smoke into the outside world. It's been raining again, soft lingering rain, but now the sun, startlingly warm, is teasing the vapour out of everything, so the air seems full of clouds of warm dampness, somewhat like a launderette with poor ventilation. The sweet light of the evening hangs around the trees; the smoke ventures out into stillness, hesitates and is gone.

His person is alert, waiting for the crunch of a vehicle on the gravel.

Robin is downloading a detailed map of the Norfolk Broads from a site on the Internet and explaining to him that the Battle is to Wrest the Web from the Hands of the Devil.

Fergal thinks about the Web, a great blob of matter, jelly-like, smeared all over the world, sticky when you grab at it, so you get handfuls but never the whole thing; a substance rich and disgusting, like the menstrual blood he is supposed never to have seen. Or then again a labyrinth of endlessly enticing passages, up which you are drawn until you bang your nose on a brick wall, and realise it was all an illusion, that vista of knowledge and entertainment. The Web is something which is there and not there, you have to think of it in metaphors.

How he loves metaphors ... Remember poor Mr Yeabsley teaching them about figurative language above the din. *He was like a lion in the fight he was a lion in the fight how about he was ate by a lion in the fight Mr Yeabsley. Now create your own metaphors. I was fucked by my teacher. Yes, that is a metaphor, technically, if you mean that you were destroyed by your teacher rather than had carnal intercourse with him.*

Fergal thinks of the Devil – huge and red and muscular, with a cock that dripped blood, or a tiny fat thing living in the eyes of the boys at the back. That thing in the rapist's eyes. Evil had to exist, because he had seen it. So you had to think of it somehow – metaphors were for that. The Devil and the Web – two things that were real and important but you couldn't think about without a picture.

'You got something there, mate,' is all he says.

'If you believe in the Devil,' says Robin, 'it's a short and simple step to accept Jesus as your personal saviour.'

He's like a young financial planner, his new suit as yet uncrumpled, remembering the phrases from the training video. Fergal doesn't grin outside, but he grins in his head.

'Yeah, whatever. Big business, pornographers, Microsoft, rip-off artists, politicians, property developers, the Devil, they're all after it. And only pathetic little us to stop them. Bit like the protests. Sometimes you lie down in front of a bulldozer and think, get a life, it's just so much bigger than you, know what I mean?'

From above them come stentorian crashes; May Margaret is working on something large.

'It's easier to fight the Devil. We have Forces on our side.'

Fergal sees legions of angels hovering round the farmhouses, fanning out over the battlefield, making practice darts with their shiny spears.

The green car rockets down the driveway, around in front of the house and into the stable. Theo gets out and opens the back door for the dogs to unfold themselves. That man gets out, slams his door. It fails to shut. He slams it again more violently. It hangs sullenly open. He walks away. Theo goes round and gently shuts the driver's door.

Her straw-coloured curls are damp against the collar of her coat. She's bright and shiny with wetness. On her back is a bag made of bright blue cloth, patterned with lizards and snakes and unidentifiable Australian animals in splotchy pinks and yellows. Fergal searches for the right image. He thinks of some picture where an angel turned up, another where Father Christmas was real – film actors bathed in a special light to alert the audience to their otherness. He thinks of the early fantasy films, where the fairies and monsters were before your eyes but somehow you knew they were superimposed, and that didn't matter at all. Creatures that were there and not there. He thinks of advertisements for panty shields, international airlines, florists, where unreal beautiful girls fly across various terrains. He thinks of the Doc Marten ad, where people like Fergal get to look like heroes of romances, yearning and striving to be together for love. And he sees Theodora wreathed in sunlight against a background of dripping trees, waving and smiling up at him, and thinks she can't be real either, because no one with teeth like that ever smiles and waves up to Fergal.

Fergal forgets about the police and the herons of Sedgemoor. He takes the image of her inside him and it fills all the space inside his head.

The dogs chase the hens and crowd around the man. He waits for Theodora and speaks to her. Together they go into the house. Fergal wants to tell her that something is wrong with this.

That evening while Fergal was in the kitchen drying the dishes with Theo, and explaining why Arsenal Football Club was really the best in the world, Elspeth came into the kitchen to deliver a summons.

'Fergal, Jenner wants to talk to you in his room.'

Fergal was seized with alarm, but he made light of it.

''Ere we go, 'ere we go,' he said to Elspeth and abandoned his dishcloth. 'Pack me things, will you darling?'

He knocked on Jenner's door, fighting down thoughts of headmasters and parish priests.

'Come,' said Jenner.

Fergal hadn't been into Jenner's room, but he already knew its smell. The jackal enters the lair of the wolf and all the hairs go up on the back of his neck. It was dark and stuffy. He could see sunlight through the window, but it was more like a painting of a sunlit scene for all the difference it made to the room. Jenner was sitting in a handsome round leather chair, with turned sides. He sat upright, his legs uncrossed, one hand on the small mahogany table in front of him, where his book lay open. He hadn't been smoking, but a decade's worth of pipe tobacco hung wearily on the room.

The table with the book on it was the only clear space in a sizeable room. The room was jam-packed with furniture and books and pictures, more books and pictures than Fergal had ever seen in one place. One quick professional survey told him that there was nothing of immediately nickable value, but a great deal of middle-market stealable stuff, if you had a van and the contacts. Not that Fergal had any intention of stealing anything.

In one corner between the window and fireplace was squeezed in a narrow bed, insubstantial, almost like a camp-bed, so narrow that you wouldn't want to sleep on it more nights than you had to, and certainly not take a bird into it. It was covered with a tartan blanket, pulled very firm. The space under the bed was filled with suitcases. Every wall surface was taken up. Even the space above the bed was filled with bookshelves, packed two deep with old books, the kind that clog up the boxes out the front of booksellers' shops. 20p each or 10 for a pound. Code for: Take 'em away, please.

On the shelf above the fireplace were lots of ornaments, spotted dogs, shepherdesses, naked bronze guy, china flowers, two fancy clocks, both stopped, porcelain tom tits, little girl praying, toby jug (good market for them), and there were quite a lot more of the same herded into a glass-fronted cabinet, along with Victorian flowered gravy jugs, cut-glass vases, stacks of big plates, soup bowls, that kind of stuff. There'd be about forty dinner plates in there alone.

There was a great big wardrobe firmly shut, and a big chest of drawers. And a smaller chest of drawers, with suitcases stacked on top of it. The only clothes visible were

Jenner's coats, on a big hall-sized coat stand by the door. Stockman's coat, green cord jacket, tweed jacket, with a variety of hats and sticks and umbrellas. Nice collection of walking sticks.

Taking up the space in the middle of the room were two fine antique tables, stacked with old magazines, *Punch*, *Illustrated London News*, the *Farmer*, sheet music, a couple of nice wooden workboxes, hand sewing machine, a dozen or so framed pictures in a pile, a solid toolbox, a globe, tobacco tins, dozens of them, candelabra, big glass fruit bowl, glass dome full of stuffed birds. Under the tables cardboard boxes tied with string.

By Jenner's table was an old gramophone sitting on a cabinet full of 78 records. All the wall space left over from the furniture was occupied by pictures, right up to the ceiling, cheek by jowl. Dark oil paintings of stags and mountains, and little widowed watercolours of cottage gardens, framed engravings yellowing at the edges. *The Death of Nelson*, *The Funeral of the Duke of Wellington*. *The Apocalypse* of John Martin. There was one which took Fergal's fancy. It was entitled: *And when did you last see your father?* and showed a small Cavalier boy being interrogated by Roundhead soldiers.

'Ah yes,' said Jenner.

Fergal was quite impressed by the way he was reading. One glance at the book told him that it was the kind of book he'd read one page of at a time and then not really understand, though he'd got good marks in hard subjects like Statistics and Principles of Database Design. He knew when he was outclassed.

'Yeah, well, hi,' he said.

'The death of the English language.'

'Yeah, the middle classes started talking like us and now we've got nothing left. These days they just grunt, down the pub where I come from.'

Jenner smiled. Fergal found this disconcerting. A man like Jenner Ransfield didn't smile.

'Sit down, Fergal.'

Fergal looked around for somewhere to sit. There was a settee pushed into one corner, but you couldn't sit on it, because it was piled with hatboxes, embroidered cushions, china dolls.

Fergal sat down on a trunk lettered Levy.

'Are you serious about this protest?'

Fergal considered. It was a deep question, but he wasn't going to get time to think about it.

'Me? I'm not serious about anything except saving the world from property developers, plastics manufacturers, airport executives, transport moguls, Microsoft, McDonald's and Mattel Corporation. Anything else is for the birds.'

'Do I interpret that as Yes?'

'Yeah.'

'Because if you are, it occurred to me that you might draw the right sort of attention to your cause by a more middle-class species of action.'

'Depends, don't it?'

'Precisely. It depends. Every act of idealism is a compromise of some kind. You cannot be a pure idealist and avoid cruxificion.'

'Hang on. I gotta process that.'

Jenner smiled. He knew that Fergal understood him but was objecting to the complexity of the statement.

'It occurred to me that if you were to make a play for the historical, old English aspects of the battlefield, you might engage the sympathies of the widely influential conservatives, people of substance and a certain age, readers of the *Daily Telegraph,* the uncles and aunts and godparents of Members of Parliament, the kind neighbours of bored journalists, the elder sisters of High Court judges.'

'Yeah. I'm with you so far.'

'If I were in your position, which is not as absurd as it may sound to you – and by God I envy you –'

Fergal started to drum his fingers. He wanted out; he wanted a smoke. He didn't want to be preached to by this man with the wolf's smile.

'. . . I would organise a re-enactment of the Battle of Sedgemoor. There are a dozen battle re-enactment societies in this country. Then I would arrange for the Chief Executive – *soi-disant* – of English Heritage to visit the site during the event. The national news media would enjoy that. And if you are well enough connected you might persuade a documentary television team to trail the whole event. It has considerable appeal – left-wing liberal sympathies and the affections of the young are attracted by the protests of yourself and your kind; conservative middle England is attracted by the notion of preserving heritage; the viewer without principles is intrigued by the pageantry of the battle scenes; every television licence holder in the South-west is gripped by local fervour. There is even, I am informed by the young, a sexual element in your own dubious appeal.'

'Thanks, mate.'

Jenner got up from his chair and moved over towards one of the desks that was laden with papers.

'Somewhere in this Augean stable I have a list of local landowners.'

He began to work his way through the piles of paper. Fergal speculated on his motives for helping the cause. Ransfield seemed an unlikely ally. Fergal had met several hundred well-wishers in his years on the protests, and none of them was like Jenner Ransfield.

'You are welcome to stay here,' Jenner continued, sifting through his piles of paper. 'And I am sure my son will put at your disposal his remarkable talents as a designer of Internet web pages, not to mention the more quotidian service of electronic mail.'

It was hard for Fergal to resist this offer. He felt a part of himself sucked away by the vacuum pump of overwhelming good sense. He wanted to stay. He desperately wanted to stay. But he wasn't going to let on to anybody, least of all himself.

'Yeah, but the police, they're after me.'

'I shall deal with the police. I shall take great pleasure in dealing with the police. They have no evidence against you, but I suspect they are looking for any excuse to arrest you. I would advise you and Theodora to be extremely disciplined in the matter of marijuana. The smallest trace will be enough.'

'Yeah, I keep meself clean. I learnt that early. But they'll ask questions.'

'I am sure you and Theodora are equal to the invention required, as long as you collude in your story.'

'You telling me to tell porkies?'

'Of course. Is this not war? War against the forces of commercialism, a battle against the deadly disease of greed that is destroying our country? The creeping leprosy of grasping littleness which has taken hold and can only be eradicated by extreme measures. Warriors in this battle must fight with every weapon to hand.'

He produced a typewritten list, tattered and amended, and made some more swift amendments in black ink.

'This fellow has sold up . . . the phone number is the same . . . this one consolidated . . . that farm name has changed . . . that postcode should be . . .'

Fergal was fascinated by the use of a black ink pen. He watched the lightning elegance of Jenner's hand. He imagined those long fingers pulling apart the secret grottoes of Theodora's body, and he was filled with excited hatred. He saw the list of names forming under the black magic of the pen – a beautiful project, worthy of his reputation, something to be done. The big red wave of lava, that was his passion to get out and to get Theodora out, washed up against the hard rock that was unarguably a good scheme. Marvellously the lava lapped around the rock, and stilled. Fergal went out of Jenner's room with the list in his hand.

VII

SATURDAY AFTERNOON LATE. Theo, Robin and Fergal
are kicking a football about in the yard, scattering hens
every which way and yelling a lot. Robin's invented a
set of complex rules to govern three-person football, but
the others are ignoring them. Theo says that the only rule
that matters is that under no circumstances is the ball to
go anywhere near the shiny new car she has hired, which
now sits smugly in the stable between the egg truck and
the Countryman.

The ground has dried, isolating the mud to a series of
puddles and ruts, which Fergal, being the better player, tries
to get the ball into, while the others defend. This method
of playing involves a great deal of shouting and even more
splashing, all of them quickly discovering that when you
reach a certain degree of muddiness nothing is sacred.

Out of the highest window, where the thatch would
have been, appears the top half of May Margaret. She
watches the game like a modern mother – torn between
the desire to curtail this primitive nonsense, and the sense
that she ought to join in. Fergal flashes her a grin but
she doesn't signal back. After a stunning goal, perfectly
knocked into the big puddle by the side of Fergal's shoe,
she breaks silence.

'I say, you chaps. Will you come up here?'

'Beers?' says Theo.

'Not immediately. I've a job for you all first.'

Theo and Fergal leave their muddy trainers at the kitchen door, but Robin's boots stay on his person. They bundle rowdily up the stairs to May Margaret's kingdom. Theo is curious to see how Fergal will react to the fearsome woman carved on the door – but he glances at it and grins.

'Men Beware. Should I worry?' he asks.

'I'll make an exception for you,' May Margaret says, 'because I suspect you are on the side of the angels.'

Fergal roams around May Margaret's gallery of carvings, touching everything, as if it were a blind person's section of a great museum. The blackout curtains are drawn back, and natural light is allowed in. Seen clearly, the interior is patently a notebook of ideas in wood, and as such more evidence of May Margaret's serious artistic endeavour than of a troubled mind. But without dramatic lighting and the drama of shadow, the carvings are simply work in progress, rather than emissaries from another world struggling out of the wood.

'Any new ones, Marg?' asks her brother.

'No, I don't doodle any more. I do commissions and art works. Commissions down here, art works up there.' She points to the attic. 'I'm going to show Theodora later. Sorry, boys, no show.'

'You keep promising,' says Theo, looking doubtfully at the padlocked trapdoor.

'And I am a woman of my word. Let us just get through this afternoon's ordeal first.'

'Can I put on me high heels and come too?' asks Fergal.

May Margaret glances derisively at his genitals.

'I have yet to be convinced that transsexuals are genuine women. I think they transform themselves into a man's idea of a woman. The biological version of the marbles of Canova.'

'Phew,' says Fergal. 'I'm fraid me art history's a bit rusty.'

Up at the working end of the space stands the latest commission, draped in a sheet that looks in rather better condition than many Theo has observed being humped on to the washing line. May Margaret whips off the sheet and lays bare a magnificent eighteenth-century wooden fireplace, crawling with grapes and apples and pears and strawberries and pomegranates and a forest of miscellaneous vines. Between the vines peek fat winged cherubs and fat marauding birds. The whole is carved as if in one continuous gesture in dark wood, twining up one side of the fireplace, across under the mantel and down the other side.

'Wow,' says Theo.

'School of Grinling Gibbons,' says May Margaret and laughs very loud.

On the work surface next to the carving is a venerable set of chisels.

'Genuine eighteenth century,' she says pointing at them. 'So is the fireplace.'

'So what exactly –' asks Theo.

'The fireplace is genuine; some of the carving may have been added or restored.'

'Restored!' says Robin, bent over it. 'It's all yours, Marg.'

'No, no, no! Look again. Actually, don't bother, because you'd never be able to tell mine from his. I have to assume it's a him, because I don't think they let women into carvers' workshops except to sweep the floor. It might be Grinling himself; I have my fantasies.'

'This is wrong,' says Robin. 'It's deception.'

'Not at all. It is an eighteenth-century fireplace. It is school of Grinling Gibbons. I am school of Grinling Gibbons, am I not?'

'What's wrong is wrong,' insists Robin. 'Everything else is moral relativism.'

'I won't ask who the fuck Grinling Gibbons is,' says Fergal.

'Seventeenth-century, actually,' says May Margaret, 'but someone in the eighteenth had hacked the carving about to make it fit the fireplace. I just aided and abetted him.'

'Sneaky,' says Fergal. 'Don't sound like you.'

'It's not me. It's a commission for my friend Elgin Summers. I've done several, of which this is the most ambitious. He is an antique dealer and restorer.'

Fergal walks around the fireplace, while May Margaret explains about the relative rarity of this kind of fireplace, about eighteenth-century wood carving, and the *trompe-l'oeil* effects at Claydon Hall, which naturally she hasn't visited due to the exigencies of her situation.

Fergal strokes the fruit with his fingertips.

'Never seen a strawberry like that.'

'Seventeenth-century breed of strawberry. I don't make mistakes as simple as that. And the sparrows. Copy what is there, don't invent. Don't know about the cherubs, not having seen a twentieth-century one up close.'

'There'll be people who can tell,' says Robin darkly.

'I do hope so. But not, I think, any of Elgin's *nouveau riche* customers. Middle-of-the-road rock singers gone respect-able, media types teleworking. And curiously, among that group, a work's chequered history adds to its value – they love a cunning forgery, it gives them a story to tell their guests. So Elgin tells me.'

'So this is why your parents are so disapproving.'

'Yeah verily, the male parent because everything I undertake is destined to disgust him, and poor Mother because something in her Presbyterian background impels her to agree with him. Also, poor creature, she thinks I am throwing away my expensive education and prodigious talent on mere forgeries. But then she hasn't been in the attic. He, of course, grows weak and pale with rage whenever the word "attic" is mentioned, knowing as a man of discernment that it contains beauty he can never reach.'

'Has anyone been in the attic?' asks Theo.

'Not yet. You, my darling, shall be the first. A signal honour. But first we have work to do. What's the time?'

'Seventeen-fifteen,' says Robin.

'Right, at half-five, Elgin Summers is arriving to collect this fireplace. I need you chaps to carry the mistresspiece *very carefully* down the stairs and help him lift it into whatever vehicle he brings. Theodora, my love, I want you to waylay Father, because about the last thing I could endure would be him ranting at Elgin. That would be so shaming that I would prefer to die. Does anyone know where he went?'

'Well,' says Theo, 'he took the dogs and a straw basket and a hideous old hat and a stick with a point on the end and said he was going to imitate the action of Isaak Walton. Is that code?'

'In his convoluted mind, everything is code. Alas, alas, *gemetria*! You are no match for my father's mind.'

'What's she talking about?' asks Fergal.

'Actually, for once, I understand,' says Robin. '*Gemetria* is like the Bible Code – the idea that every word contains a hidden message. If you treat Greek letters as numbers, then every word in the New Testament contains a number that points to some other mystical meaning –'

– and he is out of the birdcage and off! The others watch him tear into the distance, sorry that he's out there all by himself. It transpires that he has written a software package for a Bible group in the States to analyse this very thing – and oh, the wonders unveiled thereby!

May Margaret potters round the fireplace covering it up

again, and tying the sheet in place with cords. Fergal tries to lift it.

'So what do you want me to do?' asks Theo.

'Distract him. Flutter your eyelashes or primp your curls or something, anything to delay him while Elgin is here. Do you know which way he went?'

'Towards the moor.'

'Well, off you go. You'll hear a toot when the coast's clear.'

Theo is irritated at being ordered about, and about to say that it's pretty daft expecting her to slow Jenner down for more than ten seconds. Then she looks across and sees that both Fergal and Robin are staring at her with alarm, as if she were being sent into no man's land under enemy fire. She laughs at their folly and decides that waylaying Jenner will be just an extension of the game of football – one more nutty experience to add to the photo album.

She grabs a beer out of the fridge and wanders down towards the caravan trying to think of a strategy. She's sure Jenner won't come back right now, because when he goes out, he goes out, mercifully, for hours.

She gets past the clearing round the caravan and the vegetable patch and into the wood through which the path leads on down towards the moor. It was in this direction that she saw Jenner go. She climbs up into the lower branches of a tree from where she can just see the track down to the farmyard, and can also see some distance towards the moor if she turns her head the other way. She drinks the beer.

Eventually a donkey-brown Range Rover comes slowly down into the farm and turns out of sight. Theo is consumed with curiosity to see this Elgin Summers about whom she has heard so much. In the course of several late-night drinking sessions she has found out that he is an older man, though May Margaret is coy about how much older. He is quite wealthy, divorced, and of dubious ethics. He deals in Art Works and Antiques, and has several shopfronts in different towns in the West Country. He is opening a gallery in London, in one of the newly trendy old working-class areas where he acquired a lease in the middle of the recession. Theo has been told at some length about his frequent and energetic sexual engagements with May Margaret. May Margaret encourages him in this, since any man is as good or bad as any other, and this one also looks after her material interests. She says that contrary to expectation, the sex is rather fun, except for Elgin's superannuated notion that sexual conjunction implies some sort of contract.

In the distance Theo can vaguely hear voices, probably people swearing as they try to get the heavy fireplace down two flights of stairs. Then she hears from the other direction, a bark.

O Jesus! she thinks, alarmed, although she tells herself that it really doesn't matter a sausage if she fails to slow Jenner and he does, after all, encounter Elgin Summers. He may deliver a mighty tirade, every bit as entertaining as embarrassing, or he may simply walk into his room without a word and slam the door.

Jenner's getting closer; she can see bits of his coat through the trees. Theo feels she must at least try something, mostly because May Margaret has set her a task and she doesn't like to fail. But what she finds she has decided to do takes her very much by surprise.

He's almost underneath her now, but he hasn't seen her, although Abishag has, and stops.

'Hi Jenner,' she says, dangling her legs.

'What exactly . . . ?'

'I was hoping I'd catch you.'

'Are you playing dryads now? Is this some new rite of spring you have learnt from consorting with vegetarians?'

'I was waiting for you to come back.'

The expression on his face would seem comical in another light. The intensity of his reaction gives Theo the shudder of a mistake about to be made.

'You were waiting for me to come back? Is this to accuse me of some new folly or taunt me with some new piece of outrageous behaviour of your own?'

'God, Jenner, I really don't –' then she remembers herself. Whoops. Sweet smile.

He swishes at a clump of nettles with his shooting stick.

'Did you have a pleasant walk? You were going fishing, weren't you? My father's a great one for fishing . . .'

She hears herself babble. Jenner is looking up at her in an uncomfortable way. Further up towards the farmhouse there is the sound of vehicle doors slamming, and voices, rather more voices. Jenner seems not to notice them. He concentrates his attention on Theo up in her tree, and she wishes that she could just disappear into it, the way Fergal can.

'The thing is,' says Theo, smiling, but not sure she doesn't just loathe herself, 'the thing is, I've hired this car.'

'So I observed.' Bitter, he's taken it personally. As he should, because it is entirely personal.

'And I was wondering, well, it seems a bit of a waste me having it, and all these wonderful places round here to see, and –'

There seems to be something happening up by the house, but Theo can't make it out. She daren't let her concentration on Jenner slacken, in case he should see through her and storm back in the midst of the operation. How long is it going to take them to get the fireplace into the vehicle? Theo can hardly endure herself, and she's conscious of digging herself into a pit that's going to be incredibly difficult to clamber out of.

'And?' He looks angry. Maybe he'll refuse. *Please God, let him refuse.*

'I was wondering if tomorrow, maybe, we could – you could – um, show me round some places – Somerset churches, Exeter Cathedral – Elspeth says you know a lot about them.'

'You, Theodora Potts, young wild Australian, are asking me, ancient and impossible Jenner Ransfield, to go around looking at churches with you?'

'Er – yes. Though I wish you wouldn't pull that old man stunt. You're only just fifty.'

'Fifty-two. And you are twenty-six. Perfect.'

Hurry up, Marg, for God's sake!

'It's just a bit embarrassing in front of the others. I mean Fergal – and Elspeth –'

She decides to slip down the tree. This is a tactical error, for he is so much taller that she is forced to look up. Looking up at tall men, she has discovered, always makes a girl simper, no matter what she's made of.

'Fergal and Elspeth what?'

'Well, they might think, you know.'

'I'd like you to explain to me exactly what you mean. This is uncharacteristic behaviour for you, Theodora. You always tell me exactly what it is you think. What are you playing at?'

'Well, I would like to go out for the day with you, but I would be embarrassed if Elspeth or Fergal knew, because they might imagine there was something in it.'

'*Something in it* is newspeak for a sexual liaison?'

Theo feels herself blush. *Again.* What a disgusting performance she's putting on. Why had she ever thought this was a good idea?

At that juncture, Elspeth appears above them on the

path. They both start when they hear her voice, and turn towards her in disarray. Theo remembers the yawning impossibility of explaining things away, from the time she was demonstrating to the Head of Genetic Studies what was and what wasn't regarded as sexual assault, and his secretary walked in.

Oh shit, oh shit, oh shit, thinks Theo, not having the Ransfields' large vocabulary in which to express her fury and distress.

Elspeth is agitated, sure enough, but not by Theo's blushes or Jenner's rapt attention on her.

This is what had happened.

Two days after Fergal arrived at the farm, Tuesday, the police had come knocking, bright and civil in the morning, with a search warrant. Jenner and Theo had left for college. Robin was hard at work designing the best web page ever seen, for the New Battle of Sedgemoor, while Fergal, stuck to his mobile phone, directed over his shoulder.

Fergal heard the police car arrive, and heard Elspeth answer the door. He slid immediately into the hall to listen. He had very sharp hearing and well-developed eavesdropping skills, one of the many useful things you didn't get taught in class. The policemen came inside very polite, and accepted Elspeth's offer of coffee. The visit was a formality, they explained; they were checking all the dwellings in the vicinity in case any undesirables were concealing themselves. A number of people were wanted by the police on charges ranging from obstruction to possession of illegal substances, and in general pursuance of the Criminal Justice Act of 1994. The policemen were genial and friendly, and very nice to Elspeth. Fergal got ready to run for it.

He knew he could get out the window in Elspeth's room and across to the trees in a matter of seconds, but if he ran they would know he was guilty. With the fuzz, you had two choices: to run like stink and never get caught, or to stay completely cool. It all depended on what Elspeth said.

And she was champion.

'Oh there are no undesirables here! Just ourselves, and the young couple we have staying in the caravan. That's Theodora and Fergal. Dr Theodora Potts from Australia, you know, she's come all this way to write a scholarly paper with my husband. There's no one else here. We would know, wouldn't we?'

You darling woman, thought Fergal.

The police explained that, all the same, they'd need to have a look round and speak to everyone, in case anyone had seen anything. They couldn't emphasise too much how important it was to show zero tolerance to these people, who were simply troublemakers in disguise.

When Fergal was tracked down and interviewed, he said he'd come down from London with Theo, having met her two weeks ago in a pub called the Prince of Wales in Clapham. Asked what kind of girl picked up a person like himself on no acquaintance and brought him down to stay in the respectable home of complete strangers, he replied that Australians don't see things the same way. They didn't believe him, but Elspeth stayed as quiet as a rabbit in the presence of large dogs.

They looked around the caravan, but Fergal and Theo were tidy creatures, and their sleeping bags, his with its tell-tale trademark M, were stowed in the drawers under the bed. Fergal gave his mother's address.

They will come back. *Just to corroborate the facts, you do understand, Mrs Ransfield? We will need to speak to Dr Ransfield and Dr Potts? Just a formality, my dear, I'm sure this young gentleman understands, don't you, my lad? You won't be wandering off anywhere until we've had the opportunity to speak to Dr Ransfield and Dr Potts, now will you, sonny?*

That was the mid-week visit. And come Saturday, here they are again.

Elspeth saw them coming before the others. She'd been polishing the floorboards in her bedroom when she heard Elgin Summers's Range Rover arrive. She had a look, and decided to stay out of the way, lest May Margaret introduce her to this man, whom she did not want to meet. She knew she would be nice to him, and she didn't want to be. He was the corrupter of her daughter.

But she kept an eye on what was going on. She noticed that the man Summers wore a very expensive Pringle sweater, cream trousers and hand-made brogues, which sat oddly with his gold jewellery. She noted that, in spite of elaborate attempts to conceal it, Elgin Summers was older than she was herself. He had a fanatically trimmed beard on his chin and designer stubble on his cheeks. The beard was grey with streamlets of white running down either side, so perfect they must be dyed.

Looking and not looking, as she was, she saw the police car arrive and the men get out. They were in dark suits this time, different men.

Fergal and Robin were just staggering out of the door with the heavy object bundled in a sheet. They were complaining about its weight and awkwardness, and had it half in and half out of the doorway. Elspeth couldn't actually see them from her window, but she could hear the raised voices, and the directions issuing from Summers, in his smooth television art critic's voice, and much louder and more graphic commands from May Margaret.

These two were standing by the Range Rover with their backs to the drive, watching the progress of the bundled carving.

'For Christ's sake, tell them to be gentle!' said Summers.

They didn't immediately react to the arrival of the

police, but when they did, Elgin Summers's tanned face went pale, and his hand flew to the gold chain around his neck and started to pluck at it. His body grew rigid, and May Margaret became, of an instant, quiet. The boys put down their burden with some relief.

'Dr Ransfield?' asked one of the police officers. Elspeth thought she'd better go down after all.

She didn't have to be introduced to Summers, the confusion relieved her of that. He stood pale and tense by his vehicle, darting glances towards his booty. Elspeth thought, if the police didn't smell a rat, they weren't any good at their job. May Margaret was shaking.

Elspeth occupied herself with greeting the police and inviting them inside for a coffee, or a tea, or will you have a glass of water, perhaps, or home-made ginger beer? But these men were not interested in chats. They took the name of everyone present, and showed no interest at all in what Elgin was up to. He jerked his head at the boys and they carried the fireplace and stowed it in the back of the van. He offered no explanation, and stood holding the handle of the closed trunk, waiting for his chance.

May Margaret was still speechless with some sort of terror. Her mother thought: her crime was about to be uncovered, her lover exposed, well might she tremble!

'We wish to speak to Dr Jenner Ransfield and Dr Theodora Potts,' the senior police officer said. 'Are either of those people here?'

May Margaret couldn't speak. Robin was tongue-tied, throwing longing glances at the safety of the house. Elspeth didn't know where they had gone.

'I'll go and look for them,' she said. 'Would you like to step inside, gentlemen.'

'No!' said May Margaret.

'I'd like to be toddling off now,' said Elgin Summers. 'Hop in, Maggie.'

'No, I can't come with you,' said May Margaret in a low voice. 'I have to stay here.'

'Why, for God's sake, get in girl. I haven't got time for this.'

'You go. I have to stay.'

'For Christ's sake!'

He turned to the police officers.

'I take it you don't need to detain me?'

'If you are neither Dr Potts nor Dr Ransfield, and not an occupant of this household, certainly not, sir. Good day to you, sir!'

Summers practically ran for the driver's seat, slammed the door and drove away with an alacrity that Elspeth thought would have been a clear indication of guilt. The police took no notice. The two boys sloped inside, probably to conceal evidence of their battle plans, but May Margaret stood barring the police officers from entering the house. Fortunately, they did not wish to push past her, for she wouldn't have stood a chance.

'They went that way,' she told her mother in a taut voice, gesturing towards the wood like Joan of Arc at the stake.

Elspeth went down among the trees and found Theo and Jenner in conversation. She was confused by this, for surely they spoke to each other often enough at college? But she was too worried by the threat to Fergal to pay attention to the niggle of unhappiness that this sight provoked.

Theo and Jenner made at once for the house. Jenner took such big strides that Theo was forced to run. Elspeth prayed that she and Fergal had got their story straight, even though she knew that to lie to the police was a crime, and worse, a sin. She prayed for forgiveness, and asked not to be put on the spot.

But what would Jenner say?

Theo confirmed Fergal's story. What else was she to do?

She seemed entirely unashamed of the picture of her morals that the police tried to paint.

'Yeah, I'd only known him five minutes, but hey don't you guys know about sexual chemistry and love at first sight? You should be flattered, I fell like that for an English bloke.'

They persisted with their questions with an undertone of sneer. Jenner stood silent while they questioned her, driving holes into the ground with the pointed end of his shooting stick. His dogs circled the police car hoping it would give them an excuse for attack.

'Hey, Fergal! What was the name of that pub?' Theo yelled.

Fergal's head appeared.

'Which pub was that, then? Been in a few.'

'The one we met in?'

'Prince of Wales.'

'That's right, Prince of Wales, Clapham. My cousin lives there, she took me for a drink and I met Fergal. And that was it.'

The police didn't believe her. They turned to Jenner.

'Dr Ransfield, can you confirm Dr Potts's account? Just a formality, you understand.'

'Formality! he cried. 'A formality to impugn the veracity of a scholar! To you perhaps, manacled to your rulebooks and your petty bureaucratic desks, never raising your heads to look beyond the horizon of a filing cabinet stuffed with the secrets of innocent souls – to you perhaps a scholar is nothing but a schoolteacher with leisure, you who have plodded your way through nothing more intellectually demanding than police officers' training camp, you would not recognise a scholar if Isaac Newton himself appeared before you in all his glory. Do you not understand that a scholar – and Dr Potts is indisputably a scholar of excellent credentials, or I would in no way impugn my own academic reputation by collaborating with her – a scholar is, by definition, a person of principle? Principle is what we live and die by; without it we scholars are empty husks, bought and sold by the corrupt mandarins of industry, or worse, arse-lickers, up for sale to cynical politicians –'

'Thank you, Dr Ransfield, that will be all.'

After the police had gone, without so much as setting foot over the doorstep, everybody, including Elspeth, needed a drink.

As they went inside, she heard Theo say in a low voice to Jenner, 'That was a stupid idea of mine. Please forget all about it. Perhaps if you just tell me some good places to visit and what to look for, I'll drag Fergal along.'

'On the contrary,' he said, 'I think it is a wonderful idea. Nothing would dissuade me from it. I will be waiting outside Westonzoyland church at nine tomorrow morning, come rain or shine.'

That night, Theo and May Margaret were sitting in the studio drinking wine, celebrating a victory over the forces of maleness. Below them Fergal and Robin were unsportingly at work, bent over the computer and the phone. Robin was elated because he was getting real personal e-mails from someone called Rupert of the Rhine, leader of the historical re-enactment society called the King's Westron Men. Rupert was riding hither in a sennight to spy out the land.

Theo told May Margaret the lengths to which she had gone to divert Jenner's attention from Elgin Summers. May Margaret very unfeelingly burst into long and loud laughter, wiping her eyes, and apologising and laughing some more.

'Such works of supererogation deserve a reward! Church roof bosses with Father! I shall take you into the attic.'

She took a key out of a cunningly constructed hiding place and led the way up the ladder, pausing at the top to unfasten the heavy-duty padlock on the trapdoor. The door was hinged on the outside and hung down inconveniently. She disappeared into the darkness. Theo followed her up; by the time she emerged, the space was lit by a string of powerful light bulbs in a precarious loop down the far end, casting complicated shadows across the inhabitants.

The attic had two small windows, which were blacked out with cloth. The usual attic paraphernalia were piled up in a heap in one corner like refugees' luggage. The rest of the attic space was a forest of wooden women.

Theo stood quite still. She had grown used to May Margaret's skill, and the breadth of her range, and the scale and intensity of her work, but she had never imagined anything like this – the conception was so shocking, so breathtaking, and so beautiful. Theo knew nothing about art, modern or ancient, but she knew she was looking at an *oeuvre* so impressive that no one, no matter what clever terms they might invent to disparage it, could ignore it.

The immediate impression was of a grove full of women's forms, but in fact there were only nine figures, with a tenth, under the direct glare of the bulbs, being worked upon. They were precisely life-size. Each one was constructed in the same way, the naked wooden body made up of a jigsaw of pieces, in many cases woods of different grain and texture, glued and pegged together, and smoothed off to a perfect finish so that the joints appeared like the tracings of an alternate anatomy. Though much the same height, each woman stood in a different pose and was differently shaped from her sisters, the proportions of each body different and characterful, small breasts, big hips, big drooping breasts, shelved bottom, sloping shoulders, skinny arms, bulbous calves, delicate ankles. But the bodies were no more than outline – there was no detailing of the toes, feet, calves, knees, hips, hands, arms, shoulders, ribs, breasts, collarbones, neck, throat, cheeks or brow. Though each shape was clear and distinct, it was smoothed and suggested rather than spelt out. But on each figure two parts – the hair and the pudenda – were realised with minute and loving detail, carved and then coloured with stain, so that no detail of the carving was lost. Dormouse brown, mule yellow, rat black, tomcat ginger, long and straight down the back, bobbed round the shoulder, cropped close to the scalp, escaping in a riot of curls, each head of hair was lovingly detailed, so that you felt you might pluck an individual hair from the head, so that you wanted to run a comb through the messy one, and ruffle the smooth.

But the crowning glory was the carving of the women's genitals. On most the detail was hidden, but close examination showed that it was perfect, if largely invisible to the casual observer. Each woman's secret self was as clearly different from her sisters as the curves of her body and the fall of her hair. The labia tight and close, or wide as elephant's ears, the clitoris tiny as a bud or standing out bidding for attention. In some the pubic hair curled luxuriantly over the fleshy parts, preventing further investigation.

May Margaret explained her process, as if she were in a lecture hall surrounded by a group of admiring art critics. She couldn't get hold of large pieces of wood, so had made a virtue of necessity, and would probably not use whole pieces of timber now, even if she should be able to afford or obtain them. The variation in the pieces echoed the variation over the series – the same but different. Constructing them piece by piece, she said, allowed her to carve the whole pubic area in three dimensions before inserting it into the completed figure; the hair, however, was done after the whole woman was put together. This seemed more natural, May Margaret said, though she did have to stand on a lot of boxes and things to do it. At least in a hairdresser's the subject sat down. She was wondering about doing the next series sitting down, because then you could see the whole genital area more clearly, and it would be so much easier to work on the hair.

'I'm wondering about hands too,' she said. 'I think in many ways hands are every bit as lovely and unique as hair and cunts. Maybe more. They seemed a bit of a cliché at first, but you know after a while such considerations don't affect one. Yes, I think, hands, on the whole.'

'She's the last,' said May Margaret, patting the tenth woman, 'Sigourney.'

Beside her bench of tools, in two high but very neat stacks, were hairdressing style books and pornographic magazines. A few photographs from each had been sliced out and pinned on to the plaster.

'I'd rather work from live models, of course, but I can't afford to. Not many girls I know are prepared to let one study their private anatomy for several hours for free. It's all right, Theo, I don't pay for those magazines. Some things deserve to be stolen.

'I expect you wonder how I can bring myself to touch those things, even in the cause of art? I argue thus: men are irredeemable. Objecting to pornography will not stop them making it by some means. If women did not pose, men would computer-generate bodies, as indeed they do already. Women might as well make as much money as possible out of it, since the net effect of it is not to demean woman but to humiliate man. The side effect is a celebration of woman's body in all her glory, and in useful detail.'

But Theo was not interested in arguments in favour of pornography. She wanted to take pictures to send home. She was afraid that once she was back, in the blazing openness of home, this would all be nothing but good story material, quirky, like a cleverly engineered pop-up book, you turned a page, and wow, up came a whole view of the world, little scenes with people that moved and doors that opened to reveal more scenes behind. A little place to marvel at, and shut the book. Theo didn't want to be the only person who had seen into the book. She wanted someone else out there, in the real illuminated world, to have seen what was inside. To confirm that she had indeed seen with her eyes and that it had been marvellous. Otherwise it might cease to exist.

'My friend Juliet would faint with ecstasy if she saw these. She practically worships – you know, that woman who did an installation of the wimmen's dinner party?'

'Judy Chicago. She is my patron saint. Certainly you may take pictures, on the absolute understanding that you show them to no man of any description, transvestite, homosexual, transsexual or hermaphrodite, and neither does your friend or her friend or anyone else down the chain.

'Actually,' May Margaret added, a holy light coming into her eyes, 'I've been thinking about hermaphrodites. Have you ever seen pictures of those Ancient Greek herms? They are blocks of stone with a male head and genitals. I could do a hermaphrodite series of them – male heads and female genitals. Hermaphrodite herms. In stone. O stone!'

'What are you going to do with these ones, though?' asked Theo. 'When the series is finished? Are you going to sell them or put them in a gallery, or what?'

'Well, no, actually, not. No. But I do need to put them somewhere. I am really going to run out of room here if I start a new series, and they might not get on with one another, if you understand me. I can't quite see the patriarch giving up the room his dogs inhabit. There are numerous stables and sheds here. I expect I could barricade one sufficiently.'

'I guess there are galleries just for women,' said Theo. 'But it would be easier if you let some men in. They're so beautiful, they're almost holy. I mean, like the Venus de Milo. No one gets horny over that.'

'Not negotiable,' said May Margaret. 'I don't trust the way men look at things for one second. I used to think Princess Diana was a pure icon of female beauty and then I discovered there were all these creeps lusting over her as a body. Ruined her for me. There are twenty-nine million women in the United Kingdom. I think it's only a matter of time before we have no-go areas for men in every walk of life. Art galleries will follow. As things stand, I would not want to be involved in anything that was part of this male-dominated society, even if it had a *wimmen*'s label.'

'But your other work —' said Theo.

'That's commerce. It's a form of prostitution. This is art. It matters.'

As they went back down the ladder, Theo made the mistake of saying, 'They're so wonderful you should really show them to Jenner. He ought to know how brilliant you are.'

'Theodora Potts, are you by any chance a quisling? This is war, darling. Those who are not with us are against us.'

When Theo told Fergal how she'd waylaid Jenner Ransfield and how she was now trapped into going round churches with him for a whole day, Fergal didn't find it funny. He saw Theodora face down and silent in a wood, her cheek as pale as a primrose, *Primula maculata*, her garments only slightly disarranged, while Jenner Ransfield strode about the forest, slashing at trees with his whip.

'I'd watch him, if I was you,' he said, and put his hand under the pillow to feel his knife.

'Don't be absurd,' she said, and moved in a bit closer than she ought.

That night it was too warm for Fergal and Theo to be wrapped in their separate sleeping bags. They lay side by side, almost touching. Fergal got the feeling he was supposed to celebrate his reprieve, but he couldn't do it, even though he owed her. She'd lied for him and got Ransfield to lie for him. She'd talked about sexual chemistry and love at first sight. He couldn't let himself think about those things.

But he couldn't extrude from himself the feelings and ideas that are Theodora, and all lovely things in the world, white violets, minute beige toadstools, the feathers of carrots as they push up into the light, a head of narcissus straining to go pop and spread its sweetness on the world. And the Virgin Mary, jostled by holy girls, Teresa, Agnes, Bernadette, Philomena, white smiles and eyes brimming with love and rich with promise – this is for you, we are here if you can get to us.

Some time he would have to try and explain to her the matter of his black dreams.

He's fifteen, and the taut brown buttocks of Keeshmal are before him, poking out shameless under the little black netball skirt she wears now she's a senior and about to hit the world. Her discarded panties lie where she stepped out of them; she's bent over a desk, groaning, and the buttocks shine and heave before him. And he is filled with a desire to hurt them, to seize his knife and slash the arrogant perfection of them, to hurt and hurt. And as he feels this he is overcome with loathing at himself, disgust so complete that he shrivels up inside her. Mercifully Quiche has reached the point of anonymity, where it is of no consequence whether he is a worm or a man. She thrashes and cries out, and he pretends and uses his fingers until she is through . . .

★   ★   ★

Dawn. He wakes in a sticky mess of shame and cries 'Jesus!', cups his hands over his groin and starts to get up, but not soon enough. Theodora wakes as he is struggling with his decency, is immediately aware of his state, groans in the way women do at men's grossness, and passes him a towel off the floor. He runs to the bathroom cubicle, turns on the shower, throws his T-shirt and pants under it, then parts of himself. It's pure cold water off the roof tank. They only turn on the gas to heat it as a special event. Shivering and chattering, he scourges himself dry, unable to stand still, from cold and distress. He wrings out his clothes, hangs them up to drip. Last night's are still damp and he has no other clothes. He ties the now-damp towel — brash Australian beach colours — around himself like a sarong and creeps back into the living area. Theo is standing by the kitchen bench in bare feet and a long T-shirt doing a little tap dance to avoid contact with the floor. She is boiling a saucepan of water over the toy-town gas ring. Two mugs stand ready.

She knows he has no other clothes. She takes a shirt and a pair of white panties out of her stock and gives them to him. He puts on girl's clothes uncomplaining, not even making a joke about how the panties fit him so well. He can't stop shivering. She tells him to get into bed and warm up.

When the water has hauled its way to boiling she makes the coffee and brings it to him in bed. He is shivering so much he can't hold the mug, so she puts the coffees down on the floor, gets in beside him. She puts her arm round him.

'Don't,' he says. 'Don't touch me.'

Of course she doesn't understand why. How could she?

She makes him take the coffee and drink it.

'You have to try and explain, Fergal,' she says. 'It's only fair.'

Fair, to make everything fair and lovely again. *Bless me Father for I have sinned since my last confession which was one week ago I . . . have drowned myself in beauty but still my head is full of worms . . . Our sleep was pure as angels' and I have smirched it.*

Have you seen but the white lily grow before rude hands have smirched it?

Wot's smirched, Mr Yeabsley, is that fucked? Is that butt as in arse, Mr Yeabsley?

Explaining will not make everything fair again, because it was not pure in the beginning. The worm Fergal was there for starters, and the serpent Ransfield, and everyone has blackheads and spots and fungal infections. Even Theodora, though he can't see it or believe it. He looks at her, hoping for a sign of imperfection, but finds none, nothing except the used-bed smell, which is as much him as her, and two little lines beside her eyes, exaggerated by sleepiness. He wishes to trace them with his finger, but will never do such a thing, any more than he would touch the fledgeling found on the path.

'You need to tell me what it is about sex,' she says.

Need. Now that's a better word. *Need*, the thing Fergal doesn't have any more. Need is a beggar with a scrap of cardboard; need is a white woman with a trashed toilet and the lift broken and three kids under five; need is a sad git with a negative-equity mortgage and a posh wife in a dank suburb of identical semis doing twelve-hour days to keep the kids he never sees. Fergal doesn't do need.

'Look,' she says against his continued silence. 'I don't specially like waking up and finding spunk on my back, but I'm quite prepared to forgive you if you try and explain yourself.'

'Yeah,' he says, 'yeah.'

He shivers, draws the bedding close, feels her body

almost touching, but not quite, to show that she's pissed off, but kind.

'Yeah, I need to tell you. It's a long story.'

He finishes the coffee first, still shaking, wanting to cry, because she's lovely and kind, and innocent in a complicated way, like a spider's web. But he never cries. Not since he was five and his dad thrashed him for blubbing and the more he wailed with the pain and indignity and unfairness, the more he was beaten, until he was flooded with rage so hot that it sucked up every tear inside for ever and for ever, so he would never cry again. He wants to cry, because the world is dirty and impossible and screwed, and there isn't any way to make it clean and sensible and straight, the way Theo thinks it is.

He wants a smoke, but confession requires abstinence. The body must be punished for what it has done.

'It was the job, see. I had a job. I just left college and I went on the register – the job seekers' register, that is. I got a degree in sociology and information technology. A good one, like A minus average, which considering where I came from is fucking good. Me mum worked her substantial arse off to get me through college, and I swotted up me maths that we never got at Mile End Comprehensive, and I got a good degree.

'So I turn up at the centre with me degree, right. No jobs. Course not, it's a fucking recession, right? Nobody needs a working-class git with a degree in sociology and information technology.

'So then they have this government initiative and they find me a job. It's with British Telecom, BT, right? Actually they make me a job, and I'm not complaining because I'm right desperate for it.

'D'you know what I did? Well, they had this idea that they could stop whores and sex workers from putting up their little calling cards in phone booths, if they recorded the numbers and then prosecuted them. So I got this job where I got all the little cards passed in by the telephone booth cleaners, right, and I had to classify them, enter them in this database and work out who was a persistent offender.

'Yeah, well it doesn't sound too bad, does it, till you use your imagination, right? You seen those whores' cards? I got about five thousand on me desk every day in bags from the cleaners. Naughty Miss Nineteen Needs Sir's Firm Hand. Only Twenty Years Old Open For You. TV All New – that's transvestite, not television. New hot brunette 36–28–36 genuine photo. Sixty-nine that's my number. Miss Whiplash demands your obedience. I Luv being put in Bondage with Nipple Clamps and Hot Wax . . .'

Theo frowns with disgust and gets up to make another coffee. He talks to the back of her T-shirt: BUT I SHARE. It's easier that way.

'Then after about five weeks they tell me the scheme's been cancelled, right? Like the civil liberties people told them they couldn't do it – I got all these letters to send out – Dear Sir/Madam, In accordance with the Public Nuisance Act 1887, your publication of blah blah blah. – I had first letter, second letter, response received, action taken, all that stuff, right? I had the sexiest database you ever seen.

'And the lawyers got busy on two thousand pound a day, and dear old BT couldn't send out any more letters. So there's Fergal in the office with the sex cards in these piles, right, all filed, cos you gotta keep the evidence, plus the database. And a job scheme.

'So I said to the boss, whatya gonna do? And he says, don't worry, laddie, employment service will keep paying and BT is committed to job schemes, so you just keep on doing what you're paid to. But he doesn't want any letters done or anything. So I says, what am I supposed to do, sit here and wank? Something like that, he says, only do it in the Gents.

'So I come up with schemes. Like I could write a paper on the distribution – like is there more S&M round the Strand? No, they said, you can't do that, this data is governed by privacy, whatever that means. I mean, what's private about flashing cunts all over Kensington? So I keep coming up with schemes, writing papers – like how to design a whore-proof phone box, another one on legalisation of the sex industry and giving them a controlled space to advertise. Gotta stay sane – I mean, you think about it, turn up to your desk at nine every morning and open your mail. Open your filing cabinet – all those boobs.

'It got to me see, it really got to me. I started to get really strange. All those women. It made me go sick – all that sex as commodity, know what I mean? Turning the most beautiful thing in the world into this cheap vicious supermarket where you work out your nastiest fantasy and get some poor bloody girl who's desperate for the money or terrified of a man to do it. They took sex away from me. I couldn't see any difference between what me and my girlfriend did, for love, and all that – them bums and cunts and great fat boobs, and whips and masks and women sticking out their fucking tongues, and women grinning and offering themselves. I couldn't see where mine ended and theirs began. I couldn't have sex without thinking about them, so I couldn't have sex. I wasn't going to dirty up the only lovely thing in human life with them. So I gave up sex.

'Me girlfriend threw me out, but by then I didn't care too much. By then I had free access to the Net. First I used it for research for these bum-wipes I was writing. Then I discovered the direct action sites, and then I got involved, and started organising. BT didn't give a shit. As long as I sat at that desk and filled a job scheme, they didn't give a shit. It was like, when McLibel was hotting up, there was loads to do.

'I coulda stayed in that job. The boss liked me. I didn't do a single thing, but I always turned up in me tie and sat at me desk and made everyone cups of tea and put in a monthly report and got me timesheet signed and went to the pub on Fridays and bought me round. There were guys there who had been making up what they did for years. I coulda stayed.

'Then I was walking along the street one day, looking out for shit on the ground, reading all the little sex cards, like you do, except I read them like a connoisseur, and I passed this guy selling the *Big Issue* – you know, that street magazine the homeless sell, yeah? – with his dog and he had this little cardboard setup up with a hand-written poster – Buy the *Big Issue* and Help the Homeless – you know, all written in coloured pen and covered in plastic for the rain, and I stopped and talked to him, cos I thought I could do a nice colour printed one and laminate it courtesy of BT, and he said, no mate, I'd be selling me soul.

'And I walked along and thought, fuck, I'm selling me soul. This is how you do it, and you mightn't even notice till it's too late. The priests never told us this at school. You mortgage your soul to get a job and then you sell it to stay in one.'

'O poor Fergal,' she says, and puts her coffee mug on the floor and snuggles up around him with the innocent finality of the cat who curls up in your bed and does not propose to be moved.

Sunday was a poor choice of day to tour churches. Jenner and Theo had to sneak in and out of church services in order to look at the buildings. Theo didn't really care;

she was only doing this tour because she couldn't get out of it. She was no more interested in the minutiae of roof bosses than she was in the rhetorical devices of the preacher. Jenner was fascinated by both. He was also highly emotionally charged. The awkwardness which occurred on their daily journeys to and from work was intensified. It could hardly have been otherwise, for Theo was driving the car and Jenner abhorred being driven by a woman. He had nowhere for his irritation to go, if he could not take it out on motorists and road kerbs. At each place they visited he would be reminded of another they must see, so they criss-crossed the county in crazy segments. Jenner held the map, and his battered copies of Pevsner's *Buildings of England*, the Somerset volumes, and tried to navigate. He found this quite difficult, for all his gifts of recall, perception and analysis, and he encountered cause after cause to be annoyed – from the modern language of church services, through the plain architecture of service stations, the poor state of roundabout signage, the fifty-seven different varieties of potato crisps on sale and the food colouring in orange juice.

He would lapse into black silences, and Theo couldn't decide whether these were worse than his speeches. When he was silent she thought it would be better if he talked, and when he talked she wished he would shut up. He could not endure anything on the radio except classical music, and she was damned if she was going to trail round old buildings and listen to dreary music as well.

Worst of all was the unmistakable sexual undercurrent which infused everything he said. She had thought she was getting used to this; she thought she had developed, in her dealings with Jenner, the same non-stick surface that had got her through Vet School. But Jenner's sexual innuendoes were so mixed up with everything else he said that Theo was taken by surprise every time, and every time found herself reacting with some cheap parry, when common sense and dignity would advise her to ignore him.

In Draycott graveyard, the air thrumming with bees, the grass as green as papal embroidery, he said, 'The poet says: *The grave's a fine and private place, but none I think do there embrace.* Is it possible to conceive of love-making after death if sex does not exist conceptually without the body? And yet how can we conceive of ourselves existing without the force that drives us?'

On Glastonbury Tor he said, 'The ancient world, it's here, it's in the fabric of the stones. Unadulterated man, his driving passion, thrusting up to the sky, his untrammelled sexuality. How far we have fallen, we poor emasculated modern men.'

In Isle Abbots, the cradle of the world, 'You can smell it in the air,' he said, 'orgasm in the very essence of things.'

Driving back, on a lovely mistake of a back road, he said, 'And in these villages, in Laurie Lee's immortal phrase, incest quietly flourished.'

She reckoned she'd had enough.

'Ever have an interchange that doesn't involve sex, Jenner? Implicitly or explicitly?'

A long silence followed. Theo watched the variations of green, green layered against other greens, no words in English to tell one from the other, although the colours were quite distinct. Curious that – what did that tell one about the effectiveness of image analysis, if the English language, evolved over centuries of observing greenness, couldn't differentiate between one green and another, even though the difference was quite clear to the eye? Which implied that things existed in the pictorial imagination that were not correlated to an object in the linguistic model . . .

'In a sense,' he said, after long meditation, 'every inter-change is about sex.'

Jesus!

'It all comes down,' he went on, 'to saying that a flower is just a seed's way of getting another seed. Or alternatively, a seed is just a flower's way of getting another flower, which is rather prettier, though logically identical. If the purpose of life is life itself, and the only currently known method of creating life is sexual, then it follows that the purpose of life is sexual. It then follows that anything that is relevant to life is necessarily sexual, and anything that is not sexual is irrelevant. Therefore every interchange is about sex.'

'No! False deduction – A implies B does not mean that not-B implies not-A.'

'The first mistake was coming down from the trees. The second was letting women into our universities. Have you ever seen a chimpanzees' tea-party?'

'Why do you hate women so much?' she said, stung beyond sensible retaliation.

'On the contrary, I love women so much that anger is the only possible defence against you. In the way one hates Leonardo da Vinci for being perfect or Mozart for writing so ravishingly without effort or attention. I adore you. And therefore I rail.'

At Woolfardisworthy West, the grass grew lush around the graves. The graveyard was full of dark stone slabs. The doves chorused in the trees, and there was no one for miles. Evensong was at six. Jenner traced the engraving on a tombstone with his finger. Thomasina Harding Who Passed away in the Arms of her Saviour 1776 in her Twenty-Second Year, Having Lived an Exemplary Life Deeply Mourned by Jeames Harding.

'I have never visited my mother's grave.'

Tears came out of his eyes and ran down his cheeks. Theo looked away.

'Why not? Was she cruel to you or something?'

'Oh no,' he said, 'my mother, poor creature, was far too enamoured of her own tragedy to be cruel to anyone; she lived in a world of sorrow which made her mad but gentle.'

'Oh. Jeez, I'm sorry.'

Jenner sat down on the side of a grave and looked away into the green murk, seeing some other landscape.

'There was a selfishness about her tragedy. No doubt she had suffered, but as she never spoke of it, and only sighed – how could you sympathise, how hope to heal? A child is not designed to nurture, but to be extravagantly loved; he does not learn how to love until he is shown by example. My poor mother, locked in her wardrobe of horrors, to which she had thrown away the key, could not reach out to show me how it feels to be loved. In my fumbling childish way I wanted to love her and help her, but I did not know how. My response to her silent misery was to shout: this was what my father did. We shouted at her to tell us – why don't you tell us? Why don't you play the piano instead of weeping over it? The words would fall on her like hailstones, and she would weep more heavily, grow more silent.

'My father gave up the struggle; he could only rage for so long without an answering anger. He moved her into Monmouth, and stayed on the farm. She taught the piano, week in, week out, the same beginner pieces, no advanced students. She passed them on, so that I suppose the music of Chopin and Bach might never echo round her house as it echoed in her head.'

Theo lay full length on the final resting place of Catherine Morten, Widow. *Her children rise up to call her blessed.*

'Poor stunted creature,' Jenner said, 'she could not look on her sorrow, and so it ate her up from within. So terribly matched to my father, man of overwhelming simplicity and passion. She was beautiful, you know, in that dark defiant way of Jewish women – that splendour which cries out to a western Gentile: dare to find me beautiful! Tall, and slender, with long black hair – in plaits until the day she died. A child, my poor mother, always a child.

'I don't know where they came from. The family were refugees before the war, fleeing from some earlier terrors, but bound up in all those that came sweeping across Europe. She never admitted to being Jewish at all. She would refer to the Jews as *them*. I commented once upon Grandma Levy, whose photo I liked, longing as children do for a proper family of cousins and grandparents, saying that surely Levy was a Jewish name. Oh no, she told me, silly Grandpa wanted a name that was easy to pronounce – his foreign name was too hard for Englishmen to say. He took the name from the first shopfront he saw on his arrival. Besides, she said, our name is Ransfield now, a good English name. I objected that we were Welsh. No indeed, we are English, that is the safest thing to be.

'Silly Grandpa Levy – he was always silly Grandpa – I think he made the fatal mistake of returning to his homeland to rescue brothers or nephews or nieces – Father thought it was some such story. Grandma Levy pined away from the bitterness of silence, never knowing whether he was a bundle of bones with a watchchain, face down in a muddy ditch outside Bratislava, or struggling back from a Russian labour camp, one foot in front of the next to make his way home. She would never move house, though the East End collapsed around her, in case, in case – how will he find me? she said, when they took her to hospital. He was never heard from, nor the cousins, nor the uncles and aunts and nephews and nieces.'

'I thought you could trace people. I thought there were huge centres for that.'

'Oh yes indeed there are. But you need the will – my poor mother denied it all – as though her cousins were still alive in our house, playing the piano, playing games, plaits flying, hoops and balls flying – they could not be admitted to be dead. And poor Grandma Levy – I don't remember her. She would not leave London, in case, in case, and Mother would not leave Wales.'

'How did she come to be in Wales to start with?'

'Now there's a very curious thing. Why did she fly all the way to Wales? You could never ask her such questions, and as a child I never thought it odd. That was where we lived, for better for worse, for richer for poorer, because my father was a Welshman. But when I started out in life as an adult, and flew as far as I could from Wales – Australia, Papua, Zimbabwe, ironically enough, Poland – I began to see what might have driven her. Far away your woes do not grow smaller; rather they take on an epic quality, are steeped in storytale, and you yourself are elevated by exile. You become romantic.'

Theo, lulled and entranced by the music of his voice, thought she could lie in this graveyard and listen to him talk for ever.

'And now I am old,' he said, 'I understand a little of her tragedy, but now it is too late.'

Jenner stood up and walked about the churchyard. There was no sound except his footsteps over the long-dead. A dragonfly the size of a small bird whirred above Theo's head. She closed her eyes in the sun and tried to think about Tom, but he was too transparent in this dark rich light.

When she opened her eyes, Jenner was standing above her, holding a stem of wild roses. The flowers were not yet open.

'Buds of perfect beauty for a bud of perfect beauty.'

Theo did not care for this; she sat up almost at once.

'Sod off, Jenner, don't patronise me,' she said.

'Ah, but you patronise so well, so little, so pretty, so young, so clever. Your very being represents a temptation to patronise that I cannot resist. It is in the genes, you know. Men are programmed to dominate women, and as they grow older, to dominate younger and younger women. It is a combination of sex and territory.'

Theo frowned, but found she had taken the flowers.

'I think your attitude to sex is contradictory,' she said. 'I mean, you try and have it both ways – you talk as if sex was about as close to heaven as humans can come. But then you throw in cheap excuses like genetics, in which case, to be consistent, you should take a purely physiological angle, and say that the pleasure we experience is a convenient side effect of the genetically programmed need to reproduce.'

He was still standing looking down at her; he must know the effect of this.

'In my heart the scientist is at war with the romantic,' he said. 'Sometimes I think my life's work is to forge a peace treaty between them. At present I believe that the mind adopts a different set of beliefs depending on circumstances, and it is our goal as scientists to understand how each set operates, and the effect of the contradictions on our thinking, but not to do away with inconsistency. It would not be humanly possible. For example, you remember my preliminary work correlating the penile sensitivity of bulls with the frequency and length of their copulation? When we discuss that work, and other issues surrounding the mating behaviour in cattle, you and I, as scientists, think of human beings as behaving in fundamentally the same way – males programmed to mount as many young females as possible, and conceive as many healthy offspring as possible. But you and I would not hold that view if we were conjoined in the worship of Aphrodite, climbing together towards that state of ecstasy where words fail. We would abandon scientific interpretation of our behaviour along with our clothes, and not to do so would be inhuman.'

'Oh Jesus,' said Theo, 'here we go again. I liked you

a lot better when you were talking about your mother.'

'A very good reason to surcease. I do not want you to like me.'

What did Jenner Ransfield mean by the words *I do not want you to like me*? Like most of the man, the living breathing paradox, entirely fit for the freak show that is the modern novel, it was entirely contradictory. He did not pause to analyse what he said, but we may. He meant that if she liked him, he would be deprived of the sexual *frisson* her antagonism provided. That was the surface of his meaning, but there was more. He understood the concept of liking and found it dangerous. He had no experience of being liked, for he was a man who was worshipped or lusted after, but not liked. Liking was too close to understanding, and therefore too close to love. It was the thing most to be desired, and therefore the thing not even to be contemplated. He knew that if Theodora liked him, he would be in hopeless danger of exploiting that liking to hurt her and damage himself. And though he lusted to punish her for being a young and desirable woman, yet he wanted above all things to nurture and protect the perfect, clever being thrust into his care.

It's as well Theo understood none of this.

VIII

ALL DAY JENNER Ransfield sat at his desk. Before him on the bare surface lay a copy of *Nature*, open all day at the same page: 'The Apine Eye: An analysis of patterns in the communication processes of the bee.' He had not read a single word.

In the bottom drawer was a bottle of whisky. He had opened this drawer three times during the day to fill his glass. In the top drawer was the letter. He had opened this drawer only once to shut the piece of paper away.

But by doing this he had not succeeded in effacing its contents.

He had known from the first moment what it must contain. The Bursar had come to his door. This alone was alarming, for none of Jenner's colleagues came to his office. They knew from long rejection that he invited no staff member through the door frame. Nor any student. Except.

The Bursar knocked on the door; he waited, knocked. Jenner was forced to answer. The Bursar handed him the envelope, saying that the Principal didn't want the letter to go through the internal mail. He said it with a little smile that betrayed his connivance and went away. Jenner shut the door on him, tore open the letter.

He held himself together long enough to call Theodora on the internal telephone – though she was working not twenty feet away – and say that he was suddenly unwell. He asked her to take his morning lab and afternoon problem class, mortified that there was no one else to ask. He was mortified too that she said yes straight away without any fuss, and mortified that she offered to drive him home at lunchtime. Mortification that, compounded with the stark reality of his other sins, led to catalepsy.

He could not move from his desk, for every creature in the outside world cried out to accuse him.

From the evidence so far, you might expect Jenner's study to be the academic equivalent of his room in the farmhouse – dark, oppressive, crammed with items of antiquity without particular value or beauty, obsessively anachronistic, wilfully comfortless. Not so. His room at the farmhouse, the farmhouse itself, is a tribute to the life of his forefathers. All their toiled-for worldly goods are kept there, piled together, because he cannot bear to part with any of them, lest he seem to betray their values. Everything is preserved except one item: his mother's piano, which he could not endure to sit silent as it sat silent all his youth.

But Jenner's study at the Agricultural College is a masterpiece of minimalism and beauty. His desk is dark shining brown, completely bare except for the paper he is reading and a slim white Danish vase with its customary handful of fresh flowers. The walls are bare but for one laminated poster, acquired in Australia in the sensuous days of the late seventies. The poster has travelled with him from study to study all over the world. It is life-size, a photograph of a naked girl so young as to be only marginally acceptable to the law, lying on her side with her back to the camera. She looks back at the viewer, resting her blonde head on one hand, and drops the other arm back so that one breast is outlined against the black background. Any suggestion of erotic content is side-stepped by the solemn sweetness of the girl's expression, and the grainy finish which proclaims this photograph as art.

In the early days, when Jenner was dashing and brilliant, this picture on his study wall provoked fascination and debate. He keeps it as a luscious *aide-mémoire* to the time when the world was different, and he was differently regarded within it, a symbol of and participant in the freedom of his youth; and, according to his paradoxical nature, he keeps it as a hair shirt, a prick to his conscience, an unrelenting goad to his memory. *This has destroyed you; this will destroy you.*

His bookshelves are almost bare. Years of packing up and leaving behind have pared the collection down to the beloved classics. Every university, after all, has a library. He has his *Principia Mathematica*, volumes of Bourbaki's *Elements of Mathematics*, Knuth's *Fundamental Algorithms*, *The Natural History of the Sheep*, *The Grammar of Science*, *Postscript to the Logic of Scientific Discovery*, *Biometrika* . . . And in the bookshelves also, his one valuable possession, his Bang & Olufsen sound system, as perfect in design and sound as he could achieve, as simple as he could contrive. Above it a slim collection of compact disks – Richard Strauss, Philip Glass, Michael Tippett, John Taverner. A little Mozart and Bach – instrumental only. No opera, no choral works. These are confined to the farmhouse with his father's memorial.

He sits all day with Strauss's existential lament, *Metamorphosen*, on continual play, the multitude of strings winding in and out of each other again and again, their angst unending, inconsolable to the end of time. His inclination is to turn the volume up to unbearable beauty, but he knows that this will provoke loud hammering on the adjoining walls and general unpleasantness. He is acutely conscious, particularly now, that he must not provoke any non-specific wrath. You may think from his behaviour that Jenner is blind to his effect on others, but this is not so.

Like the music, the thoughts that torment him wind around and around, repeating themselves, variations on the same agony. *I have done this. I cannot blame anyone else. Only God, who made me as I am, too vile to live decently in this world, too weak to change.*

Why have you done this to me, God? Why have you made me so I have done this to myself? After all my struggles – I have succeeded in the test you set me – I have not touched one hair of her head, not one word, not one gesture, against terrible temptations. You might have rewarded me for passing that test – but no, instead you have poured burning oil on my head. This! This which was nothing!

God had set a trap in his way, but he knew himself to be the perpetrator, and knew that he could not blame the girl – he must make the effort to remember their names – Caroline Hayes; must not blame her, in spite of the treachery of it. The decayed familiarity of that look – tears trembling in the eyes, the breast quivering, the hands wrung, the absurd importance of this grade, this assignment, as if life itself will end if she gets an F. To avoid which shame she will – she can't say it, she can barely think it – but she offers it anyway, though she'd deny having done so, with every shred of her conscious mind. But this one, this Caroline Hayes, how can she pretend coercion? Unless she credits him with some hypnotic power. Impossible to force a girl, no matter how impressionable, to fall on her knees and scrabble with the fastening of one's trousers, to take it in her mouth, with every appearance of eagerness, and though one tries, tries in the miasma of wanting it, to explain that this is not what one wants, no not at all, but rather to fall down and worship at the temple of woman, to minister to, not be ministered unto?

But neither he nor God is fooled. No, there was no

coercion in that first encounter. She waited for him, that evening, all alone as darkness fell, waiting and waiting. He knew immediately when he came out of his office and found her there. From the posture of her body and the expression with which she glanced towards the door and came immediately towards him, he knew what she wanted, and he knew where it would end.

He hesitated while locking his office door, let his hand rest on the handle, knowing he would open it and allow her to step in, knowing that he would not switch on the light, knowing that she would stand too close, touch his arm in supplication. He had a moment, caught on the threshold of his room, when he might have chosen otherwise. But after that moment, so short as to have no real duration in any moral scheme, he was lost – *surely, surely, you cannot judge me on that split second?*

No, it is not that split second by which you are condemned.

It was the second encounter that destroyed him, and by which he stands accused, in heaven and on earth. It was the second, combined with the paltriness of her reward, that sent her scuttling to the council. And having failed the first trial, the insignificant, the shruggable offence, having had his warning, he played wilfully deaf to the word of God. Of course she returned. She could hardly fail to, to whine over the restricted pass he had given her – so much better than she deserved and so much less than she had expected.

She was bold now, because she had already crossed the threshold of his room, and his body. She was angry because of her poor grade, but also because he paid her no heed, jealous of the attention he lavished on Theodora. Perhaps she had thought she might have an affair with the great Dr Ransfield. Perhaps she had not thought at all. This was the more likely. Such a girl would not in her conscious mind think of Jenner as sexual territory.

It was the second encounter that brought down vengeance on his head. He could not enter any plea of diminished responsibility. He had known immediately after the first time that what he had done was appallingly dangerous. He knew that the girl was manipulative, and he understood that she was aggrieved. He had read the invitation in her crossing of her legs and then the bafflement and spite in the tossing of her head. He recognised her power – the power that all young women exercised over him; he acknowledged also the intense anger that their power and his powerlessness ignited in his heart.

He knew all these things, understood himself intimately and still he must let her into his room – knowing at each step what would happen. Close the door, block the exit. Remonstrate. Show anger at her for tempting him, anger at her for ingratitude, anger at her for being young and coming into his orbit in jeans and a T-shirt. And the anger takes hold, and forces her against the desk, over the desk, down, begging her to give him what he wants, not the mean currency she offered before. He is cruel, he is rabid, offensive.

But he did nothing, in effect nothing, pushed her against the desk, kissed her on the mouth, tried to undo her jeans. Realised at once her resistance, the terrible stupid danger, and let her go. But his violence, his need is enough –

To hang him.

But all this seems so insignificant beside the temptation to which he has not succumbed. He rants at the Disposer, the great Jehovah, who has set it up in such a way. He cries out in his head, though he sees no reason why anyone should answer him. *How can you be so spiteful? To plant this very one in my household – this young woman of all of them the most difficult to resist. You know how little it takes to ensnare me* . . . All women, all young women he worships. And God had put this one in his way – day in, night out, young, vigorous, sexual, the skin, the teeth, the young body – spring in her step, breasts held high, meeting his eye, challenging, teasing – clever, kind-hearted, innocent. *Could you devise a temptation more cruel?*

That Sunday she invited him to drive with her – Why? *Why did you contrive that? Why did you set that trap for me? What did I do to deserve it? To test me – yes, and I passed your test. And this is how you reward me?*

Mile after mile, watching her drive, watching how she held the steering wheel, imagining – no, rather knowing – exactly what the steel button of her jeans would feel like as his thumb disengaged it from its buttonhole, knowing exactly what the zipper would sound like as he drew it down, knowing exactly the rasp of his skin on her dough-soft belly as he peeled back the cloth, knowing how far his hand would stretch, from her navel almost to the hip bone, and how much further across her stomach, a line drawn in the snow, his thumb would travel as his hand curved over the hip and down the buttock.

All of this in his mind, mile after mile, while she cheerfully refuted his anger, swallowed his antagonism, making a joke of geographical confusion, exclaiming over vistas of velvet green and treelines studded with blossom, and two-a-penny Tudor farmhouses.

And then into overhung churchyards, dark with secret places, the air thick with spring, doves curdling and fluting in the trees, the sunlight steamy with promise, the dark undersides of the trees begging for a man and woman to make love under them.

I never laid a finger on her. I never made so much as a gesture that a father or priest might not have made.

I passed the test and this is how you reward me.

Thou the Lord God art a jealous God.

So round and round and back to the beginning.

*　　*　　*

It was perhaps half past six – the light beginning to slant and slacken – when Theo appeared in the car park. From his office window he could see his car, parked so that he could keep an eye on his dogs during the day. He must have been staring at them, or perhaps at the lovely brick wall beyond – all that remained of the fine walled garden that once adjoined the house. He must have been thinking about his dogs or his need to return home, for he saw her immediately she stepped into his sightline. He was shocked. For there she was, quite real, quite ordinary, when she had been all day a character in the *psychomachia* of Jenner Ransfield.

She walked up to his car, coat unzipped but wrapped round her by the pockets, as the young do, ready to go home. The dogs recognised her and roused themselves. The back door of the car was left open for their passage; they climbed out, as far as their leashes permitted, and barked at her. They were hungry, poor creatures. They, like their master, must suffer today. It was a day of fasting and sackcloth.

Theo didn't go close to the dogs; she didn't care for them; he understood it as the natural antipathy female creatures have for each other. She picked up their water bowl, took it away and returned it full of water from the tap way over by the wall. The dogs drank with enthusiasm. She went away again, this time for much longer, and returned with a blue plastic bag. He recognised this as containing by-product of the small slaughterhouse where experimental animals were dismembered after they were finally laid to rest. His mind ranged over the chances of his dogs developing a new strain of some hideous disease from consuming this meat. He toyed with the idea and discovered that their fate weighed nothing in the greater arbitration.

Theo fed the dogs the proscribed meat, and vanished once more from view. Ten minutes later came a healthy knocking at his door, and her voice muffled beyond it.

He did not move. More knocking.

At last a sheet of paper slid under the door, firm capitals on squared paper.

I HAVE FED THE DOGS. I AM GOING.

He made no response.

Another sheet. R U OK?

He squatted on the floor to read it, knew she was inches away, warm and sweet, vestal of the inner sanctum, guardian of the sacred hearth.

IT MUST BE TRUE THEN.

O avenging fury, I hate thee.

He opened the door. She was already packing her pad into her bag to go away. He let her into the room.

'Jeez, you're drunk!' she said. 'Don't you dare touch me, you old sod!'

'I wasn't – I wouldn't.'

She shut the door, put out her hand.

'Keys.'

He shook his head.

'I'm taking you home, Jenner. Whatever has happened, you need to go home. The fucking dogs need to go home, and I'm not taking them in my hire car. I'll leave it here.'

He took the keys from his trouser pocket and handed them to her.

She went over to his desk, put the whisky glass in any old drawer, switched off the music, checked the windows were locked, picked up his bag, and took his coat off its hook. She caught sight of his picture.

'Doesn't help your case having an underage bimbo on your wall.'

He said nothing.

'Come on,' she said.

He stood in the middle of the room, unable to move.

'I love this. You've run out of words. I never thought I'd see the day.'

'I have not run out of words. The words are spewing out of me so thick that they form a log jam in my mouth.'

He felt sick with the frustration of it, and the anger which he felt towards her for managing him, and the anger he felt towards her born of gratitude. She thrust his coat and bag into his hands. He found that he took them from her and followed her out of the room.

He could not believe that he suffered himself to be driven in his own car by a woman. But his hands were shaking, and objects in the middle distance would not stay stable. He must be silent, for in this state he could confess anything, and what was said could never be unsaid. Nor must any part of his person stray in contact with any part of hers, nay not so much as his coat must brush her foot, lest he be undone.

'You'd better tell me, Jenner,' she said, driving far too slowly out of the college gates. 'Spit it out. The story's gone right round anyway. That airhead Caroline Hayes has shafted you to the council. Tell me the truth. Did you fuck her?'

'Don't –' He found he had raised his hand in the air like a prophet.

'Sorry,' she said, grinning like a fairground doll. 'I mean, did you have intercourse with her?'

'No. I did not. I would have done so, exultantly, even though she is a cheap creature, I would have done so, had she offered. I am a man without self-control. I was made without that portion of the mind which exercises restraint.'

'So why's she mad at you?'

'Because she believed that I would look on her indulgently. In the matter of her Biometrics unit.'

'Because?'

'Because some sexual converse had passed between us. I cannot bring myself to talk of these things, Theodora. I am drunk, I am distraught. I am driven in my own car by a woman, a young woman. I am not myself.'

'Well, screw it, mate, I took your classes today, and very embarrassing it was too. They all laughed when I said you were sick. Real nasty laughter. I think I was the last person on campus to hear the goss.'

She changed gear with exaggerated care.

'Please don't tell my wife. I cannot bear her tears.'

'Why would Elspeth be upset? Has this happened before? No one mentioned an earlier case – they usually can't wait to fill you in on past history. Especially the secretaries. Very sympathetically of course.'

'My wife is obsessed with the idea that I might lose my position. More than anything she clings to the idea of the family home, the children clustered round. She is terribly afraid that I might find it more congenial to work in a different establishment. Which is why I am condemned to stay in this third-rate jumped-up school for hedgehog-lovers.'

'I can understand how she feels. I'm very attached to home.'

A vision of Theodora's likely home rose before him. He saw Melbourne, its gracious streets and wide green lawns, sun streaming through broad windows into living rooms where life was lived with vigour. He saw a big clean white kitchen, whiteware gleaming, stainless steel pans on hooks, copper bottoms serried outwards. He saw the fridge fall open to spill out cans of beer, straight to the sweating palm, contact cold. He saw girls all limb, on the lawn shaking long hair in laughter at the sporting antics of boy-men with bodies but no conversation and no technique, and turning back to talk to him. He saw weathered faces, white smiles, heard ribaldry and laughter, endless Pommy jokes, Welsh jokes, vet jokes, professor jokes, taken and given in good part. He saw brown skin sleek as egg yolk, crumbed with wet sand, flaunted, innocently flaunted, up and down the beach, and the waves crashing on to him, and drowning his concupiscence, washing him clean from sin.

'Hate this car,' she said. 'Can't you afford anything better?'

'In England it is not considered polite to talk about money.'

'Yeah well, in Australia it is not considered polite to touch up students.'

'I know.'

He had never forgotten Australia, where they told you exactly what they thought of you. And after the first horrific shock, like the first slap of a wave on an off-season swim, you grew to love it. Why had he not contrived to stay there, where girls like Theodora sizzled out of every lecture hall, taking the piss, as they called it, but enjoying you for your exotic brilliance, your wonderful old-world glamour, your Lawrentian sexuality?

God in heaven, send me to Australia when I die.

'What are you going to tell Elspeth?'

'Why should I tell her anything?'

'Well, she'll think it odd, won't she, if you're pissed as a newt and I've driven you home?'

'She may think what she pleases. I do not distress Elspeth by sordid truths.'

'Precisely what is the sordid truth, Jenner?'

'In this case, that I have drunk too much whisky because I am deeply upset by developments at this so-called college.'

'And that's all Elspeth needs to know?'

'There is nothing to know.'

'So there's nothing in these accusations.'

He found that it was beyond him to put the matter into words that would not compromise his veracity, nor destroy him in her eyes. He could no more lie than he could fudge a result, but nor could he endure for her to spit on him with that modern woman's look in her eye, the look that said: *You pus-infected toad, you fetid black scum, you particle of scurf.*

If only it were possible to make her understand.

The next day, Wednesday, he awoke in his truckle bed, wondering what had possessed him to drink the bottle dry. He knew this to be the case because he could see the bottle lying empty on its side, accusingly, for all the world as if it were a plain girl who had failed to consider contraception.

But he knew he had before him something far more serious than a matter of generative carelessness.

The ghastliness of the council meeting reared up before him. The sordidness of it all; the necessity to describe in detail, standing on the synthetic carpet, before a group of middle-aged men, who dare not dream beyond the fortnightly conjugal ritual, conducted under cover and in the dark, to describe in detail the delicate transactions that make up sexual advance, and the crashing indelicacies that make up sexual acts.

If only there were something worth owning up to – three days of abandonment, naked in the hills, never sleeping, worshipping at the shrine of Aphrodite! If only he had not improved her grade – the one inalienable fact. The men who will judge him like to deal in facts. Did you touch her on the breast? *No.* Did you ask her for intercourse? *No.* Did you promise that you would improve her grade if she had sexual intercourse with you? *No.*

But these Noes mean nothing; you are asking the wrong questions.

There are questions which he knows to ask, but which he prays do not enter their mediocre heads.

Is it not true, Dr Ransfield, that the raw grade of her test paper was an E, but that you awarded her a C minus? *I am forced to award marks for nebulous matters such as presentation skills and teamwork, to which I am fundamentally opposed; I can award marks in these areas as I see fit.* Is any other person involved in assessing term work and laboratory results? *No, but you have on file my repeated suggestions that there should be, to minimise the personal, subjective element which is bound to infiltrate these areas.* Is it not your custom to deal with student problems in the laboratory, in common view? *It is well documented that I have often suggested this Socratic practice, to encourage understanding and reduce misunderstandings.* Why did you change your practice for Caroline Hayes? *Because Caroline Hayes insisted on privacy, for what end I could not understand. But a student in apparent distress imposes certain behaviour, even on someone as rigorous as myself.* Why would Caroline Hayes bring this charge against you if it were not true? *Because Caroline Hayes cannot endure the idea that I am not her slave, that I am prepared to withstand her venial compromise. Because Caroline Hayes is resentful, to the core of her being, of the existence of others prettier, cleverer and more self-possessed . . .*

A knock. Theodora came into his room, wearing her coat, ready to depart, hair and shoulders streaked with rain. She looked about her, looked at him in bed, his striped pyjamas open at the chest, sniffed.

'You should open a window. You'd sleep better.'

He groaned at the impertinence as much as the irrelevance. She pulled back the curtains and muttered foully about the rain.

'I guess you're not coming into college today, so I'm catching the bus. D'you want me to take your classes?'

Oh the sweetness of her, oh the cruel indignity inflicted by her not waiting to be asked.

'I am chairing the postgraduate seminar at ten. In the afternoon I have a laboratory session with the Master's students on statistical programming and from half past two onwards the first-year zoology students are booked in for ten-minute chats about their execrable genetics assignments.'

'I can manage that. I warn you though, I won't be horrible to them.'

'Tomorrow I shall be as normal.'

'I should damn well hope so. When is this wretched council meeting?'

'In ten days or so – the Monday morning. Then my fate is sealed. They will dismiss me, you know.'

'Nonsense. Don't give in to them, Jenner. They're a pack of mean-minded second-raters, most of those guys. You can buy and sell the lot of them. OK, you led that bimbo Caroline Hayes on, but you haven't done anything unethical that I can see, not anything that merits dismissal. I mean, they might give you a ticking off for inappropriate behaviour.'

'Tell me, Theodora, have I ever behaved inappropriately towards you?'

She looked down at him, pinned and pathetic in his bed, the shabby middle-aged pyjamas, the shabby middle-aged body. He realised suddenly from the way she looked at him that his body had lost any power it might once have had to affect the outcome of a transaction. He had understood this theoretically, knowing that the body decayed year by year, fibre by fibre, until it was impossible to pretend that it was as it had been when young. He had not quite been prepared to believe that he had lost his physical effect, for all his other functions – his powers of recall, retention, synthesis, analysis, his fluency, his accuracy – were undiminished. As for his sexual energies he had few opportunities to test those for deterioration, but he had no objective evidence of their decline. Still, the mirror and his common sense had told him that his body had spread and puckered in a manner that was unattractive. But knowing it in one's mind was nothing compared to seeing it in a young woman's eye.

'Well,' she said, her accent as raw and chromatic as a pre-school concert, 'well, you *say* a lot of inappropriate things, but to be honest, you've never done anything that my dad wouldn't do, and he's a decent bloke. And there's no way you would ever give any girl an A for a lay, no matter how good a lay she was. You're far too hard on students to do that.'

'I am relieved to hear that, even expressed so grossly.'

He pulled his pyjama jacket closed over his chest. He looked away from her, through the window at the greyness beyond. He was ashamed of what he was about to ask.

'Is it possible – would you be prepared – would you repeat that before the council?'

'Well, not in so many words, but yeah, why not?'

'Then I have a glimmer of hope.'

'Oh for Christ's sake, Jenner, stop over-dramatising your situation. If you're innocent, you have nothing to worry about. Good-looking guys in positions of power get complaints made against them all the time by overwrought twats. I read a couple of very good papers on it not long ago. Every case has to be investigated, even the unlikely-looking ones, because about two-thirds of them are genuine, but there's no pattern to it. It's like child abuse – well, it's a form of child abuse.'

'Will you say all that also to the council?' said Jenner in a voice that sounded hollow to his own ears.

'I guess so.'

After she had gone, banging the door behind her unnecessarily hard, Jenner was left with a bitterness in his mouth. How he had come to this? How had the mighty fallen! And yet, when he looked back, step by step, it was obvious how it had happened to him, and he could blame no one except himself and God. Some people, he supposed, might blame Fate or Fortune, but he preferred a more interested, active partner in his tragedy. He was in no sense a religious man, having no truck with gospels of love or inner harmony. He required his God to be a Jewish God – jealous and demanding. A hard, relentless divinity who pushed His creatures to the limits that He Himself inhabited. Jenner did not see how love was consistent with burning justice.

How petty life had become. You steal a kiss and a girl cries rape. You are dependent on the kindness of a child to save your career. You fritter away a brilliant mind teaching girls destined for suburban marriages how to count fish in a tank.

He could not even get out of bed to put on a record. Indeed he found he had lost patience with the limitations of the 78 record, and berated himself for his stupidity and obstinacy in clinging to the wreckage of history. It was music he needed now, not nostalgia. His father's memory was of no use to him, except as a black pool of failure set in his way. Music would lift him above the trivial, the girls with painted mouths, the rabbits and the hamsters, but music required him to get out of bed.

Elspeth came to his aid. He knew it was her knock, by its timidity. She waited for him to answer. Sensibly she had not brought him anything. She sat down on the end of his bed, and smiled sadly at him, in her way. His heart was torn with irritation and sadness.

He couldn't bring himself to contemplate the accusation that would appear in her eyes when he lost his job. *Again, oh Jenner, not again*. Her misery would never be voiced, and so would allow him to pretend ignorance. He would do almost anything not to see that look in her eyes again.

'Theodora says that you are staying in bed. What can I get for you?'

He groaned, knowing that the groan was offensive, unable to control it before it oozed out of him.

'Did Theodora explain that I am not sick, but suffering from an excess of alcohol?'

Elspeth only trusted herself to nod. By now she knew well enough the sorts of things that incurred his wrath.

'I need a jug of water and a radio. At ten-thirty I want dry toast and a pot of weak China tea. I shall get up in time for lunch, and then go for a walk.'

'Fergal has some parsnips we were going to bake for lunch, but I don't suppose you will fancy them?'

'No, emphatically not. The thought of any food turns my stomach; the thought of Fergal's parsnips repels my mind also.'

'We'll have them tomorrow,' said Elspeth and went away.

IX

THREE DAYS LATER, the Saturday sennight as promised, the farm was visited by none other than Rupert of the Rhine on a bay mare to spy out the land.

He had explained in copious e-mail messages to Robin that he would park the horse conveyance at the battleground and ride around the field of battle and then down to his headquarters at the farmhouse, to install, he said, the layout of the terrain in his system. Hence his dramatic arrival through the trees, teal silks and blond locks flowing, the ostrich feathers in his broad brown hat bowing graciously in the breeze of his approach.

Robin was looking out for him. This was not any sort of clairvoyance, though afterwards Robin would have liked to think it was. It was simply that Rupert had called from the Sedgemoor battleground on his mobile to say he was on his way, and his ETA was fourteen-thirty. So Robin was more than looking out, he was suspended from the window. He was practically goggling with excitement, for the steady approach of the rider confirmed what the telephone call had already suggested. Rupert of the Rhine was a woman.

Fergal heard the sharp intake of breath, peered over his shoulder and started to laugh. But Robin was in distress. Before him, a vision of cinematic cross-dressing, a female Cavalier, every curved surface gleaming.

'What am I to do? What am I to do?' cried Robin. 'I was going to put him up in my room.'

'Just carry on. I'll tell y' dad that she's a lesbian. Probably is.'

'Oh I do hope not!' Robin cried swooningly. 'Oh please, Lord, let her not be!'

'Nothing He can do about it now, me old mate.'

'O how wonderful!' Robin continued, unable to take his eyes off the vision of Cavalier silks. 'But she can't sleep in here with me, it would be wrong!'

'Yes, she can. Me and Theodora do. Good for you.'

'I just couldn't! I couldn't lie there all night thinking of her lying right here, hearing her sleeping, I mean. I couldn't bear it. Look at her!'

She did look good, Fergal agreed. Hard to tell on horseback, but she must be fairly tall, and the hair was definitely long and genuinely blonde. Face was hidden under the big hat, might be a bit horsy. But real breasts under the jacket, with a very unsoldierly bounce. Needs a sports bra for battle.

'O dear Lord, what am I to do?'

'Pray?' said Fergal.

Robin, unable to take his eyes off Rupert's advent, clutched behind him for a bible, of which several lay to hand. He opened it at random and stabbed his finger down at a passage, without taking his eyes off his guest. He skewed round, keeping his head outside, and thrust the book at Fergal.

'Read the passage, will you, Fergal?'

Fergal read: '*For if there come unto your assembly a man with a gold ring, in goodly apparel, and there come in also a poor man in vile raiment; And ye have respect to him that weareth the gay clothing, and say unto him, Sit thou here in a good place; and say to the poor, Stand thou there, or sit here under my footstool.* Yeah, very relevant.'

'Well, it must mean something. Think, think. We'd better go down. Please come with me, I don't know what to say.'

Rupert had ridden into the yard and was looking around for signs of life other than the furiously scattering hens.

'For fuck's sake, don't blow my cover. I'm Fergal, right? Moonbeam has been and gone, and left us in charge.'

'I don't like deceptions, Fergal.'

'Listen, mate, think of it like the French Resistance – allo allo and good moaning and all that.'

'I suppose if you think of it like that . . .'

Fergal was already down the stairs and into the yard, leaving Robin to ponder the shiftiness of morality.

He couldn't afford to laugh at Rupert, his ally, however unlikely, in the war against Mammon, but when the voice came out, his grin had a struggle – that accent, only heard on low-budget TV dramas when some jobbing actor is supposed to be Lord Muck, though no one except an American would be fooled. He managed to control the grin into a big cheesy welcome smile.

'Hail, friend!' she cried. 'Goodfellow, I presume?'

On closer appraisal, she was older than the figure suggested, into the dangerous part of her thirties when the insecurities start to cry out, while the mirror gives ambivalent messages. Fergal saw the brave glimmer in her eye, the wriggle of deliberate youthfulness, the defiant cheerfulness. She had a poor complexion, rather pocked if anything, a beaky nose, and a complicated bow mouth, with something pouting about it, which he didn't care for. But she had lovely breasts, clearly her own, a flat stomach and wonderful gripping thighs. Fergal saw all this, and read a potted life and sexual history in thirty seconds, between the 'Hail' and the 'Hi!' with which he answered it.

He stood well clear of the horse. Horses were alien creatures even in concept. The only horses he had ever

201

seen up close were police horses, designed to intimidate him. He noted that Rupert, however hilarious, still was astride that thing, had paid its vet's bills, groomed it, stabled it, managed it, and had got it here from whatever bit of the Westron Land she ruled over. The horse, in spite of everything, gave Rupert instant cred, as legitimate possession of a credit card confers status. You have to have done *something* to get it. Fergal had neither horse nor credit card, and knew precious few people who had.

'Nar, I'm not Goodfellow. I'm Fergal. Goodfellow is Robin and he's upstairs. Praying, I think.'

'Heavens forfend! Is one so alarming?'

'He's got a lot to contend with, that boy. Let's go for a drink.'

'I rather wanted to have a council of war.'

'That's what I mean. Down the pub, meet some of the others. Take the phone. Got some maps, have you?'

Rupert patted her big leather saddlebags.

'Every map and chart and battle plan conceivable. It's not a battle I knew, Sedgemoor, but by God, I know it now! I could win it, you know.'

'Are you s'posed to?'

'No, alas. I'm the tragic James, Duke of Monmouth, only son and rightful heir to the throne of England, handsome, brilliant and doomed.'

'Better than Rupert, then?'

'No. Rupert was better in the field. James made too many mistakes. Hop up.' She patted the animal's rump.

'Oh no! Not me. That's too high.'

He moved away from the horse but in full view so not to startle it, and threw a stone at Robin's window.

'Get down here, Goodfellow. General needs a drink. You want to change,' he said to Rupert, 'or is them clothes all right for the pub?'

Silly question, should've known, they live in these

costumes. Rupert of the Rhine in *jeans*. Like a priest in a flowery frock. He had recently discovered, through many visits to websites and numerous e-mail exchanges, how many people all over the world spent every waking moment being someone else. From seven till seven each weekday they were grey Louisa McArdle or grey John Clarke, flat people squeezed between the train and the desk; but the rest of the time, in the evenings, in their beds, in their gardens, on their weekends, holidays, in their dreams, they were the Empress Matilda and Caius Publius Cincinnatus, centurion. These were not deranged people, they were not even what Fergal called sad people. They used sewing machines to run up their costumes, designed beautiful web pages to publicise their events, drove to them in cars, brought their supplies in plastic bags, and erected tents with aluminium poles; they made compromises with reality. All the time, the alternative reality, the court of Empress Matilda, the XXth Legion, was in session, each participant knowing it wasn't real, and completely comfortable that it was.

Fergal's style of life – how is that different? Perched up in trees, staging a protest, knowing it will fail, holing up in a tunnel knowing you will be ferreted out, rallying the locals round their bit of common, knowing the surveyors are already at it. Protest gets a bit of headline, a bit of footage, developers roll in the security guards, buy off the media bosses with a quiet word at the club, and it's gone. Then on to the next one, and the next – how can you keep on pretending that it's worth it, eh mate? Well, what choice have we got – her up there on the horse an' me? What else am I going to do about the filth and the broken lift, and kids trapped in front of the telly and the world choking us to death? What else is she going to do, stuck with her nice flat and her car and her steady job and her store cards, and a life going nowhere? We look at the world and we make what we can.

Two more stones at Robin's window before he emerged from the house, struggling into his brand-new leather jacket, hair all over his face. He took Rupert's hand, without looking at her directly, and seemed for a moment about to kiss it. Fergal made him get up behind Rupert. Robin tried not to hold on to Rupert's waist, but as she started off he had no alternative.

'But the *pub*, Fergal,' he said. 'Do I have to?'

'Get on with it, mate. Hold on tight. I'll follow yer.'

Robin hadn't been in the pub before. Fergal knew he'd never had sex either, and even thought wanking was a sin, poor bugger. Trouble with innocence, Fergal thought, people who've got it don't know how precious it is; when they find out, it's too late. You can't go back under the shower and walk out again without your experience.

Fergal couldn't remember innocence. There must have been a time before sex, those twelve tumbled years of running and fighting and moving flats – but even then it was everywhere, the big boys, the sisters, the talk. The videos, the mags with their weird ugly pictures which you couldn't help looking at. Like cigarette smoke, in everything, had me first smoke, when? The taste had always been there. Poor old Mum smoked and smoked, and nagged us all narrer when she caught us.

Can't wash it away, any of that. Theo's clean country and clean hair and perfect skin – it doesn't rub the grime out of the pub wall or wash away the shit ingrained in the stairwell. You can walk away from all that, find trees and the sea, but you can't clean it out of the system. Poor little Robin. He'll never get the smell out of his hair, not so long as he lives.

'Directions please,' said Rupert. 'Nice firm grip, please,

Goodfellow, there's a good fellow. I don't want you toppling off into the drink.'

Fergal thought it politic to smile. ''S called the Bleeding Heart. Down the path, first right, hundred yards, first left. There'll be some of the others down there. You'll recognise them by the crazy gleam in their eye. I'll bring the rest of the papers an' that. Don't worry, Robin, I'll speak to y'dad.'

Off they went, Robin clinging on behind, torn between the peril of clasping the womanly form in front of him and the indignity of falling off. Fergal went in search of Theo. He found Elspeth on her knees among the laying boxes, reaching in among the progressively nastier layers of straw. As she found an egg she drew it slowly and lovingly out, as if it were a newborn creature, and without looking round laid it in the basket behind her. Inside Fergal's head images of a woman on her knees elbowed each other for air time – wrapped in prayer before the black Virgin, scrubbing the floor of the school toilet block, sloshing up the shit and blood and semen; other images, swiftly suppressed.

'Wotcha,' he said. 'Rupert of the Rhine turned up on a bloody great horse. We're just going down the pub. Seen Theo?'

Elspeth straightened up, looking unhappy. Fergal had a moment's fear that Theo had gone off with that man again, though her car was still in the stable.

'She's upstairs with May Margaret I believe, in the attic.' She sniffed. 'Are you all going to the Bleeding Heart? Is Robin also gone?'

'Yeah, come with us.'

'Oh no no no, I have too much to do, and besides what would Jenner have to say to me if I went off gallivanting on a Saturday afternoon? You can imagine.'

'Yeah, can.'

'I'll give you a little something. I don't want Robin to be embarrassed before company.'

Fergal never turned down offers of money. He carried the egg basket as carefully as if it were the Archduchess's hot chocolate.

'Now don't look,' said Elspeth, in the sort of voice that suggested you were supposed to look, and she opened several cupboards in an attempt to put him off the scent, before extracting ten pounds from a cache in the cake tin in the top of the linen cupboard. Fergal had been stealing from poorly hidden stashes of money since he could move a chair from a to b. He had no intention of touching Elspeth's, but he now knew where it was, and roughly how much was in it. Heaps.

'What you saving for? New truck? One that starts?'

'I don't know. I worry about the future – if Jenner were to have an accident or lose his job. I don't think we have any savings or a pension.'

'You come on the protests with me, you won't need a pension.'

You'd swear she blushed. Must've been dreaming about it.

Fergal pocketed the ten pounds and went up, past the carved woman chewing balls, and into the studio. It was empty, but the attic trapdoor was hanging down. He could hear the girls' voices from above.

He didn't call Theo immediately. He roamed about the studio a bit, to see what he could see. Old habits die hard. There was so much to look at in the wooden picture books. It was like play school, the first time he went, so many things to look at he felt sick. Marg's latest commission was a wooden Virgin Mary, though there wasn't much to see yet. He had a look at the working drawings to see how she would come out. They were lovely drawings in themselves, full of careful detail of hands, eyelids, things you didn't think about unless you were a real watcher. Fergal recognised the earlobes in the drawing as Theo's, and surprised himself by badly wanting to nick the drawing.

He went half up the ladder and called out. He didn't go any higher because he knew the attic was absolutely forbidden. He thought Marg a bit daft and sad, but at the same time he understood why a girl brought up in this household might decide to hate men. Fergal wasn't specially keen on them himself.

Theo's head appeared upside down through the trap. Fergal's heart did something out of line.

'I'm taking photos,' she said, 'to send to my mate Juliet. I had this stroke of genius and borrowed the college's digital camera, so I can send the pictures over the Net.' She lowered her voice. 'Plus then she can use them as desktop wallpaper and screensavers and all sorts. Only don't tell Marg, cos computers are a man-thing, apparently.'

Fergal told her that Rupert had arrived, and that Rupert was a woman. He described Robin, on the back of the horse, clinging on for dear life, teal plumes in his face. Theo started to laugh, told Marg, and the women's laughter rolled around the floor of the attic.

He wanted to dance a little jig, like his grandad did when something particularly absurd came on the telly. He'd get up from his old chair by the gas fire, cast his newspaper on to the floor, scream with laughter and dance. He'd say if you don't laugh at the bosses and them politicians, you're dead and they've won. They hate it when you laugh at them. Margaret Thatcher had him in stitches.

Fergal recognised suddenly in himself his grandad's dark happiness, the same thing his mum had, all her jokes about hardship and violence, she could make a joke about anything.

'This I've got to see!' Theo said, still laughing.

'Fancy a drink? Look what I scored!' He waved the ten-pound note at her.

'Definitely. Just a few more pix though. I've got to make the most of it. I've only got this camera by cajoling and simpering. Just hold your horses, mate, and I'll be down.'

She blew him a kiss. Fergal did his little dance after all. He had the key to happiness, he did, and it was a joke, and a cigarette you hadn't paid for.

In the Bleeding Heart, Rupert held Robin enraptured, enlarging on her battle plans, on her forces, both cavalry and foot, on the treacherous behaviour of certain parties within Sealed Knot, Sir Thomas Muschamp's Regiment of Foote, and the West Country Historical Re-enactment Society, while Fergal's earth-coloured allies, temporarily out of their burrows, were watching Manchester United thrash Liverpool on the telly. A huddle of middle-class well-wishers were pretending not to watch the football while they sipped their local-brewed cider and discussed vital matters of transport, education and health.

Fergal, nothing if not a pragmatist, waited for the game to finish before he called the meeting to order. He explained to the group that the Battle of Sedgemoor was important as a symbol of freedom, because it was the last battle fought on English soil, and so represented the freedom from a certain sort of oppression – the threat of civil war that once haunted everyone, but now was entirely a matter of history. In the same way, he said, the terrifying way that faceless big business ate up people's homes and green spaces and the habitats of rare creatures and places of ancient importance was going to be a thing of the past. In the future, mindless destruction of nature would be as unthinkable as armed insurrection.

Of course he had practised this speech beforehand like anything, being a man of relatively few and simple words.

The genuine Battle of Sedgemoor took place mostly at night, which, as Rupert pointed out, posed a problem for the re-enactors. The Westron Men would be there overnight, of course, encamped in the fields of various friendly farmers, but few members of the public could be expected to show up. And since the underlying purpose of the event was publicity rather than historical verisimilitude, it seemed the battle would have to be staged in daylight.

Inconveniently, very little of note happened during the engagement, except for Monmouth's creeping up with wonderful daring on the King's camp during the night. After that came nothing but the sorry halting of the rebel troops when they encountered a fairly shallow dike, and their subsequent rounding up, slaughter and imprisonment. Another problem for Rupert's men was posed by the ungallant behaviour of the Duke of Monmouth in fleeing the field at the first sign of trouble. The Westron Men, being West Country patriots, did not entirely favour the official version of events, and were all set to instate an alternative reading of history. Rupert rather inclined to think that Monmouth led a magnificent cavalry attack which had somehow been omitted from the history books.

Fergal and Robin had already had intimation of these problems through the exchange of e-mails which had been going on daily since the approach was first made. And Fergal had suggested a compromise whereby Rupert became Lord John Churchill, who, although on the wrong side, was a cavalryman, a leader of dragoons, which had the right sort of panache to it. Churchill was successful in the encounter and his dashing title made up for anything. This left the way clear for Rupert's arch-rival, Sir Thomas Fairfax, daytime job economics teacher, to be the coward Monmouth.

By great good fortune one of the well-wishers worked

for South West Television and had sold the idea of following the re-enactment to a team of documentary makers, loosely attached to the company. She had vaguely let it be known that she might have some say in the documentary's purchase. The documentary team were represented by a pencil-thin man dressed entirely in black, with a diamond stud in his left ear. In measured tones he explained that he personally was ecstatic about artistic shots of Westonzoyland church tower, mist rising off the peat bog, horses sweating and armour clinking, but the dumbing down of television in general meant that he couldn't commit unless they guaranteed him Moonbeam naked in his tree top. No arse, no show, he said.

Fergal said that he'd get him that guarantee, or the deal was off.

Theo and Fergal walked back to the farm unsteadily, several pints to the wind, cracking jokes and laughing at everything. Fergal was worried, though.

'Shall I give them Moonbeam? I mean, once they got me on camera, they'll know me face. That'll be the end of cover-up stories about the Prince of Wales, Clapham and sexual chemistry and love at first sight an' that.'

'How do you know all of that was a story?' she said, but didn't give him time to answer. 'I think you've got to do it. One day soon you'll get caught on camera by accident, with the same effect. You might as well give your anonymity away in a controlled manner and for a sensible cause.'

'Yeah.'

He needed to keep her talking. When she talked he found it addictive, hearing those ripe diphthongs, that accent associated with crude comics and bold adventurers, shaping serious words, the words and the accent lending each other colour because they seemed not to belong together.

'The *Evening Standard* just offered me a thousand pound

to show me arse in designer underwear. Don't think I should, yeah?'

'Shit, I'd model feed sacks for the *Evening Standard* for a thousand pounds,' said Theo.

'Yeah, but they wouldn't ask you, would they?'

'Love you too. They might. Clever girls with blonde curls might get trendy like tree-top nudies.'

Just keep on talking so I can enjoy the sweet and sour of it.

Rupert and Robin rode all the way back to fetch the horsebox and station wagon.

'He's a lost cause,' said Fergal as they disappeared into the trees, Robin's long black locks on a background of teal silk. 'Hardly out of nappies and a woman's nabbed him.'

'Lucky lad.'

'Y' reckon,' said Fergal, feeling the jig go out of him.

Elspeth was terrifically excited. She had laid the table for seven and peeled a huge mountain of potatoes. She had never entertained seven people in her own house before. Theo made Jenner come out of his room and drive down to the off-licence to choose the wine.

Rupert stabled her horse in one of the outhouses, put her bags in Elspeth's room, and changed into jeans and a red sweatshirt emblazoned *The King's Westron Men*. Jenner was unaccountably civil to her, pouring her a drink and enquiring about where she normally kept her horse. She sat at the kitchen table explaining to Robin how he could make two thousand pounds a week as a Web designer in London, and giving him minutely detailed advice on agents, accountants, VAT and tax regimes. It turned out that she was called Christine. She told them she was a systems analyst in Bristol, but she said the rates were almost twice as high in London; she gave chapter and many verses.

Elspeth, clutching her pre-dinner sherry, listened with glazed awe. Then she remembered herself and served up boiled potatoes, cold roast chicken, boats of gravy, lettuce, radishes and carrots. Rupert told Theo all about digital cameras and how to use one effectively and how to download pictures and the new developments in digital camera technology, and Robin listened attentively.

Jenner was almost silent during the meal, pale and polite. He drank a great deal of wine. Fergal did not understand what was going on. He accepted that he had no right to Theo's secrets, but, all the same, not understanding what went on between her and Jenner upset him like blood on the bedsheets.

Rupert treated them all to anecdotes about campaigns she had fought. Elspeth served up bottled pears and real custard. Rupert described to Robin exactly how to use a Global Positioning System. Then the two of them went out for a walk. Jenner did not go into his room. He stayed on, silent, ignored, as May Margaret and Theo joked and argued about the use of body parts in modern art, and whether this was different from Caravaggio breaking into the morgue to study anatomy.

May Margaret scraped back her chair and said she had work to do in the attic. Elspeth and Fergal cleared the table and started on washing the dishes, talking about the truthfulness of television documentaries, and whether Fergal should blow his cover in the interests of wider publicity for the protest.

Theo and Jenner sat at the table finishing the wine and debating genetics and behaviourism in the low sort of tone that warns you not to join in.

Elspeth said goodnight and went upstairs to a stretcher bed in the corner of May Margaret's studio. Theo and Jenner remained by the wine bottles talking in the same intense way. Fergal reckoned they'd have kept at it all night, but he couldn't bear to leave her there.

X

AFTERWARDS, WHEN THEO thought about that week, she saw that she had been stupid, if not downright reckless, to put anything in Jenner's way that was likely to inflame his passions. But how, she argued, could she even have guessed the tension pulling him apart?

She had allowed herself to forget how unpredictable and unbridled he was. The sight of him defeated, all rumpled and half naked in his bed, had misled her. This was not the man she had demonised. He was not terrible at all, but rather like a stuffed lion seen at close quarters in a zoological museum, glass eyes and fixed growl and tufty bits of fur. The black hair on his chest, resolutely marching to grey, the middle-aged folds of his stomach, the straining around the tendons of the neck, while physically unsettling, told her that Jenner Ransfield was merely a man.

He had been quiet for days, painfully anxious not to offend her. She saw afterwards that she had fooled herself into believing that this was a permanent alteration. How could she have been so stupid?

Of course he should have been kept away from the pictures of May Margaret's carvings. How could she have imagined that he wouldn't somehow, as she was moving them from camera to computer to Internet, get to see them? It was almost as if she had wanted him to see them, as if in the undercurrent of her person there was a quite different Theo, out to make all kinds of trouble.

It was quite late in the day, Jenner's first day in public since the news broke, a day of awful silences and lowered voices. He had been busy all day catching up on days of administrivia, dealing with students from previous days who thought Theo too lowly for them. He had no time for dark silences and glowering walks around the lake. He looked thin and sick, which Theo thought entirely appropriate. She talked at her normal volume all day and put up a brave pretence that things were as they had been. But the pale face and bitten lips of Caroline Hayes signalled that they were not. Caroline wore jeans and a baggy sweatshirt, and eschewed all make-up. She formed the centre of a huddle of admiring girls, some with feminist badges, who shot Theo *traitress!* glances across the caff. Theo didn't care for this one tiny bit, having been the staunchest of sisters all her life. She was deeply unsettled by the way she had been cast on the side of the masters and the men, just like that, without her saying a word – she who had put up with so much crap from Jenner and argued the feminist case every millimetre of the way.

So Theo wasn't having a good day, even before she started copying the photographs. Technically she could have transferred them from camera to web without anyone having to open them up and have a look. The heroic figures, those hairy, secret women, could have stayed locked up inside anonymous filenames, Group1.bmp, Sigourney.bmp, Alathea.bmp, vista2.bmp, Kunegund.bmp.

But she knew it was never like that. Somehow you just have to check, to have a peek, do a Pandora. And there they were, lovely, complicated perfect artefacts, separate and conjoint, the saints together, every one with her own martyrdom and her own symbol of sanctity, the band of sisters, Mary Wollstonecraft, Ada, Countess of Lovelace, Sojourner Truth, Emmeline Pankhurst, Simone de Beauvoir, tricksy as stained-glass windows, simple as stones on the beach.

All the other students and staff of Animal Husbandry had gone off to the college local, the Old Barn Owl, to celebrate a birthday. Theo said she'd join them as soon as she'd finished what she was doing. Jenner had not been invited. It was silent in the lab, the way they both preferred it, washed clean of students.

It took her a few minutes to realise what had happened. She was busy with the undertaking. She had succeeded in transferring the pictures from the camera into the computer and had stored them away in a suitably discreet place, where she hoped no one would think to pry. Jenner was reading his e-mail on another computer across the bench.

Just a quick look, then, just a thumbnail gallery, while he's busy. And there they popped, one, two, three, four, enticing little squares, peep-shows of beauty. He couldn't possibly see them, could he?

It was suddenly extraordinarily silent, for Jenner had gone. And then the building shook to its paltry foundations as he slammed the outside door. His session on the computer was left hanging open.

At first she thought perhaps he had received an e-mail that disagreed with him, or been overcome by the general awfulness of the day. Jenner's behaviour on a typical day was unpredictable. He might slam a door because someone spelt *dependent* incorrectly. He might stump around the lake because funding had been denied to a new journal in German on cognition and behaviour. You got used to it, learnt to work around it. It was so extreme as to be funny.

But the joke was dead in the water.

Only for the time it took her to close down the peep-hole viewer did she think nothing of his violent departure. Then the truth dawned on her. He knew she had been looking at photographs of May Margaret's carvings, hidden away in the attic of his house. She ran to the door and saw his car lurching off in the distance, driven on an even more manic course than usual.

What was he going to do? In his current state of mind, there was no way of knowing; assuming, she thought grimly, that you could ever guess what he might do when he was his normal self. She remembered that May Margaret told her that he'd taken to the Warriors at the Gate with a saw. *What am I doing in this madhouse? I want to go home.*

She started to dial the Nightingales Farm phone number, but it was engaged. Rang and rang it, six or seven times, and then accepted that Robin never got off the line. She was dashing to close everything down in the lab, log off the workstations, lock the doors and turn off the lights, when she remembered Fergal's mobile number.

'Get May Margaret. It's an emergency.'

Fergal thought it very funny. 'Man Gets Wild and Threatens Statues,' he said. May Margaret was not there, but he fetched Elspeth.

'Hide every saw and axe on the place,' Theo said. 'I'm coming straight away.'

As she dashed out of the Animal Husbandry department, slamming the door with Jenner-style vigour, she thought how hilarious this would all sound when she recounted it to Juliet, and yet how dreadful she felt at the plight of Elspeth, scurrying around her outhouses hiding sharp implements. The panic she felt in her stomach was real enough. She also felt real fear for the effect of Jenner's wrath on those lovely creatures in the attic, and she could hardly bear to think about May Margaret's fury at her, and how she'd have to eat humble pie and make full confession of her stupidity. These emotions were as real as the reckless way she drove home, every bit as cavalier with regard to road rules and signs as Jenner. But at the same time, she heard the account of it as she made it to her friends, and it was pure *Rocky Horror Picture Show*, nothing you could possibly take seriously.

Get a grip, girl!

As she screamed into the farmyard like a boy racer, shortening the lives of a few hens, she saw Robin and Fergal hanging out of the window with a cigarette each, enjoying the show.

'Go, Theo!' cried Fergal. 'He's got ten minutes on you! And there's effing and blinding and banging in the kitchen.'

'Don't you buggers care at all?' she shouted, wild at them.

'She was asking for it. It's a shame she i'nt here to die on the barricades.'

Theo met Elspeth in the hall, her face sail–white.

'I thought I had found them all. I hid the axes and the saw in the linen cupboard, but I forgot the fire irons in his room. He has a poker.'

A poker, for God's sake, what could he do to Marg's women with a poker?

She took the stairs two at a time. Fergal and Robin were standing in the doorway as she went past their landing, cheering her on.

'Bastards!' she muttered.

The door to May Margaret's studio had been unlocked, so Jenner had not needed to use force. It seemed that there had been nothing in the studio to offend him. He could hardly take offence at an almost completed Virgin Mary at the end of the room. The poker was lying on an apple crate. Theo's relief when she saw this was momentary, for the trapdoor was hanging open, not by its hinges, but suspended crazily by the padlock. Jenner had used a chisel to unscrew the simple hinges from the wood.

They dangled from its edge, spilling screws on to the floorboards.

Theo took the poker and dropped it out of the window, which seemed perfectly consistent with the general nuttiness of what was going on. It fell on to the mud with a satisfying thud. But of course the space was full of chisels, as was the attic above.

Theo gripped the bottom of the ladder; the runnels of carving were unpleasant on her hands. She wished there was a nice motherly Virgin to pray to for a bit of extra help here, someone sane and jolly. Nothing in her background had equipped her to deal with this farce.

She could hear his footsteps on the floor above her, and she felt afraid. But he was walking about quite slowly, and he wasn't hitting or destroying anything. Still, there was plenty of scope for it. She didn't forget that he was six foot two inches tall, and broad-shouldered, with a complicated grip on reality, and might be armed with a chisel.

I am not a coward.

She had never regarded herself as a coward, and she wasn't going to start now. She was Theodora Potts who took on the world.

Round his footsteps went, and stopped, doing the gallery crawl. Theo forced herself on to the ladder. She climbed up, feeling very vulnerable as her head popped up through the opening.

He was standing in front of one statue – the woman called Joan, Theo thought. All the wrath had sagged out of him, his shoulders looked tired. Theo felt exhausted by him, exhausted by it all. *I want to go home.*

That was always what you did, when things got impossible. When they cut off the power to the flat, you went home. When you needed some peace and quiet for finals, you went home. When you had the flu, you went home. Home was a variable place, several places at once, Mum and

Dad's place, the flat, Australia. You curled up in your own bed, the one you had as a little girl, or the one you'd bought from the Swedish pine place, either would do, in your own sheets, safe and warm where everything made sense, where every mark on the wallpaper had a history you understood and every footfall in the hall was explicable.

Jenner looked at her, but he didn't say anything. He was crying. Theo found this excruciatingly embarrassing, and wanted immediately to retreat, but dared not leave him there alone.

She saw the array of Marg's chisels lying in their place on the bench, and went and sat down on them.

She felt their awkward edges cutting into her bottom, and felt really stupid. She wondered why she was sitting here, doing this. No one would ever believe her if she tried to describe it. Imagine trying to explain to Mum how she came to be sitting on a row of chisels while her host prowled around his daughter's studio in tears.

Well, he's clearly mad, Mum would say. *That's all there is to it, dear. You should just pack your bags!*

But you see, she explained, *he isn't mad. Everything he says and does is driven by a logic in his head. An emotional logic, but a consistent one. It's just different from ours. But so is the set of principles that drive Fergal, and we don't call him mad. I don't think I understand any more.*

He moved slowly round the figures one by one, putting out his hand to touch them, then pulling it back, as if they were real women and he dare not touch them. He came to the carving closest to where Theo was sitting, the almost finished Sigourney. She watched his fingers trembling as he reached towards it.

She looked up at him, and tried to see him clearly. She had become accustomed to his Gothic aspect, which at first had seemed such an affront to the senses; she was starting to read the glitter in his eyes as a kind of visor that he could raise or lower. She looked at his hands, long and shapely like the hands of a Renaissance angel held up in praise. Coated with dark hair on the backs, with soft, pale brown palms, the index fingers held apart, not jabbing but crooked as if querying, digits flexible, but with a grip you might think twice about. She was working on a hypothesis that a man's hands tell you everything you need to know. She liked Jenner's hands. Which was contrary, because she was quite sure she didn't much like the man.

Jenner's fingers quivered across the outline of the breast with such tenderness that Sigourney would surely have shuddered had she been flesh and blood. He let the tips of his fingers touch the ink-thin, almost imperceptible lines where one portion of wood in her armpit was smoothed into another, tracing the line as if it were a scar that particularly excited and moved him.

Theo watched this process, and watched the tears running down his cheeks, and felt deeply uncomfortable. *Creepy* was the word she would have used, but even as she thought of the word, she felt that somehow it demeaned Jenner's emotions. Creepy, weird, unbalanced were the sorts of adjectives she'd have come up with once upon a time, because she didn't have an adequate way of dealing with what she saw. She could no more imagine her brothers or Tom weeping as they touched a piece of carving than she could imagine them dancing around a funeral pyre.

She wanted to tell him that the woman wasn't real. But of course he knew that. He responded to something in his head conjured up by the carving. It shocked Theo that anything inside your head could have so external an effect. Tears. He touched the hipbone of the woman, and trailed his fingers across her slightly swollen stomach and down towards the pubic hair.

She felt she ought not to be there. The turmoil inside

Jenner was not her business. But she daren't go away now. It was she, Theodora Potts, who had done the damage to May Margaret's privacy and she'd have to see this scene out, whatever it cost her in discomfort.

'It breaks my heart,' he said, 'to think such beauty is locked away from the very people who should see it.'

'Aren't you proud of her?'

'Proud?' he said. 'How can I be proud of her? What have I done to produce this exquisite beauty, except pass on a genetic inheritance which includes an outstanding ability to create with the hands? I am not party to this.'

'That's a really depressing thing to say about your own daughter.'

'It would be dishonest of me to claim part of this. I wish I could.'

'Will you at least tell her how beautiful you think they are?'

For a while she thought Jenner hadn't heard what she said. He walked around behind Sigourney, where the work was unfinished and her body was not quite smooth, and dribbled his touch over her. Then he sat down next to Theo and ran his fingers through his hair. It was odd, she thought, that she'd never seen him perform so simple a human act as that.

He rested his hands on his knees like a working man at the end of a long day.

'I cannot talk to May Margaret.'

Theo felt so sad and angry with him that she wanted to cry too. She wanted to tell him how easy it was to say *your work is beautiful*, but then she saw that it was not. She had begun to catch a glimmer of the psychic quicksands that made it impossible for this father and his children to give or receive praise. She had begun to see how primitive was her knowledge of the human heart.

So she said something pretty dumb.

221

'Well, I guess we can repair the hinges.'

Very slowly he turned his head, and stared at her as if she were a stripper who had interrupted a funeral. His voice was so violently loud that it hurt her.

'This is my house. This is my family, my household. I shall rule it as I see fit. I shall not be barred from parts of my own house. I shall not be told how to live my life by a child with no experience of life and no understanding. Get out.'

'I fucking well will,' she said.

She went to Robin's room and entered without knocking. She was so mad she couldn't keep still. She walked up and down and swore like a swagman. Fergal watched her with a grin.

'You need a drink, darling,' he said and went off downstairs.

Theo threw herself down on Robin's bed. It was immaculately made, in harmony with the rest of the room, which was monastic-tidy, each book perfectly in place and not an adornment to be seen, except for a lovely wooden crucifix on the wall above the computer. Robin watched her from behind the ropy curtain of his hair.

'I'm leaving,' she said. 'I really have had enough.'

'Oh please don't,' he said. 'Please don't. Please wait until after the battle.'

'Why? Just give me one good reason why I should put up with this bloody awful farce.'

'Because – please don't tell anyone – we're – I'm – Rupert's organised it all.'

'Oh, *Rupert*.'

'After the battle, next week – well, I'm leaving. Please stay until then.'

'Why me?'

'Because Father is just less –'

'Less horrible to you because he's too busy being odious to me.'

Fergal came in with a milk bottle quarter full of whisky purloined from Jenner's room.

'Stealing a bloke's secret booze always makes you feel better.'

'Did you know that Robin was leaving with Rupert, after the battle?'

Fergal's grin was so wide you could post a parcel in it.

'Yeah, fucking great, innit?'

Robin blushed.

'I just have to get out of here,' said Theo, 'but Robin doesn't want me to go just yet.'

'I don't, neither.'

'Oh *you*! Aren't you the last person whose feelings I should consider?'

Fergal gave her a special quizzical look, like a gnome that is wondering about turning human.

For Elspeth there followed several of the worst days of her life.

She had known already that something awful was afoot, from Jenner's aspect of sickness, his lowered voice and withdrawal even more extreme than usual. But nobody would tell her the cause. Jenner would not even admit to there being a difference in his behaviour, and Theodora tried bravely to act as if all were well.

That was how things were until the day that Jenner went into the attic; after that things got much worse. Jenner grew so ill-looking and agonised that Elspeth feared for his sanity. Theo simply absented herself. She said she was busy helping Fergal with preparations for the battle, but Elspeth knew that she had quarrelled with Jenner and could not bear to be in the house.

Worst of all was May Margaret.

When she came home and found her trapdoor hanging open, she exploded into a fury the like of which had never been seen. She came downstairs into her father's room. Elspeth was in the kitchen, getting supper. She heard shouting, prolonged and violent, from both May Margaret and her father, and then smashing and crashing, which went on and on and on.

She felt it her duty to go into Jenner's room, though the furious wrath between them and the threat of violence drove her back. But there was no one to turn to. Robin would not help her. Fergal and Theodora were somewhere else. So Elspeth went alone into Jenner's room.

May Margaret was raging about, banging into furniture and smashing things. She had the poker in one hand, and in the other, Jenner's father's records. She was cracking them and throwing them to the floor, and shouting at him the while. Then she stopped breaking the records and flailed out at the pictures, and went back to breaking the records again, flinging them about the room as she broke them. Jenner roared back at her, but he stood absolutely still, clasping the back of a chair with such fierceness that his hands were ice white. May Margaret was very strong. There seemed no limit to what she might achieve.

She finished with the records and started on the china cabinet, telling her father in his own rhetoric what unredeemable misbegotten depraved refuse he was.

Then Elspeth, who had never shouted at anyone in her life, raised her voice.

'May Margaret, stop that at once. Go upstairs and calm down.'

May Margaret stopped in her destructive track. She stared at them both. Jenner's hands were shaking so much that the chair he was holding rapped against the table like an insistent spirit.

'You!' she said to her mother. 'You –'

She went to the cabinet in which Jenner kept his alcohol, and filled her arms with bottles. She went upstairs.

They heard her nailing up the door with great hammer blows.

Elspeth fetched a rubbish bag and a broom. She cleared up all the broken fragments, picking up the big pieces and sweeping up the small. There were so many shards of black shellac that she had to fetch a second bag. Jagged pieces cut through the plastic. May Margaret had broken every one.

All this while Jenner stood stock still, except for the shaking. He had shouted at May Margaret, but he said nothing to Elspeth. He allowed her to clear the wreckage from the room entirely, without saying a single word. Elspeth wished she had the strength to upbraid him for his silence and the courage to tell him he must apologise to his daughter. She felt that whatever parings of goodness had been in her life till now were melted away in the senseless heat of their rage. Why, why? said her heart, like a record.

For three days May Margaret stayed in her room. At night Elspeth heard her walking backwards and forwards, stumbling downstairs to the bathroom and the fridge, back up to her room, hammering in the defences, and then walking back and forth. Sometimes she shouted.

Elspeth wondered how you knew when someone was going mad. She came from stock of such sanity that madness was like a troll in a legend. You understood the word, but it had no relevance to anyone you might meet on a dark night.

Jenner prowled around sick and silent. May Margaret pounded the floor. Robin was no help at all. He had suddenly given up his newspaper rounds, and spent all evening on the phone in the hall talking to Rupert. Fergal came in around breakfast time looking busy. Theodora simply did not appear; Elspeth heard her car come and go. She felt more alone than she could remember.

On the Thursday morning May Margaret came downstairs. She was filthy and both pale and flushed at the same time, and so gaunt that she resembled her father. Her clothes were streaked with matter, her hair hung dank like the ends of a rag rug, she smelt of alcohol and vomit. Under her eyes were great black spiders' sacs of black. Her mother was ironing shirts in the kitchen.

'May Margaret, you will take off those filthy clothes and have a bath!'

'Yes I will, Mother, and then I will leave. I cannot stay another day in this house.'

She picked up the telephone, cutting off Robin in mid-session, and dialled Elgin Summers.

Elspeth stoked up the fire in the kitchen so that there would be hot water. She did not mean to overhear, but May Margaret was shouting into the telephone.

'I need to speak to him now.

'I don't care who he's engaged with. Tell him if he doesn't speak to me now, my next phone call will be to the police.

'You need to get me out of here. Today.

'Very well, tomorrow.

'I don't care who you are having lunch with tomorrow. If you don't come and fetch me with a carrier, I shall get myself out, and you can lose your fifty per cent for ever. I shall starve and struggle initially, but I'll still make it, with or without you.'

The voice on the other end grew querulous.

'I have been raped.

'My father.

'No, of course not. Figuratively speaking, but do not for one second underestimate the effect of that. I shall never speak to him again.

'Yes, a carrier. The best carrier in the West of England. The women go with me. You can set them up and show them to whomsoever you please, as long as you charge steeply for entry and I get half. And yes you may show me at work on the herms, as long as you get me the best Ham Hill stone and sell the herms for astronomical prices.

'I am turning to prostitution. Since the old Bluebeard himself has had his fill of me, there is no intrinsic reason why the lesser Bluebeards may not as well. One man, several, hundreds – once virginity is gone, does anyone count the penetrations thereafter?

'No I shall not think differently in the morning. It has taken me three days to come to this conclusion.

'Of course I have been drinking – what do you take me for? A martyr?

'You will be here tomorrow morning or you will never speak to me again.'

Elspeth made her coffee and toast thick with butter and treacle, a nursery favourite. May Margaret wolfed it down, and seemed grateful. Then Elspeth said the wrong thing.

'Perhaps you should talk to Theo before you finally decide –'

'Theo? cried May Margaret. 'Theo! She is worse than he is, if that is possible. She held me down while he did what he did. She is on their side. She pretended to be my friend, wormed her way into my confidence, and betrayed me to him. All the time she was looking for ways to betray me to him, so she could ease her passage into his bed.'

'Oh May Margaret, don't say such things.'

'Mother, if you won't see what is stinking under your nose, there is nothing for me to say to you. Get out of here, get out and leave them all wallowing in their corruption. Get out before he destroys what's left of your womanhood.'

Elspeth went upstairs to run the bath for her daughter. She would save up her tears until later.

In the morning, Elgin Summers came, wearing a velvet

jacket the same shade of scarlet as his Jaguar car. Under the velvet jacket he wore a black grandpa shirt with four black buttons, three undone, which Fergal said was quite suitable since he was old enough to be a grandpa. He smoked small cigar things, one straight after another, but he didn't light them one from another. Instead he used an art deco cigarette lighter made of mother-of-pearl.

Fergal hung around prepared to help, but the carrier's men did all the heavy lifting, swathing the sacred women in bubble wrap and manhandling them down the stairs into the van. Fergal stood in the attic and watched, feeling the absence of Theo. He filled his head with images of the wooden women.

The red Jaguar carrying May Margaret, with one bag of clothes and two cases of tools, crept up the track, conscious of its low-slung exhaust. The carrier's van followed. As the tail lights disappeared into the trees Elspeth went inside. Fergal found her standing in the hall by the great big sideboard with her family bible open in front of her.

'What did I do so wrong, Fergal,' she said, 'to deserve this?'

XI

FERGAL THOUGHT THEODORA was right. He was bound to lose his anonymity some time, so he might as well choose his own terms. He called the director of the documentary and said Moonbeam was guaranteed, bum and all. He called the *Sun* and told them that an exclusive was available (EXPOSED! MOONBEAM BARES ALL!) provided they turned up at the site with a photographer and five thousand pounds in hundred-pound notes. He called the *Evening Standard* and sold them 'Moonbeam as you've never seen him before!' for their fashion supplement. He rang his insider in South Western Television and said he was available for one interview.

Five days before the battle was due to be staged, the camera crew turned up on the moor, to find no protest and no developers, let alone any chaps in seventeenth-century armour. The scattered protesters were summoned by mobile phone from tents, sleep-outs, bed-and-breakfasts, mates' flats and hay barns. A camp was hastily assembled, using the debris of the security fences, and Fergal was duly stripped and sent up a tree to be informally photographed. He obliged the camera by swearing quite a bit, and smoking a suspicious-looking Rizla, because he knew they would have to bleep him, and skirt coyly round the spliff, as well as his nakedness. The crew required him to practise his specialised form of protest by the hour, for their convenience, so that a flash of him might be in the camera shot when something else was being filmed. Even though the sun was shining and he'd selected a nice tall leafy tree for his hammock and chains, he found that keeping it up, in a manner of speaking, for hours at a time, was chilly and inconvenient. But the crew went off to their hotel after dark, allowing Fergal to dress and sneak home to the caravan. His friends, huddled in their tents, no longer warmed by the spirit of the protest, grumbled that he was nothing but a media tart.

On Friday afternoon the clerks and postmen and computer programmers who made up the Westron Men started to trickle in and set up a very different sort of camp. Their tents managed to give the impression of being quite primitive, constructed of canvas and cowhide, while incorporating high-tech joinery, insect screens and cunning concealed lighting. The enacters, unlike the protesters, saw no virtue in being uncomfortable. They tethered their horses, banged their drums, set up their cooking pots and made excellent footage, especially with the security men and protesters for contrast and instant drama. Little bit of conflict, little bit of human interest, Moonbeam putting on his pants because a woman with small children has objected, Rupert losing her temper because the dragoons have been allocated the wrong field. Great stuff.

Then the head of English Heritage turned up to make his plug for the preservation of the battlefield, and to pose importantly for the national newspapers. His speech was repeated several times for the documentary makers, who were trying to get cavalry into the background of the picture and security guards in the foreground, without of course making it look the least bit contrived.

Fergal, besieged in his tree top, is amazed and delighted that so small an effort on his part can produce so large an effect. Weeks up a tree holding back the forces of

Mammon had produced nothing. A few cheerful hours on the Internet, three boozy gatherings at the Bleeding Heart, and here's the whole of Britain rooting for the preservation of the King's Sedgemoor.

At the base of his tree, three teenage girls in mildly seventeenth-century dress are clamouring for his autograph, and the camera crew want to capture this tender scene. He slides down, dressed, to oblige. The crew do not wish to film the follow-up, in which the girls try and persuade him to take off his trousers. Fergal, removing their playful fingers from his belt, thinks this is rather better TV than the autograph bit, though much less pleasant for him. He is sincerely pleased to be relieved by Rupert, alias Lord (Brigadier) John Churchill, who comes riding up on his bay mare, his page behind him.

'Having fun, Robin?'

'Fun!' cries Robin. 'This is all right!'

'Sure it's not forbidden somewhere?'

'Don't mock the boy,' says Rupert, Lord Churchill.

'Watch out,' Fergal calls to the horse's arse. 'Dangerous stuff, sunlight.'

He watches them wheel out on to the field where Rupert is marshalling her dragoons – a sorry bunch at this point in the proceedings – but Rupert will whip them into fighting trim. Fergal's heart dances a little jig. He's made all this happen. And he has money. He can take his girl out on the town.

The reconstruction was billed to the public and press as taking place on Sunday, and so it did, but Sunday was the day when Westonzoyland church, a prime arena in the drama, was inconveniently in use. No amount of media preening could persuade the vicar to shift the Sunday School May Parade from two o'clock on Sunday, nor postpone evensong to a more convenient weekend. Consequently, the aftermath of the battle, the herding of prisoners into the church, the groans of those bleeding on the floor, the dramatic escape of one Dutch rebel through the north door by picking the lock, the Royal commanders (Lord John Churchill and his page included) standing on the church tower surveying the bloodied field, and the rebels hanging in chains – all of this took place on the Saturday before the battle, rather confusing any observer with a decent sense of history.

Fergal had the task of mediating between the Westron Men, groaning and dying very dramatically on the church floor, but unwilling to do so repeatedly, the camera crew, who wanted plenty of evocative footage of dirt, agony, old stone and weathered tile, and the good ladies of the parish who wanted to do the flowers and set up for the Sunday School May Parade.

It was fun.

It was fun of a more serious kind when they staged the night attack for the benefit of posterity. *Remember we are five thousand strong, and fight for God only!* Monmouth exhorted them as they set out, rather fewer than five thousand, and certainly not motivated by religious fervour. Fergal, Theo and other camp followers were allowed to put on buff coats and floppy hats, and grab a pike. About four in the morning, the infantry were conveyed in four-wheel-drive vehicles, trucks and estate cars to the outskirts of Bridgwater, whence with Monmouth and the camera crew they crept up on the forces of the King, encamped on Sedgemoor. The march, in all its deadly seriousness, was without sound or light, but even the most fanatical of the King's Westron Men didn't expect a crowd of young people in a jolly mood to walk four miles in silence. Besides which, the stray cars and street lights rather spoilt the illusion that they might advance on the King's men undetected. As they approached Westonzoyland, a certain confusion arose among the leaders as to the route through the village, occasioning the drawing out of Maglites and maps. But they were off again, now almost in darkness. Somewhere out there, undetected except by the following camera, their cavalry was moving in on the unsuspecting soldiers, tucked up for the night with hardly a watch set. The moor was silent under their feet, as it had been for Monmouth's men, and a certain eeriness crept into the march.

Lost causes. Palm Sunday procession. The back door of the church is unlocked and out goes the man with the incense, which instead of billowing up to heaven melts away into the grey air. Out goes the man with the cross and either side the two altar boys, Fergal and his mate. Their candles blow out straight away. Down the road, the singing straggling and diving into schism as soon as you can no longer hear Father booming. People stand at their windows and look out, mystified. Fergal studies his shoes, letting his hair drop over his face. The procession and its celebration, palms and olive branches, hosannas, the lot, collapses into a cardboard cutout, a funny old fusty stage set being carried along in the light of day. All the glory flies away with the clouds of incense into Borridge Road, and what was powerful and important and beautiful is not necessarily so at all. But as the procession re-enters the church, lights extinguished, hair disarranged, singing the hosanna hymn as a round in many ragged parts, the colours leap right back into the banner, the boat boy ladles incense into the thing, and clouds of smoke shoot right up to heaven, the organist insists on the tune, and everyone's together again – as if the outside bit was the dream and this is the reality. It wasn't long after that Fergal got sacked as an altar boy for getting his cotta ripped in a game of tag.

In the darkness, silent on Sedgemoor, the layers peel off some more. They'd started to peel, long ago when, smoking outside the prefab, waiting for Quiche, he saw cuckoo flowers in the little garden, and saw a whole miniature paradise sprout between the stones by the pond like a magic-eye picture, there, and then gone. It was lovely, aching, but it wasn't reassuring. They'd kept peeling off, so that every year there were fewer things he could take for granted, and truth was closer, but harder to see. He reached out his hand for Theo's. Her hand was small, smaller than you'd expect from such a definite person, quite soft, belying the things she did to bulls. Holding her hand was not something he'd intended to do. Holding hands with girls wasn't something he had ever done, being too tough and cool for such practices. Theo might have been as surprised by this gesture as he was himself, but once done, neither let go.

The troop of rebels came to a stop. The cavalry at the front (or in the van, as Monmouth confusedly called it) had reached the infamous Bussex Rhine, which the rebels had obstinately refused to cross. They stood along the edge of the ditch. In 1685 the rhine had been coursing with evil black water, which tonight had to be imagined. Drought and water management had dried it up, and they stood barred from committing wholesale slaughter on the King's army by a mere depression in the country-side. On the other bank, disposed through the fields of those farmers who were prepared to co-operate, were encamped the King's men. And rather a lot of women, but hey, this is equal opportunity warfare. Light and conviviality streamed out of the tent flaps. The King's men, true to historical precedent, were getting stuck into the cider. Only one or two were even more authenti-cally asleep.

It was rather lonely standing silent by the dry ditch waiting for the enemy to notice. Only the dragoons of Lord Churchill were aware of their advance. Silently mounted, they twitched in the dark further down the field, waiting for the signal. They were to move forward in darkness, and charge at first light.

Conflating various bits of historical incidents in the interests of drama (though Monmouth explained to them once again that, tomorrow, in communicable daylight, they would do it all exactly by the book), one of their number fired a pistol shot. This was the agreed signal to the King's army that hostilities were to be commenced.

They shuffled and waited. The rebel horse under Lord Grey of Warke took off along the rhine to start the attack from the flank. Over the rhine, the partying continued. Some wag in the rebel army suggested reversing history and going for it. Nathaniel Wade reached for his walkie-talkie.

'Feversham. Do you read me? Feversham? For God's sake, Jason, we're here. We'll come and do you over. Over and out.'

Soldiers tumbled out of the tents. The cry was heard clearly through a megaphone (sound system in place tomorrow): *Beat your drums! The enemy is come. For the Lord's sake, beat your drums!* And the drums duly started, bang bang bang in the dark, impersonal, terrifying.

We're going to get done, Fergal thought, *we're going to get slaughtered. We thought we'd slash em up in their tents and put Monmouth on the throne, and now we're going to die. I don't want to be shot or be hung or be sent away from home for ever.*

Cries went up from the rebel army – *St George and Old England! King Monmouth and the Protestant Church!* And shots started to be fired all over the place. Horses came dashing down the bank of the rhine, only to disperse and gallop away in the other direction, due to the cowardice or incompetence of Lord Grey of Warke.

Theo and Fergal stood still, as they were supposed to do, and waited to be mown down at dawn. They kept on holding hands, a very unsoldierly thing to do, but motivated by an authentic misery.

'I don't think I like this very much,' she said.

In the trees nearby, trees which long post-dated the battle, the dawn chorus cut in. The birds, not knowing what to make of drums and firing and the flurry of horses over the peat, got on with things.

Prime! Fire! And then soldiers rushing the rhine, swords out, and *Hold for the passion of God, if you be men!* shouted Monmouth. Swords banging on armour, quite realistically, people falling down, groaning, puffs of smoke, and then behind them a kind of roar, and Churchill's cavalry were on them. Then it was definitely safer to lie down and play dead.

Sunday morning, church bells, blackbirds, Fergal's in some-one's tent, being Moonbeam with clothes on. He's woken and driven out by the sounds of love from the sleeping bags next to him. He goes walkabout on the battlefield and finds Robin emerging, hair awry, from Lord John Churchill's tent.

Together the two young men walk across the encamp-ment towards the coffee stall kindly set up by Harris's Village Teas whose little shopfront and traditional way of life is threatened by the hypermarket car park. Mr Harris, who is close to retirement and who knows perfectly well that his shop has to go, is a well-wisher. He's out to get as much fun out of life as possible and putting a spanner into the works of the mighty is a major source of fun. Fergal knows him well, having patted Mrs Harris's flowerbeds into shape. He greets the young men and gives them coffee and stale buns. They lean on a barrel, sticky with beer and soft drinks, to have their breakfast. 'I'm so glad I resigned from my paper rounds,' says Robin with great satisfaction. 'Sundays were the worst. The papers get heavier and heavier. I did an analysis. Do you know the average Sunday newspaper has increased by three grams in a year?'

'Got more time in bed? How was it then? As good as you thought? Best thing in the world, innit, better than football.'

Robin blushed and ducked under his hair.

'Oh no, we didn't. It would be wrong. It's expressly forbidden in St Paul. *Flee fornication. Every sin that a man doeth is without the body; but he that committeth fornication sinneth against his own body.*'

Fergal's distracted by the idea that bad sex might be a sin against yourself rather than another. He doesn't hear the first part of Robin's speech. He feels a bit apologetic, because Robin has obviously been rehearsing this for his benefit.

'. . . so you see, it must be meant. I laid so many fleeces before the Lord. Look at the chances against it all − first Theodora comes here − and that in itself must be the Lord's work. Then because of Theodora you are here. A five-minute difference in our Sunday dinner, and you and Theodora would never have met. It has to be the hand of the Lord. And then because of you, we made contact with Rupert, and again you can see the Lord's work, because if I hadn't thought she was a man I wouldn't have invited her to stay and wouldn't have met her − and then, wonder of wonders, we fell in love! What a miracle. Praise the Lord!'

'Yeah,' says Fergal, confused to find himself part of the Lord's Scheme for Rupert and Robin when he was just trickling through life as he did.

He wonders why he never heard Father Mahoney say fornication was a sin against your *own* body. Maybe Father had only ever imagined fornication − saints with half a breast showing or boy angels lifting up their cottas?

Good man, that Father, but you had to be a sinner to understand sin.

'. . . let the Bible fall open three times, and each time was a message . . . and above all, love like ours, it's got to be from the Lord.'

'Why?'

'Have you ever been in love, Fergal?'

'Dunno. How would I know?'

'It's like faith in the Lord. You just know.'

'I think I missed the gene. Faith and that. What's it feel like?'

'If you had been in love, you would know. I can't possibly describe it – you feel that anything is possible. The world looks completely different – everything is the same but sort of holy. Everything makes you want to smile or cry. You are completely taken over – you can't eat, you can't sleep. I almost can't work for thinking about Rupert – I mean Christine. And even her name!'

Fergal sighs inside at the notion that Rupert's parents connived with the creator in the naming of their child. But then what does Fergal know about such things? God could be a turtle holding up the world, for all he knows.

'I promise you, Fergal, when you find Jesus, when you fall in love, you just *know*!'

Fergal watches a heron take off across the moor, a long slow plunge of flight. He wonders what it would be like to know anything for sure.

Robin is still talking.

'You see, it has all worked out so beautifully. I'm going to work for her in Bristol. She's just created a new position for a junior Web designer – you can't put that down to luck, can you? The timing is just too miraculous! Then we are going to get married. Very, very soon, but don't tell Mother. Rupert says that there is no point in waiting since we are both so sure, and she doesn't want to tempt me into something I might think is wrong. You see, she doesn't share my beliefs yet, but she absolutely respects them, and I am sure in time the Lord will open her eyes too –'

That Rupert, Fergal reflects, knows a thing or two. He estimates the age difference – twelve years? But when you want a man for yourself, any strategy is acceptable. There's no Geneva Convention in love to protect the innocent.

Not far away the troops are lining up to do battle. Fergal and Robin finish up their coffee and disperse once again to be trampled underfoot in the cause of God and the Protestant religion, or the Godly Maintenance of the Law and King's Order, depending on whose side you're on.

That night, the Sunday of the battle, the official end of the protest, Fergal woke in the dead of night. Nothing has been gained, he thought, the big old trees will succumb silently to their fate, the foxes and badgers disperse to other thickets, the retail superstore will seep relentlessly on to Sedgemoor, and the herons will flap away for ever.

Fergal wondered if they were always bound to lose, if the march of plastic and faceless corporate man was a historical inevitability, whether he himself was a prophet or a reactionary. He didn't know whether he was the first flags of a new dawn, or the dying tatters of an old way. He didn't know, and in a sense he didn't care, because the battle had to be fought. You couldn't tell at the time, could you? The peasants who followed Monmouth couldn't tell that they weren't part of a great groundswell of the Protestant proletariat. The people who lined up behind William of Orange three years later, for much the same cause, didn't know they were the midwives of a great new world, a world in which you made political change without spilling blood. Fergal had read a bit of history; he knew that if you were an embattled minority, it was almost impossible for you to know at the time whether you were at the end or the beginning of something.

He went for a piss and a long drink of water, and settled down again. He had to climb over Theo to get in and out of bed, having been assigned the colder spot, next to the unlined wall of the caravan. When he lay down again, curling himself around her for warmth, he found he had lain his hand over her stomach. The long T-shirt she wore to bed was rumpled up, and his hand made contact with her skin. Usually he didn't allow this to happen, but tonight he let the hand lie. He didn't know why, any more than he knew why he had held her hand on the battlefield. There was some sort of inevitability about it, which troubled him.

He knew he had to move on to Norfolk. No point in lingering when the battle was lost, it just got you depressed. And the police would be round any day now, once they'd figured out what to do. He needed to get going.

He didn't like this, his arm around Theo's body. It felt too good, too much like happiness, something way beyond his budget. It was like thinking about a nice dry flat with your own bed in it. Not to be thought about. He pressed his nose against her back. She smelt way beyond his means, of expensive but animal-friendly shower gel. As he lay struggling to get to sleep, he heard birdsong. Though he'd spent many days living in woods of varying degrees of denseness, he didn't know much about birds. They flew about. They dropped poop on cars. They nested. Sometimes they were endangered and you had to protect their habitat. They sang.

And how they sang. The darkness was full of music, so rich and complex that it seemed improbable. Trills and runnels and streamlets of sound poured out in such profusion that you'd think a door into heaven had opened. The song was tricksy, complex, lulling the ear with exquisite melody, then darting into a different key, a chattering, atonal, percussive passage, folding without warning or unease into another lyric passage, shots of pure sound pealing over the trees, up into eternity. Perhaps there were only two birds, but the breadth and depth and just plain noise of the singing suggested a wood full of them. Gratuitously beautiful, unstinted, ravishing.

This was no short burst of glory. The singing continued, as if time had hung up in the dark. There was no midnight, no dawn, and the music of heaven would never slacken or cease. Living water, thought Fergal.

There was a risk it would vanish if he tried to share it. Turn out to be a dream, turn out to be quite ordinary, nightjars or owls or blackbirds before dawn. Sod's law dictated the birds would stop as suddenly as they'd started, the moment he woke Theo up.

He lay rigid, his hand touching and not touching her skin. He wanted to cry, he wanted to drown in it, he wanted never to move or speak again. He didn't want to expose it to speech or analysis or even thought. He didn't even want to say *nightingales*, for that might contain the experience, reduce it to something other people had heard, as in *Thou wast not born for death, immortal bird*, and other second-hand feelings.

He felt the cold tin of the caravan wall on his back and the warm body of his friend sandwiching him in; he told himself that he lived in the world, that sad old Keats floating out of Mr Yeabsley's record player on a hot bored afternoon, and Theo's skin, and Elspeth's second-rate welding, and Fergal's need for cigarettes were all material things of this world, and there was no door into the other world except through them.

He needed to get through to that world.

She stirred, muttered something, made those endearing

noises which betoken unwillingness to wake and pleasure in doing so.

'You OK?' he said.

'Mmm. Sort of. No, not really. I just had an awful dream about Jenner.'

She didn't say anything about his hand, so he left it there.

'Going to tell me about it?'

'I should have told you before. It's been so awful, but I'm trying to keep it secret from Elspeth. Jenner's in trouble at the college, over a girl. The council hearing is tomorrow. I said I'd go as a character witness, but then I changed my mind because he was such a bastard. But there was a bureaucratic stuff-up and I'm still down to appear. And if I don't appear, it will look even worse for him. Now I don't know what to do. What should I do, Fergal?'

It was difficult to think; he couldn't think about that man and the blackness that oozed out of him. The only things in his head were strawberries and thick cords of water, and, for some reason, sand dunes.

'I dunno. I think you should just listen.'

She lay still and listened. He thought her stillness as lovely as the birdsong. She lay rapt for so long he began to go to sleep, holding her against him.

She said, in a whisper, 'That's the loveliest thing I ever heard.'

'Me too.'

'I don't want to sleep. I might not hear them again as long as I live.'

'No, that's for real. When they cut down all the thickets, there's nowhere for the nightingales to go.'

'That's what you live for, isn't it? Giving the nightingales a place to sing?'

Not only the nightingales, he thought. This moment, this moment to last for ever.

* * *

She is sitting in a padded chair, covered in orange vinyl, seventies university chic, looking at the serried white faces, bespectacled to a man, their shirts, white and light checks, their ties, plain, patterned and Disney. A moustache, a beard, sideboards nurtured perhaps since they were last fashionable. Hair carefully poised over the bald bit, or scruffy and irregularly washed, or neatly regimented to give the minimum trouble. Their hands, clasped before them, or fiddling with pencils or touching the cheek or the lip or the hair behind the ear. Wedding bands, clean fingernails, short or bitten. Freckled hands, narrow pink hands, big stubby ones, nicotine-stained prying ones.

'Now, Dr Potts, we understand that this is a difficult and embarrassing matter, but it is vital that we arrive at the truth . . .'

Theo feels sick – sicker than she felt at the oral for her doctorate, sicker than she felt before she gave her first lecture. She's been waiting outside for two and three-quarter hours, watching first Caroline Hayes go into the room with a toss of her hair, then Jenner, crumpled and a foot shorter than usual, then Caroline Hayes's study tutor. She doesn't understand why she couldn't have been called for two hours after the start time. Her anger at Jenner fuses with anger at the stupid bureaucratic system, but as soon as she gets into the room and sits down, the anger bursts open and mutates into nausea.

She's got to talk about Jenner and sex. And this is a subject she is about as tired of as she is of blonde jokes. She hasn't voluntarily spoken a word to him since the outburst in May Margaret's attic. Happy to see him stew in his own mess, she had not intended to be here.

But here she is. She looks at the long rank of faces, and wonders what there is about these men to make her so nervous that she's sick. Who are they anyway?

Nobodies. What do they know about scholarship, or sex? *Fuck all*.

Yet they hold in their mediocre hands the fate of a remarkable scholar, a man tormented by sexual temptations they cannot comprehend. They will take it upon themselves to judge him, and almost certainly find him guilty.

She is still angry with Jenner; the bruise hurts just as much when she touches it. But looking around her she thinks that, for all his manifest faults, he does deserve to be defended against ignorance and prejudice.

This gives her the courage she needs, and she gets stuck in straight away, taking the high ground. She stands up. They're not going to treat her like a girl witness. She'll tell them the way it is.

'Well gentleman,' she starts, nice and loud and just a touch strident, 'you have to understand certain things about Dr Ransfield. I am sure you all know that he is an exceptionally distinguished scientist, credited with ground-breaking work in three different disciplines. His publications are quite few, but if you've read them, you will agree that they are remarkable. You will also be aware that Dr Ransfield is working on a major theoretical work on perception and communication theory which has in principle been accepted for publication by MIT Press, an honour not often afforded to British scientists.

'But Dr Ransfield, as you all know, is not an easy person to work with. He is extremely demanding of others, but he is equally demanding of himself; he doesn't suffer fools gladly, as we have all found to our cost. One ill-considered remark to him and you wish you'd kept your mouth shut. He expects the highest standards of scholarship from everyone around him, even the lowliest first-year student.

'I have to admit that this makes working with him pretty hard at times, but so far I've found the results to be worth the hardship.

'Now, the students do find Dr Ransfield fairly surprising, as I did myself when I first met him, because he talks in a very unusual manner. But I have come to the conclusion that this is the side effect of an extraordinary mind. He also comes out with a lot of what you might call inappropriate remarks of a sexual nature, but I have to say, gentlemen, that that seems to be a generational thing. Men of Dr Ransfield's generation seem to find it hard to know what is offensive to modern young women. And it is pretty hard to get it right all the time, isn't it? For example, I particularly dislike being called a lady, and yet I address you as gentlemen.'

Polite laughter. They are just lapping this up; she can practically hear the slurping sounds. She doesn't feel sick any more, just powerful.

'Now, there's another issue which you have to take into account, which I'm very interested in, as a woman in academic life, and it's what's called the Oleanna Syndrome, referring to the controversial play of that name, which I'm sure you've heard of. I can refer you to some papers on the subject, co-authored by male *and* female scholars, by the way, one in particular from the *Journal of the British Institute of Psychological Medicine*, Volume 31, August 1995. The syndrome, in brief, is exhibited by young women in conditions of stress, towards older men in positions of authority, especially teachers and pastors. They frequently misinterpret what is intended as kindness or jocularity as a sexual advance, often because of a traumatic previous experience.'

She pauses, but they are too stunned to interrupt. *Ha!*

'Don't misunderstand me, though, gentlemen. I'm not suggesting that sexual harassment isn't a very serious matter. I'm not suggesting that sexual harassment isn't very wide-spread and shouldn't be dealt with very severely. I'm not suggesting that remarks of a sexually suggestive nature are acceptable to modern women. I'm not suggesting that you shouldn't continue to be absolutely vigilant in protecting the young women and the young men in this college from any kind of abuse, sexual, social or physical.

'But I am saying that my dealings with Dr Ransfield have convinced me that while he is a most unusual and difficult man, he is not a rapist, nor even a sexual molester or harasser. I've worked with him closely for some time now, and observed his habits, and it's my considered opinion that any sexual fantasies he may entertain about his students remain firmly locked up inside his head, as I think they do for most men these days.'

That one hit home; some of them looked away. She'd have sworn the pink one blushed. This might turn out to be the best lecture Theodora Potts ever delivered.

'I am, in conclusion, firmly of the opinion that Dr Ransfield has far too high a regard for academic standards to alter a student's mark in return for a sexual favour. Thank you for your time.'

She was so tired that afternoon, what with fighting for the Protestant religion all Saturday, lying awake half of Sunday night listening to the nightingales, and then on Monday morning giving her all in the defence of scholarship, that each time she stopped talking she'd start to drift off, even though she was standing out in a field, in brilliant sunshine, taking video footage of a bull at full throttle.

She was working with a veterinary assistant, a sharp youth with a shaved head and two studs in each nostril. They made little jokes about the porno movies they would have to sell, and how they should distribute the profits. She was grateful to be doing something so simple and time-consuming.

Although she was exhausted, she felt terrific, and wished she could brag to the vet assistant about how she'd made the council see the light on Jenner Ransfield. She wished she could bottle the looks of appreciation on their faces and take them home to show Fergal. She wished she had a video of her speech to play over to Jenner, so he'd know how great she'd been.

But she smiled all over and inside, loving the exhaustion as evidence of what she'd done, the way you revel in the fact that you're totally knackered after a great night's sex.

About the middle of the afternoon Jenner came out across the field towards them. In spite of her spirited defence of him, the moment she saw him she wished he'd go away. She had absolutely no desire to talk to him.

He walked across the field with his head down and stood a little way apart from Theo and the young vet, looking completely out of place. She ignored him for a while, but this unsettled the young man, who kept staring back at Jenner as if shooing him away.

Jenner was not to be shooed. From behind his back he brought a bunch of flowers from the college gardens, stocks, cornflowers, Canterbury bells, sweet william and rosemary. He offered these to Theo.

'Thank you,' he said.

Theo wished the bright green field would suddenly fissure and swallow her up. She took the flowers from him awkwardly.

'It's OK. I didn't really do anything. Just talked a lot. I'm good at that.'

'They will place a letter on my file,' he said in a low voice, 'which will influence any issues that may arise in the future, but they will take no further action. Will you walk around the lake with me?'

Theo felt really uncomfortable. *Flowers, for Christ's sake!* She glanced at the assistant, who gave her a mean smile, adding to her discomfort. He had overheard what Jenner said, and now it would be all over college that she'd rescued him and he'd brought her flowers. She thought perhaps she would walk around the lake, and leave the veterinary assistant to put the old bull away, to serve him right.

Jenner set off at his cracking pace; she trotted beside him, clutching the flowers he had had given her and feeling about twelve years old. She wondered how to start the conversation. But he was quite content to be silent for a while.

They crossed the fields of the home farm and took the path that led through pleasant groves of grand old trees towards the lake. He didn't look at her, nor she at him. They passed through a wall of rhododendrons, just starting to squeeze colour out of their buds. The path led gently downwards, cambered in a leisurely age, for leisurely walking.

On the lake a tidy pair of black waterfowl slid hopefully towards them. There was no sign of any other people on the blanket of green under the trees on the lakeside. By the ruined temple that had once been Milord's boathouse, a disconsolate rowing boat bobbed; access to it was denied by a wall of orange plastic fencing around both boat and boathouse. They walked towards a stone bench set in a bank of yew, with an uninterrupted view across the lake to the island in the middle. There was nothing to be seen except splendid plantings of oaks, ash and beech, waves of rhododendrons, azaleas, japonicas, dotted with colour, and broad bright swathes of lawn. They sat down on the stone bench in silence and lovely sunlight. The sky was perfect blue, frothed up with little clouds; enough to enhance, not enough to threaten.

'I think I could grow to like England,' she said.

Then he apologised. In his beautiful voice, the apology sounded far more potent than the two words *I'm sorry* had any right to do.

'What for, exactly?' said Theo.

Jenner sighed before he answered.

'I can think of no more damaging response to an apology. Either no offence has been noted, or far too many.'

'Yup.'

'The death of the English language.'

'Don't play the old fogey with me, Jenner. I'm sick of it. When you were a wild young man about Melbourne, not that long ago, I bet you didn't entice girls into your bed with laments for the English language. I bet you offered them dope.'

'*Touché*,' said Jenner, and smiled. 'Please accept my apology.'

'When you tell me what you're apologising for.'

'For drawing you into my nightmare world. For being who I am, and forcing you to engage with that appalling person.'

Theo closed her eyes and sighed at the impossibility of him. How on earth was she supposed to respond to that?

'Well I have to say, Jenner, that after the awful bizzo with May Margaret, I really did *not* want to say affirming things about you to the council. And I don't think I would've if it hadn't been for Fergal.'

'St Fergal the Green.'

'You can scoff at him, but that only makes you look bad. Last night when we were in bed –'

'Don't –' he said, holding up his hand.

'For God's sake, Jenner, I go to bed every night. Just listen, will you? Last night, we heard these nightingales singing. It was so beautiful – and if you make another cynical remark, I shall get up and walk away.'

Jenner shook his head, as if struck dumb by the enormity of the suggestion.

'I lay there, and thought, this is what Fergal lives for, his whole life is dedicated to keeping this country beautiful and wild, so that people like us can hear nightingales. I mean, nothing in books or recordings could begin to convey what it was like to hear them for real.'

'I know. I know. I used to hear them often when I first came to the farm. Latterly I hear them less. It breaks my heart to think of it.'

'And if people never get the chance — if they have to go to theme parks to have the Nightingale Experience and the Walk in the Bluebell Wood Experience — then they are permanently impoverished. And I thought, Fergal's prepared to give up everything that matters to other people — security, comfort, love — for this.

'And I thought if he's prepared to sacrifice himself like this, for everyone's future, then the least I can do is to fight a little battle for the integrity of scholarship, which is really important to me.'

'Do I represent the integrity of scholarship in your mind?'

'Yes. Your work is disinterested, and ground-breaking, and however I feel about you personally, you should be let alone to get on with it. Because academic freedom is one of the most important things we have. Academic freedom, freedom of the press, and what's left of the natural world. They are the only things we can be sure about fighting for now.'

'Yes, Theodora, yes,' said Jenner. 'In this, you are absolutely right.'

XII

SUNDAY MORNING. ELSPETH wakes in her white bedroom, a woman adrift. For in the night, to her delight and
amazement, Jenner came into her bed and made love to
her, the first time in so long she had no longer a reckoning.
It was an occasion of unsullied happiness, because Jenner,
as passionate and tender a lover as always (though Elspeth
had no means of comparison), did not exhibit anger or say
a single hurtful word. He hardly said a word at all, but for
this Elspeth was grateful; instead, when it was over, he lay
in her arms and cried, without explanation.

When she wakes, therefore, she feels wonderful, but
confused. All week Jenner has been unnaturally kind. He
has smiled, he has talked to Fergal over the dinner table.
He and Theo are friends again. It is as if the dreadful
departure of May Margaret, and all the nightmare years
before, have been a figment of her imagination. But her
imagination is not up to breeding that.

It is early, no one is stirring. She will go to the kirk.
She bathes, dresses smartly, goes downstairs and writes a
note. GONE TO KIRK. PLEASE FEED HENS. She takes the
car keys from Jenner's coat pocket and drives off as pleased
with herself as if she were a film actress sliding out in her
sports car. She will walk about the deserted town by herself,
along the waterfront, have a cappuccino, as she had with
Fergal the other day.

Something is stirring inside Elspeth. After kirk, she walks along by the water, her head full of hymns, excited by the changes in her life. For last week, as well as the miraculous change in Jenner's aspect, Elspeth received her first e-mail. Robin peeled it off the Net for her, and Fergal came down and presented it to her. She feels she has entered a new world, just getting an e-mail, quite apart from the pleasure the message gave her.

The message was from Zachary Bryce in Norfolk, her old sailing mate and rival. He runs a sailing school, with camping chalets attached, and it is his quarters in which Fergal and his mates are to stay while setting up the new project. Zachary said that if she ever thought of coming up this way he'd love to catch up with her to chew over old times. Also, he added (though how he knew to mention this is anyone's guess), if she had some time to spare over the summer she'd be a godsend to him, as he could never find good women sailors to tutor on his summer schools, and in these difficult modern times, parents really preferred it if the tutors were women. Elspeth could name her conditions and her price.

She prods the idea of a summer in Norfolk teaching at Zachary Bryce's sailing school to see if it proves sinful and self-indulgent. She is surprised to discover that even after an hour and a half at kirk the idea still does not seem intrinsically wrong. Fergal thinks it a good idea, Theo thinks it a good idea, even Robin has nodded and urged her to go, saying that Christine believes that women are only fulfilled if they have a profession.

She stares at the water and knows that she will never be happy unless she is out there, by herself, being herself. She has long understood that people are mostly not happy, but she begins to think that deliberately not to be happy is almost a sin. She has withheld herself from simple pleasure, harmless, inexpensive pleasure, for so long, thinking it would make others happy. But all she has succeeded in is making herself more miserable.

She reflects, as she walks slowly and contentedly along by the water in the sunlight, that she does not know what would make Jenner happy. Perhaps after all he is one of the elect – elected to be damned.

. . . she remembers . . . a broad brown river . . . she is half a mile upstream from Bucklers Hard, conveying her love across the wide Beaulieu river. The sun is shining around his dark head, and his dangerous hands hang loose on his knees. He looks out to the far shore, fair and wooded, and she can gaze on his profile to her heart's desire. He says nothing; the spring of words is stopped; he allows himself to be taken wherever she wishes to take him. Such compliance will never occur again, but at the moment, which is forever in her daydream, she does not know this, and exults in the ease of this passage. Surely he must love her if he allows himself to sit so quietly in her company, agitating for no outcome, laying no restraints on where they go or when they return. The responsibility for making him happy settles on her shoulders; she is happy with its weight, happy now, for surely he will love what she loves, the riverside walk, the riparian pub, the slap and rattle of the gear, then maybe tomorrow, out into the Solent, around the Isle of Wight, a taste of sea, then later perhaps, further on, more exciting expeditions in the Channel and beyond . . . This is the first and last time he suffers himself to be ferried about by her; but her sacramental recreation takes no account of this; in her re-enactment the moment is unclouded by the dreariness of the future; the Jenner of then is preserved in his calm and physical perfection, and endlessly content to be in her presence and to be at her disposal. He turns and smiles. Jenner has never been seen to smile, and the breaking of this smile is a miracle, to which she has clung long weary years.

> O would I were where I would be!
> There would I be where I am not:
> For where I am would I not be,
> And where I would be I cannot.

The River Parrett at Bridgwater is broad and brown, and although the town has a nautical flavour, the sea seems a long way downstream. But as Elspeth stood by it, watching the currents, she saw that they were all going at their own pace and in their own ways towards the sea. Nothing was going to stop them. So in a way, she thought, the river is already there. But the river knows where it's going; it's drawn down to the sea by an inevitable progress, evolved over years and years, a general consensus of streams growing together into a river, which finds the best route down to its desired end.

> I must be going, no longer tarry
> The burning Thames I have to cross
> O I must be guided without a stumble
> Into the arms of my dear lass.

Elspeth never cared much for rivers, always being a sea person, but she wondered how it was that all these years she had allowed herself to live so close to water that was so close to sea and done nothing. She wondered how much of her life had been and was still like that — so close and yet so far away. She was not given to thought, it was too painful a process for her; easier to dream and remember and recall a verse of a ballad. Even now, as the doubt crept into her mind, she tried to shake it off, preferring to remember Jenner's head on her breast, his body and his hair dark against the white of her body, the white of her sheets. The power of his sobbing against her ribcage, which felt as if it came from inside her own body. As if she herself were weeping and did not know the cause. To wallow in these beautiful romantic feelings always used to be much finer than to engage with the complication of analysing her misery.

But now she admitted that the pavement was stone-hard real, and her good shoes thin-soled, and the sheets would need to be changed and washed and laboriously dried. Her life was not primarily Jenner sobbing in her arms, it was Jenner shouting and slamming the door of his room, and treating her like a domestic.

Think of him as a wave, Fergal said. *You hold your breath, don't you, and it goes over your head.* Sitting with Fergal outside a little café on this waterfront, sipping wicked coffee out of a tiny cup, Fergal had said, *You need to look in the mirror some time. You're lucky, you can wear jeans. My sisters would kill you if they could have your hips.* He wasn't a flatterer: he said it because he meant it, that was why Fergal was so infinitely lovable. He was like the son or son-in-law she had wanted. But then, she thought, she didn't really want Fergal for a son, she wanted him for a friend, her own friend; it was better than sons. Children left home and had their own lives, but friends were for ever. *My friends*, she said in her head, *my friends Fergal and Theodora. I am going to stay with my friends Fergal and Theodora in Australia.* Tasting it, enjoy the taste. Maybe somehow the family would fall into place if she had the friends as well. She used to have friends, but she didn't see them often these days, Jenner being Jenner and Somerset being where it was. She'd never found it hard to make friends, and even now there were always people smiling, making the approaches; she knew how it was done, you got involved in the kirk, joined the

Junior Sailors, offered to help with the Girl Guides. She could make friends here, or she could go to a new place and start all over again, rent a little flat, buy a new white washing machine on the never-never, just as Fergal urged her to do, and make friends there, without the burden of constantly justifying herself, of waiting for the random application of her husband's anger.

Fergal said she should take a job and get a woman to do. Three pounds an hour, and you never have to think about floors again. His mum, he said, often joked that she was a freedom fighter, setting women free from guilt over their floors.

But Jenner would not like it. He would not like her gadding into town. He would offend any help she found. Such silly reasons, looking back over the years, but so compelling at the time. Of such trivial things is life built up, misery and happiness, little things.

The coffee bar on the waterfront is closed – Sunday morning is a gloomy time to look for civilised pleasures. But Elspeth is determined. She walks further, finds a swanky-looking bistro, too smart for her. Walks away sadly, stands by the window of Marks and Spencer's and peers in. New clothes. She looks at the prices, and thinks about her savings, all those ten-pound notes nestled in her tin, and thinks, why ever not? Sees her reflection in the glass, the shape of her head, and thinks Fergal is right about that sharp new haircut. And why not? Why not? Other women do. We are not paupers. She turns around and walks back to the bistro, goes boldly inside and asks for a cappuccino and a croissant. And amazingly they serve her as politely as if she were the Princess Royal. *What a silly I am!* She reads a magazine full of celebrity photographs, and smiles at its inanity. Anything is possible.

When she gets back to the farm, the notion of unlimited

possibility begins to shrink and cower. The hens crowd around her, for a moment you might think with affection, but in fact with a version of affection called hunger. They have not been fed. Nor has Jenner.

She enters into the house, through the front door, head up, Fair Isabell of Roch Royall, and out of his chamber comes her lord, her true love, pipe in his hand and wrath in his heart. The dogs raise their heads as she goes by, to listen to the affray.

'What is this, woman?' he shouts at her in the hall. 'What do you mean by going out gallivanting and leaving not so much as a cold potato in the house? What sort of wife are you? Every day of the week free to go out and dally, but no, it must be Sunday she chooses, when she should be at home. When it is customary for a family to eat together, if there were any family left. What have we here – a cold oven, an empty larder, no meat prepared, no pudding, no vegetables, nothing *to* prepare, indeed.'

The onset of disappointment gives her courage. Perhaps after all it is not possible to do anything, go anywhere, drink coffee and be urbane under any circumstance. Perhaps not, but she does not have to put up with this – this diminution of her person. Maybe she will not be a famous yachtswoman with a private marina, but she is still a hard-working, faithful and loving wife, and she does not deserve to be treated like a skivvy.

Elspeth takes a deep breath, waiting for the wave to break and exhaust itself. She is horrified instead to feel tears rush towards the surface, and longs for Fergal or Theo to walk in through the door and save her. But she struggles with these wasteful tears, and makes his voice fade into a watery distance.

> *I'll show you where the white fishes swim*
> *All on the bottom of the deep salt sea.*

The impossibility of protesting about the unfairness of his criticism, distress at the return of his anger, the old sense of isolation and weakness . . . these feelings wash over her as his voice washed over her. But then she knows something has changed, because she does not apologise.

'Are the young folk here, or have they all gone out?'

'I neither know nor care. Tracking their whereabouts is a waste of my attention and a drain on my resources. You may pursue them since you are so besotted by them.'

'I must feed the hens,' she says and goes into the kitchen without looking at him. He is the same man whose head last night she nursed at her breast, as he wept with inarticulate misery. She understands that the words issue out of his mouth with the same randomness as his tears. She understands that his anger is not directed at her, and it is quite conceivable that he believes he loves her. She wishes it were possible to make sense of Jenner, just once, to put a grid up over him and see why he does what he does, and says what he says. But as she passes through the cold kitchen and out to the shed where she keeps food for the hens, she knows that it is too late for that. What Jenner does and says has become a series of emotional reactions to triggers long gone. She knows that she lacks the strength and wisdom to work through the layers and arrive at an understanding of Jenner. She once believed that loving him was enough.

In the comfortable dark of the feed shed, surrounded by the practical, homely smell of the grains, she stands suspended, the plastic measure in her hand, the feed bucket in the other. She bends over the sack of combined chicken feed, a nameless farrago of reprocessed matter, with its smell of nothing definable. She has too much feed, she notices, bought cheap at the market, but proving on closer examination to be time-expired. Damp is creeping into the bottom of the sacks, and there are weevils abroad, and possibly rats. She realises, bending there, that her life is a complete sham. She hates hens; she hates farms; she hates this dark tree-bound corner; she does not understand her husband; and therefore she cannot be sure she loves him. It is possible after all that he is the demon lover.

> *She hadna sailed a league, a league,*
> *A league but barely three,*
> *Till grim grim grew his countenance*
> *And gurly grew the sea.*
>
> *O hold your tongue my dearest dear*
> *Let all your follies abee*
> *I'll show you where the white lilies grow*
> *In the bottom of the sea.*

She had bought an idea of love. And now it had reached its use-by date.

What Jenner had failed to tell her, among the many other things, was that Fergal had been summoned that Sunday morning for an interview by South Western Television. He and Theo had driven over to the site of the battle, where Fergal was to meet a representative of the developers, and be shown their revised plans for the Sedgemoor site before the eyes of the world.

Theo combed his hair for him, and then ruffled it up again. She leant against the car in the pleasant Sunday sunshine and looked across the moor, where the debris of the battle was being tidied up by a group of Brownies. Fergal was introduced to a man in an expensive grey suit, who seemed to tower over him. The camera crew swarmed around the two of them as they shook hands, looked at some drawings and plans, and walked around the moor pointing to landmarks and stopping beside trees.

Then Fergal led the man in the grey suit into a copse to demonstrate the thickness of growth required as a habitat for nightingales. The camera had a bit of trouble following them, and the grey man wore a rumpled air when he emerged. Fergal explained that nightingales will only stay, even for a night, in copses so thick that a man wearing a white shirt is invisible ten feet away. He explained this in front of the cameras as if he'd known it all his life, though Theo had pulled the information off the Net for him not twenty-four hours before.

He was just brilliant.

The developers, scenting bad publicity, had drawn up a proposal to preserve some trees and stretches of moor and water, as part of the development. Fergal had been trundled up to say thank you in front of the nation.

When the walkabout and the interviews were over, the grey suit drove off in his Mercedes. Fergal, grinning like a hound dog, lit a cigarette and leant on the car next to Theo.

'He can keep his Merc,' he said. 'I've got a smashing chauffeur.'

'You were great,' said Theo. 'They'll be trotting you out now every time that they want an alternative comment. I'll get to see you on TV in Australia.'

'I practised what I said like anything,' said Fergal. 'Eat your heart out, Leonardo DiCaprio.'

'You were remarkably gracious,' said Theo, 'considering what a nasty cheap compromise it is.'

'Yeah, well that's the trouble, innit? I mean, I want the whole copse, not some fucking specimen trees. But then I thought, well, one tree saved is better than no tree saved. And maybe that jerk's wife will watch him on TV and get interested in nightingales, and ask him why she's never heard one. And then she gets to be a local councillor, and next time, next time . . .'

'It's quite funny really,' said Theo. 'There weren't any trees at all when the battle was fought.'

'Yeah, trees grow again. Given time.'

Theo thought, in that case it wasn't fair, because she and Fergal didn't have time. They only had this one chance, and Fergal was going to let it slide. But she didn't say anything.

That same afternoon, not one to miss his opportunity, Rupert turned up in her station wagon, without sword, plumes or horse. She unloaded twelve flat-pack cartons from the back and carried them up to Robin's room, where the two of them packed up Robin's books and papers with Elspeth's assistance. Robin couldn't look at his mother directly.

Theo and Fergal lounged against the doorposts watching the activity. Elspeth was trying to pack Robin's clothes and press household linen on Rupert. Robin took his crucifix off the wall and swathed it in bubble wrap. Rupert looked at it with a grown-up frown, as if it were a teddy bear he had insisted on taking with him. Robin began to disconnect his computer.

'I'd like to show Father my website before I go,' he said. 'He's never seen it.'

'You mean your Jesus page?' said Theo. 'Oh, but he has seen it. We had a look at it at college. It's amazing, I have to say. Though it got kinda embarrassing when this big Jesus figure started to grow out of the screen with his finger pointing and talking to us.'

'But what did Father say?'

'He said it was a magnificent example of misapplied engineering, and when did the notion arise that Jesus of Nazareth was a white man. But actually he was enormously impressed.'

'He's right about the pictures of Jesus,' said Robin. 'But the sponsors have certain ideas about how He looked.'

'Well, I dunno,' said Fergal. 'On that shroud thingy he looks white to me.'

'Forgery,' said Theo. 'Crude forgery.'

'Well, fuck me,' said Fergal, 'I remember a sermon on Easter Day when the priest brought along his bedsheet to show us what the shroud looked like, and told us all how God had confounded the clever with this miracle. You just shattered my faith.'

'Do you think you could continue this discussion elsewhere?' said Rupert.

Theo and Fergal went for a walk in the woods, so Fergal could have a cigarette.

'I'll show you something,' she said, a phrase that used to get you going when you were a kid.

Theo led him up towards the gate, and then into the trees. It was a dull purple afternoon; the light was fading fast. Inside the copse was a premature twilight, sprinkled with late snowdrops and brave bluebells and a few pale primroses.

Fergal felt excited by the secrecy of the place, but she hadn't brought him into this wood to steal a kiss or cop a feel. She threaded her way through the trees and then crouched down. He joined her, down there among the leaf mould, and saw the gnome family sprouting under the trees, the most amusing mushrooms you ever found.

'Poisonous, I'd say,' he said.

She laughed. Her laughing was so lovely he wished he could make jokes continuously, so she would crinkle her eyes and show her teeth and make that raw Australian sound. He looked at the gnomes and wondered if they were funny at all, whether what was at Nightingales was cruel or funny.

He asked Theodora.

'Maybe it's both,' she said.

*　　*　　*

Monday, Fergal went up to London for his mum's birthday, and a spot of modelling. In the car to the station Theo was very quiet, so he told her all about his mum and her birthday parties, and the surprises he and his sisters concocted, explaining how when they were young and poor, his mother had always managed a jolly time on nothing, setting up practical jokes and treasure hunts, mainly for her own entertainment. No one could get more mileage out of a fag, a good joke, a bottle of stout and a hank of crêpe paper than Fergal's mum. She loved to organise an outing, even had the old farts from Camden Calligraphers going on mystery bus trips. Took all these faded schoolmasters and arty-crafty ladies to the dogs one time. Talk about laugh. So Fergal and his sisters like to do one for her. She always acts all surprised.

At the station he made Theo smile again. He let her buy him a return ticket.

'Course I'm coming back,' he said. 'I owe you a pint.'

'What shall I do when you really go?' she said.

'E-mail,' he replied, quite cheerfully. 'Robin give me an address on his account. Moonbeam@easy.net.'

'How will you get to read it?'

'No sweat. There's always a well-wisher with an Internet account somewhere. Anyway, colleges are full of unguarded computers. And there's cyber cafés.'

Theo imagined her cheery little messages, full of news approximating to what she wants to say, streaming across thousands of miles of network, bounced from one server to another, none of them conscious of, or interested in, the unwritten words in the stream of characters they pass on.

She sees herself sitting in her sunny office with its nice view of the gardens and pool, her state of the art computer placed square on the glossy surface of her desk, her flourishing collection of CDROMs in the shelf to hand, with rather fewer books, her colour laser printer purring in its specially built cabinet, next to the glossy picture of a Charollais bull, his noble body demarked with cuts of meat, which she has designed and printed, sheet by sheet, on this very printer. She's sitting there at the end of the day, waiting for Tom to drop by and take her for a swim and a pizza, doing her e-mail to fill in the last moments, reading, answering, and scanning her inbox one more time, fetching new messages one more time, just in case Fergal has answered. But he never does.

She wants to cry, like a child who has never been denied before, for whom the affront hurts as much as the deprivation. Theo is wise enough to see that her tears are unreasonable and petty because she does not even know what she wants. She doesn't want Fergal to be other than he is. She doesn't want him to lie down and be tickled by anyone who offers to scratch his belly. She doesn't want him to be a tame performing monkey, and do what she wants. She wants him to be the completely self-articulated, detached person that he is. But she cannot bear the thought that he will be lost to her.

I can't bear this, she cries in her head, confronted for the first time in her life with suffering. *This isn't right!*

In Theo's mind, there must always be a solution, a tidy way out. It is only a matter of application. Do the research, keep on at the problem, get more data, enlarge your hypothesis, and the solution will appear.

She left him on the platform and drove from the station on to college and cheered herself up by composing an e-mail to her friend Juliet, in which she didn't mention Fergal even once. She reckoned this was OK, because their e-mail dialogue, full of jokes and gossip, often left out large matters. Juliet never expressed her philosophical disdain for Theodora's professional work, which she described to other e-mail correspondents as *doing things to animals so that the men can get more meat off them*. Theo in turn never suggested that she felt that her friend should get out and earn a decent salary doing a proper job. Friendship, they both realised early on, requires both parties to take a selective view of the other, and hold it firmly in place. Every week the latest instalment in the Jenner story – comic book or high drama serial – provided Theo with ready material. She was conscious that she downplayed her own part in some events. But she rationalised this by thinking that stories are better without the bit players.

That week Theo wrote:

I'm finding JR more and more of a puzzle, and wonder whether he could be saved for the nation. After Marg left home, I took my life in my hands and asked him how he felt. He said he was proud yet sorrowful that the Temple of the Sacred Mysteries had been removed from his house, for in that place (i.e. Marg's attic) he felt unclean and yet freshly absolved!!!!!

This is typical of the JR rhetoric – completely OTT but I wondered if there wasn't a shred of hope. Then again, I guess it could be an indicator of that But-I-*Adore*-Women syndrome which is the most insidious form of sexism. I'm glad most sexism is easier to detect and classify than his. For example, much though I hate to admit it, I've never had my work treated more seriously by anyone – male or female. No crap about co-authoring the paper either (though anyone else would, even Prof. Betsy). He takes my ideas, even the half-arsed ones, seriously, listens when I speak, argues intelligently, and concedes if I win.

If I only worked with him and didn't know him, I might think he was all right. Though having got to know him, I find it a lot easier to take the outbursts when they come.

Since he got off the hook with the council, he has been quite human and has smiled once or twice, though a fair bit of overbearing nonsense still comes out over coffee. At home he still locks himself away in his room, and emerges to snarl. The other day he came out when Elspeth and I were having Sat. morning coffee – bare-chested for Christ's sake! – all hair and flab (must've been a hunk once though) – holding out a shirt for E. to iron, without even a word. I told her not to, but she did it anyway.

I think he does things like that for a reaction – to get E. to say no.

But is he really worse than the others? You get so many men these days who never say a word out of line, but treat your work like a girl's hobby to keep her occupied till she gets married. And steal your research and put their name at the top of your papers. Akshly, I thought Dr R. was paranoid about having his work stolen, but I'm wondering whether there mightn't be a grain of truth in it. He showed me the notes for his address at the 1983 IAAS Conf. and they definitely broke ground on maternal prion transmission, and also on cross-species mutation of prion diseases (i.e. predicting that BSE in sheep is not the same disease as scrapie, and therefore suggesting the appearance of a human form different from CJD) yeah, I know, dead boring. And quite a bit of work to back it up – not just scribbles on envelopes. And people who were there went away and followed up and never involved him in the loop. But I wondered whether being cold-shouldered and stolen from and left out of the club isn't only done to women, but to guys like J. whose faces don't fit for whatever reasons.

Do you remember that little fat Jewish guy in the English Dept, with the way cool blonde wife? He was super-bright and his stuff was massive (all about cross-cultural dialectic) but the straight white guys in English didn't like him. They used to tell scurrilous stories about him (and her) and start rumours and deride his scholarship, which was lunacy, because he could buy and sell them. But he left after a year – remember that farewell party at Pascal's? They wore glitter on their cheeks and danced all night. That was the one where I – no, let's not remember that!!!!!!!!!

Anyway, I'm beginning to wonder whether JR might not be basically on the right side after all . . .

This e-mail was destined never to be sent, for while she was composing it, a communication arrived from Juliet which changed everything.

Juliet wrote:

. . . I've been doing some research. No, not like yours babe, life's too short for that. But when you told me about your JR and that harassment case, I knew that name rang a bell, akshly, tooted a bloody great hooter, but I thort I had better check first in case I was wrong and bad mouthed him unfairly – tho' from what you say that seems impossible to do!

I remembered an article from *Lot's Wife* about sexual harassment cases at the unis and how they got swept under the carpet in the seventies. His name came up. I arst around sisters I knew in the department at the time, and they confirmed it. Akshly it was worse than I thort. Apparently he was a legend in his own lifetime. There was this joke called Dr Ransfield's Terms Test. In those days you had to get a thing called Terms before you could sit an exam – if you hadn't been to enough lectures and labs you failed Terms and couldn't sit, even though you might easily pass. JR would routinely waive the Terms requirement on his courses for girls who slept with him. It was common knowledge apparently. Well he'd been screwing his way through Zoology One for several years before the shit hit the proverbial. A third year student who had passed the Terms test once or twice complained to a female staff member that he'd practically raped her. And then had the gall to give her a restricted pass in a paper, so she couldn't do honours. It went to the council and all that crap, but nothing got public and JR left the country quietly and nothing was said.

So I decided to check this story out. I went to the records man in the registry and terrorised the shit out of him by saying I was preparing a position paper on sexual harassment for the Students' Union and needed access to council minutes. I burbled about the Official Information Act and stuff, until he lay down and cried *take me!* So I got into a room with all these brown folders, and micro-fiches, and a funky old character mode computer. And he sat there and *sweated*, babe. You wouldn't believe the things I found out – like who they've got files on. Time for that later. I think I'll write a paper on it all. I zeroed in on JR, and it's all true, only there was heaps more, but he wouldn't let me photocopy it, so I had to takes notes which is a pain.

He sure got around. Not only Zoo but also Computer Science where he was seconded because they were short of experienced (!) staff. There were pages of minutes from council meetings. Apparently his defence was that Terms was an antiquated concept which ought to be abolished, and he saw nothing wrong in allowing people to sit the exam if they were willing. He said that the main complainant was motivated by revenge, because he had ended their affair, which was quite above board, because neither of them was married, and he didn't believe the university forbade sexual relationships between staff and students. Her grades had been entirely unaffected by their relationship, and any other staff member could be called to bear witness (see I got the jargon).

But there were heaps of minor complaints, orchestrated by your mate Prof. Betsy, who wasn't a prof. then but a radical young thing, and she'd got about and collected statements. Apparently the main complainant was devastated (sic) because she found out that JR was simultaneously screwing about three other students.

Basically the council gave up. They didn't summon any of the girls to give evidence, Betsy argued that it would be too gruelling for them with all those white middle-aged men sitting behind a table salivating, and they might take fright and withdraw their statements. So instead they closed the whole affair, and told JR to pack his bags and leave – and this is the good bit – *by the end of the next academic year.*

I went and saw Betsy afterwards, didn't exactly accuse her of sending you into the lion's maw, though it kinda came up. She reckons that you are just the woman to slice off his balls and fry them before his eyes for breakfast, as he richly deserves (I quote!) Apparently (and this is the worst bit in many ways), according to Betsy, he got a job at Southampton, and got railroaded out of there in exactly the same way.

She reckons he's quite dangerous, and almost certainly unreformed. I told her a bit about the doormat wife and the nutty children and the dogs and the third-rate college in the middle of Dullsville, and she laughed and said *There is a Goddess!* . . .

XIII

EVERY DAY THAT Fergal was away, Theo was unhappy. She supposed that this was because of Juliet's message, which filled the front of her mind every waking minute. She felt isolated and homesick. She longed to escape from the farm, from England; she wished she had gone up to London with Fergal. London, once a dirty jostling disappointment, now was a place of fascination.

She did not know what she wanted, and had mislaid the ability to analyse her situation.

She had stepped up her work at the college to such a degree that Jenner attempted to reprimand her for working too hard. She had taken to staying so late that she fell asleep at the bench – anything to avoid going back to the farm, to the sight of Elspeth's eager face, to accidental encounters with Jenner, to the emptiness of the caravan. Each night she dropped into her bed miserable, but too tired to care; she got up as soon as she woke and drove to work. To avoid catching Elspeth's eye, she had no meals at the farmhouse. She looked in the mirror in the college shower room and saw that she had grown pale.

If questioned, she'd have claimed it was all because of Juliet's disclosure about Jenner. Elspeth assumed it was caused by Fergal's absence, and kept smiling. Jenner made no such assumption, and began to crackle with alarm.

At first Theo was overwhelmed with disbelief – that

Jenner could practise such deception on her and behave in so unforgivably underhand a manner in sending her before the council on his behalf, when in fact he was as guilty as sin. Then she became suffused with anger that he had caused her the excruciating embarrassment of being the champion of her arch-enemy.

Why had she done it? In her misery and confusion she tried to call back the sense of rightness that had inspired her to defend him. She was still faithful to the principle she had espoused, that academic freedom must be preserved as passionately as the nightingales, but the principle wavered and distorted in the glare of her humiliation. When word got around in Melbourne, Theo would not be able to show her face at wimmen's events. She would be the Judas, the secret spy, the pig in panties. She'd never get a chance to defend herself; the defence would sound so feeble anyway. *And you believed him?* they'd say and all laugh in that way she remembered from school. Only then Theo joined in; she was never the butt of that laugh. *And you believed him?*

Only she hadn't believed him, not really. Underneath, in her private parts, she had known he'd done it. *Why, for God's sake?* the wimmen cried. *Why would you want to defend him? What are you?*

She couldn't understand why she had so readily accepted his devious denial, which, on reflection, was not a denial at all.

You could say he'd skirted round the subject. Even if she was reluctant to trust her intuition, she should have realised his guilt from the extremity of his reaction. A man who has committed one minor indiscretion does not cancel all his classes and spend the whole day locked up in his room drinking, not even when that man is as unbalanced as Jenner Ransfield. Now she could see that his reaction was violent because he saw before him the ruin of his career, brought about by his own weakness and lust.

Well deserved, Theo's friends would say. She thought she agreed. When men like Jenner Ransfield got their just punishment, she rejoiced. Theo knew of several cases; overbearing sexually predatory men in positions of power who had used their power to obtain sexual favours from women, but who at last had been cast down. Within the academic world such men had the greatest difficulty in securing a position after they had been disgraced. Even outside that world their chances of suitable employment were slim, and they could scarcely appear on any public platform, for fear of being boycotted or shouted down. *Just deserts!* Theo cried when she heard of this revenge.

But he was not some Old White Man who had felt up young women. He was Jenner Ransfield, with all his history and his complexity, into which she was beginning to gain insight. She didn't want to ruin him. She accused herself of pusillanimity, of slewing away from the cause. Her duty was clear, yet she couldn't do it.

She could hardly bring herself to speak to Jenner at all. This was especially difficult because they had so recently resumed communications that to break them off again required explanation. Last time he had known why she was angry. Now she could not explain without opening up the whole disgusting subject.

She decided to start writing up her results, although she wasn't quite ready, so that every time he came by she was strenuously engaged. She allowed him to pretend that her low spirits were caused by Fergal's absence. Well, let them both pretend that for the time being, while she worked out what she was going to do.

Perhaps she might do nothing – swallow her anger and shame and go home? Yet sisterhood cried out for justice, and her pride called out for revenge.

Sisterhood, yes, but at what cost? Her kind heart rose

up in protest at the thought of Elspeth in despair at her husband's ruin.

Justice, yes. But for whom? Would Caroline Hayes get a different grade? Did Caroline Hayes deserve a better grade? Would any of those girls, the whole pale blonde procession, get a different result? Would they get back their self-esteem? Would they suddenly gain the respect of their bosses and their partners?

Revenge – yes, but when she glanced at Jenner, hovering at her shoulder, his forehead pitted with the effort of respecting her silence, painstakingly keeping his distance, she saw a tragic fool, a Humbert Humbert, a pitiable victim of himself. She did not know how she would find the strength to crush him, and she asked herself, when he was broken, who would be healed?

But he had done wrong. He must be punished. It was the duty of Theodora Potts, holder of the secret of his last offence, to ensure that he was punished. It was unthinkable that such a catalogue of crimes should stand uncensured. Juliet expected it, Prof. Betsy expected it, all the sisters and women yet unborn expected it. This much was clear. But how was she to do it?

The council was the just and proper place to handle Jenner's case. It was the college's code of conduct he had breached, and there was some satisfaction to be had from seeing the enemy destroy himself. Theo believed in structures; if she were in power, she would replace the council with a gender-balanced, elected body, and the meetings with long facilitated workshops, but she would not do away with a council. She was sure that there had to be a recognisable authority for any body to operate.

But taking Jenner before the council was a half-arsed solution. The council was white, middle-aged men, somewhat like him, only none of them held an intellectual candle to him. They would cheerfully destroy him out of feelings of intellectual inadequacy, sexual jealousy, and deeply suppressed anti-Semitism, not for the sake of justice and the rights of women. Theo felt quite sure that if he were truly one of them – flabby, second-rate and decently English – he would be excused. But being as he was, brilliant, Jewish and sexually threatening, the council would rush to condemn him, to make an example of him, thus fulfilling two goals in one: to get rid of a person who did not fit, and to demonstrate publicly their commitment to social and sexual justice. Theo didn't see why you should play along with the enemy when he pretended to be on your side.

Perhaps she should tell the sisterhood at campus, and let them take unofficial revenge – slogans on the car, posters on his door, warnings circulated to his classes? She'd seen that done plenty. A man subjected to such campaigning lasted a semester, no more. He got out long before he could be pushed. It was crude, it was cruel, but it was terrifically effective and in some ways more just than letting the men blow one of their own kind to bits to encourage the others to more discreet forms of sexism.

But Theo didn't have any time for the sisterhood on campus. She thought them a bunch of wimps, playing at feminism while they waited to get married. Not that she'd spent much time with them, but then you don't spend time with people you don't have time for, do you? Delivering Jenner into their lily-white hands seemed another half-arsed solution – they'd discuss his case at meetings, draw horrified breaths, look at Jenner with fascination, put themselves in his way, and then end up by going to the council anyway. The fact that he had betrayed Theo would go unpunished, for her defence of him would stand as evidence of her collaboration. *After all*, she could hear them say, *she didn't have the guts to deal with it herself, and it's in her interest to stick with him, isn't it?*

I mean, he has his academic reputation, for what that's worth. Well, it obviously matters to her. They're probably lovers, look at the amount of time they spend together. His poor wife. You think that Theo Potts would have better taste, but then you know what Australians are like . . .

Which left telling Elspeth as her only course of action. But sister or no, Theo could not quite face the awfulness of facing a woman of middle years and telling her she was married to a raping, lying bastard. A woman, moreover, whom she liked, whose hospitality she had accepted and whose friendship she had nourished. A conversation of that kind took real courage, and the absolute conviction that you were right.

Round and round go her thoughts, and she longs for Fergal, so she can ask him what she should do. And then despises herself for being so poor a woman that she must ask a man to make up her mind for her.

When Fergal sees her standing on the platform, he knows at once that something is wrong, and he assumes that Jenner is the cause of it. He thinks that Jenner has finally gone and done it to her, and he kicks himself for leaving her there at his mercy. He's been telling himself she's OK, a grown-up, doesn't need his protection. He's been trying not to get involved, trying not to think about her, and then this happens.

Then she catches sight of him and smiles. The great big difference he had imagined between them vanishes. The gulf he'd conjured up, cut by class, circumstance, nationality, aspiration – it isn't there. There's clear ground all the way.

He thinks he never wants to be greeted off a train again, because it will never ever feel as good as this does. She opens her arms out wide, and they kiss each other, properly, on the mouth, though he really wasn't expecting to do that.

'Jeez, I am so glad to see *you*,' she says.

He tells her all about his week. He wants to tell her so bad, and he knows she won't come out with it straight away, whatever it is that's troubling her. He's wearing his new Armani jeans and a little black T-shirt that depicts Tintin smoking a joint. There's real cash in his pocket. A great big wad of it. He's been having a ball. They drive along to the supermarket, and he tells her all about it.

'It's like a new world up there, with this new government an' that. All the old lefties are dancing in the streets. It's like the new broom got to everything. I come up the stairs at the station by me mum's place, and they was clean – like someone had taken trouble over it – bothered to wash them an' that, like they cared. And then I come out the station and there's one of the buskers from the Tube and the bloke who sells the *Big Issue* bent over laughing like they was Dean Martin and Frank Sinatra. And when I walked over to Mum's I only spotted one condom and one decent-sized shit on the pavement. And when I got there, the council done a facelift on the blocks, and they were all painted poncy colours, with push-button locks on the front doors and little gardens. An' I saw me mate Homer in the garden out the front, doing the flowers.'

'Homer? You're kidding me.'

'Yeah, he's Sri Lankan. Lovely man. One of God's saints. There he is, watering the flowers, and smiles at me. An' I say, Wotcha Homer, and he says, Innit lovely, Fergal? Innit lovely? I mean, here we are in a mean old dirty street, all the shops got grilles on the windows, blocks right on top of each other, about a thousand cars a minute going down Gray's Inn Road pouring out shit and six square inches of garden per resident and he says, Innit lovely?'

It's such a warm and generous day they decide to have a

picnic. Fergal buys cold chicken and white wine and nice crusty bread and pickles, and they borrow a rug and a picnic basket from Elspeth. They invite her along as well, but she declines, not because of Jenner, she says firmly, but because she doesn't want to play gooseberry.

They find a pool of sunlight among the woods. No one is about. They set out the rug and the food, open the wine, sit cross-legged and drink to each other. It's a perfect day – too early for wasps, too mild for sunburn, perfect for getting pleasantly pissed and seeing what happens. She sits, knees by her chin, watching him as if he were part of the picnic, the really delicious item left till last.

Though she looks at him like a round-eyed kid contemplating her party table, Fergal can see the misery in her face, underneath the shininess of her. He thinks of the brown fingers of his friend Homer in the garden, holding up for his delight a new poppy, common as muck, impossibly red, creased from its confinement, about to spread itself to the sun for its own moment of glory.

His heart is full of love and full of hatred. He can feel the knife in his pocket pressing into his flesh. He knows that Theo needs to talk, but he understands that a woman does not want to confide in a man when another man has damaged her. He thinks that men understand inflicting pain better than surviving it. Fergal does not want that to be true of him.

He lights a cigarette, the first he's bought with his own money in months. She's generous about smokes, the way she puts up with them. In every respect, a gorgeous person.

'Don't taste as good when you paid for them,' he says.

She smiles at him. His tiniest intestine twists itself into a knot of pleasure. In response, he makes the effort.

'Are you OK?' he says.

So little it takes. Three words, and she's in tears, not just in tears, but in his arms. Sort of. Arms round him, and his round her, tricky with the fag, not very Mills & Boon, but shit we're past that.

'No,' she says, 'I'm not. I'm very not OK.'

'You can tell me,' he says.

She tells him. It's not what he expected at all. That Ransfield, sure, he's at the core of it – but in a far meaner and more complicated way than he'd have guessed. Theo's misery turns him inside out – she is so high-minded, full of pity for Elspeth, and consideration for that man.

. . . the invisible worm that flies in the night . . .

'Not you, though?' he says. 'He never touched you? You sure you're not covering up for him?'

He strokes her hair; he's never done that before, though he's woken with his nose stuffed into it. The smell of it, hay mixed with vanilla shampoo, he'll never forget it as long as he lives. It's springy, resistant to caress, as she is herself. She wants his comfort, but maybe she knows what lies behind it – maybe she's got a viewfinder, with little snapshots of the inside of his head, the flowers and ferns and baby birds that portray her, the buttocks and cunts that betray him.

'I don't know what to do,' she says.

Poor Theodora, she who always knows where she's headed. For him it's the normal state, indecision – might do this, might do that. But for her it's like being a kid lost in a funfair – what was a glorious day out is suddenly hell, and all the jollity is a cruel joke. Life has been sweet to her, and she has responded by being sweet; now life has done the dirty, and what is she to do?

'Sometimes,' he says, 'you have to do hard things.'

'Yes, but which one?'

He has many ideas of hard things to do. Diving on a digger, locking yourself on to a crane, climbing the last ten feet of Silbury Hill – these are images that float into his mind, but they're nice TV images, not his. His images are the last three flights of stairs in the dark when the lift's broke; the extra-high wall you climb on by scrambling over the waste bins when they're after you; the cigarette you deliberately light when you should scarper.

'What you have to work out –' he begins.

He's distracted by her loveliness. He wants to tell her how it is: that she isn't pretty – though that isn't something you ever say to a girl – but so lovely that he wants to devour her, the way he wanted to crush the emergent poppy Homer showed him, just because it was too precious to endure. He didn't crush the poppy – he hardly touched it – but the feeling was there, and the feeling constrained him from saying what he should have. Just as now the feeling constrains him from holding her and telling her. He struggles to be wise.

He thinks things would seem simpler lying down, but he doesn't want to let go of her. He eases himself backwards, and her with him, without jarring. He lies on his back, looking at the trees and the sky, the best things, and holds her against him, so she has her head on his chest. He knows what this is: classic romantic stuff, but he likes it. It feels good, violins notwithstanding. This is the scene from the Merchant-Ivory movie, where the low-born hero embraces the upper-class heroine in grainy autumnal tones. And they live happily ever after.

He draws on his cigarette.

'You have to work out who it's all for.'

She's sort of crying still, but the rhythm is changing, it's more regular, manageable. He has one hand on her head still, on the springy hair, and the other, with the fag in it, further down. He can feel the line of her bra. He knows where this goes, and it isn't going to help. How can a bra strap be allowed to distract him, when he's slept with her every night for weeks? But he stubs out the end of the fag and puts his hand back.

'What I think is this,' he says, looking up at the trees. 'When you do something, whether it's me up a tree or you shafting Ransfield, you gotta know who it's for. Like, is it for yourself? Or your mum or your girlfriend? Or is it for Elspeth? Or that girl he poked?

'You gotta ignore people getting hurt, people suffering. Someone always gets hurt. Stop a bypass, the poor buggers on the through road get choked to death. Old lady comes out to help save a tree, she gets thrown to the ground, breaks her hip. People get hurt. And you have to ignore suffering – cos Ransfield suffers too – he knows he's done wrong, that burns him up, doesn't stop him, but it hurts him. Then he loses his job. He burns in hell. He might suffer more than anyone. You ignore that. You just ask, who am I doing this for?'

She doesn't say anything, but she's stopped crying, which means that she's thinking it through. He finds that he wants to make love to her more than anything else in the world.

'You be pissed off if I have another fag?' he says instead.

'Don't be ridiculous,' she says, 'after all this time? How many cigarettes have you smoked since we met?'

'Yeah, but this is different.'

She pulls herself up into a sitting position. He doesn't want to let go of her, but she's smiling as she looks at him, head on one side, a sharp sweet robin-redbreast look. He cranks himself up to sit opposite her, wishing she were still in his arms, in a wonderful innocent fifties movie clinch. But here they are, eye to eye, possibly the most dangerous posture for two people who sleep together to adopt.

'So,' he says, completely distracted, 'I.'

He leans forward and kisses her, because he can't not.

She tears the kiss off before it's finished.

'What am I going to do?' she cries, but he isn't sure what she means.

He wriggles a cigarette out of his back pocket and lights it to buy himself time.

'It's for the girls we don't know,' Theo says. 'Caroline Hayes isn't an innocent, but there are girls we know nothing about, girls he's screwed in the past who might have been damaged emotionally. And as he gets older and madder, he may do more serious harm. Even if there's only one who's innocent, just one, who goes to see him in tears because other people have said he's helpful, in an ironic tone of voice that she didn't get. He puts his arms around her, gets out his handkerchief. You've got to bear in mind that quite a lot of women think of him as a sort of Heathcliff. Very sexy.'

'Pull the other one.'

She reaches out and messes up his hair.

'Can I have another kiss?'

'What is this, Fergal? You're not like this.'

'Well I am today.'

'This little girl – the one we are postulating – likes the attention, but then he puts his hand on her breast, and she doesn't like that. But there's no one about and she's too timid to scream and slap his face, and one things leads to another, and she never quite says no, although she seriously doesn't want sex. Maybe she's a virgin, or unprotected, and too shy to explain. But it's too late to escape, or maybe she tries and he starts to get angry, and accuses her of leading him on. His anger is pretty horrible. You feel like a six-year-old cowering in a pew.'

'Yeah, I've heard him. Me dad used to hit me mum, and she'd say, Well, I've got me war wounds to prove service. What she meant was, he showed what he was, because he hit her. That Ransfield doesn't leave any bruises, but he hits you just the same.'

'And he doesn't even realise he's hurting anyone,' says Theo. 'They don't, these sort of men. Their world view is unshakeable: man at the centre, filling up all the available space, and girls on the periphery, adjuncts to their being.'

'How d'you know that, then?'

'Received wisdom.'

'Not experience, then?'

'What exactly are you driving at, Fergal?'

'Dunno.'

He strokes her cheek because now he's started touching her he can't stop. He knows exactly what he means, but putting it into words precise enough for her is too hard. He means that knowledge about people and how they operate must be based on experience; you can't get it second-hand. Because if you do, you end up believing that little ladies like staying home and doing housework, and women don't really mind being beaten and girls who get raped were asking for it. He can't express this clearly enough for Theo's mind, but it's so important he almost wants to cry with the frustration of not explaining.

Also with the need to put his arms around her and keep her safe, but she needs to keep talking.

'Let's say, for argument's sake, let's say there exists, or may exist in the future, one girl he's coerced into sex – she's the person I've got to do this for. We can't make it better for her if it's already happened, we can only stop him doing it again. But that's what she'd want me to do.'

They pour out the end of the wine, though it's getting a bit warm by now, standing out in the sun. Fergal lies back on the rug again; he hopes Theo will join him, lying as she did before, but she remains sitting, cross-legged. By the slow progression of the sun, a shadow now falls over his face. But she puts her hand on his stomach where his T-shirt has rucked up.

'You English are so *white*.'

'Come on, you seen me body before.'

'Half the country has seen it. But I never looked at it this way before.'

'Don't rush a bloke.'

It's nice that she's teasing, but she still has the lines on her forehead . . . cracks in the windscreen, tear at perforations to detach . . .

She's stroking his stomach. It's hard to concentrate.

'Listen up,' he says.

Her hand stops moving. She listens.

'Where is Ransfield least dangerous? What place?'

'In a monastery. On the moon.'

'Here. In this college he's at. Where he's scared shitless even to look at a girl. One more strike and he's out. If you get him thrown out of here, and he gets another job, some tutoring outfit or some dump in Eastern Europe, he'll start all over, won't he? It'll be a shitty job in a shitty place and they probably won't care what he does to the girls, so long as he's got Doctor on his door. He'll think he's safe again, and he'll be into it like a pig in shit. Here, at this college, he's scared, cos the minute that council got a whiff of knickers, he'd be out.'

'I guess you're right.'

She starts those fingers moving again. He puts his hand down over hers to stop distraction. He has to get the words just so, and she isn't helping. It's all very well for her, she could probably participate in a conference call on the future of the beef industry while riding some lucky sod to delirium. Why does he think these horrible things, when she's as close to Holy Barbara as he'll ever find on earth?

'So the one thing you *don't* do,' he continues bravely, 'is nark on him. If you want to stop him, your best shot is to leave him where he is.'

'You're a clever little chap, aren't you, Fergal?'

'Middle-class bitches, same the world over,' he says, and she bends right over and kisses him.

But true to type, she won't just get on with it. She starts the kiss, sweet and complicated as a rope of liquorice, but then straightens up again.

'Yes, you're right, that will stop him, but I want him to suffer.'

'Well, he hates it here, don't he?'

'That's not enough. I have to punish him.'

'*You* do?' he says, blown away by this middle-class assumption of authority. 'Why you?'

'Because I have the information, and the right. He has abused me too.'

'But you said —' cries Fergal.

'No, no, he never touched me. I'd have run him through with his bleeding shooting stick and fed his cock to his dogs, he knows that. But he deceived me in the most disgusting manner.' She starts to cry again. 'The humiliation of it. He had me standing there before those wallies on the council, and saying what a good bloke he was. You should have heard me. What a dick I made of myself! When in reality he is the absolute opposite — the fucking bastard.'

Her anger gave Fergal a great surge of sensual satisfaction; if she hated Ransfield this much, she wasn't ever going to let him near enough to harm her.

'Well,' says Fergal, 'what I'd do is, get Elspeth to leave him. She's all ready to.'

'But women don't leave their husbands just like that.'

'They do where I come from.'

'Yes, well, exactly,' she says.

He ignores this; besides she's just run her hand up to his right nipple. It's too fucking hard to keep the thoughts straight when all his senses are racing towards annihilation.

'I'll take her with me. Up to Norfolk. I know she wants

to go. She's got that mate up there, give her a job. All that messing about in boats.'

'I can't do it,' she says. 'I like her too much.'

'Well fuck me, *you like her too much*, so you leave her in this hole with a cheating husband who fancies totty young enough to be his granddaughter, and doesn't care what he has to do to get it, when she's got her best chance ever to get out. Well, if that's liking someone, I hope you never like me.'

'I think I'm well past *liking* you,' she says, but he's not going to let her say it, he's not, no, anything to stop the rest of that sentence. He rushes on, round that dark bend, anything to get away from this danger.

'You tell Elspeth everything you know, cos if you don't I will, and then you'll feel even worse, and Elspeth will think you're screwing him and I'm only telling her because I'm jealous, and she'll leave him anyway, but then she won't know how to stay friends with you.'

She takes her hand away. She's mad at him, just a little, because he's right, and she is too honest to deny it. And because she's a bit irritated she's going to hold off from anything sweet and loving.

Danger averted.

XIV

THEY MADE A pact. First thing Monday morning, as soon as Jenner had left for work, Theo would tell Elspeth everything. To avoid encountering their hosts on Sunday they planned to get up early and go to Cheddar Gorge for the whole day and get home late. But when they woke up on Sunday morning it didn't look as if they were going to be able to get out of bed. In the end Fergal showed disappointing strength of character and made her get up without anything much coming of it all. In the evening they stayed in the pub till closing and he got so pissed he was absolutely no use.

Monday morning starts out suitably grey. Theo is so nervous when she wakes that she wants to get up straight away, and certainly doesn't want to dally with Fergal. So she dresses and plays games on her notebook computer until Jenner will have gone to work.

They walk up to the house holding hands. Theo is sick with apprehension, but Fergal won't let her out of it. Elspeth is outside feeding the hens.

'I'll do this,' says Fergal, taking the bucket from her. 'Theo needs to talk to you.'

'You'll be needing breakfast? Shall we make some porridge, Theodora?'

Theo bites her bottom lip, and follows Elspeth into the house, grateful for some activity. She lays the table for their breakfast, placing the knives and spoons just so. She doesn't know how to begin.

Elspeth busies herself over the stove, her back to Theo.

'Is it a tea or a whisky chat we need to have?' she asks.

'It's not what you think,' Theo says, aware that this sounds really stupid.

'I'm not at all sure you could guess what I am thinking,' says Elspeth, but she smiles a bit, to show she is not upset with Theo.

'It's not what you think,' says Theo again, unable to look up.

'No, no, I understand that. Don't take on so much, Theodora. But it is about Jenner, is it not?'

'Yes. How did you know?'

Elspeth puts a big brown pot of tea on the table and a milk jug in the shape of a cow.

'It's about Jenner and students,' she says. 'Girl students.'

'So you know? You already know?'

All the hours of worrying and debating, the nights of fitful sleep and the days of strain, and she knew all the time!

'No, no, it is mere supposition on my part. Jenner lets things slip. I used to tidy his room once upon a time, and sometimes there were hints. There had to be a reason for events. Over the years, you know, a picture builds up. We used to mix a little, at one time, socially with the other staff – and people say certain things, kindly meant, of course. And I am not so foolish as to believe that Jenner, and Jenner alone of all university teachers, is so persecuted that he is hounded from place to place.'

'I only know about what happened in Melbourne. And here.'

'So it has happened again. I cannot say I am surprised. I am only relieved that it was not, after all, you.'

Theo looks up, and meets Elspeth's eyes, which are

startlingly and beautifully blue. Why has she never noticed this before?

'Why? Why would it be any different if it were me?'

'Because with the other girls, I did not know their names. Nor what they looked like. I could shut a door on them in my mind. I could pretend they were painted hussies who entrapped him. It was possible to believe that it meant nothing.'

Theo pours the tea, but finds that she is shaking. This chat isn't going right at all.

'But if it had been you – well, I couldn't have borne it. Because you are not a temptress out to snare him, you are a real, warm person, and my friend. But I didn't think you would do that.'

'I certainly would not. And he has never laid a finger on me, never made a suggestion. Of course he says things which you could take the wrong way if you were ultra-sensitive – but I suppose I've gotten used to him *saying* things – but he didn't *do* anything. Which is why I was prepared –' She takes a gulp of the spirit. 'Oh God, this is so awful. You know what he made me do?'

Elspeth starts to look troubled. Theo hastens on with her explanation.

'He asked me to go before the council on his behalf. You see there was a complaint of sexual harassment from a girl called Caroline Hayes, and he implied that there was nothing in it. I believed him. He also let me believe that this hadn't happened before. I thought he was innocent, the victim of that girl's maliciousness, because she is a bit of a painted hussy, and I knew she was after him, so I agreed to go and speak up for him to the council. And he'd lied and lied and used me in the most calculating manner. I'm sorry, Elspeth, I know he's your husband, but he's behaved like a bastard to me.'

She starts to cry. Elspeth pats her hand.

'No, no, it's all right. But you see, I don't think he is a liar. He has a great many faults, but dishonesty is not one of them. He may have expressed things in a roundabout, biblical manner. He is upset by explicit speech, poor creature.'

Now Theo doesn't know whether to laugh or cry. She tries to think back. Perhaps he didn't quite lie. He certainly denied having intercourse with Caroline, but that didn't mean other things hadn't happened, and it didn't mean he hadn't tried to force her as she claimed. He had admitted to Theo that he wanted to screw Caroline, against his better judgement. He had admitted to what he called sexual converse.

She thinks that perhaps she believed he was innocent because she hoped he was, because she didn't want him to be so tacky and disgusting as to get the hots for a second-rate nobody like Caroline Hayes.

'But he expected me to go and lie. I can't forgive him for that.'

'No, no, that's not what he expected at all. He wanted you to tell the truth to the council. To tell them that you had lived under his roof, and worked with him for long hours, and still he had committed no indiscretion. That will figure very large in Jenner's mind.'

'That is so sick! As if not touching me somehow makes him a good guy. What am I – Sharon Stone or something? Irresistible? Not touching one ordinary girl doesn't mean he's not harassing other girls. It just means that girl doesn't turn him on.'

'Oh no, I am quite sure that he asked you to speak up on his behalf precisely because behaving decently towards you costs him great moral effort.'

'Oh God, I feel sick.'

'You had better tell me everything you know. It's a funny thing, Theodora, isn't it? All these years I have hated this matter and tried to push it away, but now it's in the open, I feel such relief. I am so glad you have some facts to tell me. After twenty years of suspicion and rumour, a fact becomes a lovely thing.'

'They're not very high-grade facts, I'm afraid. I haven't read any documents or spoken to any witnesses. But I'll tell you what I know.'

So she lays it all out, Dr Ransfield's Terms Test; the other complaints in Melbourne; Prof. Betsy's catalogue of grievances; Jenner's defence; the enforced departure; the allegation that he had done it again at Southampton. Then the complaint of Caroline Hayes that he had tried to force her to have sex, the arraignment before the council, Jenner's vehement denial, and his acquittal.

'That's all,' she ends; 'everything I know on the subject.'

'After Southampton,' says Elspeth, 'there were a number of contracts, and two other positions. The children were babies, I didn't get a full night's sleep for five years. We lived in horrid places. I didn't have energy left over to notice. But his contract was not renewed, and people – made implications.

'A girl rang up once, very drunk, and started to make accusations. He grabbed the phone from me and then went out. He didn't come back for hours. I was too upset to sleep and then too exhausted to talk about it. He never said a word – not directly, but for some time he was pale and quiet and wept. He weeps, you know, a great deal.

'I know there were other girls, other incidents, but I know no names, and we never spoke of it, not directly. But at night, he would weep and say what a terrible sinner he was. Poor Jenner, as if I was an avenging angel. I understand that there are demons that drive him. I wanted to be confided in, not confessed to – do you know what I mean?'

Theo nods.

'I am a foolish forgiving woman, Theodora. I accepted his weakness for girls, and their weakness for him. I see how women look at him, and his angriness makes him more attractive to some. I used to walk into a room with him, in the days when we went to parties, and you could see the hungry ones looking at him and at me, and their looks said *What did he marry her for?* and the second glance said *So she wouldn't get in our way.* And you know, I am not possessive. I asked for so little from him, a few crumbs of affection, a little effort at family life.

'So, you see, none of this comes as a shock to me; rather, a relief. But it confirms what I had begun to fear, which is that he cannot change. I have held out the hope that one day he will mellow, that my life will gradually improve.

'It is a strange matter, unhappiness, is it not?' says Elspeth, getting up to stir the porridge. 'All my married life I have told myself that I have little to complain of. The children are in good health, we have a roof over our heads, we never starve or go without shoes. Jenner has never struck any one of us. How can one be unhappy, when the true causes of misery are removed? And yet, you know, one is.'

'Yes,' says Theo, 'it's something about a hierarchy of needs.'

'Each morning I get up and listen to the radio, and hear the terrible things in the world, and I thank God that my family is so blessed. And I try to get on with each day, telling myself I have no argument to be unhappy.'

'Oh Jesus, you are a saint, Elspeth.'

'No, Theodora, I am a fool. I have made nobody happy by my self-sacrifice. Jenner would be happier with a woman like yourself – who would stand up to him and demand that he control himself. He wants to be driven, to be forced to goodness, to be told he is unreasonable. He would be happier – insofar as Jenner is capable of happiness.'

'Well it's time you looked after yourself. You can't change him, and he's dragging you down. You don't owe him anything, you have given him the best part of your life. Now it's time to reclaim it.'

'But what am I to do?' Elspeth asks. 'I cannot imagine myself looking Jenner in the eye and telling him I'm leaving.'

'Just decide to do it. If you go to Norfolk with Fergal you have a definite time and place, because he really is going up there. Once you name the day and start packing, it becomes unstoppable.'

'Have you done such a thing yourself?'

Theo remembers leaving home. Her mother's distress was palpable, not because the darling daughter was leaving, which was only right and proper and everyone did it, and you didn't want your children hanging around getting in your way until they were thirty, did you? but because the flat was so nasty, darling. There was, for example, a corroded washing machine (*It functions perfectly adequately, Mum. We put the clothes inside, see, like this? The rust is there, on the outside*); the only toilet bowl was in the bathroom (*Imagine if one of them is in the bath and you need to go*); and a motorbike in the hall in the merry company of six dozen empty beer bottles. (*Actually Mum, there are seven doz now*). Theo heartily agreed that you ought to live in a *nice* place but Juliet needed a flatmate, and there was plenty of time for nice places when you had a veterinary practice and car and all that crap. She thought about that first flat, and the adventure of it, lying on the mattress on the floor with the morning sun coming in, and Tom's brown head undisturbed on the pillow, and the birds chortling to one another out in the trees, looking at the posters all over the walls and ceiling, stuck on with drawing pins and sticky tape with gross disregard for the wallpaper.

'No, I've only lived with one man, and I haven't

officially left him yet. But I don't see that is any different from leaving home to go flatting. You make the plans, you stick to them, and because you promised your friends, you end up just doing it. I guess that's why most people find another lover before they get out.'

'I don't think I shall do that. I think I might forgo love of that kind. Jenner is enough for a lifetime.'

'Of course you won't. There's plenty of fish in the sea.'

Elspeth shakes her head vigorously.

'You're lucky really, you've got a job offer from your old friend, and a friend to go with.'

'Yes, I am lucky, aren't I?' says Elspeth.

She smiles, a curious faraway smile, as if she's already headed out to sea.

'Your navel is the most beautiful thing in the whole world,' Fergal says.

'You can't even see it.'

'My tongue can see it.'

They are lying in bed in the darkness, most mellow, having shared a joint some time earlier. This is the night. Theo is naked, and Fergal in a T-shirt. His cheek is flat against her stomach, and his mind is full of eggs – the ovularity and shameless warmth of new-laid eggs. He gathers them for Elspeth, burrowing into the straw, each time a minor miracle, a fillip of surprise, the warm treasure lying in his hand, perfect, promising, expendable. Never forgetting the first time – the farm visit before time began, group of snotty kids, awed and bothered by smells and the feet of animals, and little Fergal, with his elf-child eyes, allowed to put his hand into the box, into the straw – what would he find in there – some disgusting dead thing, some sharp exciting object? His child's hand draws out the egg, and its loveliness fills him with pain, so much that his hand has to close on the egg and crush it, so that it becomes disgusting and the other kids laugh.

Theo's navel is the egg he cannot bear to crush; Theo is the loveliness he cannot bring himself to destroy by smearing it with himself. And it has come to the point where he must, you know, put up or shut up. His inability not to touch Theo has wound him up here, his tongue in her navel; her expectation, and her rights and her body and his body all drawing in one direction; the streams and channels and ditches full of rainwater dashing down to the sea.

Trouble is, he can't. Physically, no problem, it's crying out for it, and not likely to fail him. Never has. But to do it, to actually bring himself to the point where he puts himself into her, absorbs himself into her body, he has to be clean. He can't do it dirty, she is too precious and lovely for him. But to get clean he has to tell her about his dirty past, and he can't. He doesn't want to talk about skipping dinner and sitting in class with cunty fingers and dreams of nipples and knowing that after school he might or might not be wanted, and doing it and wanting to do it again almost at once, and being disgusted and miserable like a bit of cheap meat in the butcher's window, flies just hovering waiting to strike.

He doesn't want to relive the constant presence of that stickiness, the impossible tension between the beautiful secret of Quiche's inside, pink and tender and endlessly capable of pleasure, and the violence and smell outside. And the sweetness of getting to her, peeling back the layers he'd been dreaming of, and finding her, and then finding someone else had been there, and she's bragging about him, saying how big he was and how big his cock was, and Fergal better look out. And the wild rush of freedom when she said that, coupled with the fear of not having this secret life. Then after that, all the pictures pursuing

295

him, months and years afterwards, into adult life, pictures that he liked so much he couldn't stop looking at them in his head, though he hated it all. Pursued him even here, when he stood in May Margaret's studio surrounded by those lovely carvings, which were so beautiful, clear and holy, purged of the slime, and yet, there, right there, on her pinboard, and in piles around, the mags, the sources she used to make them, the same pictures, the pouting, pressing, demanding, oozing.

There's something he can't get – there's the wooden ones from Marg's reverent hand, and then there's the sticky pink photos, and as well there's Theodora, pubic hair neatly curled over the opening, everything perfect and in place, as you knew it had to be, just from looking at her. All the same thing, and overlapping in his head, he can't detach the images from one another. He can't work out whether they are the same thing differently represented or different in essence.

He needs to understand, and to tell Theo all of this, wash before he can touch her with his fingers. But the words refuse to come out, stuck beneath the gigantic slaghead of thoughts.

'You OK?' she says, stroking his hair.

'Mmmmm.' The great statement of ambiguity.

She wants him to get on with it, but she's too nice to make a fuss. It was like the way she got undressed, modestly, hiding herself in the act of removing her panties, even though it was dark, and they'd slept together all these nights. A shyness is hanging between them like a mosquito net – hardly anything, but just enough. It need only hang there for a moment, whipped away by a single stroke of the hand – his hand into her cunt. Soon as he's done that, it will all be over, the rest will follow. His fingers slide up the inside of her thigh, his tongue begins to creep downwards, his cock rises. It's coming from all directions.

But he can't do it. Inside his stomach along with the lust is some kind of pain, a tumour that blocks and confuses all the signals. That reminds him of a way out.

'I need a piss,' he says, and scrambles up.

Grabs his cigarettes and today's underpants on the way out. Plan ahead, Fergal. Always take the right tools with you on a job. Cigarettes to explain the delay, pants to clean up the evidence. Got to remember to wash them out before she sees.

He doesn't think about her at all, out there, head pressed into the bark of a tree, only Quiche's secrets and Miss Bountiful 48DD All for You. Thinks of them, and feels sick, and loses it. Everything falls away from him, sucked back inside, like baby rabbits inside the doe.

It is so delicious to be out there, in the complicated darkness, the sounds you can't quite identify, that may not be anything at all, just disembodied noises. The smell of earth and grass, not nice and comforting, as you'd expect, unsettling, exciting, like anything is possible. Everything smells older and more complicated than cities, older than people.

He wants to linger, fade into it; it's like being on the protest, up a tree or on the ground in a tent, you felt you were gradually growing these little wispy roots, down into the country, dozens of little ones. Adventitious. Nice word. What are you, Fergal? I'm adventitious.

What are you, Fergal?

Smokes quarter of a fag, to solidify the illusion.

'God, you were ages,' she says. 'Was there a nice obliging tree?'

He nestles up against her, his hand on one breast, his body along hers. She can feel from that, that he's no good.

'I can't do it, Theo. I'm no fucking use to you.'

She holds him closer.

297

'It's OK. I understand.'

How could she possibly? *Understand.* That's one of the things girls say to be kind; and you wish they wouldn't.

He knows that she wants him to do something for her, but he can't do that either. Can't right at this minute think of a plausible excuse, but then maybe she won't actually ask, just hope and wriggle and drop hints. The gauzy shyness comes in handy here.

'Cigarette,' she says, burying her nose in his hair. 'You are incorrigible. I can just imagine what my folks would say if I took you home.'

'But you aren't goingta.'

'No,' she says in the sort of tone that could mean almost anything. 'No, I'm not.'

He needs to touch her, but he also needs to distract her. These may be incompatible aims, but he gives it a try.

'What you going to do, then, when you get back?'

'When I get back.' She has to pull herself into another mode, think herself into another person. 'God, it's happened along so soon. At first I couldn't wait to go back, and now I can't bear to think about it. It seems completely unreal. I suppose I shall finish this paper, send it off to the right journal, rewrite the findings in plain language as a report, print it beautifully with coloured diagrams, bind up a dozen copies and send them to the beef industry boys who paid for me to come over here.'

'Yeah, but after that, like with your life.'

'Oh, my life. *My life.* I think I'll stay in academic life for a couple of years, then go for a big government job in Canberra. I suppose I shall marry Tom and he'll go into private practice as a vet, then when we've made some money and done OK we'll move. You just can't stay in Canberra too long. I'll go for a job in an institution, close to home, so Mum can help me out, have a couple of kids, close together to minimise the pain. Then go back into the meat industry, cattle breeders, pork industry, there's lots of options, plenty of dosh. Then move back and forwards, academic, industry, government, going up the ladder. I might go back to Canberra, a bit later, when I'm established, if they offer me a posting to Washington or Brussels. Good for secondary schools too. Then eventually I'll get some cushy number in a university and we can buy a stud farm and breed horses and sell them to rich Japanese people.'

He can't think of anything to say for a bit.

'Is that what you want, then?'

There's a long slow silence.

'Yes,' she says, but there's something wrong with her voice. 'Yes. That's what I want. Good job, stable marriage, family life, heaps of money, heaps of variety. What more is there?'

'Dunno. Doesn't sound enough though.'

He's having trouble dealing with the reality under his hand, the apple perfection of her breast, at once insistent and demure, and the picture she presents him. He can see the perfect house, swimming pool glinting in the sun, the lawn, flowering shrubs, handsome husband and children, Theodora in a suit and with a briefcase, charming and impressing all the big guys. He can see that, though he's never experienced anything like it; and he can feel her breathing under his hand, her warm skin, her wanting him.

How can she want him and want that house and garden? It doesn't make sense. Fergal's used to things not making sense; he doesn't often try to work anything out. But it's not often that contradiction matters as much as this contradiction appears to matter.

'And you,' she says, 'what about you?'

'Me? Just keep on doing what I'm doing, organising, hanging out of trees, trying not to get arrested, yeah? Then

I s'pose I'll burn out, rust out. One day I'll just drop in to do a spot of gardening for someone – nice divorcee, grown-up kids, big old garden in the country, and I'll end up staying there, doing her garden, feeding the cat, hanging out the washing. Nice, yeah?'

'Nice. Is that what you want?'

'I told you. I don't want anything.'

'No, that's not what you said. You said, and I quote, *I want to want nothing*. That's not the same.'

The sharpness of Theo's mind is just another of her glories.

'Nar,' he says, 'you're right. It's not what I want. But it's what I'll end up with, and that's OK.'

'So we're both happy.'

Funny how unconvincing it sounds.

'Yeah, ecstatic.'

She puts her arms right round him, tight. He thinks she's going to cry, but she doesn't say anything, and neither does he. He can feel the unspoken words and undeclared feelings hardening up inside him, like the semen and the tears, clogging him up inside like lime in a kettle, so there's getting to be no room for Fergal.

XV

JENNER OBSERVES.

They think that he is unaware, but he misses nothing.

He observes that the bedrooms are tidied. That in itself is nothing. The children have left, ripped themselves unnaturally out of his hearth. She may reasonably tidy their rooms. But it is the nature of the tidying, the speed and thoroughness. The banging and the thundering as Robin's books are taken out, dusted by slapping them together as if they were so many tiresome children, and ruthlessly restacked. The thumping of cardboard cartons, filled to the brim with paper, screeched with broad brown tape, and bumped down the stairs to stand in the hall, boldly labelled for an address in Bristol. The advancing swish of black plastic rubbish bags through the house; the mighty pile at the gate on Tuesday morning, rubbish day.

Then the clumping comes from further up, as the broom and rubbish pan are applied with the same evangelistic energy to the leavings of May Margaret. A bonfire smoulders in the yard, of wood shavings and pornographic magazines. Jenner finds a burnt fragment of female pudenda on the windscreen of the car on Wednesday morning.

Yes, surely, to clear out the children's rooms is a logical reaction to their departure. It is what Elspeth might reasonably do – though she has not shown such rigour in the pursuit of domestic ends, excepting always the puritan keeping of her own room. It is an appropriate rite of passage. Purge them from the heart as from the hearth, sever the cords and cauterise their ends. They are ungrateful nestlings, not even a word tossed back to ease their father's heart.

But from this activity, she has moved on – or rather they have moved on, for the boy is at her side constantly like a combination of robot and gigolo – to the bathroom, from which emerge generations of soap slivers, ziggurats of toilet rolls, empty sanitary protection wrappers, discarded razors, tiny sticky bottles of body lotion trophied· back from conference trips to hotels, untouched offerings of aftershave bought for Christmas out of last-minute desperation, bath cubes crumbling to coloured dust, tubes of prescription anti-fungal ointment, caps astray, fifteen-sixteenths squeezed, but still just alive, hot water bottles perished with cold and age.

Next in the edulcoration of the house come the hall cupboards and dressers and hooks, their years-long burden of coats and scarves and ropes and boots and cracked china and ugly glass and floral table mats and salt shakers and ends of coloured candle and interesting stones found on walks and keys widowed of any lock . . .

. . . followed by the sheds in all their variety, and most terrifying of all, the kitchen.

Every newspaper clipping, photograph, brochure, newsletter, postcard and ancient calendar has gone. The floor is bare and swept, the cupboards stacked with neat piles of crockery. The miscellaneous packets of flour and sugar are decanted into new plastic containers labelled Flour and Sugar. The bread bin is cleansed of its venerable crumbs and contains one loaf of fresh bread. With great daring, Fergal has investigated and distilled the contents of the freezer. When Jenner becomes aware of this exercise, it is too late to save the dogs from whatever hideous botulism lurked therein.

From time to time the telephone rings, a sound which makes everyone start. Jenner is always too late to answer it, hears half of animated conversations in which Robin describes at length the wonders of his workplace and the business of his brisk new life. He does not ask to speak to his father, but sometimes Fergal is summoned. Often Jenner is forced to retreat from earshot, by the lowering of tone. Conversations become monosyllabic until his door is shut, but his pride would in any case prevent him from trying to listen further. May Margaret also rings; Jenner gathers from the scraps that are flung his way that she is living in the gallery workshop, which is very large and very chilly, and is therefore entirely comfortable. She has requested quantities of bedding and crockery, which are duly bundled up and dispatched.

Even if he had been both blind and deaf to the ransacking of his home, he would have been alerted to the advent of trouble by Theodora's behaviour. For what seems to him an unendurably long time, she has been distant, rationing her conversation and her smile, bent over the computer. And then, overnight, she is sweetness itself, asking him for advice, joining him for lunch in the cafeteria, engaging him in chat. Another man might have said that she was flirting with him, but Jenner reads sexual manoeuvres as other men read racing form. He sees that she is not flirting with him, but about something altogether more devious, if only he could conceive it.

Nonetheless, as a side issue, he detects her sexual hunger, which is not knowingly directed at him, but which introduces a dark element into the sweetness and light. He has surmised, quite correctly, that she is accustomed to constant and vigorous sexual activity, and that her body

303

is recognising its absence; he has assumed, also correctly, that the boy Fergal has provided her no sexual comfort. He sees that the boy has ignited and stoked sexual passion in her without being able to relieve it, and that she has not allowed herself conscious acknowledgement of her state. He considers whether Fergal might be homosexual, or whether he is suffering from an unpleasant condition. Neither of these hypotheses satisfies him by fitting the observed phenomena.

The complexity of the truth – that Fergal, through unresolved guilt and disgust, is psychologically unable to consummate his and Theo's shared passion – is excluded from Jenner's hypothesis not because it is too subtle for his comprehension, for that deals daily in philosophical and logical niceties which would make lesser minds buckle; the idea is excluded because the one thing Jenner cannot conceive of is refraining from making love to Theodora, were one physically empowered to do so. Her pretence of innocence drives him to angry withdrawal. The more she smiles and charms, and ignites him with her sexual hunger, the more he hates and is silent. What is her game? What is their game? He cannot decipher it.

On the Thursday he is browbeaten into accepting a lift with Theo to college, because Elspeth's truck is to be overhauled. On their return to Nightingales, she prattles about politics and race relations and weight gain in castrated animals; anything that might entice him into conversation. He stares ahead out of the windscreen, smelling her, refusing to look. They arrive bumping down into the farmyard; he knows at once something is wrong; Theo tells him that Elspeth has sold all the hens to a farmer over in Middlezoy who is expanding into free range.

During this week of cleaning up and clearing out, he tries to think only about his current work, his masterwork.

He finds it easier than ever to shut the door on the concrete and lift off into the stratosphere of the idea. He is constructing a philosophical synthesis, an abstract theory of communication, whereby the cognitive processes of language and seeing are generalised and classified, so that it becomes possible to consider all forms of perception of meaning in one theoretical model. He has begun to understand the potential application of his model to images, and now he has turned his attention to language and is striding his way through works on the psychology of speech and practical and theoretical linguistics. He has worked in these areas before, as consultant on various naïve projects to produce translation engines and speech analysers, all doomed to failure because based on too flimsy a model of speech and understanding. He thinks now that his new theoretical model will postulate that cognition and recognition are perpetual, ultra-rapid processes of hypothesis and data gathering, that the mind and the eye, in all animals, operate in a mode of constant re-evaluation – setting a framework or paradigm, testing this against the data and the data against the framework, altering the paradigm, retesting, again and again from the first stirring of the foetal thumb into its mouth to the last exhilarating scream into light. At which point the model may become irrelevant. Or possibly not.

His mind at present is engaged on the paradox by which a processor, that is, a mind or eye, selects data for the evaluation process. How, he wonders, can a processor even collect data to test hypotheses which lie outside the paradigms that make it up? If the processor has no concept of the datum, how can it exist in any experiential world?

He keeps the secrets of his mind under lock and key these days, for fear of plagiarists. Nonetheless he finds himself lusting to expound them to Theodora, partly for the pleasure of the exposition, the pearly lightness of the ideas as they take shape in words, partly for the sheer sensuous enjoyment of watching her intelligence engage with his ideas. Her mind is sharp and logical, and while not strongly theoretical, is well tuned to detect inconsistencies in any argument. She is, cursed be she, ideal. This alone ought be cause enough to shun her.

Friday night, Saturday morning. Unable to sleep, he sits up in his narrow comfortless bed, sucking on his dead pipe and reading linguistics. He has long forgotten why he cannot sleep, but as the chorusing of the birds cuts in outside his window, and no rooster joins them, he jolts to and remembers that Elspeth has sold the hens, and Elspeth is preparing for some event.

Today will be the day to which the frantic preparations have been leading. He must be ready also. At five o'clock he goes upstairs and runs a bath, washes himself with ritualistic care, and shaves with the same precision, without cutting himself, though his hand will barely obey his commands. He watches himself in the mirror emerging from the foam, and fails to recognise the middle-aged bedlamite, his eyes huge, dark and staring, the sacs under them rather improbably black.

Terror and distress churn through his body; he is shaking, he is sick, he doesn't know which way to turn. He struggles to finish shaving, examines the result. Yes, he is handsome enough to meet his fate, poor Petrushka.

He goes down to the kitchen to make himself a coffee. His feet protest at the bare kitchen floor. He finds only one jar of instant coffee, tidily on a shelf above the kettle, next to the tea bags and the drinking chocolate. Why was it not always like this? She, so puritanically clear and clean in her own space, and he, so perfectly minimalist in his? And yet between them in their living quarters this clutter, which one week's labour has swept away. Only one week's labour, motivated by what?

When he goes to dress, any doubts he might have had, that a climacteric has been reached, are swept away. He takes a folded shirt out of his drawer, and finds that it is the last. The supply of laundered, dried, mended, ironed and folded shirts has dried up. This is the end.

He has no records to play any longer, May Margaret spared not a single one. Her passion and extremity of action are his own. He cannot be angry with her. He feels relieved to be rid of the nonsense of the old records. But he wishes he might, just for today, listen to *E lucevan le stelle*, the aria of the condemned man about to die, but clinging to his hope and his love. Jenner has no hope to cling to, and the only love on which he can rely is that of Elspeth, who even now – he will not think on it; that way madness lies.

He sits at the desk by the window and reads. He smokes his pipe, filling the room with sweet savour. He waits.

Elspeth knocks and comes into his room. Her face is shiny washed, her hair, newly cut short, is combed. She is wearing jeans, a white sweatshirt, white sandshoes with white soles. She looks shipshape and handsome. He looks up, and then directly back at his book. She picks her way across his room to the fireplace. She sifts through the accumulated stuff on the mantelpiece, and there, behind the spotted china dog, she finds the envelope, containing the letter she wrote to him the night after he made love to her stark loveliness in that pure room. He has not forgotten. The letter which he opened with curious and dismissive fingers in the university mail room, and had to take back to his room to consider, the letter in which she offered him her total devotion. *I have nothing else to offer you*, she wrote. *It is perhaps not something you looked for, but it is real, and it is yours.*

He remembers with absolute clarity how he felt when he read those words. He had been rescued. His salvation from himself had arrived, from the most unexpected quarter.

'I'm taking this back,' she said. 'I am leaving now.'

He puts down the book and the pipe, stands up and walks to face her.

'It's not possible.'

'I have to, Jenner.'

They stand and face each other, across the hearth. She folds the envelope and puts it into her jeans pocket.

'You can't revoke it,' he says. 'It's a virginity: once you have given love, you can't take it back.'

'But it's not. It's not an item that was mine and then became yours. Love isn't a precious jewel, it's a process. And in our case, the process has failed to work. I am sorry, terribly sorry, because my heart and soul belong to you. But I made a stupid, romantic mistake.'

He looks at his hands. They shake violently of their own volition. Words start into his mouth, great rhetorical torrents of them, but as they gush up they drain away. Everything he thinks to say seems less adequate than the next sentence, and that too seems weak and ineffectual. All his words will be powerless against the engine of the preparations.

'Where?' is all he can manage.

'I am going up to Norfolk with Fergal. I shall take a little job in the sailing school there, for the summer, and then I shall see how things are. I have some savings. I don't need very much.'

'It's not possible.'

'You see that it is.'

'No. No. No. Don't do this to me.'

'You mustn't weep now, Jenner. You must listen to me. You must try and discover what it is you really want. Theodora has told me about the girl students, this Caroline Hayes and all the trouble in Melbourne. Things you never saw fit to confide in me. You must decide whether that is what you want, young girls, a life of secrets and guilt. When you have thought things through, and I have thought them through, then if you want to talk to me, I have left Zachary Bryce's number by the telephone, with Robin and May Margaret's numbers. You might want to ring them up, perhaps go and see them. Theodora will stay for a few days, so you will not be alone.'

She has rehearsed all this. It's a terrible sham piece of acting. This is her voice but not her words.

'You're only going for a break,' he says.

'No. Don't think that. Think that I am going away for good.'

'But you love me.' His voice has shrunk to a whisper.

'Yes, I believe so, but I canna be sure any more what it means.'

'How can you do this to me?'

'I don't suppose any of us really understands another person. It is hard enough to understand ourself. Goodbye, Jenner.'

She can't look at him or kiss him; she turns and walks, half runs out of the room, head down.

He might run after her, grab her around the waist, fall on his knees, weep, beg, howl. He does nothing. He cannot conceive that this is happening to him.

When Theo seeks Jenner out, it is more to seek solace than to give it.

Inside her head is a set of phrases that has become stuck in an endless loop which she cannot break. *Fergal has gone.*

*He has gone away. I shall never see him again. I shall never
see him again. Ever. Ever as long as I live. He just went away.
Just like that. And he never made love to me. Not even once,
not even once to remember him by. It doesn't matter anyway.
He doesn't matter. In the scheme of things it doesn't matter at
all. He wasn't anything in particular. How could he do that?
Just go away. Not even make love to me. I shall never see him
again, not ever. I can't believe it. How can I get on without
ever seeing him again?*

And so, on, round the loop.

Jenner has made it as far as the kitchen table. She
expected him to be barricaded in his room, and has
been trying to think of excuses to disturb him. So when
she comes in through the kitchen door and finds him
sitting at the table, glass, bottle of whisky, she's taken by
surprise, and doesn't know what to say. It feels like the
first day at high school, she so confident about the world,
the new and shiny schoolbag, *it's going to be great!* then
the awfulness of not knowing where to go and nobody
caring, and big kids rushing about, laughing, in groups,
and confusing messages in chalk on blackboards telling
people to go places they don't know how to find. And
I will not cry I am a big girl.

Before, when they were planning it all, she'd thought
that when Elspeth left, smiling at the wheel of the truck,
Fergal next to her, waving down the road, on to new
challenges and a new life, Theo thought she'd feel terrific,
as if she'd done the right thing, and triumphed over the
dark powers. She cannot quite believe how terrible she
feels. It's like being taken over by an alien – this is not
Theodora Potts, possessed by this dreadful sense of loss
and wrongdoing.

He is drunk already. He looks at her and says nothing.
She can't meet his eye, because of the awfulness inside
her. She thinks if she feels so much like death, because

Fergal has gone, how much more unknowably terrible must be the thing inside him? She feels as if the sun has gone in for ever; he must be plunged into a dark beyond her imagining.

And here lies the criminal who must be punished, the oppressor who must be taught a lesson, liquefying before her. She is panic-stricken by the spectacle of his grief.

She makes herself a coffee, too trembly to initiate conversation. How do you talk to a man when you have just engineered his wife's departure? Why hadn't she thought of this? *Course I'll be all right,* she'd said to Fergal, *I'm an adult. This is not a melodrama. Don't worry about Jenner,* she'd said to Elspeth. *I'll make sure he's all right. I'll look after him, take him out, get him to talk. Don't worry about him.*

Oh, your wife just left. Let's have a chat.

Then he starts to speak, the stream of lovely sound tumbling over the whisky towards her.

'Why have you done this to me? You have no animus against the world, no cause for hatred. Nature and circumstances have been kind to you, you are one of the darlings of God. Having everything in abundance, and never punished for it. Why then? I have done you no wrong. Why have you set about to harm me? Is it because being so lavishly favoured with health and beauty and cleverness and good spirits – a great cornucopia of material and personal gifts – yet you are not satisfied, and instead of looking within, at the shrivelled gnome of a soul, you look out and search for a victim? It must be man, not mankind, but men, who are at fault, since there is no shortcoming elsewhere – you cannot blame society or poverty or lack of opportunity – but life is not quite as it should be. It is dark and dirty and unhappy, and I am also dark and dirty and unhappy. Therefore I must be blamed, I must be punished, I must take on my back the stripes due to all men, who are the perpetrators of life's unsatisfactoriness, then when I am duly chastised, the world will be perfect.

'Or it is perhaps stupidity rather than wilfulness? Is it that you have not looked, you have seen that the world is not quite what you expect, and think that a quick fix from the handywoman's store will set it right? That all men and women and their bleeding suffering selves and crippled minds, their pathetic bloodied broken hearts, can be set right with a tube of feminist superglue and a handful of dowels. Are you then a behaviourist, that most superficial of thinkers, who imagines that human life can be sorted out by better breeding and good food? Clean up the house, get the woman a job, tidy that man away – that'll be the ticket. Everyone live happily ever after. You, you call yourself a scientist – have you not looked, have you not heard with your ears or with your heart – are you deaf to the massiveness of suffering, the silent pleadings, the tangled rope of need and dependency? Is it possible that you have learnt nothing?'

Theo stands with her back to him, pressing the hot rim of the coffee mug against her lip. She cannot believe that he is saying these things to her.

'And you have such power to do good – such strength of character and charm – all wasted, perverted and stinking of decay. You alone could have turned my children's hearts towards me – a word from you, a persuasive argument, an act of mediation, you could have taught them to see me as a human being rather than a monster. But what have you done? You have engineered their desertion – because of your interference, and with your encouragement, they have gone away without a backward glance, without a kind word being spoken. You might have changed that.

You alone. No one else in all the world, neither before, nor in the future. But you threw that chance away, and now it is gone for ever. They will grow away from me, I shall be a dark memory, a lonely old man, lurking in their past, to whom they cannot speak, with whom relationship has become impossible. I know, I remember.'

If she starts to cry, will that make him stop? She'd do anything to make him stop, anything.

She does not let herself imagine what that anything might include.

'How can you be so ignorant, so obstinately blind? Have you not seen that there is only one thing that human beings crave, one thing that all their instincts and their intelligence drive them towards – and that one thing is to be loved? We are crawling in the mud and faeces of life, grasping desperately at any love that might pull us out. We are impelled towards love in any form – the pretend love of the body, the false love of admiration, the purchased love that power confers – anything, anything so that we feel that we are loved.

'And all my life beneath all my longings and strivings, my achievements and failures, my struggles, my angers and my lusts, there was only one need – the need to have a human being wrap her arms about me and love me. Love me without ghosts, without provisos, without guilt, without conditions. Love on which I could absolutely rely, love in which I could lose myself, and purge myself of guilt, and rise washed and new each day.'

Theo can't turn round and face him. He is a disembodied voice, saying things she cannot bear to hear, and that is bad enough. But if she were to see the man himself, and watch his face as he says these things to her – not a stranger, but Jenner Ransfield, now so familiar to her that she will never get him out of her bloodstream, she does not think she could endure it.

He doesn't allow her even the small comfort of avoidance.

'Face me, when I talk to you. Are you ashamed of what you have done? Of course you are ashamed. How can you look on me whom you have destroyed? Turn around.'

She obeys him, shaking.

'Yes, well you might quiver and grow pale.' He pours himself another deep shot of whisky, and drinks most of it down. 'Well you might be afraid to look at me ever again. You must listen. You must understand what you have done.

'I am a wicked man, Theodora, but you already knew that. I cannot control the demons in my loins and the demons in my head. I am desperate for love with the longing of a beast that is starved and deprived of light, but my sinful nature drives me to acts which make others hate me. As I hate myself.

'When I was a young man, I thought I was wildly happy, ranging across the world, brilliant and admired, fornicating and free. I had the world at my feet, on occasion quite literally. I was pursued and desired and courted by everyone.

'But when fortune turned against me, I saw that it was I who had destroyed myself, that I was addicted to the pursuit of love in the lowest of forms, a disgusting, gangrenous, gaping wound in me, that unless I repented I would always be carried along on a wild ride by my demons, and that I would never be loved as I need to be, for myself alone.'

Theo feels as if something in reality has slipped. Real people do not talk like this. Not where she comes from. But Jenner does talk like this. All this time, she thinks, these awful things were inside his head, and this great, terrible need inside him, and she had been blind.

'You who are secure in always having been loved, whose grip on sanity is so sure – what can you know about the torment in the heart and body of a man like me? And the daily torture conducted in my mind – burning with ideas, unable to fulfil myself and my gifts, because I cannot control these demons that have driven me? No, you cannot comprehend these things, but you do not even see what there is to understand.

'When I returned from Australia, it seemed to me that if I could marry and force myself into a conventional life I had a chance – my only chance – of redemption and fulfilment. If I had a good woman who loved me, my wife, I might be purged and forgiven. I went out to find her, and I did. Such a good woman, so innocent and pure of heart. Even after I had desecrated her purity, foul creature that I am, even after that, she did not abandon me to hell. She wrote to me – a promise of devotion of such simplicity and honesty that I saw the stars had all come out in heaven. I knew I was saved.

'And all the rest of my life, all the twenty and more years of my marriage, I have been the recipient of that love. I have fallen again and again, I have failed and battled and gnashed my teeth at the world, and grown to be hated by everyone – but all that time I was sure of one thing – Elspeth's love.

'I was sure that I, Jenner Ransfield, was loved. She gave it to me. Without condition, after what I had done to her. After I had torn her body, had all but raped her, in the purity of her own room, she bicycled, poor sacrificing loving creature, all those miles to leave me that letter.'

He is starting to cry now. His voice, with all its beautiful rivulets of sound, breaks its banks and cascades all anywhere. His face is contorted. He rubs his face with his fingers, as if to smudge out the thoughts. He gulps the whisky, he is clearly growing drunker, but in spite of tears and drunkenness and anguish, the words pour out of him in ordered phrases.

'I have never forgotten that letter. It has been my rock. One day, one day, I tell myself, I will grow mellow, I will stop generating hate, I will cease to consume myself with lust, I shall be an old man, and my wife will be beside me loving me, as she has always done, my rock, my haven, my home.'

He weeps, his hand over his eyes. Theo is unable to move, consumed by a misery so great she can't see the end of it. These emotions are completely outside her experience. She has never been involved in scenes, steered well clear of other people's miseries, concentrated on cheering people up and getting things fixed. There is no cheering up or fixing possible here. Such ideas seem an insult to Jenner's agony.

Nor has she herself ever felt so dreadful. The minor disappointments of her life have not prepared her for the desolation she feels, both on Jenner's part and her own. There are no words in the vocabulary of her emotions to contain or react to what he is feeling and causing her to feel. In among the ghastliness of his accusation, she realises that she too is a creature compelled to love and be loved, and that she has let her one true love slip away.

She feels a desolation open up all around her, as if she had camped all night in a pleasant field and woken to find herself in the middle of a wasteland strewn with rubbish. There is no one to turn to for help, no track out, no sign of habitation or life, and a mean wind is blowing.

Now his fluency has deserted him also.

'You,' he says, smearing the tears, 'you might have made the difference. You might have helped her to understand me – she needs so little – to be happy, so little. You might have – poor Elspeth – but you drove her to it – extremity – she loves me – I could have tried – why did you all not – give me the chance?'

Here is a man, as old as her father, sobbing out loud. She has never heard a grown man cry. It seems so unnatural, as if a horse or a bull were to weep.

'I am alone. I am quite quite alone. I am done for.'

He slumps his arms on to the table and bends his head on to them and weeps into the darkness of his own embrace.

She will tell herself later that at that moment reality was completely suspended, that all sensible precautions and normal behaviour ceased to have meaning, that everything she had lived by burst open to doubt, that all of Theodora and her measured world scattered and reformed itself into a single point in time and space – into the need to comfort him.

She will tell herself this later as a way of rationalising what followed. She will tell herself that she knew, from the split moment when she put forward her hand, what the consequences were – that she weighed them and came down on the side of madness.

But she will never be able to decide whether the days of delirium and ecstasy that followed were a good exchange for a life sentence of resolutely suppressed emotion, and an enduring sense of emptiness. She will never be able to decide whether the gaining of painful knowledge of her heart and body stacked up against the equally painful knowledge that she had misunderstood the most important things of all.

'I'm so sorry, I'm so sorry. I didn't know. I didn't understand.'

She also has burst into tears. She puts down her coffee mug on the table, and puts out her hand. She is too far away to touch his bent back, rising and falling in the unnatural paroxysm of weeping. She moves the few inches which remain between them, and stands beside him, so that her hip, her knee, her body is pressed against him. She strokes the middle of his back, round and round, and then his shoulders, as if he were suffering some minor pain that might be soothed away by amateur massage. He makes no movement of response. It seems to her such a futile gesture to express her contrition and the tearing in her heart. She lifts her hand slowly, slowly, as befits motions outside history, and strokes his hair. He raises his head from his arms, puts one arm around her and buries his face against her.

She weeps as she cradles his head between her breasts, and bends down to kiss his hair.

I think we must accept that she understands what she is doing.

Elspeth experiences the lightness of heart that often accompanies setting out on a journey, no matter how grim the circumstances. Now that the parting is over, she sits up straight behind the wheel, looking about her bright-eyed, as if she'd never seen the environs of King's Sedgemoor before. She feels free to sing, her own ballad.

> *Take bak your love, now Lady Elspeth,*
> *And my best blessing you baith upon!*
> *For gin he be your first true love,*
> *He is my eldest sister's son.*

'Happy ending, huh?' says Fergal. He has not spoken for miles, but he doesn't know why. In his lap he cradles the lovely expensive personal cassette player that Theo has given him. Its neatness and perfection remind him of her. He swears he will never lose it. He's excited about the new adventure, satisfied that Elspeth got away safely, that there were no tears, no scene. He is even managing not to worry about Theodora's safety. He does this by struggling not to think about Theodora at all.

Inside him is a cheerfulness, like Elspeth's, a new-journey, bright-day cheerfulness. And inside that, like the yolk inside the white inside the shell, is something else. No, he thinks, it's a different sort of egg – one of those special ones with dark chocolate outside and white chocolate lined inside that and inside that a space with a surprise toy in it. But he's got the space without a toy.

He can feel the emptiness inside the inside shell, and it feels more like a tumour than a nothingness. A tumour or a great bubble of foul gas that's going to swell and swell and explode and destroy his membrane-thin inside shell of happiness and the impervious shell outside that.

He says nothing else. He wants to nurture the little seedling of Elspeth's happiness, knowing how hard it must be, setting out to nowhere, leaving home behind, the darkness and the guilt. He thinks she is brave as an alley cat, but he's learnt to expect that kind of courage in women.

Elspeth chats; she is excited about everything. She can't believe that she is doing what she is doing, that this is her, Elspeth, free as the sea and sky. Three hundred miles to drive, she, who hasn't been out of the West Country for years. Fergal has the map Zachary faxed over, with directions as clear as sheet music. They'll get there by nightfall, and there's a good place for Fergal to stay – Bryce's Sailing School has a barn with bunks and ablutions. Elspeth has been invited to stay in the big house with Zachary and his wife and daughters. Fergal knows that fear and worry will cut in later, but once she is free of that man, she can start again, as his mother did.

He'll never forget how the cheerfulness grew back into his mother, month by month.

Elspeth chats about any old thing that will keep her looking ahead and not back. Lot's wife, pillar of salt. Fergal won't look back either.

'And when is Theodora coming up to join us?' she asks.

'I dunno. I don't think she is. She's going back to Oz, i'nt she?'

'But you made some plans.'

'No, don't think so.'

She stares at him open-mouthed. Not a pretty sight. He's embarrassed and looks out of the window.

'I am amazed.'

He knows what Elspeth is getting at. He's not sure he can believe it either. But that's how it happened. *Goodbye*, Theodora said, *I thought you might like this. Goodbye and good luck with everything. Yeah, you too*, he replied. *Thanks for everything*. And that was it. He'd thought she'd say something different. But then he thought that he would say something different. He thought she must know what was inside him and have decided against it. But what if she didn't know?

'I thought you and Theodora were made for each other. I didn't think you'd be able to bring yourselves to part.'

'Yeah,' says Fergal, realising this himself. 'Yeah, I didn't either. I thought something would happen. Like in the pictures.'

She shouldn't have brought it up. He was OK before, but he isn't now.

As they drive along, he starts to sink into the emptiness inside, like he's gone into his own stomach and it's a great big cavernous grey place, and he sees things in there that make him want to die. He sees an Indian woman in a bright, bright sari, smothered in an old pink cardigan against the cold, picking her way through a narrow street of grey houses against a grey sky. He sees the sun going down beyond Brighton beach, stitching up the grey sky into the grey sea. The grey stones at his feet go all the way into that grey water, and it's getting cold, and he's got to go back, get the train, face school, back to his squalid duties and his grinding life, and never being able to escape, his mum's face furrowed with worry at him running off and getting into God knows what, worried sick over him and his sisters, and no money, and Fergal having money he shouldn't. He thinks he could just walk down those grey stones into the grey water and keep on walking towards the nothing, cos he can't swim and he wouldn't last long, and then it would all be over.

Elspeth has stopped the truck.

'We have to go back,' she says.

His heart leaps.

'I forgot the family bible. I can't leave that behind. It belongs to my family.'

Fergal thinks that a fucking great Victorian bible is the last thing you want in a protest camp. He understands that it's important to her, but more important than the bible, she simply has to create an excuse for him to go back.

'Will you fetch it for me? I can't bear to go in.'

'Yeah, OK.'

She laboriously turns the truck around and retraces their journey. Fergal feels absurdly happy.

She stops the truck a hundred yards from the farm gate.

'I can't go in,' she says again.

''S OK.'

He jumps down and runs back along the road. It's almost like skipping. He gets to the gate, jumps over it. *Abandon hop all ye who enter here.* OK, he thinks, I won't hop, but I can hope. He creeps into the wood. He's going to make sure he doesn't encounter Jenner: no way. He makes his way silently through the copse, past May Margaret's plaster statues of the family, as silent and out of place as he is himself. He'll get the book first, tricky if Jenner's out of his room, but a diversion might be created. Stir up the dogs, ring the doorbell, start a little fire in the barn, easy stuff. He creeps under the trees and arrives at the yard, strangely dead without the flurry of chickens. He doesn't like fowls as a general thing, but he misses them now. The stillness of the yard spells out that things are not the same in this place. It isn't that he wants them to be the same, because he thought it was sick here, sick and creepy. But the very difference, the beating of the sun on hard earth, the silence – that isn't right either.

He walks towards the house, making a big circuit so the dogs don't sense him. He needs to find out where Jenner is, and then where Theodora is. It's all quiet round the house. The dogs are chained up outside, dozing in the sun. Stupid animals. He swings around the yard, well beyond their ken, and approaches the house from the side, so that his first point of contact is the window of Jenner's room.

He sidles up to the window, listens for breath, the sucking of a pipe, creaking of a chair. Nothing. He chances a sideways look into the room, a split-second glance. Empty.

He continues slithering round the proliferation of sheds to the back door, like following your left hand round a maze, bloody silly business unless you're convinced of the need for it. Gets to the kitchen door and listens. Nothing. This strikes him as curious. Both cars, Jenner's old crate and Theo's Japanese car, are in the shed, but neither person is in evidence.

He enters through the unlocked kitchen door, and sees on the table a bottle of whisky, a glass with some whisky in it, a half-drunk cup of coffee. All is quiet in the downstairs of the house.

He pads into the hall. The bible is there all right, large as the marble slab Moses hauled down from the mountain. Bloody pointless stuff, trying to write it down. As if we understood enough to write down. What the fuck do you think you are doing, author?

All is quiet, but there is something about the silence of the house that perturbs him. Fergal has been in many houses when he oughtn't to have been, mostly for the thrill of it, though the cash and small electronic items came in handy. There are all kinds of silence in houses. There's the silence that persists over noise − like when they've left a radio on to fool you. There's the silence that noise makes, like when they're having such a good time in the front room that they don't hear you in and out the french windows. There's the silence of a deeply unoccupied house, with maybe a cat or a budgie breaking the spell. Then there's the silence of a house which is occupied but in which the occupants are too far away for you to hear them with your ears, but you pick up their presence on a different channel. Fergal knows these different silences; they are part of his education. And he freezes in the hallway, knowing they are in the house.

He has a vague sense of voices, movement. It seems that Jenner and Theo are upstairs, in Marg's attic perhaps. He hadn't expected that. He thinks he will take the book and go back to the truck. Maybe it's just as well. He's said his goodbye; he can't say any more to Theo, what is there to say? Elspeth's romantic hopes for him will have to wither on the branch.

But he hesitates; he doesn't want to go now. He wants to see Theo again, to say the things he should have said, make a pact, a commitment to the future, try and knead into words the feelings in his heart and the pictures in his head. Suddenly he knows that this matters more than anything else in the world.

He's heading back across the hall, to deposit the book outside in case he needs to make a quick getaway, when he catches sight of something on the stair. He missed it first time across, because it's round the bend, where the stairs hang a left and go on up. He swallows the bile that rises in his throat, puts the book down, and creeps up the stairs.

On the stairs, beyond the landing, he finds her trainers and jeans abandoned in a heap. Two steps further up, her panties, tiny and white.

He makes no sound. It's there in his pocket, the knife that's been waiting all these years for this moment, the moment when the rapist knows a terror something like the terror he inflicts. But Fergal knows it's beyond his power to inflict the indignity, the shamefulness of being raped. The pain he will hand out is nothing to the humiliation of being used and smeared upon.

He moves step by step. He can hear clearly now the disgusting grunts and groans of what is called love-making. Elspeth's room. Yes, it would be, wouldn't it, the dirty pig. Elspeth's lovely clean room, with its white curtains and broad white bed.

At the door to the hall, shoes and socks, *his* trousers, fucking old men's trousers, corduroys. And white under-pants, big old baggy ones, slightly shitty.

He crouches down by the door, his spine against the jamb, straightens his back. Waits. There is no advantage in rushing in. You wait for the right moment. He takes out his knife. Opens the blade. It snaps rigid. He feels it against his cheek. Yes, you could shave with it. He knew that. It is always ready.

This moment is pre-ordained, has been with him for as long as he can remember. He crouches ready, he who is destined, it now seems, not to save the planet, not even to save one stand of ancient trees, but to slice the balls off a rapist and watch him whimper as he bleeds.

He listens for his moment.

He listens.

'O Jesus,' she says, 'O Jesus.'

'A garden locked is my sister, my bride,' Jenner says, 'a garden locked, a fountain sealed. Your channel is an orchard of pomegranates, with all the choicest fruits, with all trees of frankincense, myrrh and aloes, all the chief spices, a garden fountain, a well of living water, and flowing streams –'

His voice is muffled. She groans. Fergal prepares, locks his hand around the knife handle, braces himself against the door frame. Already he can see the blood gushing out on to the white of Elspeth's bed, hear the screams . . . already he hears her voice saying his name – *O Fergal!*

He hears what she says next.

'O Jesus, don't stop, please don't – I never – O Jesus.'

He listens. He tries to hear it different.

'Yes,' she says, 'yes, yes yes.'

Fergal feels the door frame rigid against his spine. He presses the back of his knife against his cheek. The pressure of the steel gives him no comfort, but it assures him that he is still alive. He is alive and conscious and this is happening to him. He wants to get the fuck out, but he doesn't move. He doesn't know what he is feeling inside, it's like everything he ever felt all at once, hatred, desperation, lust, love. He notices that the palm holding the knife is sticky with sweat.

'O I am sick with love,' says Jenner.

Fergal also feels sick, but whether it is love he doesn't know. There are no pictures in his head, only sounds, the sounds of two people who are unequivocally making love. He hates hearing it with violent disgust and envy and jealousy, but he can't move. Just in case he's wrong, just in case she's faking it, just in case he can, after all, rush in and do what he wants to do.

Why do people always take so long over it? The minutes tick over in his head; he thinks vaguely of Elspeth waiting in the truck, singing to herself, smiling because she will think that the longer Fergal takes, the more profound and lasting the contract of love. Fergal feels that he will be sick.

He hears.

'O Jenner, I never realised . . .'

'No, you didn't understand,' Jenner says.

Fergal hears that his enemy's voice is tender and closes his eyes. He can see the hands on her naked skin that accompany that voice.

'You young and lovely creatures understand nothing at all. And those of us who are old enough to understand are raddled and marked for death.'

'O Jesus, don't say that. You're wonderful.'

'No, I am old and evil. I eat my honeycomb with honey, I drink my wine with milk. But, O God in heaven, I adore you.'

Fergal snaps shut his knife. He can no more protect Theodora from Jenner Ransfield than he can protect her from her own kind heart and loving body. He has failed her, though it now is clear to him that he loves her more than pictures or words could tell. He starts to slide the knife into his pocket, as silent in defeat as in revenge.

In the bedroom the lovers are not yet finished. Fergal feels for a cigarette, thinks he will not stay. He wonders how he will compose himself for Elspeth, from whom all this must be hidden.

Then.

'I'm sorry, Jenner,' she says, 'I just can't, I'm sorry, I'm going to cry, I don't know why, I don't mean to. I'm sorry.'

She starts to cry, and she sobs and sobs in the noisy ugly manner of true grief.

Fergal can tell that Jenner is holding her and stroking her. He hates Jenner for it, but still, he is glad that someone tries to comfort her.

'I understand you,' Jenner says. 'You love that boy deeply, but you have hidden it from yourself and from him, and now he is gone. You have tried to suppress it with kindness towards me, but your heart has won out against your kindness.'

Theo is still weeping.

'How am I going to live?' she says, through her tears. 'He was so *special*.'

Fergal wonders what is happening to him. He thinks he has cut his cheek, puts his hand to his face, brings it away wet, but not with blood. Tears are pouring out of him; it is all he can do to stay quiet. He starts to slither away towards the stairs, so they will not hear him crying, but he also desperately wants to hear what she will say.

'He is so special and I never told him,' Theo said. 'I never said anything, and now he's gone away. There'll never be anyone like Fergal. I'll never see him again, and he'll never know.'

'We can never put into words what is in our hearts,' Jenner says. 'No matter how many letters I write you, and I shall, they will never convey the loving kindness of what you have done for me today. Unless you see what is in my heart, you will never understand what this means to me. It is like grasping a concept in mathematics. And so, you might tell him that you loved him, but still never communicate the heart of your love.'

Fergal listens to her crying. He feels his own chest suck and heave with crying like the tide on the stones. Words and ideas have deserted him, he is pain and love. But they have not deserted Theo and Jenner.

'So what you tell me,' she says, dragging the words out, 'is that I could never have expressed how I feel anyway, so it's just as well I didn't make a fool of myself.'

'Oh no, no, no,' says Jenner, 'we do grasp concepts, in spite of and because of words. That boy Fergal knows that you love him, even though you said nothing and he said nothing in return. How could he fail to know?'

'Because, I told you, I told you! I didn't say anything,' she wails.

'You said nothing – but what did you do? You have shown him every possible face of love, and today you have succeeded in its ultimate test. You have let him go away. You might have tried to tangle him into a middle-class marriage or kept him as a tame domestic pet – but you let him go, to be who he is and to do what he must do. You read his true nature; that is the greatest expression of love.'

'It doesn't make me feel any better. I never knew you could hurt so much inside your head.'

Fergal listens to her crying. He wonders if you could burst and die from heartbreak, like appendicitis. It hurts as much. It hurts more.

'Not now,' says Jenner, in his stroking voice, 'but later when you think about him, you will see the truth of what I say. Now you must grieve. Let me hold you while you grieve. It will comfort you only a little, but the memory will give me happiness until the day I die.'

'I'm sorry, Jenner,' she says. 'I meant to comfort you.'

Fergal bites his lip until he tastes blood. He wonders

how they are unaware of him, reaching for breaths, as he is flung through a nightmare ride by his emotions.

'Sweet child, comfort yourself with this: you have shown your love, and in his heart he knows it. He will never forget you.'

Fergal hears these words from the man he most wishes to hate, the man who has most cause to hate him. There's nothing left inside him.

'How can you be so sure?' she says.

'Because, loveless sinner that I am, I understand love when I see it and I feel it. Weep also for me, sweetheart, banished to the outer darkness.'

Fergal takes out his knife once more, crouches by the top step of the staircase and on the broad brown post at the top of the stairs, where it cannot be missed, he carves the picture of a heart transfixed by an arrow. Underneath he cuts FERGAL + THEO 4 EVER. Then he goes down the stairs, cigarette in his hand, spring in his step, to make the earth safe for nightingales.